PENGUIN BOOKS

Small-Town Girl

Claudine Cullimore was born and raised in Waterford, Ireland. She has lived in France and the UK, and now lives in Belgium with her husband and their daughter. Her two novels, *Lola Comes Home* and *Small-Town Girl*, are both published by Penguin.

Small-Town Girl

CLAUDINE CULLIMORE

PENGUIN BOOKS

PENGUIN BOOKS

Published by the Penguin Group
Penguin Books Ltd, 80 Strand, London WC2R ORL, England
Penguin Putnam Inc., 375 Hudson Street, New York, New York 10014, USA
Penguin Books Australia Ltd, 250 Camberwell Road,
Camberwell, Victoria 3124, Australia
Penguin Books Canada Ltd, 10 Alcorn Avenue, Toronto, Ontario, Canada M4V 3B2
Penguin Books India (P) Ltd, 11 Community Centre,
Panchsheel Park, New Delhi – 110 017, India
Penguin Books (NZ) Ltd, Cnr Rosedale and Airborne Roads,
Albany, Auckland, New Zealand
Penguin Books (South Africa) (Pty) Ltd, 24 Sturdee Avenue,
Rosebank 2196, South Africa

Penguin Books Ltd, Registered Offices: 80 Strand, London WC2R ORL, England

www.penguin.com

First published 2003
1
Copyright © Claudine Cullimore, 2003
All rights reserved

The moral right of the author has been asserted

Printed in England by Clays Ltd, St Ives plc

Did you ever feel like you were exactly where you belonged? I did. This was where I belonged, in this town, with these people.

I'd never felt the need to swap small-town life for the bustle of a bigger city, or the desire to hightail it to foreign parts on a one-way ticket.

Not me.

Because I truly belonged here, in Waterford, surrounded by my family and friends, and married to Richie, my good-looking soulmate who had saved me from a lifetime of scouring the town's limited mating grounds in search of that someone special.

I looked forward to our future together now as much as when I'd first met him. We shared our dreams with each other and one day we'd fill the house with children and I'd make a wonderful home for everyone, and what I lacked in technical expertise on this subject matter I'd make up for with enthusiasm.

I liked living in Waterford. I was born here, as were my parents and their parents too. I liked walking down the street and being sure of meeting someone I knew. I liked going into a shop and being able to pick up what I went in for even though I'd forgotten my purse at home. I liked never having to explain who I was. And I liked having my family within walking distance.

My mother and three sisters formed a stable part of my emotional diet. We laughed a lot together and when the world was falling apart for one of us the others would pick up the pieces. And, just as importantly, we were living testimonies for one another that my father had been with us, if only for a short while.

If there was something in my life that I could change, it would be that. I would bring my father back. He died when I was barely ten years old, from an undiagnosed heart condition. He'd measured well over six foot and weighed about seventeen stone, so when he suddenly disappeared his physical absence from around our small semi-detached house was appalling. But the intangible gap he left in our lives was even more so. I kept expecting him to reappear. I'd hold my breath and warn God that I wouldn't breathe again until He gave him back.

He used to clap the loudest at school plays and came first in all the parent races because he had by far the longest, quickest legs. He allowed us chocolate before dinner and to go to bed without brushing our teeth. He even pretended not to notice when Hannah, the eldest of his four girls, started wearing a teen bra and took to stuffing it with cotton-wool balls. If he wasn't perfect he hadn't lived long enough for me to find out.

Richie and he had one thing in common, and a

strange one at that. They both had really long earlobes. My father used his to make us laugh by modelling my mother's clip-on earrings, but Richie didn't like his at all because he was teased mercilessly at school.

It was the second thing I'd noticed about him when we met, right after his smooth voice with its confident Dublin tones, and I'd immediately decided that sharing this trait with my father was a very good sign for us.

In the first month we were together, we did so many things that I'd never done before I thought my life had only just begun with his arrival.

Naked in bed we ate sushi that he had brought down from Dublin. We rented French films from the world-cinema section of the video shop that I hadn't even noticed up to then, and actually spoke about them after. We swam in the freezing Atlantic at midnight under a full moon, clothes discarded on the damp sand, and we climbed to the top of the Comeragh Mountains and left our names there for everyone to see, written with stones we'd gathered on the way up. How could I not have fallen head-over-heels in love with him?

During those early days I often found myself wondering what he saw in me. I knew exactly what I saw in him. He was handsome, confident and he lived life to the full. He was the sort of person I thought my father would've approved of. My father liked people who always had something to say for themselves, and that was Richie.

When I finally summoned up the courage to ask him what he saw in me, as we strolled though the park in early spring, he simply said, 'You should see what I see.'

Not an effusive answer but he said it with such reverence that I soared above the treetops with joy. No one had ever made me feel that way before, and he seemed as happy as I was.

How could it ever go wrong?

I

'Is that Richie on the television?' my mother bellowed, her voice loaded with disbelief. Her colourful Lyons-tea apron bulged, the seams straining sympathetically. 'Is that your Richie?' she roared again, as I sat behind her idly flicking the pages of a glossy magazine at the kitchen table. The kitchen had been recently decorated and boasted all-new cupboards in a light distressed-wood effect, an embedded panel on the front of each one covered in a pale-green wallpaper that matched the tiled splashback behind the sink, the fabric blinds on the windows, the newly painted walls and the covers on the chairs. There was a new cushioned vinyl on the floor that matched everything too.

'Answer me quick. Before he disappears again.' She was frowning hard at the television screen in concentration.

I looked too, not expecting for even one second to see Richie. A fireman, his face covered in sooty smudges, stared back at me from the screen in the corner of the kitchen, nestled between a stack of cookery books and a small lamp. I grinned knowingly. It couldn't have been Richie, because he'd gone to Lough Derg for a few days on some kind of pilgrimage.

He'd left the evening before and it was nowhere near Cork airport.

Richie had been going on all kinds of pilgrimages and retreats this past year because, he'd told me, he felt the need to start taking care of his spiritual self as he got older. I'd been openly dubious at the beginning, when he'd first announced his intention to dedicate some of his free time to his spiritual development, because it wasn't the kind of thing he'd ever shown a shred of interest in before.

But now, at the age of thirty, he was going on about one a month and, even though I still thought it all a bit strange, I'd decided that I should look at it differently. It didn't feel right to badmouth this kind of Godly pursuit. It was, after all, very admirable of him, and I felt like a sinner of the lowest class when on occasion I doubted his sincerity and bemoaned his weekend absences. Nonetheless I sometimes wondered why he bothered.

'You're seeing things,' I told my mother and couldn't resist teasing her. 'Have you been at the magic mushrooms?' It was well known that they were growing on a tiny patch of undeveloped land on the edge of the sprawling estate of semi-detached houses where she lived. Built around twenty years earlier, the estate was mostly full of families, with the odd house now rented out as student accommodation. You could easily spot which ones: the limp net curtains on the windows never matched, the gardens stood neglected and the wheelie bins were usually overflowing with beer cans.

The other houses on the estate were all well looked after. When we first moved in, a while before my father died, they'd all looked the same. One row of houses differed from the next only in their street names. But over the years they'd become monuments to their owners. Walls were repainted, inside and out, front doors were changed and elaborate doorknobs fitted, gardens gutted and rebuilt and windows upgraded to double glazing, and to top it off quite a few had been awarded their own house name by the proud proprietor.

That one patch of land with the magic mushrooms was the only thing that my mother didn't like about where she lived, and the comment I'd just made was bound to get a reaction.

Her nostrils flared accordingly. 'I'd never touch those narcotic fungi.'

Then the television screen blinked again and suddenly a face that looked remarkably similar to Richie's appeared. Same cheery round cheeks, sandy hair and eager smile. I jumped up off the chair, involuntarily stumbled backwards, then rushed forward until my nose all but rubbed against the television screen, the static tickling the tip annoyingly. He was gone again. 'Was that Richie? No, it couldn't have been.'

The man on the television had clearly been in the company of a woman; he'd been standing beside her, an arm around her elegant shoulders, and smiling at something she was saying. 'It definitely wasn't him,' I decided, simultaneously reassuring myself and scoffing at my own silliness to even think that it could have been.

'Well, it certainly looked like him,' Eilish, one of my sisters, said over my shoulder as she shrugged her thick coat from her shoulders. She'd walked into the kitchen a minute earlier. 'And with a dolly bird, too.' She pulled her head back sharply. 'It wouldn't surprise me of him.'

She said this with such unfaltering conviction that it ignited a flash of anger in me. 'Just what do you mean by that?' I demanded. Richie had never given anyone cause to make such a disloyal comment.

'You can't deny that he's got a sly side to him,' she replied, tugging her fingers one by one out of her leather gloves. 'Like that time he never told you about going to Dublin overnight when we went away for my birthday.'

'That was nothing,' I insisted. 'He doesn't have to tell me everything.' I just wanted him to. Besides, he had been organizing a surprise for me. He'd commissioned an artist friend of his living in Dublin to do a painting of the two of us from a favourite photo and he'd gone to check on its progress.

In the background the fireman was describing a small explosion, which was big news, at Cork airport and suddenly the camera veered away from him again and honed in on the crowd momentarily.

'There.' My mother's finger flew into the air and towards the television with the sharp hunting instincts of a hawk. 'There he is.'

Three heads cracked noisily as we jostled for the prize spot right in front of the screen. '*Holy fuck!*' I shouted into the room. The words seemed to reverberate off the new cupboards and bounce back up at me from the vinyl flooring.

'*Holy fuck!*' Eilish shouted too.

There was no way I could mistake him this time. It was Richie. A woman's head rested on his shoulder as he tried in vain with one arm to shield them from the camera he'd spotted was turned on them. The other arm was wrapped protectively around her shoulders, drawing her close.

I felt my heart come to a thundering halt.

'Very Hollywood, Richie,' Eilish commented, her voice hard. 'Very d-r-a-m-a-t-i-c.' She was squinting at the screen, cold murder in her eyes. The camera moved on and he was gone again. 'I never liked him anyway,' she tried to comfort me.

'It's a pity you couldn't tell me that when I married him four years ago,' I shot back, wondering why she'd waited so long to tell me. It wasn't like her. 'Anyway, I'm sure there's a very good reason for this.' I paused to think of one such reason to tell her, an acceptable excuse for what we'd just seen, but couldn't find one.

9

'Of course, there's a good reason,' I went on. I would make myself believe this. 'Why wouldn't there be?'

Eilish and my mother exchanged eerily knowing glances that unbalanced me further.

'I never liked him either,' my mother announced, sounding the death knoll for their mother-in-law/son-in-law relationship. 'You're far too good for him and I've always said it.'

If I was too good for him, I fumed silently, it was the first time I'd heard of it. And anyway, I certainly didn't think I was. Richie was the love of my life. I planned on seeing my days out with him. The two of us would sit side by side, surrounded by framed photos of children and grandchildren, laughing and drinking sherry, and looking back at how good life had been to us. That was how it was going to be.

I wanted to tell her this but the image of Richie with some woman's head on his shoulder silenced me, robbed me of the strength I'd need to say anything with conviction. It was an intimate gesture, the way she was leaning against him. She wasn't simply some passer-by he was comforting in the wake of the fire at the airport. I stood by helplessly as the image magnified itself a hundred times in my mind until it was billboard-size.

'I'm sure there's an explanation,' I ventured again, voice hollow. I couldn't deny the dreadful ache in the pit of my stomach owing to desperation, uncertainty and shock. To make matters worse, I realized, I'd have to wait until Richie got home the following evening to confront him, to get an explanation. He never turned his mobile phone on when he was away on these weekends. I swallowed the hard lump in my throat.

The fireman was coming to the end of his interview when the camera fleetingly swept over the crowd one last time. 'It's them again.' Eilish warned us. 'She's turning around. Look at her.'

Shoulder-length dark-brown hair, Jackie O-style sunglasses and a sophisticated red lipstick. She wore a floor-length wool coat with a shawl thrown casually around her shoulders and we all stared in silence at the elegant figure. The image only lasted a second or two.

My mother folded her arms across her chest and declared, 'She's no spring chicken, despite the fine feathers.'

I nodded gratefully, as I'd noticed this too. Regardless of her careful appearance, she looked to be at least fifteen years older than Richie. 'Yeah, she's much older than him.' I allowed myself a sigh of relief and ran a hand around the back of my neck, lifting the damp tendrils away from the clammy skin, a sure sign of my heightened state of emotions.

'There's definitely a good explanation, isn't there?' I forced myself to smile at them. 'Nearly had me worried there for a minute. Before she turned around. But there's no way Richie would be up to anything with an older woman, would he?' I waited for an answer but my mother and Eilish said nothing. 'Would he?' I had to insist.

'She wasn't even that beautiful,' Eilish then said by way of a reply. 'I mean, had she been extraordinarily beautiful, well, you know, that might have been an acceptable reason.'

A constellation of tiny anger spots flashed in front of my eyes. 'What?' I snapped at her, wondering what had just happened to sibling loyalty, 'I suppose he'd be allowed to two-time me with an older woman if she was in any way good-looking, but not someone who looks like one of Mammy's friends?' She didn't really look like any of my mother's friends – too self-possessed – but I couldn't think of another way of putting it to get my point across. 'And before you say anything,' I turned to face my mother, pre-empting a defensive comment in favour of her friends, 'there's nothing wrong with any of your friends. They're just not Richie's type.' I really liked most of them but this was true.

'My friends are all beautiful,' she said nonetheless. 'Fabulous-looking girls,' she emphasized, 'and not an ounce of interest in Richie Maloney between the lot of them.'

'I think the revival of the older woman is really great, Mam,' I assured her. 'I just don't think they should go running off with my husband.' Suddenly my mouth went dry. 'What am I talking about? No one's run off with anyone. I'm sure there's a very good explanation for this.'

Eilish slipped her arm around me, warm and solid beneath a black wool jumper. 'That's about the tenth time you've said that,' she said softly.

I half-sobbed then, because I knew this was true and that constantly repeating myself was not going to change the facts. My conviction was beginning to crack. 'I thought Richie was in Lough Derg.' Said aloud, this sounded pitiful and unbelievable because the reality was that my husband was standing with his two arms wrapped around some woman at Cork airport and I didn't know why he was there and I certainly didn't know why *she* was there.

My head began to reel as I desperately tried to make some sense of all this but couldn't. Everyone in the whole town will have seen the evening news too, I suddenly realized with dread, so I made yet another attempt to rally my thoughts.

There must be an explanation for this. But more to the point it must be an explanation that I wanted to hear because I couldn't bear to think about the consequences if it wasn't. Richie was my life. He was what I did. I'd only ever wanted to be married, to belong to someone, and to have someone belong to me.

Before Richie had come along this had been a problem, unsurprisingly. It meant that I could get serious quickly, often from the very first date, if I decided that things were looking good – compatible star signs, same favourite food. This wasn't the kind of behaviour that endeared me to the young man about town. Among my friends the joke was not to fall asleep sitting beside me in case you woke up with a ring on your finger.

Then one day Richie had turned up. He was from Dublin. And we'd clicked immediately. He was different from all the rest; he somehow knew more, had done more, and he made me laugh. He revelled in the intensity of our relationship and that suited me fine. I deemed us a perfect match and I decided that this was the person I would settle down with, right here in Waterford because I didn't want to be anywhere else. We'd get married and live happily ever after. It was a cliché but I didn't see it any other way.

'Huh, they didn't look like they'd been to Lough Derg to me,' Eilish said, intruding on my thoughts. 'They were looking a bit too well fed,' she decided. Lough Derg was a place of fasting. 'Too well sated,' she then added meaningfully, 'if you get me.'

Before I could think of anything to say to this the door to the kitchen burst open and Hannah appeared, flushed and tittering with excitement. Gerry, her one-year-old, curly-haired, cherub-like son was clasped under an arm and her three-year-old daughter, Katie, was perched on a hip, in near perfect symmetry.

Hannah, my eldest sister, lived next door to my mother. She was a real home bird and it had taken careful plotting on my mother's part to get Hannah to move out of the family home when she married her husband, Dennis Healy. She thought Dennis could just move in with them – there was enough room, with the rest of us gone – and they'd all live happily ever after. 'Richie Maloney was on the six o'clock news,' she gushed. 'Did you see him? Did you see him? Oh God, I hope you didn't miss it.'

'Why was Uncle Richie on the news?' Katie demanded from her round perch, oval-faced and wide-eyed. 'Did Uncle Richie kill someone?'

Eilish smiled at Katie. 'It's more like someone's going to kill Uncle Richie,' she corrected her in a saccharine-coated voice.

'And who *was* that slapper with him?' Hannah turned to me. 'It certainly wasn't you.'

'Thank you, Hannah, we'd already figured that one out.' My mother glared at her for not knowing better than to rub salt in my already smarting wounds.

'She was much older. Much, much older than you,' Hannah rattled on pointlessly.

'You don't think it's one of those *mother* things?' Eilish suddenly grimaced, clearly disgusted by the thought. 'You don't think that Richie has a mother-complex-syndrome thingy? God, that's *vile*!'

'I saw her nibble his earlobe,' Hannah said, presumably hoping to be helpful. 'Right at the beginning.'

'Could you sink any lower, Hannah?' I asked her, convinced that she was making this part up.

'No, that's the bit you missed, Rosie,' my mother interrupted.

I let my face collapse into my hands and moaned. The situation was going from bad to worse. The sound came from deep within. It was a kind of half-baked rumble crossed with a pitiful howl. I held a hand out to my mother, looking for her familiar comfort, and she rushed towards me. 'Sssh now, Rosie.' This was awful. It couldn't be happening to me. I didn't deserve any of it.

'No, let her voice her emotions,' Hannah advised the room. 'She needs to acknowledge the pain.'

'Shut up, Hannah,' Eilish snapped tersely. 'What do you know about pain?'

'I gave birth,' she snapped back. Hannah became almost savage when the subject of childbirth came up. We were all agreed that it had something to do with getting to the hospital too late for an epidural both times she gave birth. But I didn't want her to bring all that up now.

'What am I going to do?' I sobbed. I didn't know how I was going to get through the next minute, never mind the next hour or the next day.

My mother looked at me with an expression of such raw concern that it unhinged me further. The dam of tears I'd been fighting to hold back was about to burst. Everyone could tell. 'Get the sandbags,' Eilish called out.

*

Richie wasn't due back from Lough Derg, or wherever he really was – probably Florence, or Paris, or somewhere equally fitting – until the next evening, so he'd have no idea that he'd made the national news. No idea whatsoever that the television camera he'd spotted at the airport had projected him into the homes of everyone we knew, ready for a public scorching.

Waiting for him to come home I knew I'd have a fight on my hands to stay sane, fraught with not knowing what was going on, where he was. A part of me longed to believe that somehow he'd be able to convince me that what I'd seen had meant nothing, that he'd be able to present me with the perfect explanation. But another part of me knew that there couldn't be any perfect explanation.

It was as if someone had thrown lighter fuel on my emotions. They were blazing like Bonfire Night, the fiery flames of hurt, anger, betrayal and confusion. And I knew I wouldn't be allowed to suffer in isolation, in dignity, because the whole town would have seen the evening news too. The love triangle that Richie had drawn me, unwillingly, into did not hold only three people. It held the population of Waterford as well.

I'd lived here since the day I was born. It didn't feel like Ireland's fourth-largest city to me. As I got bigger it got smaller. My mother and father, and their families, had lived here since they were born, too, which meant as children we didn't get to escape to anywhere else to visit relatives. Lucky friends trekked off to exotic places such as Galway and Donegal while we traipsed across the bridge to Ferrybank.

We did things our own way in Waterford. Like when on 31 December, for instance, we opened the back door to let out the old year, and then the front door to welcome in the new one.

Everyone was involved with everyone else's lives and now they'd want their say in mine. I wondered how much intrusion I'd be able to take. All in all they were a hospitable bunch, I had to remind myself, and they only had my best interests at heart, mostly. My mother always said that the woman who boiled her cabbage in Waterford would always loan the water to her neighbour to boil hers. I hated cabbage.

I can still remember how everyone rallied around when my father died nineteen years ago. An awful silence invaded our lives and for a while the suddenly all-female household withdrew from happy, normal life. But our friends and neighbours kept us going. Their support didn't wane until it was decided that we were ready to fend for ourselves again.

In all this time my mother didn't have to cook one meal. We had so much food around the house that we had to hide it in cardboard boxes under the beds in Eilish and Hannah's room because people were always popping by unannounced and my mother didn't want to risk anyone thinking we were being ungrateful by not eating it.

The upshot of this hoard was that we got mice,

which with no man around struck up as much terror as discovering a colony of man-eating goblins beneath the beds. Rory Summer came around and took care of the problem for us, and ended up becoming more than a friend to my mother.

During the time after my father's death, the grass was cut regularly, the outside of the house was repainted (though no one thought to ask if we *wanted* yellow walls, as grief supposedly rendered a person colour blind), the cat was anonymously fed several times a day and grew to the size of a Tyrannosaurus rex, we were collected from school by someone with a car whenever it was raining, and so on.

All the little things were taken care of but, no matter how grateful we were for this help, in the end it was a huge relief to be left to fend for ourselves again, to get on with life – something I was starting to realize I might have to do myself.

For the last four years I'd worked in one of the busiest taxi offices in town, on John Street, between Harney's bakery and Kearney's butcher's, which is why Richie used to complain about having sausage sandwiches for dinner four times a week. The office was near all the liveliest pubs and nightclubs, which was very good for business.

Beside the bakery was a small alley, the side entrance to St John's church, where I used to stand for a quick cigarette before I finally managed to kick the habit six months ago with the help of self-hypnosis tapes. I wondered now whether I'd be able to stay off them. Whether I'd end up back in the alley again.

I manned the phones in the office with an English woman called Susan Gray. We always worked our shifts together and got on brilliantly. It wasn't a well-paid job, nor had it what I could call 'good career opportunities' – unless you wanted the experience to set up your own taxi firm, and that wasn't on my agenda. I wasn't career-minded but, more to the point, I valued the use of my legs too much. The last one of our drivers who left to start up on his own had ended up shortly afterwards with one of his legs in plaster of Paris, swearing blindly that he couldn't remember how it had happened, didn't know.

But I did. Danny and Lucas Furey, the two brothers who owned the taxi firm, were responsible. I over-heard Danny telling someone that they'd just given him a little tap to ward him off. They weren't to know that he had brittle bones, he'd said. Danny and Lucas Furey were like that, a bit rough around the edges.

Susan was bursting with sympathy when I dragged myself into the office for work at seven o'clock that evening. The dark, worn industrial carpet, the jaded paintwork, the cheap though practical furniture did nothing to lift my spirits. She leapt up from her seat and wrapped her arms around me.

'Don't be too nice to me,' I warned her, quite

honestly. 'I don't think I could stand it.' A very fragile willpower was keeping me from breaking down completely. I was trying my best to make it last until Richie came home.

'We all know,' she admitted, looking down at her feet gingerly. They were big feet, inexplicably big. Size-eleven planks. But the rest of her made for such an attractive package that people hardly ever noticed her feet. She was a six-foot redhead who believed in painstaking attention to detail with her appearance, even for work. 'Johnny was watching the six o'clock news before his shift and saw him.' She sounded like she would rather choke than actually say Richie's name. 'I always thought there was something a bit funny about him but I didn't like to say anything.'

'Who? Johnny?' I asked. I was stalling, pointlessly I knew, because I didn't want yet another person to reveal what they really thought of Richie. Richie had been my choice.

Johnny Power was one of our drivers. He was sixty-one and lived with his two sisters, who cooked for him, cleaned for him and ran a busy florist's shop called Flower Power on Parnell Street, just around the corner from the taxi office. None of them had ever married and they all seemed perfectly happy and normal. I knew she wasn't talking about Johnny. There was nothing strange about him. He was a lovely older man.

'No. Richie,' she corrected me, a distinctly disdainful expression on her face at having to say his name. 'But I didn't like to say. He's just not nice, Rosie, too full of himself for starters.'

'Too full of himself?' I echoed. 'That's only him being confident.' Even now my first reaction was to defend him. I'd liked that confidence. He wasn't afraid to say what he thought and didn't ever feel insecure, which in turn made me feel more secure.

'Believe me, I've known enough not-nice men to be able to tell,' she continued. The subtly painted lips pulled into a rueful smile at the recollection.

I dropped my chin on to the palm of my hand and it lay there, propped up by my elbow. 'Not you as well,' I sighed, unable to feel anything but deflated by this disapproval of Richie that seemed to follow me around.

She nodded.

'Doesn't anyone around here like him?' I knew I sounded desperate. A picture of Richie was beginning to appear, one that was very different to the picture I had, and I wanted the old picture back and everyone else to have the old one too.

I wanted to be able to tell them all again and again, as I'd done, about the time we'd watched Kurt Russell in *The Soldier* on television, and I'd waxed lyrical throughout about his tight army trousers, the torn vest that revealed hard muscle, and his strong, silent, very silent – he said less than twenty words throughout the whole film – persona, and how Richie had jumped out of the bedroom wardrobe two nights later, dressed in cut-off army fatigues, body glistening and smelling of baby oil, and on his exposed chest – half the breadth of Kurt's but I didn't care – he'd written 'The Soldier, Part Two'.

I'd laughed so hard that I bruised my innards and I'd told everyone about what my funny, thoughtful husband had done.

'Not really,' she answered.

I didn't know how I was meant to feel. Betrayed because none of my friends liked Richie? Stupid because I'd had no idea that they didn't? Or angry because they'd never told me?

I think I felt all three.

Rory Summer walked through the door at that point. He tipped his peaked cap respectfully towards Susan, and Susan smiled pleasantly in acknowledgement. They liked each other. 'Your mother told me,' he said. Rory Summer was my mother's partner. They'd been living together for the last ten years and had gone steady, as they called it, for five years before that. They started seeing each other, in the romantic sense, about four years after my father died. It had been too soon for my liking. But I now realized that it would always have been too soon. My father occupied a place in my heart that no one else could ever share. I measured every man I met against him, and that's where Richie had come up trumps. As well as the funny earlobes they shared, I'd sensed other similarities. They were both talkers with a big appetite for life.

At the beginning of Rory's relationship with my mother, as well as being angry that he wanted to take something away from my father, I was mortified because it meant that my mother was having sex, or 'horizontal shenanigans', as she liked to call it. Needless to say, for years I did my utmost to avoid any talk of 'horizontal shenanigans' with her.

Rory was a good man. He worked hard setting up the music systems in nightclubs and hotels all around the southeast and acted as DJ at weddings and parties and other functions locally, where he was very much in demand with the older crowd. His white van was emblazoned with his company name, Summer Sounds.

Rory had discovered weightlifting two years ago, at the age of fifty-five, and now his muscles bulged like a range of small mountains beneath his coat jacket.

'I suppose the whole town knows by now?' I asked him.

'They do,' he agreed with me, using his words sparingly, sensing that there was no point in lying to me. 'I called into the pub and it was the talk of the place. Someone had it taped and they were showing it.' The pub he was talking about was his local, the Oak Cask, about a fifteen-minute walk from the house where he lived with my mother, and run by a friend of his, Mitch Fitzpatrick.

'*What?*' I gulped. 'They were fast.'

'It was only on the small screen behind the bar, Rosie, because Mitch hadn't seen the news,' he tried to console me. 'You wouldn't have seen it if you weren't looking.' A muscle beside his mouth twitched and I knew he was more than vexed with Richie. 'It wasn't on the fancy one they use for the big games. They'd never do that to you.'

I glanced sceptically at Susan because we both knew better.

'He's a very unpopular fella in this town today, that Richie bastard. Bloody West Brit.' Rory's hands were bunched into tight balls in the pockets of his cord trousers.

To call someone a West Brit was not a compliment. It happened when a person's behaviour was deemed to be more British than Irish. Rory must've decided that, given Richie's newly revealed penchant for adultery, he was now taking his moral cue from across the water, when in fact, knowing what I knew about what went on around the town, he really didn't need to look that far at all.

'It's maybe time for him to go back to where he came from,' he decided, and the muscle beside his mouth thumped tellingly again.

Richie was from Dublin. He'd told me that he was a 'successful entrepreneur' masquerading as an office-supplies sales rep for a short while when I first met him, here in Waterford five years ago. It was Christmas time, St Stephen's Night, one of the biggest social happenings of the whole year in the town. It would be fair to say that only those locked behind bars didn't go out that night.

Eilish and myself were standing on the edge of the crowded dancefloor in Preachers Nite-Club, shoulders pressed tightly together, swaying to the music, waving to everyone we knew and drinking copious amounts of alcohol to be in keeping with St Stephen's Night tradition.

I was wearing a black halterneck dress and had a length of silver tinsel wrapped around my head, which I was tightening when I suddenly felt someone standing very still beside me.

'Which tree did you topple from?' a voice asked, laughing and sounding intrigued. The owner of the sexy voice had to stand very close to me in order to be heard above the din – so close that the point of his nose rubbed against my cheek. I tipped my head back and looked straight into his boyishly handsome face, open and encouraging and, remarkably, with the same funny, almost flabby earlobes that my father had had. His engaging smile won one back in return straight away.

Eilish was leaning over my shoulder trying to listen in because she assumed that if he was talking to me then he was talking to her too. 'The one in the lobby of the Tower Hotel,' I quickly answered. They had a fabulous tree there, especially imported from Norway, and it was the talk of the town. I'd never noticed him around before. Maybe he wasn't from here. And if that was the case he wouldn't have a clue why this tree was so special. I felt a bit stupid then.

It didn't seem to make a difference. 'Fancy a drink, angel?' he whispered, very loudly, into my ear.

In the other ear, I clearly heard Eilish chortle. 'Looks like he wants to be married by the New Year.'

I stuck a well-aimed elbow into her ribs. 'I'd love a drink,' I told him, despite the fact that I'd already had too many.

'Don't leave me here,' Eilish ordered as I linked my arm through the stranger's and prepared to walk off with him. 'Do not leave me here on my own. Don't you dare,' she warned.

I shouldn't have. But I did. I just couldn't help myself.

And that had been the start of Richie and me. He moved to Waterford soon after and now he owned a busy shop on the Quay selling mobile phones and accessories, and he supplied office equipment, too, and he was doing very well.

'Well,' Rory continued, 'he can give me my money back for this.' He pushed a small black phone, neatly folded in two, into my hand. 'I don't do business with no *philanderers*.' The word hung ominously and I guessed that he was simply repeating something he'd heard someone say.

The office phone rang, shattering the heaviness of the moment. 'I'll get it,' Susan said immediately.

I was nearer. 'It's OK,' I assured her. 'Triple-A Taxis. How can I help?'

'Is that you, Rosie?'

'Yeah, who's this?'

'Carmen.' Carmen, twenty-one years old, was my youngest sister and still lived at home with Rory and my mother. Carmen's real name was Carmel but, ever since she started flamenco dancing lessons four years ago – about the same time I'd married Richie – she had refused to answer to the name of Carmel, having become increasingly smitten by this new world she'd discovered.

Her hair was dyed crow-black and she wore a thick layer of dark eyeliner and clicked her heels and stamped her feet a lot. Needless to say, we all despaired of Carmen. Utterly, utterly despaired. My mother worried that she'd inadvertently taken some drugs she shouldn't have while she was carrying her in the womb and that it was somehow all her fault.

'Well, is it true?' she demanded.

'Yes,' I said, betraying none of my internal hysteria.

'*Caramba!*' she wailed. 'I never liked him.'

'Yes, I know.' Bloody hell. Another name to add to the list. 'Did you need a taxi?' I asked pointedly.

She ignored me. 'You know, older Spanish women are very beautiful. Yes, *muy guapas*,' she added. 'So I could understand if she was Spanish or something.

But an old Irish hag? I haven't seen her but I can imagine. God, what *is* the world coming to? Eilish says he's got one of those mother syndromes. Did you know about that?'

'No, Carmen, I didn't.' My voice suddenly sounded tired and hollow even to my own ears. I placed the receiver back on its cradle without saying another word to her.

'I'll be off again,' Rory said, sensing the growing tension in me, and swiftly disappeared.

The phone rang once more and I automatically reached for it. Habit. I'd been pestering the Furey brothers for hands-free telephone sets for Susan and myself for nearly a year now. They gave us pink fluffy earmuffs with pipe-cleaners attached to the ends of them for Christmas a few weeks ago and thought it was hilarious. They were now stuck to the notice board as a reminder that we were never to think, act like or aspire to anything above our stations.

'Is that the girl who answers the phones whose husband was on the six o'clock news?' an unfamiliar voice asked.

'Yes.' I wished it wasn't. More than anything in the world.

'You'd want to tell him that people this end of the country don't behave like that,' the voice went on. 'That's what I'd say if I were you.'

'Thank you.' I wanted to cry. I wanted to tell this person that Richie would have a very good explanation. I was trying so hard, so very, very hard, to hang on to that possibility. Why didn't anyone else want to believe it too?

'I have a very nice son who'd never do something like that to you.'

'Send him in to see me,' I said, flatly, my voice devoid of any trace of humour.

'Well, you see,' and then the mystery voice faltered, 'that'd be somewhat tricky. He's married himself, to a fierce bitch, and we'd have to get rid of her first. But he'd never do something like that to you.'

I hung up but the phone rang again almost immediately. 'Hello, Triple-A Taxis.'

'Rosie Flynn?'

'Yes.'

'My husband left me for another woman sixteen years ago. An out-and-out slapper she was, too. Now, what you need to do and what I should've done is . . .'

In our small town everyone felt entitled to their say, as I'd known they would. I just didn't know how it was meant to make things any better.

Susan handed me a fistful of hastily scribbled messages. I glanced at the first one. 'Bloody hell,' I swore into the phone. 'Doesn't anyone around here just want a taxi tonight?' There were all kinds of incredulous messages. Was this what people really thought of Richie? And what did it say about me?

2

After what seemed like a lifetime, Sunday evening came.

Richie was due home.

I hadn't slept at all the night before. Fuelled by rage and desperation, I'd spent the night on a listless circuit of sitting room to kitchen to bedroom and back again. I could find nothing to busy myself. Everything had lost its appeal and the lavender-scented candles I'd lit in an attempt to find calm had made my empty stomach heave. I sat in the dent in the cushion on the cream sofa where Richie had last sat, hoping to feel somehow closer to him, but it didn't work. I carefully stroked the dried blob of shaving cream on the side of the washbasin where he'd washed himself before he left, looking to understand. Not a hope. I took his work shirt out of the laundry basket, stared at it for ten minutes, and then I checked the pockets. Nothing.

In the morning, with a faint level-headedness brought on by the appearance of the pale January sun, I'd promised myself that I'd stay calm when the moment came. I would hold my head high, and keep my dignity, when he walked through the front door.

But that was hours and hours ago, long before I

heard the key turn in the lock, scratching the metal for an instant before it found its niche. Richie was home. That's when the real jealousy, the insecurities, the uncertainty surfaced and all the talk really got the better of me.

'Who was she?' I roared, rushing into the hallway, tripping over the sisal mat and sliding clumsily towards Richie. Any hope of preserving my dignity was in smithereens. I was purposely wearing one of his favourite outfits. Figure-moulding black wool trousers and a fitted black jumper with dainty three-quarter-length sleeves that tied with a small bow at the end. Would he notice? Would he care? Probably not, I admitted to myself and glowered at him.

The wide but false smile on his face slipped slightly, but only very slightly. 'What kind of welcome home is that for your husband, Rosie Flynn?' he said, trying to be playful, for some strange reason.

'What's your definition of husband, Richie Maloney?' I asked him sharply.

The smile dropped further.

'Did you not promise to love, honour and cherish me out in that church in Crook four years ago, in front of everyone we know? Love, honour and cherish, Richie.' I stabbed at my chest with my finger. 'I don't feel loved. I don't feel honoured. And I certainly don't feel cherished.' I took a deep breath. 'I feel gutted.'

'Rosie, you're a howl,' he said, kind of cautiously.

'Wait till I show you the soles of my feet.' His shoes and socks were then pulled off in a guilty hurry. I really didn't know why he was bothering. 'We walked around the island in our bare feet,' he told me, wriggling his toes accordingly. 'Our bare feet, can you believe it?' He grabbed hold of the radiator and pulled up a foot by the ankle to show me a very slight pinky-redness. Pathetic.

'And just where is that meant to prove you were, Richie?' I demanded.

The smile vanished completely. 'You'd better tell me what the hell you're talking about before you say something you really regret because,' and he raised his voice, 'I do not like your tone.'

'And I do not like to see you show up on the six o'clock news with your arms wrapped around some wrinkly hag at Cork airport when I thought you were on some mission for God out on Lough Derg,' I fired back at him. He opened his mouth to protest but I quickly cut him off. 'I wasn't born yesterday, Richie.' I felt stupid and angry for ever believing him.

'And do you blame me?' he blurted.

'What?' A hand flew to cover my cheek. It actually felt as if he'd slapped me.

Somewhere deep inside of me, where anger and all those other wretched feelings couldn't dictate to me, I'd been waiting for him to deny everything. But he didn't do that. 'So who is she?' I asked, because I now knew for certain that there was a 'she'. My mouth

33

was dry, my tongue crumbly, and it felt awkward to talk.

'She is not a she,' he said, sounding offended at the way I'd referred to her, and sending a jolt of pain through me. 'Her name is Ellen Van Damme.'

'She's not Irish with a name like that.' Thank God, I thought miserably. At least I'd be able to say that she was one of the more exotic species, that I'd been betrayed for a foreigner.

'Yes, she is Irish,' he said, dashing my limp hopes. 'Her husband was Dutch and they lived over there for many years.'

As I looked at him, way too imploringly, I sensed, something strange happened. His face, even though it still looked exactly the same – the same fair, freckled skin, the same pale-blue eyes – began to lose its intimate familiarity. Richie began to look less and less like himself, and more and more like someone else's lover. He looked colder, and somehow older too. I couldn't see him in the same way I used to because *he* didn't and that stopped me. It was all happening too fast.

'She's certainly past her heyday,' I muttered in bitterness and confusion.

'She's not,' he replied, in the surly voice he used when something irked him. The surliness was something that I'd never really liked but always chose to overlook in favour of the better things. 'She's in her prime.'

It struck me sadly that the dynamics of this conversation were all wrong. Richie was defending the wrong person. The person he was meant to defend was me, his wife, but there he was taking someone else's side. How could this be happening? I had a normal life where normal things were meant to happen, not things like this, not to me. It wasn't even something I'd ever worried about. I'd felt sure of him, of us.

I looked at him. He was standing in front of me, in his bare feet, with his arms folded stubbornly across his chest and his socks stuffed into the pockets of the leather jacket I'd bought him for Christmas a few weeks earlier. Comical. Dismal.

'Richie,' I suddenly sobbed, 'this is ludicrous.' I took a few gulps of air because I felt as if I might suffocate. 'What are you doing?'

'I love her.'

'You love her? You love her?' I repeated and I knew I'd started to raise my voice. But my head was inexplicably itching from the inside out. A scratch I couldn't reach. 'I thought you loved *me*. I thought it was me you loved.' I needed him to explain to me how this had happened, to take away the confusion, to make me see what I'd done wrong, to hit me with the hard facts. I needed the undiluted truth to make me understand.

He shook his head with apparent sorrow and regret. 'Things haven't been the same between us for a while, have they, Rosie?'

'*What?*' Things couldn't possibly have changed in the serious way that Richie was implying without me even noticing. Yes, I'd sensed some kind of shift. We'd downgraded from a fast-living relationship to a more comfortable routine, but I figured this probably happened in most marriages after the first few years. It didn't change how I felt about him. To me it didn't seem to be the fatal problem that Richie was trying to suggest it was.

He nervously raked his fine sandy hair with his long, neat fingers and I sensed there was worse to come. 'I've loved Ellen from the first moment I saw her,' he said with candour. 'I don't love you any more, Rosie. I'm sorry.' He winced at his own honesty. 'We just don't want the same things.'

I knew that if Richie wanted something he went straight for it and if he didn't want something he moved away from it. And now he didn't want me any more. He wanted someone else. The realization hit me with the dead weight of a slow-crossing freight train.

'Who is this Ellen Van Damme? And why? Why her? Why did it have to be anyone at all?' I wanted to cry. I wanted to scream. I wanted to attack him just to get him to react to me physically. And at the same time I was so frightened.

'She walked into the shop one day, about a year ago,' he admitted.

I'd expected a much grander beginning. People

walk into shops every day of their lives. What was so different about this time? What had she got? Was she so much more than me?

The hurt and anger, and a determined, detrimental curiosity, fanned the desire I had to know everything, exactly what had happened. I was hungry for the details even though I knew I would be much better off without them, better off unable to relive their first moments with them in the dead of night when I couldn't sleep.

'And what did you say?' I insisted. 'Something like, "My name is Richie Maloney and I have a wife who loves me but I've just fallen in love with you"?'

Richie looked very uncomfortable but that didn't stop him shaking his head at me as if he couldn't believe how badly I was taking this. What had he expected, my blessing?

I should've stopped then but I just couldn't. I continued aloud with the ridiculous conversation I imagined them having. '"We won't tell her anything and then we'll just appear on the six o'clock news and she'll find out about it at the same time as the rest of the country. And by the way, if I may say so, you are in your prime." Is that what you said?' A note of hysteria had crept into my voice, making it squeaky. '*Is that what you said?*'

'No.' He twisted his smooth hands together. 'Rosie, I'm so sorry but these things happen.'

'Not to me they don't,' I contradicted him. Everything was ruined. He'd ruined everything. 'You're a bastard, Richie Maloney. A bastard of, of . . . dra . . . dra . . .' the word escaped me.

'Draconian?' he meekly suggested.

'*Draconian?* What's draconian? No, *drastic* proportions!' He always seemed to know bigger words than me. 'You'll have to go,' I told him, unsteadily, pointing to the door. 'Go.' I didn't want him to go; I wanted him to stay here with me and fix this, but I knew that wasn't what he wanted.

'Look, Rosie, Ellen's waiting for me. I was just coming back to tell you about us, to tell you that I wasn't coming back, so to speak.' He paused. 'I never wanted it all to be so public but that, at least, wasn't really my fault.'

I bit my tongue.

'I'll get my stuff another time,' he told me, and turned to leave. I looked on in horror at the obvious spring in his step as he strode down the garden path. He was relieved to be leaving me. Richie was actually relieved to be leaving me.

'You haven't thought this through, Richie,' I warned him shakily, praying that this was true. 'I know you haven't.' I decided to play my only card. 'What about babies, Richie? She'll hardly be up to producing a horde of them.' We'd always wanted a big family. It was all I'd ever dreamt of.

He turned around to me and shrugged. 'Things are different now, Rosie. Anyway, it was you who always wanted children.' There was an edge to his voice as he said this, as if implying that he hadn't really wanted them.

Of course I wanted kids. Everyone I knew who was married had kids. I wanted to experience for myself that special look etched on Hannah's face when she held her son and daughter, and I wanted Richie to cherish our children in the same way that my father had cherished my sisters and me. How dare he ridicule me!

Without thinking, I picked up one of the pots of frozen geranium stalks sitting at my feet in the outside porch and lobbed it after him. I missed and the pot landed in the middle of the garden path, a pathetic patchwork of broken terracotta and tattered geraniums.

In desperation, I once again wandered around the house that we'd shared, trying to find a hint that something had been really, really wrong, something that I'd overlooked, something that would help me to understand what I'd done to make him do this to me. There was nothing. The house looked like it always had. Bright but narrow hallway with a sisal mat that ran the length of it. Sitting room decorated in supposedly restful cream colours. Small dining room with blood-red walls that Richie had decided on. And a much lived-in kitchen that held the paraphernalia of our life together – household bills, old shopping lists, photos, holiday brochures, decorating magazines.

The ringing of the doorbell eventually pierced the shroud of despair I'd wrapped myself in, sitting on the top stair, my head buried between my knees, and sobbing. I vaguely realized that it had been ringing for a while. Reluctantly I went down to open it, hoping that it wasn't Richie again, because I didn't want him to see me like this, but at the same time desperately wishing it would be.

The outside light, bought by Richie in Woodie's DIY for £19.99, cast dim shadows on the huddled figures of my three sisters, a bundle of sibling solidarity, standing shivering in the January wind. Hannah, Eilish and Carmen.

'Well, let us in before we freeze out here,' Eilish begged, her words followed by a trail of mist, her white nurse's uniform peeking out from under her wax jacket. 'Carmen saw Richie and his tart together at the Cosy Inn,' she said. 'That's why we're here.'

Carmen worked part-time, albeit reluctantly, as a receptionist at the Cosy Inn, an upmarket hotel in the centre of town.

I still didn't let them in. I couldn't. While I kept them on the doorstep, I was still in charge. And I needed to feel in control of something in my life, even for an instant. Once inside, they'd take over completely because that's what sisters did in times of crisis.

Carmen looked at me, her darkened eyes bursting with sympathy. 'They booked in earlier for an indefinite stay,' she said, trying to sound very matter-of-fact, as if it was of no real concern to me. She thought this way she might lessen the damage. 'Did you know?' she added.

'Kind of,' I half wept. I hadn't spoken to anyone since Richie left; I'd ignored the phone several times. I didn't want to have to say that he'd gone. But when Carmen saw them together at the hotel she'd have known immediately.

I opened the door wide and one by one they brushed past me, crossing in front of the enormous hanging mirror in the hall, the one that I'd spent three whole days sanding, priming and varnishing to the exact shade of 'rustic' that Richie had wanted, ignoring the irritated voice in my head that reminded me I hated all kinds of DIY work.

I quietly studied the parade in the reflection. We'd all grown up to be small and fair-haired with bigger chests than you'd expect to find on such petite girls, inherited with gratitude from our mother. For years at school, I remembered, they called us the Brady Bunch, which over time had become the Booby Bunch. The recollection brought on the tiniest of smiles.

Carmen was now a bit of an exception to the rest of us because of her desire to look like an authentic flamenco dancer. Her hair was dyed jet black, her skin was tanned from overexposure to the sun-bed at Images beauty salon on the Quay, a few doors away from Richie's shop, and her eyes shone like beacons from between two thick lines of black eyeliner. Strangely, I barely remembered what she looked like before.

I stood before them and knew I looked a sight. To be honest, standing is too positive a description of what I was doing; I just hung there, suspended in my misery, shoulders stooped, in my old green towelling dressing-gown with the missing pocket, chunky knitted socks swimming around my ankles, wet tissues stuffed everywhere.

'Get changed,' Hannah ordered me. 'We're going out. Head high, chest out . . .'

'She'll topple over if she sticks that out,' Eilish laughed dryly.

'. . . and chin up, Rosie,' Hannah finished, unwinding her long, tasselled scarf from around her neck.

I pouted at her and told her in a hoarse voice, 'I'm not going out ever again. I don't feel like it.'

'And that is exactly why you are,' she insisted in the same no-nonsense voice I'd heard her use so many times with her two children.

Carmen was smirking knowingly behind her back. 'I'll come with you and help you decide what to wear.' I was clearly beyond doing this for myself. 'And you'll need to give Eilish something to wear too because she can't go out in that uniform and those clogs. She'll drive the men wild,' she joked, refusing to become infected with my moroseness. She then caught me firmly by the elbow and propelled me up the stairs, into the bedroom that I'd shared with Richie. She winced and shook her head like she did every time she looked at the purple walls – Richie had wanted a regal colour scheme for our bedroom, and he'd been so enthusiastic about it I'd agreed.

'Get the snakeskin trousers out,' she ordered me.

I barely mustered up the energy to nod. They were a mottled snakeskin effect and extremely figure-hugging, and they usually caused a small riot whenever I wore them.

I pulled the trousers off their wooden hanger. I didn't want to go out, face the whole town and pretend that I was strong. The man I loved had left me. He'd left me for another woman. She was older than me. And she was here in my hometown. I was feeling understandably humiliated.

Throughout the day, waves of anger had been promptly followed by waves of raw desolation before more waves of anger enveloped me. But right now I was feeling bereft and very humiliated.

'Get them vipers on,' Carmen ordered me again.

I simply didn't have the strength to argue.

There was a new wine bar near the marina, an up-and-coming end of the town with lots of recent development, and that's where we were headed. It was called Wino's and everyone went there, especially those people who wanted to be seen. I didn't want to be seen. But Eilish, Hannah and Carmen all wanted to be seen and wanted me to be seen.

There was a moment of ear-shattering silence as we pushed four abreast through the double doors. I gazed around the room. I knew most of the people there, at least by sight. I was staring into the distance, trying not to make direct eye-contact with anyone, when at the opposite end of the bar two figures caught my attention. The outline of one was so familiar that my gaze had automatically honed in on the lean frame. It was Richie and he was with Ellen Van Damme. He must've decided that he wasn't going to hide himself away at the hotel, which was very brave – and cocky – of him, and made things all the more awkward for me.

My snakeskin trousers turned to slime on my legs and I froze.

'Don't look,' Hannah commanded.

It was already way too late.

Richie was stroking Ellen Van Damme's hand and he hadn't even noticed me. I wanted to die. We found a table and had just sat down when a bottle of Australian Shiraz appeared in front of us, along with four long-stemmed glasses, delivered by one of the waitresses. 'Courtesy of that table over there,' she explained and pointed a slender finger adorned with an array of Mexican-style rings.

I looked around. Susan was sitting a few tables away with a man. 'Pig,' she mouthed contemptuously, and then slid her eyes towards the good-looking man sitting beside her and staring my way, for me to take note. I'd never seen him before. He had bed-rumpled dark curls and devilish good looks. He reminded me of what I'd always imagined a South American revolutionary to look like.

He said something to Susan and they both stood up, the steel legs on their chairs scraping the wooden floor, and began to walk towards me. He was taller than Susan and a temporary distraction from the unnerving presence of Richie and Ellen Van Damme.

'Where is he from?' I heard Carmen whisper from behind her hand.

We all assumed he wasn't from around here because he wouldn't have gone unnoticed in a town this size.

'The land of the physically perfect,' Hannah sighed, strangely echoing my own thoughts as I looked at him.

Jagged high cheekbones sat above the day's growth of thick black stubble, and deep-set eyes blazed with intensity. He was wearing faded denims displaying strong thighs and a plain round-neck top that wasn't loose enough to hide the hard muscle beneath. There was no denying his magnetic physical attributes. I wouldn't have expected myself to notice, given how I was feeling at that moment, but I did – and quickly.

I guessed that Susan hadn't known him for very long, because she'd never have kept him a secret from me.

'Hi,' she breezed, with a bright smile that encompassed all four of us sitting at the table. She was wearing her revered Helmut Lang black trousers and a crisp white cotton shirt – one of the three outfits she referred to as her 'confidence clothes' because she knew she looked good in them. A thick gold bracelet swung from her right wrist.

'Hi,' we answered in unison.

'Thanks for the wine,' I continued, standing up because it felt more comfortable than staring up at them from my chair, neck arched backwards.

'Cool trousers,' the stranger commented, looking appreciatively at my legs. 'There's something about women in snakeskin,' he said, and grinned.

I took this as some kind of compliment and felt an inexplicable flicker of delight. Suddenly I wondered if Richie was looking this way and whether I should try flirting with the stranger. Would it bother him at all?

'By the way,' Susan interjected, 'this is Hank, everybody.'

We acknowledged him with nods and smiles.

'Isn't that a great name?' she enthused, so bowled over by him that she would've thought the same of any name he had.

They chatted amiably with us for a few minutes before returning to their own table. I sat back down again and as I did so caught Hannah, Eilish and Carmen staring intently at Richie and Ellen Van Damme. They stopped abruptly and tried to assume innocent expressions. 'Oh, don't bother,' I told them.

Hannah leant forward, her chest resting on the table, and angrily whispered, 'How could he show his face here? This is your hometown, your territory. He should have taken himself and his slut back to Dublin!'

'Dad wouldn't stand for this if he was still around, I'm sure of it,' Eilish commented dryly. My father had very traditional views on marriage and the few occasions that I'd seen him lose his temper had been enough to convince me that I never wanted to be the one on the receiving end of his fury. Richie would be taking his meals through a straw for the rest of his life were Dad still alive.

I glanced at Ellen Van Damme again. 'Do you think she's attractive?' I asked them of the woman I'd only ever seen once before, on television, and who had taken my husband and wrecked my life.

'*God, no!*' they duly shrieked in chorus.

'She's a bag,' Hannah exploded.

Eilish nodded firmly. 'Yeah, a pure hag.'

'Worse than that,' Carmen said emphatically. 'Much worse.' She didn't expand on this description.

So they did think she was attractive. I stole another glance. She looked more slender in real life, and very feminine. But then again candlelight favours everyone, I told myself. The cool light of morning wouldn't be so kind to her. It wasn't even kind to me and I'd only just hit twenty-nine.

3

We didn't pay for a drink all night. As soon as one bottle of wine was finished another would miraculously appear, and it was all thanks to me being dumped. Carmen called it solidarity in a bottle.

We left the bar a few hours later, and it was a struggle to walk in a straight line or even think straight. The others decided that what was needed was a helping of fish and chips to soak up all the wine, and to make sure the night finished on a suitably greasy note. So we headed off in the direction of the takeaway on John Street, a short walk away.

I didn't want to go. I wanted to go home and wait for Richie to come to his senses. I stopped mid-step.

'Come and have some chips, it'll make you feel better,' Hannah tried to persuade me, slurring and making the sentence sound like it was made up of one big word, and dragged me up the street by the arm. Most people we passed smiled openly.

I didn't want to eat. I couldn't eat. I was feeling even more miserable than before. Richie and Ellen Van Damme had left in a big hurry a short while after we arrived. They'd slid along the side wall and I was in no doubt as to why they were in such a hurry; I could tell by the look on Richie's face. It was a look I hadn't seen in a long time and I'd wanted to shout at Ellen Van Damme that that was my look and she had no right to it, in her stiletto heels and black throw – somehow appropriate attire for a paramour, I fuzzily determined.

Hannah, Eilish and Carmen were selfishly insistent on getting something to eat because, I decided, they didn't understand what it felt like to be dumped. None of them had ever gone through what I was going through. Hannah had married her childhood sweetheart, Dennis Healy, a builder who saw the world in terms of bricks and concrete and nothing or no one else outside of that. Eilish had been going out with Jimmy Bible, her first serious boyfriend, for ten years and they'd been engaged for six of those years, and living together for four, and would be getting married when Jimmy stopped betting on horses. Carmen had never had a serious boyfriend and she wasn't the slightest bit worried by this, which was worrying enough in itself.

So how could they understand? No wonder they thought the answer to all my problems lay buried in a mound of fish and chips.

A few minutes later I was sitting on the chipped windowsill outside the takeaway, its bright plastic sign glowing a few feet above my head. The only reason that I wasn't feeling the bitter cold was that these past two days I hadn't felt anything unless it concerned

Richie or Ellen Van Damme. Gathering my parka around me, I tried to lose myself in the thick folds, to slip into oblivion, hoping that no one would notice me there.

It worked too well, certainly better than was good for me: the two girls who came to sit beside me on the windowsill, sloppily devouring their bags of chips, didn't realize who was next to them as they chatted away about me.

They'd been in the wine bar earlier. And the stingy bitches were one of the few who hadn't sent over a bottle of wine, I fumed inwardly. I knew who they were – we'd all gone to the same school – and I'd remember them.

'God, that took neck, to turn up like that,' one of them munched to the other, 'and him sitting over in the corner with the other one. The nerve of him, all the same.'

'And Rosie's not that bad-looking,' the other replied, stuffing a chip into her mouth as I sneaked a sideways glance from behind my oversized collar.

Not that bad-looking? I repeated silently. My mother had been telling me that I was her beautiful baby for the last twenty-nine years and Richie used to tell me that I was gorgeous all the time – but not recently, I suddenly realized.

'Well, she's got the Flynn titties,' the girl continued. A little snigger and a nudge. 'My brother works in the hospital with Eilish and he says that she has to have her uniform specially made for her in Dublin and reinforced at the chest.' *Munch, munch.*

She does not, I wanted to shout at them, but I didn't want to draw attention to myself.

There was an envious gasp from the other one. 'She doesn't!' She lowered her bag of chips and stared open-mouthed at her friend, a few bits of soggy chips stuck to her tongue.

A well-informed nod. 'Apparently so.'

'God.' There was more than a tinge of admiration. 'What did you think of the other one?'

'She's old enough to be his mother.'

A hazy calculation on my part ensued. Ellen Van Damme wasn't quite old enough to be Richie's mother: I guessed she was around forty-five. She was tall with thick, silky chestnut hair that fell smoothly to her shoulders, flawless skin for a woman her age, a wide, expressive mouth that Richie seemed trans-fixed by, and she was beautifully dressed. Plus she had an incredible aura of confidence that sitting in a wine bar with her lover's younger wife a few tables away didn't seem to shake. I suddenly wondered if she even knew who I was. Maybe he hadn't even pointed me out to her – maybe I was that unimportant to him now.

It was a strange thing, being left for an older woman, I mused unhappily. I'd begun to look at them all in a different light. Lined hands, soft bellies, wayward curves were suddenly desirable things, like I'd never noticed before. I was even looking at my own mother differently now, perhaps catching a glimpse of what Rory saw when he looked at her.

'What do you think he sees in her anyway?'

I sunk further into the collar of my jacket, while straining to hear the answer.

There was no delay or hesitation whatsoever. 'Well, apart from being fairly attractive, she has to be good, doesn't she?'

'Good what?'

'Not good *what*, good *where*,' her friend said meaningfully. 'That's what they say about older women, isn't it?'

'Oh, poor Rosie.'

'Yeah, poor Rosie.'

And off they went, leaving me feeling as empty as the ketchup-stained chip bags they left behind them, just as Hannah and Eilish reappeared, each cradling a bundle wrapped in newspaper. Carmen was two steps behind them and licking her lips. 'I'll dance it off,' she sighed happily.

'We've got something for you.' Eilish carefully pulled three greasy white bags from her bundle. 'One large chips and two cod in batter.' She dropped the warm parcel into my hands. 'That'll make you feel better.'

'My problem is a lot bigger than that, thank you very much.'

'Now, now . . .' she began to chide like she was talking to a disobedient child.

And something snapped, something that had been pulled taut right in the core of me. I was tired of listening to them. I wanted to be left alone. 'Now, now, nothing, Eilish. Just piss off,' I shouted at her. 'Maybe you should concentrate on weaning Jimmy Bible off the horses.'

She gasped in astonishment that I dared mention the subject aloud in such a public place. Beside her Hannah tut-tutted disapprovingly.

'And as for you,' I stabbed the air in front of Hannah's face, 'when will Dennis realize that you're not made of brick?' I was repeating something she'd often wondered herself. I knew I shouldn't be doing this, as it was a real worry to her, but I couldn't stop myself. I wanted someone else to hurt, too. 'He hasn't touched you once since Gerry was born.'

There was a heavy silence as I overstepped the line.

'Dennis knows that I'm not a brick,' she said then, very quietly and sounding uncharacteristically humble and vulnerable. 'He's just been very tired for a while. He's working himself very hard.' She looked close to tears.

I didn't stop there.

'And as for you,' this time I swung, albeit unsteadily, towards Carmen, who was looking glassy-eyed amused, 'you can keep your advice to yourself because you don't have a clue what you're talking about,' I declared.

'I won't talk to you again until you apologize,'

Hannah threatened me in a trembling voice, still dwelling on what I'd said to her.

'I'm not apologizing,' I vowed. And, with a last cutting look towards the three of them, I wedged my bundle of fish and chips beneath my arm and marched off home through the streets I knew so well that I paid no attention to them. I swore I'd never speak to any of them again. I didn't need them.

I got there in about fifteen minutes, slightly winded by the brisker than usual, anger-fuelled walk, and climbed straight into bed still wearing my thick parka. There I unwrapped my by now cold bundle of chips and ate every last morsel, for comfort because I was suddenly very, very lonely.

For the next few days I felt utterly abandoned. Where were my sisters? This was the toughest time of my whole life and there was no sign of any of them. It was almost unforgivable except that I knew I had used my despair and hurt as an excuse to be caustically mean. The house was filled with an awful silence. And time was going so slow; there seemed to be a day to every hour. I even defrosted the freezer, watching every drop plop into the plastic basin.

It wasn't as if Richie had left me any hope, I told myself, reliving my sorrow over and over. What hope can there possibly be when your husband tells you he doesn't love you any more? It quite simply means the end. There was nothing left to do but put the past behind me and get on with things. I knew that but how was I meant to do it? Who could tell me?

I'd steadfastly refused to apologize to Hannah, Eilish or Carmen because I thought they'd belittled the biggest problem I'd ever had to face in my life, and I was upset that they hadn't checked up on me. But I knew they'd be thinking that what had happened didn't excuse my behaviour that night and that I needed to be taught a lesson. Sisters could be unbelievably cruel at the most inappropriate of times, I decided.

Susan did her best to persuade me to call a truce, implying that I'd especially hurt Hannah by saying what I had to her about Dennis when I knew it was something that was genuinely upsetting her.

To hell with Hannah, I thought stubbornly. What about me? What about what was upsetting me?

Thursday evening after work we went back to Susan's, which looked like something from *Ideal Home* magazine as she was gifted at DIY and decorating. I suspected that Richie had always been secretly envious of these skills. The walls were tastefully stencilled. All the curtains had matching pelmets and tiebacks. The shelves were almost scientific in their precision.

'I suppose you still haven't apologized?' she asked.

'Nope.' They hadn't called me either, I didn't add.

She pointed to the phone. 'Why not do it now?'

She was right, I suddenly decided. It was time to signal a truce. I missed them all too much. 'OK,' I conceded, 'I'll call Hannah.' She'd be the most difficult one and she'd probably forbidden the others to contact me. 'But first tell me who you were with in Wino's on Sunday night.' I surprised myself by showing the first signs of enthusiasm for anything in days as I suddenly remembered Susan's attractive mystery man that night. Actually, he was more than attractive.

'He was gorgeous,' I told her, still amazed that I hadn't been above noticing him and then remembering the hungry way he had looked at my legs and the inexplicable thrill it had given me.

'In a minute. Any news from Richie first?' she asked, somewhat inevitably as we hadn't yet broached the subject that day.

And there had been news, of sorts. Yesterday, about an hour into my shift, the phone had rung and the caller had hung up, but not before I sensed something ominous cross the line – and when I got home I understood immediately. The house felt different; bare, even though all the furniture was still in place.

I raced upstairs to the bedroom. The wardrobe doors and drawers gaped like raw wounds. They were empty. Richie had called the taxi office earlier to make sure I was working and then he'd sneaked in and gathered his belongings. I ran around the house frantically. All his things were gone. I'd never have expected such cowardliness from him.

The smell of a strange perfume hung in the air, too,

a more sophisticated scent than my light floral one, and I knew Ellen Van Damme had been in my house and my bedroom. I felt immediately exposed. I wondered if she'd touched any of my possessions, to try and get a sense of what I was like. I'd gone on an immediate cleaning bender after that.

'So, any news from Richie?' she prompted again.

'He's taken his things and he's gone. Shacked up with the OAP, I suppose.' I said this with obvious bitterness, feeling only the slightest glee in calling her an OAP because she had my husband and I didn't and also because she didn't look like the average pensioner.

'Been down to the shop lately?'

She was, of course, talking about Richie's shop. 'Nope, I've been avoiding that end of town.' I was going out of my way to avoid the Quay area, which wasn't easy, because it ran the length of the town, but it just felt like their territory.

'Well, then you haven't seen her there.'

'*She's there?*' I'd offered to work in the shop when it first opened but Richie had gently declined, saying that he wanted to come home fresh to me at the end of every day, that he wanted to have that to look forward to. I'd thought it was the nicest possible reason he could've come up with. It was funny, but pathetic-funny, how the rules had changed for Ellen Van Damme.

'Yeah, she's there whenever I go past,' Susan said.

'Are people still going in?' I'd been relying on the people of the town to boycott the shop.

'Well, none of *us* have been,' Susan assured me loyally, meaning everyone from the taxi office. 'But I think other people are still going in. He does have the best selection in town, you know,' she said begrudgingly.

'Yes, I know. Who do you think chose everything?' We'd spent hours together looking through catalogues and trawling Websites and checking out the competition. To thank me, even though I'd really enjoyed doing it, Richie had bought me a stunning diamond cross that hung on a silver chain around my neck. It felt like a lead weight at that moment.

'I always thought there was something suspicious about those retreats he went on,' she said. 'Any normal person' – she stressed the word normal, so as we'd both know that she didn't consider Richie to belong in this category – 'would've just invented a business trip.'

I hooted with laughter unexpectedly and it felt good to laugh again when I thought I never would. 'Susan,' I whooped, 'I would've been far more suspicious if Richie had said that he was off on a business trip. A business trip doing what? He owns a shop.' Susan was English and didn't understand the Irish weakness for retreats and pilgrimages. 'A retreat was a perfectly plausible excuse.' The proof was that I'd believed him.

'Well, it wasn't the most likely of things to happen,' she conceded with a resigned sigh. 'He seemed very attached to you.' In front of me she placed the plate of scrambled eggs that she'd been preparing for supper. Susan was the only person I knew who decorated her scrambled eggs with two sprigs of parsley, arranged at precise ninety-degree angles to each other, and my mother claimed that this was a sign of Susan's innate sophistication.

Yes, he had seemed very attached to me. But not attached enough, obviously. I changed subjects. 'So where did you meet your dark stranger?' I was very curious.

'Well,' she began in a hushed tone, leaning over the plate. 'I get this monthly magazine sent to me from the UK. It's a magazine for, for . . . well, for people like . . . well, it's just a magazine and there was one personal ad in it from someone wanting to meet up with a likeminded person, blah-blah, that caught my attention. It was kind of funny, but not presumptuous, if you know what I mean.'

'Not really. Is it a dating magazine?' Susan was attractive, albeit in a manicured way, and there was no way she needed to consult the personal ads to get a date.

'Well, not really,' she hesitated, 'maybe kind of, but not really . . .'

'OK, let's skip that bit,' I said, confused, but it didn't matter. 'What about him?'

'As you know, his name is Hank . . .'

Wrong name for him, I thought. How could someone who looked like that be called Hank? Adonis would suit him better.

Susan smiled and drifted into reflection. 'Such a *man*'s name,' she sighed contentedly.

I didn't want to spoil the moment for her. 'What does he do?'

'Err . . . he's an actor.' She announced this in a sprightly manner, as if she'd just made it up and was feeling pleased with herself. 'He does plays, that kind of thing, moves around a lot. He's a bit of a nomad by all accounts.'

'Did you tell him what you did?' Answering the phone in a taxi office would sound like such a boring job to an actor. Maybe she had been worried about the same thing and had lied?

But she nodded her head. 'Yeah, I told him and he thought it was a very real thing to do.'

Our job was definitely that, I mused. We sent real cars, driven by real people, to collect other real people. 'Well, I suppose acting isn't very real, is it?' I said. 'He must enjoy the make-believe side of things.' I sipped my white wine. I was vaguely surprised that Hank's looks hadn't propelled him further in the acting world, that he wasn't a household name.

'Hank,' she murmured again. 'Such a *man*'s name.' She sounded dangerously infatuated.

'Men are not worth the bother, Susan,' I cautioned

her, though I could see how anyone would be tempted by Hank and I couldn't help but wonder if I'd ever find one who'd make me change my mind again. One who stood out from the rest.

4

Myra Barry was sitting at the kitchen table, commenting on the splendid redecoration job, when I popped into my mother's the next day to say hello, and to see if Hannah, Eilish or Carmen had mentioned anything to her about last weekend's argument. In the end I'd given in and called Hannah to apologize. She seemed OK on the phone, but sounded slightly distracted, as if she wasn't following what I was saying, so I couldn't be sure whether I was really forgiven or not but my mother might know.

Myra was an artist and in her spare time produced a local women's magazine, paid for by some grant she'd wheedled from the council. The magazine was meant to be for women of all ages but had somehow become a kind of bible for the over-fifties in the town, with tips on maintaining themselves, lifestyle changes, local events of special interest. And Myra Barry had become their icon.

Needless to say, my mother thought that Myra was the most sophisticated person in the whole world, even more sophisticated than Susan and her neatly arranged parsley sprigs. Myra wore long, flowing clothes in rich colours – burgundy, bronze and jade –

and opulent fabrics such as velvet and heavy silk. Her hair was white and she always had it fashioned into a French pleat. Her choice of jewellery was eclectic. She was wearing several strands of amber beads today.

'Here she is, Maureen,' Myra wheezed at my mother in a throaty voice that came from a cherished smoking habit of forty cigarettes a day. 'Good on you, the woman.' She stood up and slapped my back.

I was thoroughly puzzled. I didn't know what Myra was congratulating me on. I glanced questioningly over the midnight-blue velvet scarf that hung on one shoulder, my gaze landing on my mother, hiding behind Myra, arms in the air and gesturing madly at me. She looked like she was trying one of Carmen's tortured flamenco dances but she seemed to be saying, 'Play along.'

Myra lit another cigarette with the end of her old one, sucking so hard that I expected the whole cigarette to disappear into her mouth. Her cheeks went hollow. She loved those gritty sticks and both they and she had been regular features in our house for as long as I could remember. Myra would breeze in at any time, bringing with her raucous laughter. She always sat on the same chair and smoked, and drank white wine or tea depending on the time of day.

There were candles lit everywhere in the kitchen – including one flickering hopefully under the statue of the Virgin Mary that my father brought back years ago from a trip to Lourdes – in an attempt to hide

63

the smell of cigarette smoke. Judging by the heavy haze hanging over our heads, the Virgin Mary had more important things to see to than clearing Myra Barry's smoke. 'Your mother told me you'd agreed to do it,' Myra rasped, sounding very pleased indeed about this.

My mother was still looking at me imploringly and I found myself doing what she wanted and playing along. 'Yes, of course, I'll do it.' Do what? I wanted to know. I really didn't feel like doing anything.

'You're not your mother's daughter for nothing.'

I wasn't sure what she meant by this but understood it to be a compliment of some sort. 'Myra, *Mammy* wasn't very clear on the finer points.' I shot my mother a thunderous look.

Myra dragged on her cigarette, almost tenderly, and began to speak as a tiny puff of smoke emerged. I really didn't know what Myra did with all the smoke when she inhaled but very little of it ever came back out. 'Simple,' she said, 'you just tell it exactly as it happened.' Another puff. 'It'll make a great story.'

My mother was busily avoiding my stare and folding a bunch of new tea towels, colour co-ordinated with the rest of the kitchen.

'The magazine is going to the printer's any day now, so you'll have to work on the article over the weekend.' She sounded very crisp and businesslike all of a sudden. 'It'll be good for you to be able to get your side across,' she assured me. 'Get it off your chest,

64

you know. You've got enough on that chest of yours.'
She whooped with laughter.

I folded my arms across my front.

'Now,' she went on in a decisive manner, 'we'll call
it something dramatic, something eyecatching, like
"Left!"' She drew a banner in the air with her hand. 'Or
maybe "Home Alone!" What do you think, Maureen?'
She looked over her shoulder at my mother. I seized
my chance to wrap one hand around my neck and
stick the other arm up in the air in the classic hangman
pose 'You're for it,' I mouthed at her.

'Myra, this article you want me to write,' I'd gathered
that much, 'on Richie leaving me?' She didn't contra-
dict me so I knew I must've hit the nail on the head.
'Won't that be just announcing everything to the
whole town?' I categorically did not want to write
about what it felt like to be left. My horror and my
hurt were all my own.

She swirled around. 'But the whole town already
knows. It's not that big a place.' She sounded confused
as to why this would be a problem anyway. 'And that
is not the issue. I am giving you a voice, Rosie Flynn.
I am giving you wings. I am giving you your dignity.'

I threw my eyes up to heaven at her theatrical speech
and wondered why she couldn't give me something I
could really use, like a new housemate to share the
mortgage with. Because I knew Richie wouldn't be
paying his share any more and I would not lower
myself to asking him to help me out. I also needed a

car. What I did not need was more public humiliation.

'The whole town,' she continued, the words spilling out as she bulldozed on, 'has been in and out of Richie Maloney's shop all week listening to him tell his sorry tale of love at first sight, and I know that for a fact.' She took a lightning puff on her cigarette. 'This would be your story,' she flicked the air in front of me with the cigarette, 'your story and only your story, Rosie Flynn.'

Before I had the chance to object, she told us, 'I'm all for the right of the mature lady to find herself a younger man – I've had a few in my day – but in this case, Rosie Flynn, I'm on your side. Use me.'

I couldn't stand the thought of Richie telling everyone about his fantastic new life. It enraged me. Yet another betrayal and if Richie was having his say then I'd have mine. And I'd do it bigger and better than Richie. 'Couldn't trust Richie to keep his mouth shut,' I fumed. 'He always did like to talk. Well, I can talk, too. I'll do your article, Myra.'

In the heat of the moment, I didn't stop for one minute to consider the rashness of this decision.

'That's the spirit,' Myra encouraged me. 'Spill all the beans.' She clicked her fingers eagerly. 'And I've just thought of another thing. Now, I don't mean to belittle you, Rosie, but the fact remains that Ellen Van Damme is a lot older than Richie and, well, that'll give my mature readers a real boost. Lovely for them,' she decided.

66

I looked down at my hands, noticing chipped nail varnish at least a week old. Myra's last words were ringing in my ears . . . a lot older . . . a lot older. I still hadn't figured out the age thing. Richie genuinely didn't seem to care. Was the world changing? Was it now true that an elegant older woman exuding confidence and poise by your side was more of a status symbol than a frivolous young doll?

My mother spoke for the first time. 'A lot of us don't actually want a younger man,' she said, unintentionally implying that the choice was theirs to make – and this made me smile, and then frown. 'They're much too, much too everything.'

'But a lot of us do,' Myra argued back, patting her French pleat. She winked at me, lighting another cigarette. 'There's something familiar about that name,' she mused. 'Ellen Van Damme.' She paused thoughtfully. 'I just haven't been able to put my finger on it. It's an unusual name and it kind of sticks in your mind.'

Usually I didn't take any notice of Myra's musings, but this was different. It concerned Ellen Van Damme. 'Try and think,' I urged her.

'That's what I *have* been trying to do.'

'No, no, Myra,' my mother said. One of the rare times she ever contradicted Myra. 'Are you thinking of that big scandal a few years back in Dublin?' my mother asked. 'A few years back' in their lingo could mean anything up to twenty years ago, I knew. Since my mother and Myra had reached a certain age they didn't make any distinction between what happened last week and what happened fifteen years ago. They remembered one just as well as the other. 'You know the one, that Dutch man with the same name involved in that, that pyramid-selling scam.'

'Ellen's husband was Dutch,' I told them hopefully.

'Yeah, you're right, Maureen, absolutely right,' Myra conceded. 'The one with the vitamins and skin creams.'

Vitamins and skin creams? It didn't yet sound devious enough for my liking.

My mother clapped her hands together. 'That's the one. That Dutch fella made all the money and took off. The whole country was in uproar.' That's Ireland for you. 'Luther Van Damme,' she went on to animatedly exclaim. 'That's what his name was.'

'Luther Van Damme, Luther Van Damme,' Myra repeated. 'Now, didn't he have an Irish wife?' Her face was flushed with excitement. The Irish loved any kind of scandal.

'Ellen's husband was Dutch by the same name,' I insisted again, hoping against hope that this man's murky past might be linked to Ellen, revelling in the possibility that she wasn't as perfect as she seemed. Wouldn't it be an unbelievable coincidence? It was almost too much to ask for.

'Don't get your hopes up,' my mother warned me.

'I'm sure Van Damme is a very common name over there,' she said. But really she knew zero about Dutch surnames so she sheepishly changed the subject. 'Would you look at all that mess,' she complained, and fingered the little rivers of wax threading their way between the candles.

I glanced at my watch. It was nearly three o'clock. There was still time to get to the local library and do some research. 'I have to go,' I told them. I suddenly had a mission, a purpose, and it felt good.

My mother shook her head knowingly. 'Wild-goose chase.'

Myra smiled and countered with, 'Good investigative journalism, Maureen.'

It would have been pointless to try and persuade them that my sudden departure had nothing to do with Luther Van Damme. 'We'll see, we'll see,' I said cautiously, but brimmed with hope nonetheless.

'I'll pop around Sunday evening to collect that article,' Myra reminded me and I sighed inwardly, having momentarily forgotten that I'd agreed to do it just to get back at Richie for having a big mouth. How did she expect me to use mere words to describe the hurt, the panic, the sense of loss, the fury, and the way time now dragged?

'And by the way, I think you should apologize more to your sisters,' my mother shouted after me as I ran out of the house. 'I think you should grovel.'

*

69

The town library on Lady Lane had recently been sandblasted and the ugly duckling of a building had turned into a beautiful silver-grey swan. The notice board inside was covered with different-sized coloured sheets that gave details of all the various courses and events going on around the town, giving the impression that Waterford was the undisputed cultural capital of the country.

I liked the look of the Chinese acupuncture course. Myra had done an acupuncture course in Dublin once; I'd have to remember to ask her about it. There must be something very satisfying about sticking sharp objects into people legally.

The head librarian was Muriel Ryan. We used to be really good friends, right up to when I fell for Richie. We'd drifted apart then. I started spending all my time with Richie because I was addicted to him, to us, to getting us into the settled life I'd always imagined.

Since Muriel had become a librarian, after university, I'd had to completely change the dull picture I had in my head of all librarians, because she was gorgeous – with silky, waist-length hair of an unusual purple-black colour, alabaster skin and a smile that lit the deepest, darkest recesses of the old library.

I guessed that Muriel did more to promote reading in the town than any amount of advertising could ever have done. I could easily have hated her for seemingly having everything but she was too nice and I'd known her for too long – since primary school days. Besides, these days all my reserves of hatred were being used. Richie Maloney and Ellen Van Damme were exhausting my supply.

Muriel flashed me a radiant smile. 'I know what you're after,' she said. 'And I have just the thing.'

'Do you?' I asked her in amazement, wondering how she knew what I'd come in for.

She held up a thick book with a very serious-looking cover, written by someone with a lot of initials after their name. 'It came in this morning,' she told me. '*Untraceable Poisons*. I'm sure you could find something useful in there.' She winked at me jokingly.

'Muriel, how would I find a newspaper article written about a Dutch man about ten or fifteen years ago?' I asked her when I'd finished laughing.

If she thought it was a strange request she didn't show it. 'Follow me.' We headed towards a computer sitting in a square cubicle.

She sat on the swivel chair and typed some words into the computer. 'Do you have a name for him?'

'Luther Van Damme,' I whispered, leaning over her shoulder.

She nodded and played with the keys on the keyboard. 'Most of the newspapers have been transferred on to microfilm now and it should be fairly easy to do a search under the name.'

The computer whirred enthusiastically. 'Here we go,' Muriel said.

I studied the page of references on the screen.

'What are those numbers?' The string of numbers meant nothing to me.

'Oh, those are the microfilm references. Do you want to see all of them?'

'You mean he's mentioned on all of them?' I hoped the vicious glee in my voice wasn't too obvious.

'Yep.'

I gushed greedily, 'Well, I want to see all of them.'

Muriel paused for an instant. 'Or do you want me to cross-reference with another name or something?'

'Cross-reference with Ellen Van Damme,' I told her.

Muriel swung her head back towards me. 'Isn't that – ?' she asked inquisitively.

'Yes, it is.'

She looked at me in the same way she had when she'd caught me cheating in a fifth-year maths exam. I'd scribbled the formulae on to my legs underneath my uniform skirt. It was one of those pained, disappointed looks that made me feel no taller than my thumb.

Last year Muriel had split with James McGrath, an organic farmer she'd been seeing for a good while. He'd met a successful pig farmer from Cork at some agricultural mart and immediately fallen for her natural charms. Muriel was really good friends with both of them now. Vindictiveness was not her style, but I couldn't say the same of myself. Through the thick haze of hurt that had enveloped me since last Saturday, a different kind of emotion was suddenly beginning to emerge. It was the need to hurt back.

'All's fair in love and war, Muriel,' I told her in response to the wounded look.

The computer screen showed a smaller list of references this time. 'Those are the articles that mention the two names,' Muriel explained.

'Can I see them?'

'I can print copies of them, if you want.' She smiled sadly. 'Be careful, Rosie. Don't do yourself more harm than good.'

'No need to worry about me,' I assured her. I knew what I was doing. I was getting my own back, in a small way.

While I waited for Muriel to make copies of the microfilm articles, I wandered up and down the aisles, slipping books from the shelves, grimacing at the sloppy, well-thumbed love stories and nodding approvingly at the gritty realism of some of the books stocked under the heading 'contemporary literature'.

'There you go,' Muriel interrupted me, handing over several sheets of paper. 'Remember what I said.'

'I will,' and then, more seriously, I said, 'Let's get together some time soon. Really.' I knew that I'd neglected our friendship and that it was presumptuous of me even to suggest it. I'd happily given Richie all my time, thinking that anyone fortunate enough to meet their soulmate would do the same. And now my soulmate had dumped me. 'If you want, that is,' I added humbly.

It was hard to resist looking at the newspaper articles immediately I got out the door but I wanted to savour the words when I read them, languish over them, because I'd decided that the content of those articles would be the downfall of Richie Maloney and Ellen Van Damme. I was hoping that whatever was in those articles about Ellen Van Damme and what she and her husband had been involved in would be too damaging for Richie to stay with her, would destroy the perfect image he had of her. He was always fiercely scathing of unethical behaviour in business because he'd worked long and hard and honestly to get where he was.

I walked down to the bottom of Lady Lane, turned right and crossed the busy main road at the end, and then headed for Wino's to buy myself a congratulatory cup of freshly ground coffee. It was usually quieter there during the day than it was in the evenings because it was off the main shopping thoroughfare, and quiet was what I needed.

I sat at a small corner table and fingered the edge of the small pile of paper in anticipation. Then I spread the articles out on the table, carefully studying each one, and pieced together a collage of deceit.

Luther Van Damme had set up a company loosely based on something called network marketing, and had sold his own wonder creams and vitamins through a chain of independent distributors – ordinary people who invested their money in his junk. The diagram in the paper showed it as a kind of pyramid.

He made a lot of money from the products these people bought and, in an ideal world, he would make even more money when these people talked some of their friends into being distributors too and they, in turn, recruited some of their friends and everyone was buying from Luther Van Damme and selling to each other.

But Luther Van Damme's ideal world didn't include Josie Nolan, the wife of a loud Dublin politician, who thought big and used all her savings to buy his creams and vitamins only to find herself four months later with most of her stock still in the garage and no help from Luther.

Her husband, Tommy Nolan, went on a popular national radio programme to complain about Luther Van Damme's get-rich-quick scheme and there was an influx of phone calls from people around the country with unsold stocks of the same lotions and vitamins. There was a lot of hinting at wrongdoing but nothing concrete. Just plenty of vicious talk – and that was damaging enough to Luther's business because Ireland was a small place.

Luther's Irish wife, Ellen Van Damme, then launched a bitter counter-attack in the press, defending her husband's business and his ethics and his wonderful creams. But the Van Dammes had too much money and a luxurious lifestyle that most people would never have, and public opinion judged that this was their just comeuppance.

Crooks, I decided, and a great story to serve my needs.

The Van Dammes, disillusioned by their treatment at the hands of the public and the press, left Ireland and fled to the Netherlands. First-class seats on a Lufthansa flight, according to the article, which wasn't what I'd call fleeing at all.

I knew what had to be done. I fished around at the bottom of my leather rucksack and found a pen and a crumpled envelope. To ensure that Richie wouldn't recognize my writing, I held the pen in my left hand and stabbed somewhat awkwardly at the articles as I marked each one with a short comment for his attention. The message was clear: Ellen Van Damme was bad news. He should stay away from her.

I'd slip the envelope under the shop door later on, after business hours, when no one was about.

When I tried to pay my bill the waitress shook her head firmly and pointed to a table near the door. 'It's taken care of.'

The owner of the Cosy Inn, the hotel where Carmen worked part-time and where Richie and Ellen Van Damme were staying, was sitting having a cup of coffee with his wife. She gave me a wide smile and winked.

Things were looking up again for me. I had discovered that Ellen Van Damme was once married to
a near criminal, and I was never going to have to pay
for another drink in this town.

5

That Friday, Susan and I were lumbered with the night shift, which started at seven p.m. and ended at two a.m. The night shifts at the weekend were hard and not made any easier by the number of drunks who wanted taxis but were able to tell us only that they were in a house somewhere with a green front door or a broken knocker when we asked them for their address. The invention of mobile phones had made our job a lot more difficult because we frequently got call-outs to ditches in the middle of nowhere.

'I can't cope,' Susan moaned as soon as I pushed open the glass door to the office, making the Venetian blinds that afforded us some privacy rattle noisily. The two phones were ringing simultaneously and I knew that the Friday-night rush had already begun.

Susan picked up both receivers and dropped them back down again in a fit of despondency. Again the ringing grew shriller and shriller in the small, badly decorated room, and I knew something was wrong.

She wasn't usually given to depression. In fact, sometimes her constant positive attitude exhausted me. But this mood of hopelessness worried me; I needed her to be her usual self, upbeat and strong.

I flopped into the empty chair beside her. 'What's up?' I asked anxiously.

The two phones in front of us rang. We ignored them.

'Your lips are sealed?' she asked.

'Super-glued,' I swore. 'You could hang me upside down from them and they *still* wouldn't open.' I meant it, too. She was a good friend for whom I'd keep my mouth shut.

She pulled a letter from her bag. 'It's from my mother.'

That wasn't strange. I knew that Susan often got letters from her mother, though they weren't usually sent in blindingly bright-orange envelopes like this one was.

'Some boy back in the UK is looking for me.'

'So?'

'He's looking for his father.' Her face looked numb, expressionless, and only now did I notice that she wasn't wearing any lipstick and that her lips and face had melted into the one lifeless colour. 'He's looking for his *father*,' she repeated.

'How can *you* help him?' I figured she must have known his father and that he was linked to painful memories. She seemed so upset.

Our hands were working mechanically, lifting and dropping the telephone receivers with Olympic-gold-medal-standard synchrony.

'He thinks *I'm* his father.'

'Well, he's obviously got it very wrong, Susan,' I laughed lightly, relieved. 'Why are you so worried?'

'He was adopted at birth and he's looking for his father.' Her expression had grown even more serious.

'Susan, lighten up. He obviously thinks you might know where his father is, that's all.' I smiled at her. I could not see the problem. Now, if she wanted to talk about problems we could talk about mine, because at that moment we were probably the only people in town who were not busy discussing Richie and Ellen Van Damme, trying to figure out if the age difference reflected something really sinister in Richie's character, lamenting on how dreadful all this must be for me and wondering how they could help. And help, when it came, took all forms.

For example, only that morning the woman who worked in the bakery beside the office had seen me passing by and had run out into the street and insisted that I take a bagful of free blahs. The blah is a purely Waterford phenomenon, not to be found anywhere else in the whole world: a kind of soft, white, floury roll. It's thought that the name originated from the bastardization of the French word for white, *blanc*.

And one of the Cosy Inn's housekeeping girls, who was in the same class as me at school, had nipped into Richie and Ellen's room, set the shower temperature at extremely hot, rubbed the sink with the toilet brush, disconnected the television and turned on the air-conditioning to produce an icy blast. Speaking to

Carmen later she'd been really apologetic that she couldn't do more.

'I mean, how could he possibly think anything else?' I continued, and began the ritual I had for the start of every shift. I made sure the chair was at the correct height, lined up my pens in a row and rubbed the telephone receiver with a scented wet-wipe.

'Rosie, he could be right.'

I stopped everything and looked at her. In truth, I'd known that something was bothering her for the last few days. More than once, I'd caught her staring straight ahead, her eyes dim and a desolate expression on her face, while her phone rang out unanswered. She'd been unusually quiet, too, not engaging any of the drivers in the idle chit-chat that she usually loved. I'd wanted to talk to her about it but every time I started thinking about anyone's problems I ended up lost in my own. I felt awful about it now.

Susan was one of my best friends. We'd been working together for four years. I'd taken to her straight away for her ready generosity and sense of humour, and over time I'd come to really appreciate the steadfastness of our friendship. I knew all about her childhood, which had been spent in the UK and was lonely compared to mine, and about the rift between her father and her. But even though I knew her well, she was still a private person. Some things she kept for herself and I would never want to take that from her. So I never quizzed her about the inconsistencies in what she'd told me about her past.

'You don't know everything about me, Rosie. There're things that I haven't been able to tell you. Things that just aren't so easy to talk about,' and then she stalled, looking pained.

'Go on,' I urged her. I hoped she'd trust me enough.

She took a deep breath. 'Thirty-five years ago, I was born Terrence David Gray. Not Susan Joanna Gray.' She looked at me imploringly. 'Rosie, I was born a man.'

No way, I thought, no way. I expected her to burst into laughter any minute at my panic-stricken expression but she didn't and the utterly solemn look on her face quickly convinced me that she was telling me the truth.

Holy shit!

Why had she never told me before? And how come I'd never had the slightest suspicion in all the time we'd known each other? I had a thousand questions that I wanted to ask her but I couldn't. I couldn't say one word.

Susan was staring at me, begging me with emotional eyes not to overreact, not to turn away from her. She held her hand out to me but I couldn't move. The weight of what she'd told me was pinning me to the chair.

'*Rosie?*' she said, smiling tentatively.

I looked at her in disbelief. I was more surprised

than anything else. How could she look so perfectly female?

'I know,' Susan sighed, seeming to read my mind with ease. 'It's because I chose all the bits myself. I do have good taste,' she reminded me.

We both laughed, albeit nervously: Susan because of the enormity of what she'd just told me, and me because I didn't really know how to react.

'Susan, I will never, ever think of you as a man,' I told her and realized that it was true. I simply couldn't.

'Thank you. That is the nicest thing anyone has ever said to me.'

Anything else beyond her immediate predicament would have to wait; I didn't think now was the right time for more questions. She had divulged enough and I'd honestly had enough surprises for one week.

Susan was staring at the letter in her hand.

'Susan,' I said very, very slowly. 'I thought you wouldn't have any . . . any, er, fathering capabilities.'

A hard glint flashed in her eyes. 'Oh, I don't now,' she assured me. 'But I did once.' The hardness disappeared. 'It seems so far away, so long ago, you know?'

I nodded. 'And did you have girlfriends? What I mean is,' I paused as this was kind of awkward for me, talking to her like I hadn't done before, 'could you have been the father of some baby, a long time ago?'

Now it was her turn to nod, and sigh. 'Yes, yes, I

think so. But it was a long time ago,' she was careful to point out. 'And it was just the once. Funnily enough an Irish girl.'

We both grimaced wryly at the irony of this.

'And how long ago was that?' I asked. 'Were you over here at the time?'

'No, no, it was eighteen years ago, or more even, and no, she was in England on a school trip. We met at a youth hostel in Bath where we were both staying. We were both so young, only sixteen.'

'So,' I did a quick calculation, 'this boy would be at least eighteen?'

A bleak nod. 'I suppose so.'

'And did the girl ever tell you that there was a baby?' The thought of Susan with a woman was very strange. All wrong. Two bits of a jigsaw puzzle that did not fit together.

She answered with a miserable flutter of her head. 'I didn't see any more of her and no one ever said anything.'

The private office line rang. We had to answer that one otherwise there'd be trouble. It was for emergencies, or things deemed emergencies by our two bosses. 'Excuse me a minute,' I told Susan and snapped an impatient, 'What?' into the receiver.

'What the bloody hell are you two ladies playing at?' Danny Furey roared. 'Well?' he demanded. 'I've been getting complaints that no one can get a car and there are the drivers roaming the town over with no arses on their back seats. And no arses on back seats means no pennies down my wishing well.'

He really did have an elegant way with words. 'We're having a systems breakdown,' I told him. It wasn't exactly a lie.

'Well, Rosie Flynn, you get that systems breakdown fixed,' he warned, 'or I'll be over there to sort it out myself.'

'OK,' I agreed, far more concerned by the power he wielded over my purse strings than his thuggish threats. 'What an arse,' I complained to Susan as I put the phone down. It was an expression that she loved and she smiled faintly at me. 'Now,' I said firmly, 'didn't the letter say anything else? Can't you track this girl down? I mean . . . surely if there was only the one?'

Susan fingered the orange envelope tenderly. 'The letter didn't say much,' she revealed. 'Just that my name was on the birth cert and my address on file with the adoption agency. He didn't really say anything – only that he would like to meet me but that he'd understand if after all these years I didn't want him as part of my life.' She yelped the last few words, as if they'd pushed a nail into her heart. 'If I didn't want him as part of my life.' She looked at me beseechingly. 'How could I not want that?' Susan loved children. She was the only one in the office who remembered all the drivers' children's birthdays.

I wondered whether she'd already told Hank all

this, whether her infatuation with him had pushed her to the point of absolute honesty.

'I would love a child,' Susan continued longingly, floating in a pool of oblivion, purposefully blocking out what I was saying because it would draw her back to reality. But the distress began to seep into her voice. 'How could I present myself to him as his father? What would that do to him? He might already be a fragile child,' she worried.

The answer was not clear to me either and I had the feeling that, even if I could include Hannah and Eilish in the conversation, and my mother and Myra Barry, too, the answer still wouldn't be clear. 'Susan, I don't know what you can do.'

'I will not acknowledge the letter, or any other letters,' she decided firmly, as if it was the one good thing she could do for him. 'He will never find me. My mother will never pass on this address to anyone. My father doesn't even have it – not that he'd ever want it.' She paused for a moment. 'Do you think we should tell him I died?'

I shook my head sadly. 'No, you can't do that. That's going too far.' So many lies, I thought.

'I could've had a heroic death and he could be proud of me?' she suggested, martyr-like.

'Maybe he would be proud of you anyway,' I ventured.

'No. This way is for the best. No contact.' She slapped the desk sharply with the flat of her hand, announcing her resolution, and then suddenly flopped back in her chair and gazed into the empty space above her, her face glowing. 'I have a son,' she told me proudly. 'A boy.' That he was alive and part of her seemed to fill her with happiness.

But as I stared at the bright-orange envelope in her hand I could feel nothing but despair and sadness: a young boy would never know that he had the most wonderful mother in the world, simply because she was born his father.

'No, Mrs Burke, there's nobody free to go out and collect the money,' I told the shaky voice on the phone a short while later. 'You know Friday night is one of the busiest . . . No, don't cry, don't cry on me,' I beseeched her.

Susan glanced at me sympathetically, guessing the direction the conversation was taking, and wiggled her car keys at me.

'OK, OK,' I conceded and the crying on the other end of the line stopped immediately. She wouldn't even remember she'd been crying in two minutes, I knew. 'I'll do it myself but just this once as a special favour. Is it the usual? A half-bottle?'

Mrs Burke was in her late fifties and lived about four miles outside the town, on the windy back road to Tramore, in a house that bore the stamp of neglect. Mrs Burke had openly decided that she needed the help of alcohol to live when Mr Burke died, but I reckoned she needed the help of alcohol long before he passed away and I felt really sorry for her. Especially now that I knew what it felt like to be on your own.

Mr Burke had been the caretaker at the all-girls school I went to and he was always a bit too eager to clean the windows of the changing rooms at PE time or check the water supply in the showers, and he'd never miss a chance to have one of us help him out in his crammed tool shed either if he could think of a good enough reason.

He'd sometimes have us climb up his ladder in our short uniform skirts to get at a top shelf while he held the bottom of the ladder because his back was at him. Muriel had spent nearly as much time up that ladder as she had sitting at her own desk. He'd probably end up in court for such behaviour these days, or have parts of his anatomy chopped off in certain countries.

My father hadn't liked him either.

Mrs Burke rarely ventured into town to buy her drink. She'd call us up at the taxi office and one of the drivers – Johnny Power usually volunteered – would make the short trip out to her house, collect the money she'd left under the garden gnome, prop the bottle of whiskey against the battered gnome and leave again. She made no excuses for the way she was and in return we just took her like that.

I grabbed Susan's keys from where she'd dropped them beside the plastic pen-holder while she frantically tried to answer both phones. Her red Peugeot was parked on the footpath opposite the taxi office, where it wasn't meant to be, but she never got a ticket because the traffic warden lived beside her and she was always fixing leaks and putting up shelves for him. I now reckoned her aptitude for DIY must have been a handy legacy from her days as Terrence Gray.

I ran outside remembering the last time I borrowed Susan's car to drive to Dublin, late one Friday afternoon about a month ago, battling the weekend traffic to collect supplies for Richie's shop that he said were urgently needed for the Christmas rush. He couldn't go himself because he was heading off on a retreat and he'd called and begged me to do the trip for him.

Despite being nervous about doing the distance on my own, I'd agreed to go because I could never refuse him anything. I now thought about what a fool I'd been for him, but instead of crying I pressed hard on the accelerator and the recklessness gave me some slight relief.

The once brightly coloured but now faded, weather-beaten gnome in Mrs Burke's garden was sitting on top of a small pile of grubby coins. I could make out its crooked angle from a few steps away. The dampness of the grass underfoot seeped through my light suede shoes. I quickly gathered up the coins, feeling wet dirt stick behind my fingernails, and put down the bottle I'd collected for her in the off-licence.

A sudden voice made me jump backwards. 'I know what he did to you and it's disgraceful.' There was no doubting the disapproval. 'Disgusting. And bringing her here like that, too. Disgusting.' Standing in front of the door was Mrs Burke. The light pouring out into the garden from the bare bulb in the hallway behind her gave her an eerie glow.

'You know, Myra Barry very kindly visits me sometimes,' she said, explaining how she was so well informed. Myra had a mouth like a torn pocket. 'And she just happened to mention your little problem.'

'He's a bastard,' I told her. I could use bad language with Mrs Burke because she was a woman who fought her own demons and knew life was tough, not fair. 'What else can I say, Mrs Burke?'

'I hope you've got something up your sleeve to get back at him,' she said. 'Never mind all this talk of dignity that you hear these days. You hit him hard where it hurts and you'll find that your dignity will take care of itself.'

I grinned into the semi-darkness, thinking of the envelope I'd slipped under the shop door with the cuttings about Ellen's husband inside. This was the start of hitting Richie Maloney hard where it hurt: first up was the perfect image he had of Ellen Van Damme, which I was going to deface.

'Don't worry, Mrs Burke,' I assured her, 'I will.' But behind the words I still couldn't believe that this was what Richie and I had come to.

'Good girl, good girl.'

*

Once back at the office I slipped into the chair beside Susan just as the phone on my side of the desk rang. 'Triple-A Taxis,' I answered.

'Could you send a car?' someone asked. 'I'm on the bend in the road.'

'Which bend in the road?' I scribbled 'bend in the road' in the column marked 'pick-up' on the sheet of paper in front of me. Danny Furey would be furious if he caught me trying to send a driver to the bend in the road and wasting his time, but after the earlier shock of this evening, I was feeling helpful – and cheered up, too, since I'd remembered the unpleasant news that Richie was about to receive.

'Come on,' I coaxed, 'which bend in which road? I need a bit more information.' This was Ireland, after all, and we didn't have bends in our roads, we had roads in our bends.

'The *big* bend,' the voice came back, slightly indignant. 'The big bend in that twisty road.'

'The big bend in the twisty road?' I still didn't know where he was but I decided to remain helpful just a bit longer because it made me feel good. 'And where are you headed?'

'The next crossroads.'

'Of course. The next crossroads,' I repeated, writing that down too. I'd been in the job long enough to know that, funnily enough, this wasn't a joke.

'Is that the guy from the big bend in the twisty road?' Susan asked in a rushed whisper, holding her hand over her own mouthpiece as she took a call.

I turned to her in surprise. 'How did you know?'

'He's called before,' she told me. 'Send Paddy. He knows where to go.'

'But it's not Paddy's turn.' I had to be careful because the drivers got really annoyed if I sent someone else when it was their turn.

'Paddy's second next and I'm giving Johnny a fare now so it'll be his turn.' Her voice carried no hint of the anxiety that was present earlier; it had slid beneath the surface. I wondered when it would be back.

I'd accepted her news quite calmly, as she'd so wanted me to. Anyway, there wasn't really a lot else I could do, I realized. There'd be no guest appearances on any daytime chat-shows for me, despite the startling events of the past week.

'Right.' I swung in closer to the radio microphone propped on the desk. Despite Susan's assurances, I was feeling a bit apprehensive about sending Paddy to 'the big bend in the twisty road'. I'd ended up on the wrong side of him only once before and didn't want to repeat my mistake.

I'd sent him to collect someone an hour early and he was so angry at having to wait that he'd made me cry – no, *howl* would be more like it – because it was my fault. Richie was livid as he held me in his arms comforting me later on. He'd wanted to have a word with Paddy for upsetting me like that but I wouldn't let him. I was secretly pleased that he got so worked up about it. He must really care for me an awful lot, I'd thought.

I took a deep breath. 'Paddy, can you get to the big bend in the twisty road?' I waited for the explosion over the radio.

'Right you are, Rosie,' came the unexpectedly pleasant reply. 'I'll be there in fifteen. Is he going to the next crossroads?'

'Eh, yeah, Paddy, he is.'

Susan's phone rang. 'Triple-A Taxis,' I heard her say. 'Where are you?' She scribbled on her sheet, pencil deftly scratching paper. 'Can I take a name?'

A sudden chill invaded the small room. Susan's voice changed. 'Sorry, no cars available.' She looked at me and mouthed, 'Ellen Van Damme.' Her face was glacial, a frozen mask of vicious emotions. 'Is that the woman who steals husbands?'

There was the briefest of icy pauses as she waited for an answer. 'Is it or isn't it?' she snapped. A triumphant snort ensued. 'Well, there you go, you need no other reason as to why we have no cars available when, yes, we are indeed a proper taxi company.' The phone fell from her hand in distaste. 'Bitch,' she snarled.

I smiled. There could be no doubt that Susan was pure woman and she was on my side.

6

I realized that a week had passed since Richie and Ellen Van Damme had infamously made the national news, blowing my world and my marriage to bits, at six o'clock on what was meant to be a very ordinary Saturday evening.

God, it felt more like a year.

No, it felt more like ten years.

But all this had happened a mere *seven days ago*. It didn't surprise me any more that people could turn grey overnight, or over seven nights. I inspected the hair on my head daily because I really did expect to wake up one morning and be henceforth known around the town as 'Snowy'.

Of course, people were still talking about what was now being called the 'Van Damme Affair'. Several times a day I'd be stopped in the street and asked what the latest was by people who figured they'd known me and my family so long they had every right to ask the question – and, after all, as one of them explained, it was only out of concern that they wanted to know. Concern and an insatiable appetite for gossip, I thought.

I was praying for a diversion of some kind but

nothing had happened so far to steer the attention away from Richie, Ellen Van Damme and me. Susan's 'little secret' would've taken some of the heat off me but it was just that, a secret, and it had to stay that way.

Thinking about it, as I did most of the time on one level or another, I still couldn't believe that this had happened to me. ME. Sometimes I felt numb, sometimes distraught, sometimes angry, a milk-curdling kind of bitterness, and sometimes I even felt guilty, which I tried to tell myself was ridiculous. But a lot of the time I felt lonely even though there were people all around me.

The relative normality of my working-day routine, getting to the office on time, taking calls, contrasted sharply with the collapse of my personal life and I felt that I was living a split existence. I mean, what was I supposed to do now that my husband of four years and a woman at least fifteen years older than him had moved into the hotel where my sister worked as a receptionist and I still didn't really know why, apart from what he'd told me (i.e., that things hadn't been right for a while)?

What was I supposed to think when everyone now told me that what I'd seen as confidence in Richie was just arrogance? And what I'd thought of as generosity everyone else thought of as flash behaviour. I was getting headaches like I'd never had before, trying to slot round pegs into square holes in my head.

I wanted payback somehow and I felt satisfied that with the articles on Ellen Van Damme and her husband I'd taken the all-important first step.

Johnny Power dropped me home from work at around two-thirty a.m. A free taxi ride to and from the office was the only perk to my job and I used it most days, sometimes making a detour to collect my mother or one of my sisters if they needed to be dropped off somewhere too.

Since Richie had left, Johnny was going out of his way to be nice to me, always popping his head around the door to check if I was OK, and bringing me small bouquets of flowers from his sisters' shop to brighten up the office. I think he felt sorry for me. Most people did, and I was reaching that stage where their pity only made me feel worse about myself.

The car smelt of faded aftershave. 'You look tired, Rosie,' he commented.

'I am.'

'Pale and wan, too.'

'Yeah, that too,' I agreed. My tired complexion wasn't helped by the beige polo-neck I was wearing, which drained my face of the last traces of colour it had. And my hair needed a wash. It looked dirty and sad.

The grey leather of the car seat was beginning to give way at the seam between my knees and I nudged a finger inside and absentmindedly began to pick at the hard foam.

I sensed him look at me out of the corner of his eye and heard him sigh. 'You know, I've never told anyone else this before,' he began.

I was listening, but barely.

'I let the love of my life go a long time ago.'

I began to listen more carefully.

'Went off to work at sea, expected her to wait for me, and took too long getting back, too busy seeing the world and flying my kite.'

'I'm sorry.'

'My own fault,' he told me. 'She was married by the time I came home again. And you know, Rosie, I never found anyone to equal her. I still love her.'

I wondered how any woman could inspire such devotion in a man. I certainly couldn't, as everyone now knew. That particular news had made the rounds of the whole town before I even had time to digest it myself. Faster than snuff at a wake, my father would've said.

'Do I know this woman, Johnny?' I didn't think so but I had to ask.

'Lilian,' he said simply.

'Lilian who?'

'Lilian Hurley. But you'd know her better by her married name: Burke. Lilian Burke.'

'*Mrs Burke?*' The long-suffering wife of our old

school caretaker, and the woman to whom I'd just dropped off a half-bottle of whiskey.

He nodded.

I tried to hide my surprise. Her cheeks were riddled with tiny spider veins and her white hair looked like she'd tipped her head into a candyfloss machine and stood up again. Then I remembered her as she was years ago, when she'd sometimes drop by the school to visit her husband. She'd been an attractive woman who liked matching shoes and handbags.

'Just to say, Rosie, that men sometimes make mistakes, make the wrong decisions, and live to regret them for a very long time.'

When I got home I rolled myself into a tight ball and cried myself to sleep. I cried because I was trying to build a life for myself from the rubble of my existing one and I didn't know how to, and I cried because I was worried that there was only one true love for me and the bastard had just left me. And I was still only twenty-nine; what would happen to me now?

I wept beneath the bedclothes until I eventually drifted into an unsettled sleep. I woke at eleven o'clock the next morning feeling unexpectedly energetic, more so than I'd felt in days. It was as if the tears of the night before had washed away all my negative feelings. I kicked back the bedclothes, freeing my ankles from the cotton shackles, and swung my legs over the side of the bed.

Then, suddenly and for no particular reason, I felt deflated again. I flopped back on to the pillows. I shouldn't have been surprised. Unpredictable highs and lows were commonplace these days. I could not think of one good reason to get up, and flatly deduced that this was how people ended up spending years in bed.

Then I heard the key turn in the front-door lock. Only one other person had the key to the house. Richie. Fortunately I had double-locked the door from the inside last night and he couldn't open it no matter how hard he pushed himself against it.

'Open the bloody door, Rosie,' I heard him shout through the letterbox as I raced downstairs. Through the glass panes I saw him take a few steps back and look up at the bedroom window, its closed curtains blocking out the outside world. 'Get up and open the door.'

I'd been running downstairs before I even realized that I was running and I knew that my brain hadn't sent the signal to my feet to move, that it had been my heart's treacherous doing. As soon as I registered the tone of Richie's voice, I came to a halt. I guessed what brought him.

I tried to retrace my steps backwards towards the sitting room, somewhere to hide. But it was too late. Richie had spotted my blurred shape through the same glass panes that I'd spotted his.

'I can see you, Rosie. Open the door.'

I caved in immediately because it was hard to break old habits. 'What do you want, Richie?' I knew perfectly well what he wanted. He wanted to tell me in person that he knew I was behind the anonymous newspaper clippings he'd received, that I wasn't as clever as I thought I was.

'This,' he said, slicing the air with the brown envelope I'd slid under his door.

I wondered if it had had the desired effect. I stared at him brazenly. 'What's that?' I asked him.

'I know it was you.' He smiled, faintly recalling for an instant how well he knew me. Then he scratched his earlobe, waiting for an admission from me. My heart lurched at the familiar gesture.

But I held my own. 'What are you talking about, Richie?'

'You know I know it was you,' he said coaxingly and then, with tremendous effort, he began to tear the thick envelope and its contents into little pieces. 'So just admit it, Rosie.'

Of course I knew that he knew, and he knew that I knew that he knew. But I was not going to admit to it now. I had some sense left so I stood my ground and folded my arms across my chest, clutching the baggy T-shirt I'd slept in around me.

For some totally inexplicable reason this seemed to annoy him. 'Look at yourself,' he gestured loosely at me, and I suddenly realized that it was one of Richie's old T-shirts I was wearing. An old Guinness one that I'd found under the bed last night when I'd frantically searched the house for something that belonged to him that he'd forgotten.

I'd sniffed at the faint odour it held until there was nothing left to sniff. Then I'd put it on and wrapped myself in it. In the sobering light of morning, I was appalled by my own descent into weakness.

'Look, I'm going to be honest here and it's for your own good,' he told me. 'You always wander around the house looking like something the cat dragged in. No, even worse,' he reconsidered, 'if I'm being really honest, you actually wander around looking like something that the cat would never drag in.'

'Richie, I'm just a bit tired today.' I tried to explain myself to him, thinking that I didn't really deserve his cruel comments. Admittedly, my fringe was standing up like a tiara of horns on my head and there were sooty mascara rings under my eyes. But these were exceptional circumstances. It was my right to look like shit.

'No, no, Rosie, it's not just today,' he said, sounding somewhat exasperated, and I wanted to slap him. 'Once inside this door, you never make an effort. Just for me. That's always been a problem,' he added.

This hurt too much. He was hacking away at our past. 'If it was always a problem then why did you never mention it?' I shouted at him. I could've fixed it. But he'd always said that he loved the way I looked, that I'd look good in a bin-bag, that no outfit could do me justice. He'd said things like this right up to the point where he stopped saying anything at all about how I looked. I'd missed the warning bells.

He didn't really answer the question. 'It'll take a lot more than this, Rosie,' he said, shuffling bits of torn envelope and newspaper cuttings around the hall floor with his foot.

It was only then, as the wind created tiny flurries of paper around my bare ankles, that I realized the front door was still open. I gazed downwards. 'I still don't know what those are,' I persisted. In this instance, there was nothing to be gained by telling the truth.

'Oh, you know all right. I know you well enough to say that much.'

This declaration of familiarity infuriated me firstly because it was true and secondly because there was nothing I could do about it. I couldn't take it all back, everything that we'd shared, and with all that we had lived through together he'd still left me.

'You do not know me,' I retaliated.

And suddenly we were shouting at each other, furiously debating how well he knew me and how little he thought I really knew him. I blamed him for everything that had happened and he somehow shifted the blame back again. I demanded to know what had gone wrong – what, where and when – and Richie responded with babbling soliloquies on personal happiness, life journeys and the irrevocable process of inevitable change. I could barely decipher any of this and told him so in no uncertain terms. By the end I wasn't even listening to what he was saying; I was just letting rip with whatever came into my head and sounding remarkably like a banshee on ecstasy.

I gulped for air. It took a few seconds to steady myself. 'Put yourself on the other side of that front door, Richie.' I began to feel calmer. Not less hurt, not less confused, but slightly more in control.

I looked at him, watching as he patted his fine, sandy-coloured hair into place and shook the annoyance from his face, and an overwhelming sense of sadness washed over me. 'Surely it doesn't have to be like this, Richie?' For that instant, I was willing to be gracious about the fact that he had left me, and left me for an older woman.

He looked me straight in the eye, placed a hand on either shoulder, and said, 'Yes, it does have to be like this. This is how it is going to be.'

'I won't offer again.' I really hoped I meant that. I wasn't sure how firm my resolve was. I carefully smoothed my T-shirt, rearranging the wide neck and sloping shoulders. But I still looked undone.

'Isn't that my T-shirt?'

'You're right, it is your T-shirt.' Damn him for noticing.

There was a heavy silence. Richie didn't dare to demand the return of his T-shirt while it still graced my back but he obviously felt uncomfortable about leaving anything belonging to him here, anything that might link him to me.

Suddenly, my patience snapped. 'Take the goddamn thing,' I shouted, unable to bear his unease. I pulled the T-shirt over my head and flung it at him.

Without it I was naked but for big knickers. I felt conspicuously bare but I decided I had no choice other than to brazen it out, and I somehow resisted the urge to double over on myself. Instead I adopted a defiant John Wayne stance. Richie was staring. 'What are you looking at now?' I demanded, but it was obvious.

'You can certainly be proud of those two mothers.' He duly nodded at my breasts and I immediately covered them with my hands, an exercise in futility given their size.

'Oh yeah?'

'Oh yeah.'

'Well, you won't be seeing them again.' I couldn't believe the ludicrousness of the conversation. It hadn't taken all that long to reach this stage. I sighed. 'Just go, Richie.'

'You *what*?' Eilish was clearly stunned when I told her about the morning's happenings and flinging the T-shirt at Richie. 'You must've made his day,' she remarked wryly.

'Yeah,' I agreed lamely, but really thinking that all I'd done was make a fool of myself.

We were sitting at one of around ten round, glass-topped tables, most of them taken, in an open-fronted café in the busy City Square shopping centre, waiting for Hannah who was across the marble-floored aisle in the Early Learning Centre with her kids. Eilish was acting as if my drunken argument with her last weekend had never taken place and that suited me fine: with hindsight the whole thing had been a little bit childish, though I'd never admit to it.

Hannah arrived a few minutes later, pushing her double buggy, her face flushed brightly with annoyance. 'You'll never guess what this one has gone and done.' She pointed a finger accusingly into the buggy and Katie looked back at her, uncompromisingly, while her brother slept peacefully beside her. 'She's gone and got herself barred from the Early Learning Centre.' Hannah was furious. 'The first one ever to be barred. No mean feat, given some of the types in there,' she added.

Katie smiled and Hannah grabbed her hand and wrestled something out of it. It was a cocktail stick. 'Do you know what this is for?' she asked us. 'This is for puncturing the inflatable toys in the shop.'

Katie confirmed this with a serious nod.

'She came prepared. That hoity-toity Miss Blue Peter shop assistant said it was "with intent" so she barred her! Imagine that, at three years of age. God Almighty, what's ahead of me?' Her unnerved gaze swerved between Eilish and myself. 'Don't answer that. Either of you.'

We couldn't have answered even if we wanted to because Hannah had barely paused to take breath. She looked at me intently. 'What's different with you? No, no, don't tell me.' She held up a hand. 'It's the eyelashes. Jesus, Rosie,' she proclaimed, too loudly for a crowded café, 'you look like Daisy the Cow with those lashes.'

'Thank you, Hannah.' I'd made a special effort to look good today. Richie's earlier comments about not making an effort with my appearance had sparked in me a determination to spruce myself up.

I'd unearthed the Body Shop eyelash curler from the back of the bathroom cabinet and it had taken a precise sixty-second compression, with me counting, on each eye and lashings of dark mascara to get the impression of three-inch-long eyelashes. My hair was fashionably flicked out at the ends according to style protocol gleaned from a glossy magazine, and held in place with a canister of extra-strength hairspray, and I'd very carefully applied an expensive, quick-developing fake tan all over, right down to the cracks between my toes. I was taking no chances.

So despite Hannah's comment I was feeling better than before, so much so that I didn't tell her that at least it was only Daisy the Cow's eyelashes I had to contend with and not her rear end, like Hannah. But

Katie, at three, knew no such self-restraint. 'Your bottom is as big as Daisy the Cow's, Mammy.'

We all laughed and it was really nice to hear Hannah join in when I was so used to seeing a more sullen side to her, especially of late. I wondered, and not for the first time, whether her problems with Dennis were the only reason, or whether there was something else going on that I didn't know about.

Just then Muriel walked by the café. She spotted us and came in. 'The very person I wanted to see,' she said to me, tucking a stray strand of long, glossy hair behind her ear.

'Really?' I was thrilled that someone actually wanted to see me above Eilish or Hannah. Small things like this made such a difference to my self-esteem, things that a week ago I wouldn't have given a second thought to.

'This is just an idea I had,' she began, quite shyly, 'on the off chance that you might want to get away for a day or two, a bit of an escape. I'm going over to visit Imelda next weekend and I was wondering if you'd like to come along, keep me company. The break would do you good. And she says you'd be more than welcome.'

Imelda was Muriel's older sister and lived in England. We'd spent from the age of twelve to sixteen copying everything that Imelda did. We imitated her swingy walk and her hippy-style clothes, we tied our hair up the same way she did hers, two plaits down the side and the rest hanging loose, and bought macramé beaded bags like she had. We drove her insane. And considering this, it was very kind of her to say she'd like to see me.

'Hypothetically, I could go,' I pondered aloud. 'I'm off next weekend.' I'd love to escape for a few days, to go to a place where no one knew me, to become anonymous, me again, not Poor Rosie, just Rosie. I knew that Muriel wasn't short of friends to ask along and I was genuinely touched that she'd thought of me. I didn't deserve it.

'Go on,' Eilish encouraged me, slicing into her doughnut with a small knife, pink jam exploding over the plate.

My stomach heaved at the sight of the artificial-coloured puddle. 'I'll go,' I decided. The money would be very tight but I'd find a way. 'Thank you so much for asking, Muriel.'

She looked pleased. 'Great. I'll call around tomorrow evening for a chat. Can't stop now,' she explained. 'I'm on a short lunch break.'

'You wouldn't catch me going to England,' Hannah scoffed as soon as Muriel left. 'Maybe France.'

Hannah had an aversion to England that none of us could work out. She'd been once, on a school trip to Bath when she was sixteen, and had liked it so much that my mother had miraculously allowed her to take six months off school a few months later and to go stay with one of her sisters, who lived in London at the time. Without success, I'd begged to be allowed to do the same. Then she'd cried for three months solid when she came back, and now she couldn't stand the place at all. It made no sense.

'Lucky, then, that it's me she asked and not you,' I told her.

We left the café a short while later, and outside we passed two builders who worked for Dennis, Hannah's husband. They were rigged out in the predictable builders' attire of padded plaid shirts, steel-capped boots and scruffy jeans, the necessary two sizes too small. No surprises there, I thought dryly, and then made the mistake of smirking.

One of them, Titch Murphy, whom I knew to see around, caught the look and mistook it for an invitation. He nodded at me. 'Looking good, Rosie.'

I was surprised by his forthrightness, especially since he had a physical appearance that didn't let him get away with such a forward approach. 'Eh, thanks.'

'Have you done something different to your hair?'

'No.'

'Been away recently?' he asked. 'You're looking all brown. What's this they call it? *Café au lait*, isn't it?' he grinned jokingly.

I decided not to incite him further by letting him think that mine was a natural beauty. 'It's all thanks to a plastic bottle,' I said, doing my best not to get into any kind of real conversation by not looking at him directly. Anyhow, the glint in his eye would've blinded me.

'Must have been some plastic bottle,' he insisted, and took the liberty of stepping closer.

'Yeah, it was.' I swiftly lifted Katie out of the buggy, her feet dragging in the safety harness, and wrapped her around my middle as protection.

'I'm not too comfortable,' she insisted and started wriggling, slowly working her way down my legs until I had no choice but to set her down on the ground and stand up unshielded.

Titch took another step forward, getting even closer. Over his shoulder I could see Hannah and Eilish stifle grins. 'Do you have anything over at the house that needs seeing to, Rosie, now that there's no man about the place?' He'd never make the Diplomatic Corps, that's for sure, I thought. 'I can see to most things,' he told me.

I didn't say a word more than necessary. 'Nope.'

'That's a shame,' he continued, undeterred. 'Be sure to call me if anything pops up.'

'He thinks he's God's gift to women,' Hannah explained once he'd gone. 'And have you ever seen a more unlikely candidate?' she asked, shaking her head in dismay at the confident swagger of the generous showing of builder's bum walking into the distance.

'How could he possibly think that?' I was dumbfounded.

She leant in close. 'Word has it on the site that he

slept with this stunning Italian girl on holiday in Torremolinos last year, twice in a row – a major achievement for him, I imagine – and he's been unbearable ever since.'

'I didn't think the Italians went to Torremolinos,' Eilish commented.

'A stunning Italian?' I repeated. 'My God, she must've been comatose with the drink.'

'Yeah, surely,' Hannah agreed. 'Both times probably. But the other one wasn't bad,' she said about his friend, the slightly older one. 'And he was giving you the eye too.'

'He didn't even look at me,' I told her. I'd barely noticed him. He definitely wasn't in the same league as Susan's friend Hank.

'You're fair game now,' Eilish warned me. 'They all think you must be desperate after what's happened.'

'Thanks a lot.' One more thing that Richie was responsible for.

I spent the entire next morning working on the computer in the smallest of the three bedrooms upstairs, writing the article for Myra Barry, cursing my mother for getting me stuck with it in the first place, wondering why I'd ever agreed to it and trying my best to find words that didn't make me sound too desperate, too pathetic, too easy to leave.

I needed about 700 of them and they needed to be of the humorous kind because nobody wanted to read about misery unless it was seriously funny misery. I spent a lot of time staring at the blue wall in front of me and counting dust flecks on the dado rail.

Halfway through, right at the point where I was broaching the goose-pimple-inducing issue of lifelong commitment, I started thinking about Johnny Power and his venerable attachment to Lilian Burke, whom I now considered to be one of the luckiest women in the world.

I was in two minds as to whether such a lengthy attachment could be sustained purely on the limited amount of time they had shared together. On one hand I loved the very notion and I wanted it to exist. But on the other I couldn't help but wonder if it was just an easier option for Johnny than getting involved with someone all over again, starting from scratch. If he still loved her, and could deal with her penchant for whiskey, why hadn't he made a move on her now that her husband was out of the picture?

I decided to find out. I picked up the black cordless phone beside the printer on the small wooden desk and called the office. Johnny was working and I asked them to have him call me back as soon as he could. After a minute or two the phone rang.

'Rosie?'

'Hi, Johnny.' I could hear cars driving by and the sound of the radio in the background.

'What's up?'

'I'll get straight to the point. I've been thinking

about what you told me the other night and wondering why you haven't done anything about it.'

'What, about Lilian? You know how things go,' he told me. 'I've left it too long.'

'Johnny,' I argued, 'you probably have a good thirty years left in you.' Life expectancy in this part of the world was very good and getting better. That would take him to his nineties, I figured. 'Give it some thought,' I encouraged him, because I wanted to know whether true love could last. 'I'll let you get back to work now. See you at the office.'

'See you, Rosie.'

I returned to writing my article, called 'Home Alone' as Myra had suggested, and felt pleased with myself when about two hours later I hit the print command and the small HP printer ejected the final version. English had been one of my better subjects at school. I'd even won a gift-voucher once for an essay I did in sixth year on the decay of morality in modern society. I could write a book or two on the subject now. God, talk about first-hand experience, I thought.

I sat back and read it through one last time, oblivious to the fact that I'd spent far too long analysing each word, rewriting line after line of my recent history until it sounded like I thought it should, to be able to have a fresh, unbiased perspective on the work I'd done.

I knew that I'd been open and honest throughout

and in doing so had made myself feel very vulnerable. But I hadn't wanted to lie and I hadn't wanted to cower away from the truth. The article clearly demonstrated that I blamed Richie for undoing my life's plans but I hadn't stopped to think that maybe I shouldn't have hinged all my dreams on him. I'd pinpointed all my hopes and desires that were no longer but I hadn't tried to remember the last time I'd asked Richie if these were still his hopes and desires too. I'd debated why he would choose someone fifteen years his senior over me but hadn't stopped to consider that it wasn't her age he chose, it was simply her.

I was hurt, angry, bewildered, lonely, frightened and heartbroken, and it showed. But the odd joke, at my own expense, lightened the overall tone.

I carefully folded the pages in two, slid them into my bag and promptly left for my mother's, where everyone was gathering for Sunday lunch at one o'clock. This would be my first family occasion without Richie since we were married, a milestone in its own right, and it felt as if I'd walked out the door without my vital organs.

7

Myra Barry was due by the house at any minute to collect the article. The precious pages were still lying folded at the bottom of my bag where I'd put them earlier that day. I'd been hoping to get to read them to my mother and sisters, to get their opinion. I'm sure they would've loved it because it made Richie out to be His Satanic Majesty whereas I glowed with goodness throughout. But I never got the chance.

Before lunch there'd been the table to be set, the good linen napkins to be ironed and folded into swans, five types of overcooked vegetables to be drained, a lump of meat that had been cooking for three hours to be somehow carved without the help of a chisel and, most importantly, men to be waited on. The usual Sunday-lunch ritual. And immediately afterwards everyone had disappeared.

My mother went to bed to sleep off her lunchtime Martini and white wine indulgence and Rory had taken advantage of her absence and absconded to the pub to get in a few pints of Guinness.

Hannah and Dennis had a blazing row. Hannah stormed out the back door with the kids in tow while Dennis left in a fury by the front door. Hannah had made some snide comment about her mother having a better sex life than she did and Dennis had taken offence to her sharing her thoughts on their private life with the rest of the family. I didn't know what his problem was. We all knew anyway.

And Carmen rushed off to a dress rehearsal because there was a Spanish-dance show coming up, which we were all attending. Carmen took her dancing very seriously and we were expected to do the same.

Eilish and Jimmy had tucked themselves into the sitting room with the door closed and were hissing at each other like delirious snakes. Eilish had just discovered that Jimmy had taken all the money she'd put aside in a special jar to build a new patio and put it on a horse called Bound to Win because he had a good feeling about this one.

In the end I was left sitting by myself at the mahogany dining table so I decided to go home and wait for Myra Barry.

I smelt the cigarette smoke wafting under the front door even before the bell rang. 'Hi, Myra.' I swung the door back to let her in.

'Well, pet,' she sang throatily and breezed by me, coming to an abrupt halt just a few steps later in front of the big hall mirror. She inhaled sharply. 'Rustic is so *passé*,' she exclaimed, running two fingers – cigarette squashed in the middle – along the wooden frame.

'My life is so *passé*.' I sighed involuntarily. The words were out before I realized I'd even said anything.

'Your whole life is ahead of you,' Myra immediately contradicted me. 'Ahead of you, Rosie, straight ahead. Look that way, look ahead,' she pounced on me and caught my head in a vice-like grip, turning my face forwards. 'That's where it is, Rosie, ahead of you. None of this defeatist attitude.' She drew on her cigarette and eyed me shrewdly. 'I hope you're not feeling sorry for yourself.'

'No, Myra, I'm not,' I said. 'How could I be? Everyone thinks that I should be glad to be rid of Richie. And to top it off, this is the year 2000, the new millennium, women have got to be strong ... independent ... uncrushable ... unsinkable ... battleships.' I paused a moment. 'All things considered, Myra, I haven't a hope in hell of feeling sorry for myself.' I had tried.

'That's right, you haven't! Now, let's see that article.'

I led her into the sitting room and she planted herself on the sofa. 'It's no wonder Richie left,' she said, showing no reticence whatsoever in delivering this kind of barefaced opinion. 'This sofa is facing the wrong direction. And there's a dead plant in your relationship corner.' She rushed over to the other side of the room, swishing devouré and crushed velvet, and lifted the pot then dragged it with some effort out into the hall. 'That's better.' She rubbed her hands against her skirt and left traces of dried clay on her thighs.

'Well, I hope he doesn't come back again now,' I told her jokingly as I grabbed my bag and lifted the leather flap. 'Here it is.' I unfolded the sheets of paper and handed them to her. 'Tell me what you think. It took hours,' I admitted.

Myra stacked several of the small, plump sofa cushions behind her and slowly leant back like a regal matriarch. 'Get me a drink, Rosie dear.'

'OK.' I had a few bottles of good white wine stored in the fridge, chilled Sancerre, that I'd blown my food budget on because I was no longer interested in eating.

Instead of going straight into the kitchen I walked down the hallway and stopped in front of the hanging mirror that Myra had commented on, which I now vowed to do something about. Yesterday's fake tan gave me a nice Mediterranean glow. It made my hair look blonder and my teeth look whiter. I had on the same black wool trousers and black jumper as the night Richie had left. I bravely placed a mental image of Ellen Van Damme beside me in the mirror.

She was tall; I was short.

She was dark; I was fair.

She had Richie; I didn't.

Why the hell was that?

'Is that drink coming?' Myra called out. 'I'm parched in here.'

'Coming right up,' I told her, scuttling guiltily into the kitchen.

'You know,' she said, as I handed her the blue glass

goblet, generously filled to the rim, 'this is not bad work at all, Rosie.' She waved the sheets she'd been reading from and lowered her mouth to the glass to sip.

'Seriously,' she carried on once she'd finished, 'I mean, it's very emotional, but witty at the same time, and by the end of the first page the reader just wants to be your best friend and give you a big hug.'

'Is that good?' I didn't really see why any of Myra's readers, mostly women in their late fifties and plus, would want to be my best friend. I'd battled my way through writing the article, torn between putting on a brave face and telling the truth. In the end I did a bit of the former and a lot of the latter. I'd had enough of lies.

'Yes, that is good,' she insisted. 'Most of the time you don't feel anything for what you're reading; it leaves you indifferent.' She looked at me with glistening eyes. 'But this doesn't. You've done yourself proud.' Two trickles made shiny tracks down her powdered cheeks. 'Oh, Rosie,' she quietly sobbed, 'I've known you since you were a little girl, just a tiny thing, and it makes me feel so proud,' she slapped her hand against her chest, her big turquoise ring getting tangled in her scarf, 'that you're being this brave and, and . . . putting your raw feelings on paper for everyone to see, and you're being generous enough to allow people to laugh when they're reading all about it. You are something else, let me tell you.' The tears continued to roll down her cheeks as she lifted the glass and took another sip of wine.

I didn't know what to say. I had never seen Myra Barry cry. I didn't think she could. Blocked ducts or something. 'If you put another tear into that glass, Myra,' I said hesitantly, 'I'm going to have to throw you out under the decency towards alcohol rule. Salt and Sancerre just don't go.'

'You're absolutely right, Rosie. I don't know what came over me. I probably need to see my herbalist and get rebalanced. By the way, did I ever tell you that I practically introduced this town to Sancerre? They were still drinking Blue Nun till I came along.' She drained her glass and shook it at me. 'I think it's time for a refill.'

Two hours later Myra was still demanding refills. She hadn't moved or stopped talking in all that time. My ears were getting tired. She was now telling me about the time she'd won Miss Agricultural Ireland when she was eighteen, which I already knew all about.

'I was gorgeous then, Rosie, a lovely little figure and beautiful thick hair that I wore in a sophisticated chignon, right here,' she patted the nape of her neck, 'and I had just the most perfect skin you could ever imagine. And I must have had just the personality that the judges were looking for, too . . . you know, it isn't all looks . . . I had such energy and such an appetite for life!' Myra was enraptured. 'And this, Rosie, this is the way I walked when I went up on stage to collect my crown.' She jumped up from the sofa and quickly crossed to the other side of the room, where the dead plant had lived and died for many months. 'Watch now,' she warned me, and she did a slinky walk back to the sofa. 'You're in luck, Rosie, because I think I can remember every word of the acceptance speech I made.' She took a deep breath and I groaned inwardly. But I hadn't the heart to cut her off when she seemed to be enjoying herself so much. I should really learn to speak up for myself. I bet Ellen Van Damme did, I thought.

Luckily, the doorbell rang just as she was about to launch into her acceptance speech, which I knew from past experience was fifteen minutes long. Myra, my mother, my three sisters and I all knew it off by heart.

I was on my feet running into the hallway before the bell could ring a second time. Muriel smiled at the expression of pure relief on my face. 'Saved by the bell?' she guessed.

'Yes!'

'I spotted Myra's car.'

I nodded. It would be difficult not to spot Myra's car. It was an old Beetle that had been spray-painted shimmering turquoise, Myra's favourite colour.

'Come in.' I opened the door and she stepped in, looking splendid. She was wearing a long, slightly flared wool skirt in a deep-purple colour and a matching loose-waisted short jumper with a high neck. Her coat was an ankle-length sheath of purple and charcoal-grey plaid, which was definitely the work of some Irish designer.

'Why can't I look like you?' I moaned. Even in her flat leather brogues, Muriel towered over me by about five inches.

Her eyes widened and she looked at me. 'What would you want to look like me for? I've never seen you look better. That's the irony of the whole thing. This is probably the toughest time of your life, and you've never looked better.'

'I bet you say that to all the girls,' I said and hugged her.

She laughed and we both went into the sitting room where Myra was idly flicking through my compact-disc collection. She looked up and spotted Muriel. Suddenly, her demeanour changed dramatically. She became all stiff and edgy. 'Ah, Muriel, how are you?' she asked as she raced over to the sofa and grabbed her big patchwork bag. 'Got to fly now, girls.'

Muriel was standing beside me, smirking knowingly.

I didn't know what was going on. 'Myra, you can't drive home,' I said firmly. 'You've had too much to drink. Anyway what's the hurry?'

'I've just remembered I have to be somewhere,' she lied, so unconvincingly that she made herself even more uncomfortable and clutched her bag even tighter.

I tugged the bag from her and rummaged around until I found her car keys and put them in the pocket of my trousers. 'Sit down,' I insisted, just sternly enough to make her listen but not enough to rile her. 'You're not driving anywhere. I'll call you a taxi.'

Myra realized that she had no choice so, looking very awkward, sat back on the sofa again, beside Muriel. 'I'm very sorry about that book, Muriel,' she mumbled. 'I keep meaning to bring it back.'

'I know, Myra. And you must. There's a waiting list for it.' I could see that Muriel was trying to suppress a grin. 'It's a popular book.'

'Oh, you don't have to tell me how popular it is,' Myra agreed. 'I promise, I've been on my way to the library with it several times but each time I've just gotten waylaid.' She settled back further into the cushion and took a deep breath, more at ease now that her offence was out in the open. 'Once . . .'

I immediately recognized the onset of one of Myra's soliloquies and slipped out of the room to call her a taxi. When I got back she was still telling Muriel about the various times she'd tried to get the book back to the library and had been sidetracked *en route*.

Trying to interrupt Myra with mere words would be like trying to stop a fast train with my foot – pointless – so I just sat cross-legged on the floor in front of her and resigned myself to letting her go on while we waited for the taxi to get here.

Over the next fifteen minutes we somehow went from Myra's Indiana Jones-like adventures in getting the book back to the library to the catastrophic weather changes brought on by El Nino. And neither Muriel nor myself had uttered a single word.

Then suddenly Johnny Power was standing in front of us. I'd purposely left the front door open and he'd walked straight in, looking dapper – in his own peculiar way – wearing a navy suit, a butter-coloured shirt and a short, patterned tie, with his hair brushed back.

'Jesus Christ, Johnny Power, but I could really fancy you if you were twenty years younger.' Myra launched herself at Johnny and hung on to his arm while she tried a seductive drawl. 'Have you come to take me away from all this?' The result was *The Best Little Whorehouse in Texas* meets *Shirley Valentine*.

He smiled at her indulgently and nodded towards the door. 'The engine is still running,' he told her.

'I'll bet it is, Johnny boy.'

I grabbed Myra by the arm and guided her towards the front door, glancing apologetically at Johnny.

'I need to talk to you urgently,' he whispered to me so Myra wouldn't hear.

'What? What's so urgent?' I whispered back.

'What's all the whispering?' Myra wanted to know.

I propelled her forward a few more steps.

Johnny nervously worked the knot on his tie even tighter. 'Not now, not now. I'll grab you at work.'

'What's so important?' I persisted.

'Sshhh.' He nodded towards Myra's lilting figure. 'She'll hear.'

'So?'

'Well, it's a secret. Just a little one.'

My heart sank. I'd had my fill of secrets this week. The last thing I wanted was yet another one. But I smiled politely and said, 'We'll talk soon, Johnny.'

He looked at Myra. 'Come on now, Myra, in the car and we'll be off.'

Myra surprised me by climbing on to the back seat of the car without putting up a fight. 'This is just like *Driving Miss Daisy.*'

Johnny shook his head in bewilderment. 'Except I'm not black and you're no daisy.'

'What book was Myra reading that was so interesting she couldn't give it back?' I quizzed Muriel when I got back to the sitting room after waving them off. I was curious.

'*The Beginner's Guide to Tantric Sex,*' she laughed. 'Strange to see Myra flustered like that, but you wouldn't believe how some people react when they've got a book overdue. You'd swear I was the Fifth Horseman of the Apocalypse. Anyway, we've got better things to talk about.'

I knew we did. Our forthcoming trip to the UK.

I poured her a glass of wine and we set about making plans for the weekend. Muriel had gone on the Internet at work and booked our flights. We were leaving Dublin airport on Friday evening and flying direct to Southampton, where Imelda would pick us up and take us to her place in Winchester, about eleven miles away. Then she'd take us back again on Sunday late afternoon for the return flight.

It seemed strange to me to be planning something without Richie. But I couldn't deny that it was exciting too. And now I knew one thing for certain; Richie wasn't coming back to me. He'd deliberately burnt all his bridges when he brought Ellen Van Damme to Waterford, my hometown, and paraded her in front of the people I'd known all my life. The finality of this act made me realize that I had to get on with life and, for my own sake, I had to make it better than before. It sounded simple but it wasn't. It would be a battle. I sighed loudly.

'It's no good going back over things,' Muriel cautioned. 'You need to look forwards, not backwards,' she said, echoing Myra Barry's words of a few hours earlier.

'I'm dizzy from trying to looking forward,' I told her earnestly.

Her eyes dropped to my stomach. 'That's lack of food.' She curled her feet under her, her long, dark skirt draping the pale sofa and creating a dramatic effect. 'Leave Richie to worry about Richie,' she said shrewdly. 'From this moment on he'll spend every waking minute trying to persuade Ellen Van Damme that he loves her more than he ever loved you, wrinkles and all.'

I shook my head. 'She doesn't seem that insecure.'

'It's the nature of the game, Rosie. Bound to

happen. You're so close by and you'll be a constant reminder of Richie's old life. A worry to her.'

'I don't know about that.'

I wouldn't be leaving Richie alone for a while, I'd decided. I hadn't quite finished with him. I wanted payback. Muriel wouldn't have understood this if I'd told her – she'd have lectured me on the damage I was bound to do myself, and would have tried to talk me out of it. But I had plans for Richie and I didn't want to change my mind.

8

The week kicked off to a glorious start. At eight-thirty on the dot a funeral wreath arrived for Richie from the Furey brothers. It was sent from Johnny Power's sisters' flower shop and it was a skilful creation of thistles and thorns with a single white rose in the middle. The symbolism was enough to make a grown man cry.

Delighted by this unsubtle – and slightly crude – show of support, I hurried to give the deliveryman the address for the Cosy Inn, where reports from Carmen told me that Richie and Ellen were still staying, and suggested that he should make his way over there immediately. I didn't want him to miss Richie before he went to work. He grinned at me and winked. I winked back. It was a small town.

'Morning,' I greeted Susan breezily. We were starting the ten a.m. to seven p.m. shift.

'Good morning. You're sounding chirpy today. Has Richie dropped dead?' she inquired, but in a kind of lacklustre way.

'Next best thing,' I told her.

'I'm not going to ask.'

Usually she would. I peered closer and noticed the

signs of tiredness beneath her cleverly applied make-up. Her eyes were dull and slightly bloodshot and there were lines of strain etched around her mouth. Her skin was dry and pale and looked like it might crack. The day's show of grooming was superficial.

'Did you have a bad weekend?' I asked hesitantly. I didn't want to bother her if she didn't want to be bothered. Maybe she needed time to think things through after getting that letter.

'Yes,' she admitted.

'I know,' I confessed. 'You're doing your Uncle Fester impression.'

She pulled the now familiar bright-orange envelope from her bag. 'I've resealed it and today I'm sending it back to my mother for her to return it from the UK. I can't send it back from here. That would leave a trail.'

I marvelled at her logic at what was such a difficult time for her. 'Do you really think . . .'

'Rosie, I must ask you something,' she interrupted me. 'Please – that we never, ever talk about this again. I couldn't stand it.'

The plain office with its flimsy furniture and rough paintwork seemed to jar with the weight of the conversation. 'I don't think that's a good idea, Susan. I think you need to talk about things,' I urged her, even though I'd only just found how good she was at not talking about things, at keeping things well hidden, even from close friends. 'Sooner or later you're going to need to.' I really believed this. Everyone needed someone to confide in.

She drummed her nails in a sharp rhythm on the table, deliberately trying to block out what I was saying.

'I really think you should talk to me,' I continued, for once undeterred. 'To lessen the load in there,' I coaxed her, tapping my knuckles against my head. 'And in here, too.' I patted my chest.

'I have a good life the way things are,' she explained, a forced firmness in her voice. 'Finally, I've a happy life, a life that treats me well the way I am. And for my own sanity I can't afford to delve into things that are not.'

I sighed. 'OK, we'll do it your way.' This was just another way of saying that we'd do it my way but another time.

Then our phones rang simultaneously, heralding the start of the Monday-morning rush. Monday mornings were Shopping Time. Taxis sped to and from the three big supermarkets all morning, filled with hyperactive toddlers, bulging plastic bags and mothers with half-crazed expressions.

No sooner had I put down the receiver after taking one such call when the phone rang again. 'Triple-A Taxis. How can I help?'

'This is the Tower Hotel. One of our guests would like a taxi to take him to Waterford airport. He's got a flight to catch to London and he's running late, so can you send someone quickly? He's a Frenchman by the name of Pierre Beaumarchand; he's waiting outside.' The caller hung up before I had the chance to ask them to repeat the last name. French surnames were not my forte.

I leant into the mic. 'Paddy, can you get down to the Tower Hotel on the double and pick up a French guy by the name of Pierre Bo-something waiting outside?' I wondered how Paddy would take this.

'I suppose I'll recognize him by the string of onions around his neck and the baguette under his arm?' came the slightly bemused reply.

'Yep.'

Just before lunchtime there was a lull in the incoming calls. Susan quickly decided to go to the post office to send the letter back. I didn't try to talk her out of it because she had a stubborn look on her face that warned me against saying anything.

With the office empty, I slipped the weekly news-paper, the *Waterford Chronicle*, from the magazine rack that mostly held backdated copies of *OK!* and *Hello!* I went straight to the back section. I knew exactly what I was looking for. I'd already thought about this.

I grabbed a pair of scissors from the plastic pen-holder on the desk and carefully cut until I was left holding just a small square of paper in my hand. I put the rest of the newspaper back in the rack. The blank personal-ad form sat in front of me and I grinned mischievously to myself. I could have up to fifteen words published with which to harass Richie.

I sat still a bit, scratched my head a bit, chewed the end of the pen a bit, and then wrote:

New escort in town. Wide experience. Call R on 0868 335210. Satisfaction guaranteed

New escort? I chortled. He'd be the only escort in the town because it wasn't that kind of place. He'd be big news and he'd get all sorts of unwanted attention. When it came to filling out the payment details on the form, I wrote in Richie's name and credit-card number without any hesitation. I was hardly going to pay for it myself.

I eyed the completed form with satisfaction. It would appear as an ad in Thursday's paper. I'd have slapped my own back if I could've reached it, it felt that good. Suddenly, I had another idea. Why stop at one? I grabbed the office's second copy of the paper. This time I wrote:

Want to make some easy cash? Maximum wages. Minimum effort. Call R on 0868 335210

Susan was gone longer than I expected and in her absence I worked flat-out answering both phones. When she did come back her eyes were red-rimmed and the tip of her nose had tiny specks of tissue stuck to it. 'Done,' she said with an air of grave finality. 'And here's something to take your mind off *my* troubles.'

There was only one thing that would take my mind off her troubles and that was my own. 'What?' I demanded thirstily. 'What? What? What?' What did she know that I didn't? Who had she met while she was out? What had she heard?

'Maybe I won't tell you after all,' she teased.

I stared at her imploringly but she just busied herself with the drivers' rota and smiled secretively. It was her first genuine smile of the day.

'Tell me,' I tried pleading with her. 'Go on, you know you want to.'

The smile grew bigger and more secretive.

'Right, handbags at ten paces,' I yelled, grabbing my bag. This was a game we often played and I usually won because she was too scared of genuinely hurting me. I used to joke with her that she was stronger than most men I knew. Ah, the irony of it, I now thought.

'OK, OK,' she gave in. 'As I was coming back I spotted Richie and Ellen Van Damme go into Kneisel's.'

'What? Go in together?' My voice trembled and for comfort I stroked the tiny gold Claddagh ring on my little finger. It had been my father's last gift to me. He'd bought it in Kneisel's and I was so young at the time that now it only fit my little finger. I never took it off.

Kneisel's was the best jewellers in the town, and there was only one reason why Richie and Ellen

Van Damme would be going in there together. They wanted to buy Ellen a ring – and it wouldn't be just a Claddagh.

'Yeah, together,' Susan admitted. 'So I waited a few seconds and then I peeked in, very discreetly,' she quickly assured me, though being a six-foot redhead she didn't lend herself to discretion. 'The assistant was taking a ring out of the window for them to have a look at.'

'A ring out of the window?'

'Yes, a ring out of the window.'

'What kind of ring?'

'A big sparkling one'

'A big sparkling one?'

'Yes, a nice big sparkling one. With a hefty price tag, I'd say.'

'A hefty price tag?'

'Rosie, I know you're upset but could you stop repeating everything I say.'

'Sorry. It's just that, well, it's obviously an engagement ring, and he's still married to me,' I said, stating the obvious. 'What else can he do to me? I shouldn't care by now. But I do. It's just that it's a slap in the face, on top of the last slap in the face. And there's only so many slaps a girl can take,' I went on. 'He's going to divorce me,' I then declared. 'I am going to be a divorcee.' Divorce had only recently been made legal in Ireland. I would be the first divorced person I knew.

She looked me straight in the eye. 'You could always beat him to it and file first.'

'He'd be only too happy.' What a horrible thing to be able to say.

'But you might feel better,' she argued. 'At least you'd have done something, taken some control back.'

I thought about this for a minute. 'You're right,' I told her. 'I will divorce him. He deserves to be divorced.' I didn't believe these words were coming out of my mouth. What was happening to me? What was happening to my life?

'Good,' she said.

I replied as expected: 'Good.'

The phone rang and Susan answered, throwing me a resigned look. 'Triple-A Taxis.' She listened intently for an instant and then leant forward to hit the hands-free button on her phone, clicking her fingers to get my attention.

A smile was already forming on my face even though I hadn't yet heard a word of their conversation.

'I'm sorry, there seems to be some interference on the line. Could you please repeat that?' she asked politely for my benefit.

'Yes, of course,' a well-spoken male voice agreed. 'I'm in town on business and I'm looking for a prostitute and have no idea where to find one so I thought a taxi company would surely be able to point me in the right direction?'

Susan didn't say anything at first. She had her hand

over her mouth trying to stifle a laugh. But the caller thought she was hesitating in case it was a hoax call. 'I can assure you,' he continued, very politely, very sombrely, 'that this is a serious call and I would be very grateful if you could help me out.'

Susan composed herself and slipped back into professional mode. 'Of course I can, sir. If you could just call this number they will be more than happy to help you out.' She went on to give him the number for the local police station.

We got calls like this one the whole time. The city council really needed to put up signposts indicating to strangers where the local docks were, I reckoned.

'The stupid shower's not working,' I shouted around the empty bathroom. I twisted the water knob one way and then the other, and then tried pulling it towards me. But it was hopeless. Nothing I did made any difference. It was a new shower that Richie had insisted on fitting himself only three weeks ago, even though Susan had offered to do it for him. 'Why is the shower not working when I need it?' And why did he bother installing one when he planned on leaving anyway?

I climbed out of the glass cubicle and went down-stairs to phone Hannah.

'Is Dennis still there? Can you send him over urgently to fix my shower?'

'What's so urgent about getting the shower fixed?'

Hannah wasn't feeling helpful and I guessed she'd just had another sleepless night.

'Well, I need to wash properly before I go to work.' I was covering the day shift with Susan, starting at ten a.m.

'Do you think I get to have a wash every day? Let me tell you that with two small children the shower may as well be broken!'

'Look,' I wheedled, 'I'll pay him.' Dennis worked for himself and therefore never thought he could refuse a job that would bring in money – that's why he was always so busy, and that's why he was always so tired, and that's why his relationship with Hannah was disintegrating, and why Katie and Gerry thought he lived in another house. I had it sussed. I didn't know what was taking him so long.

I was really hoping she would refuse to hear any talk of money changing hands because I could hardly afford it. I had other plans for the meagre wages the Furey brothers paid me every week: my trip to the UK, the mortgage, the household bills, and replenishing my stock of proper wine because I could never go back to drinking the paint stripper I used to drink when Richie had control of the household budget.

Hannah sighed again. 'You know very well he'll do it if you tell him you're going to pay him. I'll send him over before he heads off to work.' She paused to yawn and I pictured her standing beside the phone in her flannel pyjamas, a baby's dirty bib stuffed in the top pocket, with her hair still caught in places with yesterday's elastic. 'I'm so tired,' she moaned. 'Plain knackered, Rosie. If I was a horse I'd be put down.'

I felt sorry for her. Hannah had a problem. And half of that problem was that she was the only one who was trying to fix the problem, and was getting nowhere. It was wearing her down an awful lot. She seemed constantly preoccupied and snappy.

'Why don't I come over tomorrow evening and babysit the kids while yourself and Dennis go out for a meal or something and talk?' I suggested, endeavouring to be more supportive.

'Humph,' she snorted and I knew she wouldn't be taking me up on my offer. 'Dennis has an extra job on, some new housing development, and he won't be home until gone midnight. He hasn't been home earlier than that for the last two weeks. I have to go,' she suddenly said with an exhausted urgency. 'Gerry has got hold of his bowl and is mashing his porridge into his hair. I'll just send Dennis over to you and you can do with him what you like.'

'OK, thanks.' The line was already dead.

I went back upstairs, put on yesterday's clothes and surveyed the unmade double bed I used to share with Richie. Last night, for the first time I'd taken over his side too.

I'd just finished plumping up the pillows, an uplifting exercise, when the doorbell rang. I glanced at the clock on the bedside table. Dennis had been quick. Damn, he must really be expecting to get paid for this to have showed up so fast. I went downstairs, slipping my flat oblong wallet from my rucksack and hiding it under the sisal mat so I could pretend that I couldn't find it later when payment time came, and then I casually pulled open the door to let him in.

'What are you doing here?' I spluttered. I couldn't help it because it wasn't Dennis at all. Instead it was Titch Murphy, his workman, the one who'd been coming on to me on Saturday when I was out shopping with Hannah and Eilish. The one who thought he was God's gift to women. I'd have recognized the leer anywhere.

'Dennis asked me to come over and fix your shower,' he said.

'*Did he?*' The words sounded like a saw cutting through wood. I'd kill Dennis for this. Hannah and he were probably chortling into their cornflakes right now.

We went upstairs and as we walked past the bedroom he glanced in hopefully. I was grateful that I'd made the bed, in case he mistook crumpled sheets and head-dented pillows for an invitation. I could guess how his mind worked. 'It's not that way,' I told him, adding, 'Not ever,' when this didn't seem to register.

I led the way to the bathroom, squirming as I felt his eyes travel up and down my back, mentally stripping me of my fitted blue Oxford shirt.

'There's the shower,' I said, unnecessarily because it dominated the small white bathroom, and then made to leave.

He threw back his shoulders and squinted at the glass cubicle, assessing something. 'I'll need your help, Rosie.'

'What for, Titch?'

Using his name might have been a mistake, I realized, too familiar and too promising. First he looked amazed that I actually knew it, his eyebrows shooting up his forehead, and then he looked flattered, as if he'd decided that this must be a really good sign, and his lips parted into a satisfied grin.

'It's on the side of your toolbox,' I quickly informed him, not wanting to let on that I'd already known his name, and nodding at the steel toolbox nestled between his feet. 'So what do you need me here for?'

He had an answer ready. 'I'll need to ask you some questions about the installation itself.'

I'd give him two minutes and no longer, I decided. 'Right.' I pulled the toilet seat down and sat on it but immediately jumped up again. It seemed far too intimate a gesture. It reminded me too much of all the times when I'd sat there chatting to Richie while he took a shower, of all the times he'd coaxed me in to lather his back for him and we'd ended up all over each other, of all the times he'd played join-the-dots with the freckles on my leg, tracing a pattern on my skin with his warm, damp tongue.

Titch started to dismantle the shower, dropping plastic parts into the basin. 'How long has it been up?' he inquired.

'About three weeks,' I answered.

He held a spanner in his right hand and was using all his force to undo a stubborn bolt. 'It's a stiff one,' he puffed, turning his head towards the shower wall, trying to hide the salacious grin on his face at his own choice of words.

'I wouldn't know.' If I could just hold him still for long enough, I could give him a leg wax, I mused wryly. Rid him of thirty-something years' worth of growth and cause him a lot of pain in the process.

He finally managed to undo the bolt with a loud, satisfied grunt, way too reminiscent of another kind of satisfied grunt. I closed my eyes and massaged my temples, trying to ease away the growing ache there that was all Titch's fault.

'Got it. Got the problem,' he exclaimed, examining a piece of distorted plastic. Just as well Richie decided to stick to the day job. 'This,' he said, shaking the mystery object at me, 'was not where it was meant to be.'

'Righty oh.' I hoped that meant he'd be leaving soon.

'Now,' he said, somewhat adamantly, letting me know he meant business, 'I need you to come in here for me and hold this in place while I fix it to the wall.'

He was talking about the rigid encasing that protected the inner workings of the shower unit.

It seemed like a genuine request for assistance but I was still reluctant as I slid past him, being careful not to touch any part of his anatomy with any part of mine, and took up position against the tiled wall.

Titch smiled at me and I felt a shiver run down my spine. 'This is all very cosy, Rosie, isn't it? For first thing in the morning.' He was clearly savouring the moment.

The man must crave rejection, I figured. He was probably ignored as a child. Or maybe he was just irresistibly drawn to a challenge. Although, to be honest, he probably didn't see me as a challenge. As Eilish had reminded me, I was now thought of as fair game by the town's male population. They'd reckon that I was bound to be suffering from 'jilted-wife syndrome' and would be overjoyed to jump into the sack with the first man to come along to prove to myself and everyone else that I was still desirable.

But what they didn't realize was that, while I did doubt my own desirability – Richie had, after all, left me, and for an older woman – I was just about clever enough to realize that jumping into the sack with say, *Titch*, who could probably be persuaded, would not be proof of my desirability but of my desperation.

'Titch, we're fixing the shower,' I coolly reminded him. 'There's nothing cosy about it.'

'Where's the romance in you?' he wanted to know,

busily working around my hands, brushing against them as much as possible, as I held the plastic casing in place. 'By the way, your tan is fading. You need to apply some more of that cream.'

'Have we nearly finished here?' The white casing was now back in place and to my amateur eye everything looked like it was where it belonged. Except Titch Murphy.

'Yep, we just have to – ' and with that he seemed to lose his footing. He fell forward heavily against the control point of the shower then, in a flimsy effort to regain his balance, reached out with his hand and grabbed hold of the water knob. All this happened in very slow motion because the outcome was so inevitable. The knob turned easily and suddenly there was a spray of water from above us.

'You little fucker.' I tried to push him but he slipped again in the growing pool of water underfoot and craftily placed another steadying hand on the control knob, increasing the spray of water to a downpour over the two of us.

I struggled to get out but, as he'd made sure I was pushed up against the wall when I got into the shower to help him in the first place, and was now blocking my way, I was stuck. I was so furious that no more words would come out of my mouth, I tried to get at the control knob myself to stem the flow of water but he somehow seemed to be blocking that as well.

It felt like I was in there weeks with him. My shirt

was clinging to me, and showing clearly beneath it were the pattern on my bra and two wet, cold nipples. My hair was stuck to my head and rivulets of water ran down my face, dropping off my chin.

My power of speech returned as I realized how I must look to him. '*Get the fuck out of my way now, you . . . you . . . pervert,*' I spat. 'You know, Titch, sleeping with some good-looking Italian on holiday does not make you George fucking Clooney.' I thumped his chest hard and pinned him to the glass partition. The rage I was now in gave me the strength I needed to hold him there while I slithered past.

'Jesus, Rosie,' he gazed at me lustfully, blissfully unperturbed by my anger, 'but you're fierce sexy like this.'

Hanging on the back of the bathroom door was my old bathrobe. I grabbed it and pulled it on over my clothes, tying the belt as tight as possible, and glared at him.

Titch turned off the water and began drying his wet tools with my good Egyptian-cotton bath towel. 'At least we know the shower's working again,' he said.

I didn't trust myself to say anything. I just clenched my fists and waited for him to finish up, which he did by drying himself off, again using my bath towel. He then threw it on the floor, stepped on it and used it to wipe his steel-capped boots, leaving thick, dark, mud stains everywhere.

I could take no more. 'Down!' I ordered him and

flung out my arm in the direction of the stairs, making sure to walk down behind him. He stood back while I opened the front door, and wisely didn't mention anything about payment of any sorts. He'd had payment enough.

The postman was walking up the garden path, carefully stepping over the bits of terracotta that were still strewn everywhere from when I'd flung the flowerpot at Richie as he left.

Titch waited until the postman was within earshot, then whistled. 'That was some morning we had, Rosie.'

The postman, a friend of Rory's, took one look at my wet hair and wild expression, and immediately jumped to the conclusion that Titch badly wanted him to and I knew that by lunchtime the whole town would have heard about our torrid love affair.

9

'Caught you at last,' Johnny Power beamed at me at the office.

'What do you mean, "Caught you at last"?' I laughed. 'You've been off for the last two days while I've been here, helping to fill the Furey brothers' crock of gold.' My sense of humour was only just returning after the episode with Titch Murphy in the shower.

Susan smiled. I'd been keeping tabs on her, checking on her smile to frown ratio, and she seemed OK by appearances.

'Do you have a minute?' he asked.

I checked with Susan and she nodded, looking amused by Johnny's tightly belted gabardine rain mac and matching cap. He'd come in from the rain and still had on the protective rubber slippers he wore over his shoes.

We stepped into the empty corridor.

'Do you remember that secret I wanted to tell you about the other day when I was collecting Myra Barry from your house?' he whispered.

'Yes,' I said. I hadn't given it much thought. I had other things on my mind.

'Are you all ears?' he wanted to know.

'Couldn't be more so.'

'By the way, heard the good news about yourself and Titch Murphy. Very happy for the both of you.'

'You can save your congratulations, Johnny. Because there is no me and Titch Murphy.'

He looked at me puzzled. 'Are you sure? 'Cause I heard from . . .'

I cut him off and assured him, 'Well, you're hearing it from me now,' followed by a very serious look.

'So there's no you and Titch Murphy? Straight from the horse's mouth, eh?'

'Yes.'

'OK, we'll get back to my little secret, in that case.' He looked around him and shuffled closer. 'I'm going to ask her to marry me,' he said in a very serious whisper, his posture straight and military-like.

'*Susan?*' I whispered back and felt myself go faint.

'No, y'eejit. Mrs Burke.' He seemed to relax a little once he'd said it aloud, and he cocked a leg to the side, distributing his weight more comfortably.

'Mrs Burke?' I'd almost forgotten all about it.

'Yes. I've decided that you were right. A decent mourning period has gone by . . .'

'Yeah, three years,' I interrupted him. 'Anyway, I don't think she was really mourning.' I certainly wouldn't have been, because lechers like Mr Burke didn't deserve mourning.

'I'm ready now to put the question to her. I still love

147

her. There's no doubt about that.' He was sounding like a love-struck sixteen-year-old.

The subject I was about to bring up was very delicate. He hadn't mentioned it but I felt that I should, as this was all my idea. 'Johnny,' I began, wanting to make sure he realized the potential battle facing him, 'she seems pretty fond of the bottle.' This, I thought, was nearly a nice way of putting it.

'The bottle's only there because no one else is,' he told me emphatically, because he'd already worked this out for himself. 'She doesn't need it.'

I hoped he was right.

'I've waited nearly forty years,' he said and didn't bother adding that a bottle wasn't going to stop him now but I knew that was what he meant.

'When are you going to pop the question?' I asked him, intuitively guessing that it would be sooner rather than later.

'It's the month of February,' he told me. 'There's only the one date that will do: February the four-teenth,' he announced and broke into a huge grin.

'Valentine's Day. Oh, God.' I buried my face in my hands. How could I have forgotten that it was looming? I suddenly had an image of Richie and Ellen Van Damme celebrating together, drinking cham-pagne and toasting their love. And I'd be on my own.

A tidal wave of misery threatened to wash over me. My thoughts went from colour to black and white. My humour nosedived. An empty feeling invaded the pit of my stomach. This all took about two seconds. I had perfected the fine art of misery.

With a huge effort, I fought back. I banished the bad thoughts and began to repeat to myself, 'I am a fighter, I am a fighter, I am a fighter . . .' This was something Muriel had helpfully suggested that I try when things threatened to get me down. She called it the power of positive visualization and told me that I should imagine myself in a boxing ring, wearing a pair of gloves, glowing with sweat and knocking all my life-size problems to the floor one by one. And to this picture I added fabulously toned legs and a rock-solid stomach. Amazingly the wave of misery began to recede.

Johnny was staring at my lips silently working. 'What's that you're mumbling?'

'Nothing.' There and then I decided to do something special for Valentine's Day. I didn't yet know what that would be. But, I promised myself, it certainly wouldn't be a bottle of sleeping pills and a flagon of duty-free vodka.

Valentine's Day hadn't meant anything to me before, when I had Richie. It was too contrived. I laughed in the face of Valentine's Day, scoffed at the inflated romance of it all: big cards, big cuddly toys, big bouquets of flowers, big commercial rip-off. I didn't need any of it because I had Richie and we could celebrate our love any time we wanted.

But now, suddenly single and with everyone looking

on to see how I was coping, it took on an ominous importance. It became essential to mark the occasion to prove to myself and everyone else watching that I was on top of things, that Valentine's Day, with its enormous potential for misery-making, wouldn't get me down.

'I wish you luck on the day, Johnny.' Ironically, I needed luck far more than he did. But these days my needs were coming way behind everyone else's – Susan's, Hannah's, and now Johnny's.

He was chewing on his bottom lip and biting on a tiny dot of grey grizzle beneath. 'I might need your advice on some things. I've been out of the game for too long, standing on the sideline. Would that be OK?' he asked, twisting his cap anxiously between his hands as if I might refuse.

My laughable track record in the marital arena didn't seem to concern him and this show of faith touched me enormously. 'I'll help in whatever way I can,' I said, and meant it. By then I might have discovered what I myself had done wrong, and I could steer him in the opposite direction.

'Hank called,' Susan announced as soon as I walked back into the office. 'He's coming down tomorrow night and he's taking me out to dinner.' She was breathless with excitement and hopping up and down in her chair.

I wondered whether Susan had the same effect on

Hank. And whether he was comfortable with her past – whether he even knew about it. I decided to come right out and ask her.

'Does Hank know about you? About before?' Because he might be in for a bit of a surprise if he didn't, and I thought of his handsome face being shocked rigid.

Susan waved her manicured hands in the air dismissively and laughed. 'No problem there, Rosie. Hank only became Hank three years ago. Before that he led a very unfulfilled life as Patricia, a schoolteacher,' she announced. 'So he understands,' she then confided in a stage whisper.

I managed to hold back a bewildered yelp by firmly embedding my chin in the palm of my hand. I raised my eyebrows and smiled politely at her, as if she'd just given me the weather forecast, but despite my best efforts this news was too much. How was it possible? Again. I couldn't get my head around it. He was too . . . too manly, I supposed, and too gorgeous. Surely I would've sensed something? Not that I had sensed anything with Susan, one of my closest friends, I thought dryly.

Once again, I got the distinct impression that Susan didn't want me to be shocked. She wanted someone she could be open with, someone she could confide in. And now that I was in on her secret I was that someone. It was all so clear-cut – pardon the pun – for her as she sat there beaming at me, but I was new

151

to this. She was revealing a whole new world to me and I was reeling from it. I'd never really given these things much thought. Who does?

I cleared my throat. 'And you found him in that dating magazine you have sent to you?'

'Yeah,' she nodded, the edges of her red bob dancing on her cheeks. 'It's a magazine for transsexuals that I get sent over to me from the UK and there just happened to be an ad from Ireland.' She took in my wide-eyed expression. 'There often is, you know,' she assured me.

'He's very handsome with that chiselled face of his,' I said incredulously, drawing a line around my chin to imitate his strong jaw. It would have been impossible for me not to notice how good-looking he was in Wino's, even through the haze of confusion caused by Richie's unfaithfulness and sudden departure. Though perhaps it was odd that I'd taken such notice of him, that he'd embedded himself so firmly in my memory.

'I know,' she sighed.

'Is there something going on between the two of you?' For some reason I wanted her to say no – and she did.

'We've only met once before, that time when you saw us in Wino's. But we've talked lots on the telephone and I'm very hopeful.' She winked at me wickedly then, to let me know her intentions were far from honourable.

All this was becoming quite a lot to keep to myself.

'I'm thinking about a change,' she said, switching subjects and patting her sleek bob. 'Something a bit more modern. I think this style is staid now.'

Nothing about Susan could ever be described as staid. 'It suits you perfectly.' She'd worn it like that since I knew her. It was her hairstyle.

'I always promised myself long hair one day but now I'm thinking of cutting it really short,' she continued, bunching her hair together behind her head with one hand and fluffing up the front bits with the other. 'Maybe the urchin look?'

I nearly choked on the nib of the Bic pen I was chewing. 'You're six foot in your stockinged feet. Steer clear of the urchin look,' I pleaded.

She duly considered this. 'Yeah, you're probably right. I'll just have my eyelashes permed instead.'

During the eighties I'd had enough bad perms to last a lifetime and I wouldn't dream of letting anyone near my hair or eyelashes with curlers and setting lotion. I couldn't believe people really did that. But Susan was far more ahead of the game than I was when it came to feminine wiles. She knew all the tricks. Then again, I guess she had to.

The big hall mirror was lying on a thick bed of newspapers on the floor and the can of spray-paint hissed in my right hand. I'd been waiting all day to get home to do this. By mid-morning at the office, respraying that mirror had become a vital step in getting Richie out of my system. There wasn't any real logic to this, but it was something I felt utterly compelled to do. I could hardly concentrate on anything else all day. It would be a sign that I was really moving on.

A blurred movement caught my attention and I recognized Muriel's slim outline through the glass-panelled door before she even rang the bell. It was good to be friends again. In fact, it was more than good. We had effortlessly drifted back to our old ways of impromptu visits and mindless daytime telephone chats, which were peppered with the odd bout of Muriel's philosophizing.

'I brought you these,' she held out an armful of books with titles like *Heal Yourself!* and *Positive You!* 'They'll be really helpful,' she insisted, setting them down on the floor beside the radiator. 'What are you doing?'

'I'm spraying, can't you see?' I waved the can at the frame again to demonstrate. 'I wanted to spray it silver from the start. Rustic was Richie's idea.'

Her eyes narrowed and she tilted her head reflectively. 'I see.' She paused for an instant to gather her thoughts before she set about revealing the significance of all this to me, but she never got the chance because the phone rang.

'Why aren't you here?' Hannah demanded.

'Where?'

'Don't get smart. You know very well.'

'If I knew I wouldn't ask.'

'At the Theatre Royal.'

The minute she said the words I remembered. Damn, damn, damn. I'd forgotten that tonight was Carmen's dance show, *Sueño Guitano*, or something like that. I glanced at my watch, now speckled with silver paint. It was just gone half past seven. The show began at eight and I had two tickets. When I got them three weeks ago I thought that Richie would be coming with me.

'I'm on my way. I was just waiting for Muriel.' I gestured madly and apologetically at Muriel while I said this. 'She was late.' More gesturing.

'We're waiting for you in the lobby . . . like we said we would.'

'Be there in ten minutes.'

Muriel agreed to come with me and quickly called a friend to cancel the plans she had for later. I hugged her gratefully for this and for letting me be her friend again.

I raced upstairs. My black trousers and wool jumper were still lying beside the bed where I'd dumped them on Sunday. I pulled them on and took a second to assure myself that the trench-like creases weren't too noticeable. Then I grabbed my bag and we left in a hurry.

The Theatre Royal was a recently revamped, Victorian-era venue and its brightly lit lobby was dotted with small circles of nicely dressed people, many of them familiar to me. Given that this was a small town in the southeast of Ireland, these flamenco dance shows seemed to draw inexplicable numbers of people.

I quickly spotted Hannah, Eilish and my mother standing at the bottom of the sweeping staircase; two very blonde heads and one black velvet skullcap with a long, delicate black feather attached to the side at a slight angle. The hat had been a present to my mother from Myra Barry.

'You could have taken an iron to your clothes, Rosie,' Hannah commented.

Muriel graciously stepped in. 'She had to change at the last minute. She was wearing that lovely white trouser suit but I spilt some coffee on it.' She shrugged apologetically.

Hannah was openly doubtful. 'I thought you were late getting to Rosie's? How come you had time for a coffee?'

Eilish looked at me. 'You'd hardly notice the wrinkles.'

My mother handed me two programmes. 'We'd better go on in.'

But Eilish dragged me back by the arm before I had a chance to follow the others as they moved forward. 'We'd decided not to tell you but I think you should know, in case you come face to face with them.'

I knew instantly what she was going to say and I felt the smile on my face freeze.

'Richie and Ellen Van Damme are here. We saw

them come in. He saw us too but pretended he didn't. I mean, how could you not notice that,' with a hand she gestured towards the oversized swaying feather attached to my mother's hat. 'It's practically a fully grown emu that she's carting around.'

'It's OK,' I assured her, feeling unexpectedly calm. I'd have to get used to seeing them around. I'd have to learn to live with it and then I'd have to learn to forget about it.

'It's not OK, Rosie. He knew you'd be here. He knew we'd all be here. He should've stayed away instead of flaunting himself and his wrinkly whore for all to see.'

Hannah, Eilish and my mother would be pushing hard for a showdown, I knew. They'd want to see me stand up for myself, show some fighting spirit.

'His behaviour is beneath me,' I told Eilish while I calmly wondered what had brought Richie here tonight. I was sure he had some plan.

'Eh, right, Rosie.' For a second her expression was one of puzzlement because she'd expected me to lose my head, get my knickers in a real twist. But then the puzzled look vanished and she smiled coyly as she figured that the mellow attitude was put on for show and would never last.

We took a few steps in silence, walking beneath the arch and the swish velvet curtains that led into the main seating area.

Eilish whispered over my shoulder. 'And what's this

Hannah told me about you and Titch Murphy? You his new lack?' The teasing tone of her voice thankfully assured me that she knew it couldn't be true. 'She says it's coming straight from him. Dennis told her it's the talk of the building site!'

I glared back at her. 'It didn't happen.'

'It's kind of flattering, though, that he's gone to the bother of making it up.'

'You must be joking me.' Besides being dumped for a woman who was nearly old enough to be my mother, I could think of nothing else less flattering.

I dropped down into the empty seat beside Muriel just as the curtain rose to reveal a stage lit by an enormous backdrop of flickering flames, in front of which stood the dark outline of two intertwined bodies. As they separated, taking deliberately slow steps backwards, knees rising high, I recognized Carmen's silhouette. Her head was tilted to the side, her chin held just above her shoulder, an expression of angst on her darker-than-ever face.

Suddenly her arms rose above her head and her hands began making perfect circles, her fingers moving fluidly while Antonio, her dance teacher, his long hair greased back into a ponytail, stood absolutely still, his muscled back straight, staring at her with a brooding intensity.

Then she was still and Antonio leapt into the air, crossed his legs at the ankles and twisted twice in rapid succession before landing lightly on his toes, slightly bending his knees and bringing the heels of his boots down on the wood with a clap of thunder that made Muriel jump in her seat beside me. There were microphones hidden at foot level at the front of the stage.

Carmen faced him for an instant, an unspoken torment passing between them, and looked away again. The pace of Antonio's dancing increased. My toes twitched. The first beads of sweat glistened on his forehead, tiny balls of glitter. His feet pounded the wooden stage but his shoulders hardly moved. He held one arm outstretched towards Carmen. There seemed to be some kind of imploring going on. But she was having none of it.

However, this was one of Antonio's choreographies so I knew she'd give in at some stage and they'd have an intense moment of passion together before a heart-rending end to their affair, which would probably involve the cruel death of Antonio or Carmen at the hands of a spurned love interest. There was a lot to be said for predictability.

I felt Muriel nudge me in the ribs. 'I'll have some of whatever Carmen's on.'

At the interval most of the audience, appreciative noises abounding, filtered out into the lobby and we joined them, taking it in turns to voice our astonishment at the progress Carmen had made since her last show. In a short time, she'd gone from crippled village grandmother to impassioned leading lady. I knew she was motivated by her desire to impress Antonio but she seemed to possess real talent too. I was so proud.

Out of the corner of my eye I noticed that my mother had suddenly become flustered, alternately patting her hat with the palm of her hand and smoothing the skin on her neck. She coughed nervously. 'Trouble at two o'clock.' Her addiction to American police dramas was a great help at times like this.

We turned to two o'clock while discreetly feigning neck stretches, all of us.

'Sorry, sorry,' she mumbled into her chest, 'that should've been ten o'clock.'

Discretion was abandoned in favour of speed as we spun in the opposite direction. I'd be lying if I said that I didn't already have an idea of what it was that was bothering her – or, rather, *who* it was.

Richie and Ellen Van Damme were standing picture perfect beneath the archway leading from the main seating area inside the theatre to the lobby, framed by the lush red velvet curtains that cascaded to the floor on either side of them. They had an aura of togetherness that my one stab at destroying with the anonymous newspaper articles hadn't even dented. I felt crushed but I said nothing.

Ellen Van Damme stood very close to Richie, where I should've been standing, and the lump in my throat quadrupled. Her bare arm merged with the sleeve of his suit. Her ankle-length dress of an almost indefinable silvery-white colour added to the air of mystery that surrounded her, and it clung to her tall, slender frame in all the right places, while her vanilla skin had a polished sheen.

At that moment I felt thirty years older than her. To put it simply, I felt like a hag. Her simple elegance and undeniable poise demolished the self-confidence I'd been trying so hard to rebuild in the short time since Richie had left. It was already bruised just from seeing them there, appearing socially as a proper couple.

Dressed head to foot in black, as I was, I looked like I was in mourning, which was absolutely not the way I wanted to appear that night, because when Ellen Van Damme looked at me, as she would in a few seconds, she wasn't going to see the fight in me, the determination to pick myself up from where Richie had left me, to shake myself off and get on with life no matter what. And these things counted.

Next to me Muriel was quietly chanting, 'I am a fighter, I am a fighter, I am a fighter . . .' But her well-intentioned pontificating was no match for the feelings of inadequacy that were swamping me.

Richie's eyes scanned the crowd in the lobby and fell on us with such obvious intent that I took an immediate step backwards and gasped aloud. He whispered something in Ellen's ear, to which she nodded, and then guided her in our direction.

I wanted to run away. Flee.

'I don't believe this,' Hannah hissed.

Eilish's eyes widened and her jaw dropped. 'Of all the cheek,' she stuttered, mouth ajar.

'Stay strong, stay strong,' Muriel tried to tell me, but with an edge to her voice.

Since she'd first spotted them, my mother's demeanour had undergone a complete transformation. Her initial agitation had by now metamorphosed into serious indignation. 'Do not let yourself be put upon,' she ordered me. 'Rosie, you hear me?'

There was a terrible roar of confusion in my ears. This was all wrong. Wrong. Wrong. Wrong. It shouldn't be happening to me. Who had decided otherwise?

Then they were in front of us. There were a few more fine lines on Ellen Van Damme's face than I'd first noticed. But it didn't matter. It didn't make her any less attractive. When people called her a geriatric tart it didn't really apply. They just said it to make me feel better, which it didn't. Some misguided onlookers may have been thinking that being traded in for an older woman couldn't be as bad as being traded in for a younger one, but it certainly didn't feel that way. All the usual excuses associated with the lure of youth were useless to me. I had to find new ones.

Richie looked at me.

Ellen looked at Richie.

Muriel looked at me.

My mother looked at Ellen.

I looked at Richie.

And Hannah and Eilish looked at each other.

After what seemed like an eternity Richie spoke up, coughing nervously but looking resolute nonetheless. 'I know this is a bit awkward for you, Rosie, but I thought we could all be adults about the situation. We're faced with certain facts here so let's try and make the most of them. Let's have some adult behaviour,' he suggested. This was the kind of direct approach I used to admire in him but it had suddenly worn very thin.

'I want to formally introduce you to Ellen,' he continued, and placed a hand on her shoulder. To this she responded by lovingly placing her hand, with its perfect French-manicured nails, over his, and they stood there, all very lovingly indeed, waiting for me to say something.

I squirmed. What was I meant to do, to say? Was I meant to care? Was I meant not to care? What? Up to ten days ago, Richie had been my husband and, as far as I knew, the man I was going to spend the rest of my life with come what may. And now he was trying to introduce me to the woman of his dreams.

The spacious lobby had turned into a stage with the sparkling chandeliers overhead lighting the scene to perfection. Everyone had their eyes on me, waiting to see what I'd do.

My hand curled involuntarily into a fist. I wanted to punch Richie for putting me in this situation, for subjecting me to this scrutiny and humiliation, for making me feel that I was the odd one out, and maybe for the first time ever I would have done just that. But suddenly I spotted Myra Barry hurrying across the foyer, skidding towards us in jewel-encrusted satin slippers.

'Shame, shame, shame on you, Richie Maloney,' she was saying and everyone turned to look at her. I almost sank to the floor with the relief of escaping the limelight, albeit briefly. 'There are ways to behave and this isn't one of them.' She burst into the tense circle, fanning herself with the paper programme she held. 'What are you doing here anyway?' she addressed Richie. 'You know Rosie comes to all these shows.'

Then Ellen Van Damme spoke up unexpectedly and I was surprised by her distinct Dublin accent – I hadn't expected her to sound as if she was from anywhere earthly. 'My late husband and I used to own a tapas bar in Amsterdam and I adore flamenco.' She was not at all intimidated by Myra's brash appearance. 'It's just such a passionate dance,' she went on, 'such a hot-blooded form of expression.' She glanced sideways at Richie as she said this, as if they shared some very intimate secret, at which point Eilish and Hannah openly sniggered at the thought of Richie in the role of ardent lover-cum-bullfighter.

Ellen bristled visibly at this. 'I don't think any of you really know Richie. I don't think any of you ever wanted to,' she said with an accusing glance in my direction.

I wanted to protest but didn't because I was afraid

of making myself look foolish, of not finding the right words when I opened my mouth, and I'd never felt like that before.

Eilish smiled again, genuinely amused at the ludicrousness of this statement. They all knew how I felt about Richie, what I would've done for him. I worshipped him from the outset. My mistake.

'One thing's for sure, Mrs Van Damme,' she said, correctly guessing that Ellen didn't suit being called 'Mrs Van Damme' because it conjured up images of aprons and wooden clogs. 'After what's happened we don't want to know him any more.'

My mother nodded adamantly and the long feather on her hat arched like a lethal weapon. And beside her Myra nodded too. Then, to my surprise, Muriel spoke up. 'I never really got to know you, Richie.' Because of her soft, even voice, Richie looked at her with a semi-hopeful expression. 'And I've never been gladder of anything in my life.'

Faced with such open disapproval, Richie decided to vent some of his understandable discomfort on me because I was possibly the easiest target. 'And what's this I hear about you making a tart of yourself with Titch Murphy? The whole town knows about it,' he claimed.

'My, my, Richie,' Hannah drawled. 'If I didn't know better I'd say you were jealous.'

'I am not,' he denied, but looked very much guilty as charged.

Yes, you are, I fumed silently. And how dare you be jealous? *You* left *me*! I was all the more peeved that he would actually think I'd stoop so low as to indulge in horizontal shenanigans with Titch Murphy of all people. Had I fallen so far in his esteem?

I noticed Ellen Van Damme subtly squeeze his arm.

'That kind of behaviour reflects badly on you,' he continued, trying to make it sound like he was just concerned for my sake about how the town might be viewing me. It was too late for such concern.

Ellen Van Damme's hold on his arm tightened and she began to frown because she could see that Richie was fooling no one and it put her in an awkward position.

'You really should know better than to get involved with the likes of him. He's only after one thing,' he added, seemingly oblivious to Ellen's vice-like grip.

I decided not to bother contradicting him because I was enjoying Ellen's inevitable discomfort at having to listen to Richie's jealous ranting over my supposed sexual exploits. And, in a stupid way, I was also flattered by this outburst – thinking that he still cared, maybe.

My silence, which he took as a clear admission of guilt, galled him and he threw his hands into the air. Out of the corner of my eye I noticed a few onlookers jump at the sudden gesture. 'Are you listening to a word I'm saying?' he asked me.

'I just keep remembering the words "adult behaviour", Richie. You remember, from the beginning of our conversation?'

He shifted uneasily on his feet. 'Yeah. So?'

'Well, I'd like to remind you that I wasn't the one to carry on behind my partner's back.' I couldn't believe I just said that in front of everyone, with no weeping and no hysterics but quite calmly.

There was a stunned silence. No one else thought that I'd have the guts to come right out and say it either.

'That wasn't really adult behaviour, was it?' I prodded him. I knew he couldn't really say yes, as the laws of reasoning were stacked against him and everyone knew exactly what they were.

He glanced at Ellen and reluctantly mumbled, 'No.'

'And Ellen,' I turned to face her, amazed by my own new-found audacity, 'woman to woman, that wasn't very adult behaviour, was it?' I wasn't expecting a verbal reply and she didn't give one but she lowered her eyes fleetingly, betraying her remorse.

Myra Barry could barely refrain from applauding. I saw her bring her hands together and at the last minute redirect them to her hair. And I hadn't seen my mother looking so proud since Rory won Local Businessman of the Year five years ago.

'I think the only one who has behaved like an adult here is me,' I concluded, conveniently forgetting all about the revenge campaign I was plotting, the anonymous newspaper articles I'd sent Richie and the personal ads that would appear in tomorrow's newspaper.

'Does anyone disagree with me?'

Right on cue, Hannah, Eilish, Muriel, my mother and Myra Barry shook their heads firmly. Then the bell rang signalling that it was time for everyone to return to their seats for the second half of the show and I turned away, head held high, and walked back into the theatre.

The curtain rose and Carmen, wearing a black velvet corset and a red satin skirt, was lying in a majestic heap on the stage, face pulled into an expression of pure terror as her rival in love stood above her, dagger in hand.

I'd guessed it would come to this.

But Antonio suddenly twisted his torso, leapt in front of the pointed dagger meant for Carmen and fell to the floor. Carmen's grief, though a little drawn out for my taste, was dignified but passionate, while her love rival wailed her laments amid striding and stamping, her emotions seeming to reverberate from her very core. The two women slowly parted then, each to their own sorrow and yearning.

After the show was over and we'd applauded, cheered and waved for Carmen, I quickly headed backstage with Muriel to congratulate her and the other dancers and to avoid Richie and Ellen Van

Damme. Carmen was standing at the far end of the corridor and when she spotted us approaching she began to thread her way through the other dancers and their babbling entourages.

As she got closer I could see the two thick black lines that careered outwards from her eyes to give her a sultry, smoky-eyed look on stage. But up-close the effect was the opposite; her face was caked with enough stage make-up to camouflage a small country. 'My God, Carmen, you are scary.'

'At least I get less scary when I take my make-up off,' she said pointedly.

Muriel threw her arms around her. 'You were fabulous. I couldn't believe it was you,' she sang. 'Last time I looked you were in knee socks.'

At that moment, with Carmen wrapped in Muriel's long, sinewy arms, Antonio sauntered past. Carmen reached forward and pulled him back. 'Here's the man responsible for it all,' she chimed, delighted at his appearance.

'Hello,' he said, in a voice that still held faint but very alluring traces of a Spanish accent, and draped his arm around Carmen's bare shoulders. 'Did you enjoy the show and what did you think of our rising star?'

Carmen looked up into his brown eyes and she glowed, her long-standing infatuation with Antonio lighting her from within. 'Oh, you're the star, Antonio. I only did what I could,' she gushed.

'Nothing compared to you, the real star. Your talent is wasted here. Your name should be up in lights.' She made big flashing signs with her hands. 'Tonight, you were *magnifico.*' Carmen could muse on the splendour of Antonio for hours.

'We thought the show was wonderful,' Muriel raved as soon as Carmen stopped.

He slid his arm from around Carmen's shoulder and stepped forward, hand thrust out. 'I don't think we've met before,' he said to her, smiling like a prospector who'd just discovered a nugget of gold at the bottom of his pan of grit.

Titch Murphy could learn more than a thing or two from this man, I thought.

'I am Antonio Gadez, dancer.'

Muriel did a flirty curtsey. 'Muriel Ryan, librarian.'

Carmen watched the exchange between the two with big, sad eyes. I wanted to hug her, tell her that there were plenty more *peces* in the sea. 'I'm going to find Maria,' she said quietly to me. Maria had been Carmen's best friend for years and they shrank mountains into molehills for each other.

'OK. Are you coming for a drink after?'

She looked at Antonio and Muriel again, already deep in a conversation riddled with tell-tale body language, and shook her head dismally. 'No.'

Muriel was tugging on my sleeve trying to get my attention as I watched Carmen disappear. 'We're going to start dance lessons,' she enthused as I turned around to face her again. 'It'll be good for you. Give you something to do.'

Antonio looked at me. 'Hi, Rosie.'

'Hi.'

'Antonio was just telling me that there's a beginners' class starting next week, Wednesday. We'll join up, won't we?' she insisted.

I was reluctant to agree, primarily because I had two left feet and dancing lessons would be an exercise in humiliation when I didn't really need another one for a while.

'What do you think?' she nodded encouragingly.

Naturally, I hadn't the heart to say no. 'All right. It'll be something different,' I said aloud, sounding as positive as I could at the prospect of learning how to stamp my feet properly.

'Yeah. It'll be great,' Muriel agreed.

From inside one of the crowded dressing rooms someone was calling out for Antonio. 'I have to go,' he said regretfully, staring at Muriel. 'Come along at seven o'clock next Wednesday.'

Muriel gave him a smile. 'I can't wait.'

'Me neither.' Antonio beamed back.

'Me neither,' I added but I just couldn't reach the same heights of enthusiasm. In mountaineering terms, I was still at base camp.

Muriel and I left right after that by the back door which led on to a dimly lit side street behind the theatre. It had been raining and the footpath glistened. Arm in arm, we dodged the mirror-like puddles and made our way down the narrow street to the Quay, where the river was noticeably swollen from the heavy rain earlier.

My sisters, my mother and Myra Barry were waiting for us in the plush bar of one of the hotels a bit further along the Quay. This was my mother's idea of a good place for a quiet drink where we'd all be able to hear each other speak, and everyone else's idea of a well-decorated morgue.

A taxi sped by and I recognized Johnny Power's arm as he waved out the window. We were just about to go into the hotel, Muriel still raving about Carmen's performance, when I heard a distinctive giggle behind me.

'Susan?' I glanced back over my shoulder.

Susan, dressed in brown leather trousers and a sheepskin coat, was walking down the street with Hank. She was trying her best to slot her arm through his but I thought I could see him resisting.

'Rosie, that you?' She squinted into the night and quickened her step.

'Yeah.' My eyes were still on Hank and I felt him return my stare.

'I was just showing Hank Waterford by night,' Susan said as she got nearer. The alcohol fumes ballooned towards me. 'We had an early dinner in the Thai restaurant on, err,' she was struggling to think of where it was, 'err, Canada Street,' she suddenly remembered, 'and we've been doing a round of the pubs ever since.'

She made an attempt to steady herself against the wall of the hotel, misjudged the distance, and ended up propped against it at an unnatural angle. She couldn't really hold her drink, I knew. Her legs may have been long but they weren't hollow.

Beside me Muriel giggled at the sight of Susan precariously leaning sideways with the most nonchalant expression on her face, and Hank laughed, too, a resonant, amused rumble. It was a laugh that did not sound as if it could ever have belonged to a woman. He must've found the best voice therapist in the country. I now knew that transsexuals spent money on such things.

'Susan insisted that I sample the local watering holes,' he explained while at the same time gallantly helping her to right herself and showing no signs of any of the same inebriation.

I quickly looked away. I didn't trust myself to look at him for longer than two seconds at any one time because I was sure that I'd end up staring, trying to spot some tell-tale sign that he'd previously been a woman. Try as I might I could not reconcile this fact to the reality that I was seeing before me.

Then he asked me a direct question and I had to look at him. 'There's that one pub where they only allow men in. What's it called again?'

I cautiously fixed him straight in the eye, resolved not to look him up and down, to ignore the broad shoulders emphasized by a chunky sweater and the athletic thighs wrapped in faded denim as before. It must've been a hell of a build to pull off as a woman.

'Maher's,' I answered. Maher's had been around a long time. The only woman allowed past the door was the landlord's wife, who served behind the bar. It was the town's last bastion to male domination.

'Yeah, Maher's, that's the one. But it was closed.' He slapped his thigh hard with regret. At this Susan sneaked a sideways glance at him, pulling the collar of her sheepskin jacket around her face and impishly peeking out over the rim. I was looking at him too. I couldn't help it because I was overwhelmed by his physique even though I didn't understand how I could be.

His hair was curlier than I remembered, shaggier, more unkempt-looking. His eyes were darker, not a limpid chocolate-brown like Antonio's but a mesmerizing slate-grey colour that made me think of turbulent seas. He was taller, too, about four inches taller than Susan, and more solid. He was simply one of the most handsome men I had ever seen. And, yes, it did feel very weird thinking that when I knew what I knew about him. But it was true.

'They only open a few hours a day, late in the afternoon,' I said casually but inwardly feeling uneasy because if circumstances – his, mostly – had been different I would've fancied the pants off him. But to do so now would be ludicrous. Insane. Inexplicable. Dangerous.

'Pity.' He paused then and insisted on holding my gaze. 'I'll just have to come back again, won't I?'

The question hung in the air. Was he waiting for an answer?

He dug his hands into the pockets of his jeans and executed a jerky forward-thrust pelvic movement that was altogether very male and I suddenly realized that he was flirting with me. I was thrilled but then immediately uncomfortable.

Every time he looked at me I clean forgot that he used to be a woman and then he'd look away again and it would be the first thing I'd remember.

Susan's eyes were slightly glazed and she didn't seem to notice anything going on. I was glad. The last thing I wanted was to have her upset by all this; I knew how much she liked him. But Muriel's feelers had picked up on something and she was watching the goings-on with curiosity. I wouldn't know what to say to her without divulging too many secrets.

'We should go in now,' I said, pointing to the revolving door to validate my suggestion. 'People are waiting for us.'

But Hank had other ideas. 'Why don't we join you for a drink?'

'We can't,' Susan piped up, rejoining the conversation at the crucial moment. 'I've got plans for the two of us.' She bundled the sleeve of his jumper in her hand and started to coax him away. 'Bye,' she chimed with unmistakable finality. 'See you tomorrow at work.'

For a second it looked as if Hank was going to say something but then he seemed to change his mind, guessing that it would be pointless to argue with her. He simply looked at me, intently, as if trying to pass some kind of silent message.

I surprised myself by staring right back, thinking I'd actually like to talk to him some more. I liked his easy-going style and lack of pretensions. And the more I studied him the better-looking he got.

I asked myself what was going on here. I could never get involved with him, no matter how good-looking he was. It was out of the question. Wasn't it?

10

The next time I saw Muriel after that night was at the airport to go to Winchester.

'How have the last two days been?' she asked me as the small plane that was our getaway mode of transport for the weekend taxied down the runway.

Muriel had taken the day off and gone to Dublin on an earlier bus than me to do some shopping. She'd headed straight for Brown Thomas only to emerge, barely thirty-five minutes later, £250 lighter but deliriously happy – such was the power of Brown Thomas. It should really be made available on the public health.

We'd met up at the airport with just enough time to check in and race through security to the departure lounge where the flight was already boarding, so this was our first real conversation of the day because neither of us could talk and run at the same time.

'Yeah, good,' I replied, finally allowing myself to smile after the last-minute rush to get on the plane. 'No more run-ins with Richie and Ellen Van Damme, for starters.'

'Wait until he has his wounds licked after the whipping you gave him at Carmen's show,' Muriel warned me.

'I know.' Richie was not the complacent kind. 'Oh, by the way, remember I told you that Eilish knew a nurse who needed someplace to live?'

She nodded.

'Well, they're moving in with me this weekend. I left the keys with Eilish.' I was thrilled to have found someone to share the mortgage with because I really couldn't afford to pay it on my own and I was too proud to ask Richie to help out when really he should have offered. Too proud or too stupid, I figured. But I'd get my own back.

The two ads in the paper had appeared in the *Waterford Chronicle* yesterday and, just like with the anonymous newspaper clippings in the envelope, Richie would have no real proof that the ads were my doing – and if he called the newspaper he'd find out that they'd been paid for with his own credit card. It was a good enough start. I still hadn't told Muriel about this, though, because I knew she'd just give me another lecture.

'Who's this nurse?' Muriel asked.

'No idea. They come highly recommended by Eilish, though,' I assured her when she looked troubled that I hadn't even once met my new house-mate. 'Anyway, it will be someone to help me with the mortgage and household bills, and that's what matters.'

'Yeah,' she agreed.

'And listen to this,' I went on, accepting a miniature

bottle of lukewarm white wine from the air hostess. 'Myra Barry swore my mother to secrecy but she told me nonetheless. She probably thought I needed cheering up.' I grimaced slightly. 'Myra showed the article I wrote for her to some friend of hers in Dublin and she might have a surprise for me when I get back.' I unscrewed the lid on the bottle and emptied the contents into a plastic glass.

'A surprise?'

'Yeah.'

'Wonder what that could be?' Muriel was squeezing the juice out of a wedge of lemon floating in her gin and tonic. 'With Myra you never know.'

'Yeah, I'm not getting too excited,' I told her. 'Myra's friend has probably set up an inner sanctum for women who have been dumped by their men for older women and she's about to give me the secret password to get in or something.' Rueful glance.

'Lucky you,' she exclaimed, surprising me by sounding unexpectedly wistful. 'At least there's something a bit special, a bit out of the ordinary to being dumped for an older *femme fatale*. I was just plain dumped . . . for a pig farmer. My God! A pig farmer.' She shook her head, the dismay catching up with her momentarily.

It was the first time since we'd struck up our friendship again that Muriel had made any reference to her split from James McGrath. I thought she was over him. 'But you coped really well,' I ventured. I hadn't seen much of Muriel last year, when the break-up had happened, and I felt awful about it now that I understood what it was like, but I'd heard on the grapevine that she'd taken it well.

'Mostly thanks to St John's Wort,' she confided. 'I don't think they sell it over the counter in Ireland any more. They're looking into the side effects,' she said, doing a crazed, cock-eyed look. 'But don't worry, you'll be able to pick some up in Boots when we get to Winchester.'

It sounded like just what I needed.

'You know, it wasn't easy at the time, being dumped for a pig farmer,' she continued. 'It doesn't sound good whatever way you try to put it.'

'And now you're all friends with each other?' I knew this too.

'Yes,' she replied matter-of-factly and then changed subjects. 'Isn't that Antonio lovely?'

'From what I've heard he's a bit of a Don Juan.' Carmen was a very good source of information on Antonio. 'Don Juan,' I repeated, laughing at my own choice of description for Antonio. 'Spanish? Get it?'

Muriel smiled indulgently. 'I wonder how come I've never met him around before? Tell me everything you know about him.'

So I told her. Everything. In as much detail as I'd first got it from Carmen. I was just glad that she hadn't asked me about Hank. That night in the hotel bar I'd fielded all her questions because I wasn't sure what I could say.

'Does Carmen have a thing for Antonio?' she asked as she struggled to digest the vat of information I'd just given her.

'Well spotted, Einstein,' I said at the same time that the plane hit the runway at Southampton airport.

I glanced at my watch. It was just past nine o'clock and, according to the arrivals screen overhead as we waited for our luggage, our flight was one of the last scheduled to land that evening.

Muriel's sister, Imelda, was waiting for us when we walked through the sliding doors into the main building, standing out from the others there in an off-white funnel-necked coat and tight fudge-coloured plaid trousers with a sharp kick at the bottom, a baguette bag clutched in one hand and vertiginous stiletto heels: the epitome of Friday-night glamour and the last thing you'd expect to see hanging around Southampton airport.

'Rosie, I'm so glad to see you. You're looking great.' She threw her arms around me. 'You've come to the right place for a bit of mothering.'

I had to forcibly stop myself from spluttering. She looked like the furthest thing from a mother that I could ever have imagined and even if I did look 'great', as she put it, I would never be in the same league as either Imelda or Muriel. But it didn't really bother me.

I'd grown up with them so I was used to the punch they both packed in the looks department.

'Thanks for letting me come over.' I smiled back at her and slipped out of her embrace, patting her arm in a gesture of appreciation. The soft material of her coat shimmied beneath my hand. It felt like a handful of the finest, softest sand slipping through my fingers. 'That's a beautiful coat,' I sighed longingly.

'What, this old thing? I just grabbed the first coat I could lay my hands on. You're not going to go out and buy the same one, are you?' she asked jokingly, bringing up the days of old when copying her had been the focus of my existence. She hadn't always seen the funny side of it. I remembered one time she'd been particularly annoyed with me because I'd copied her idea of wearing a pair of fluorescent socks underneath our regulation grey uniform socks for school, leaving a rim of bright yellow or green sticking out at the top.

She'd been furious with me – and with Muriel, who'd copied her too. When I tried to tell her that imitation was the highest form of flattery, which is what my mother told me to tell her whenever she had a go at me, which was fairly often, she just looked at me and said with as much indignation as she could muster that imitation was for 'sweat-shop fakes' and not Imelda Ryan. The indignation went way over my head and I stuck with the fluorescent socks until she started wearing patterned tights.

'Don't worry, I couldn't afford it,' I assured her. 'The bank manager would be very upset if I had to stop paying the mortgage for five months. He'd never understand why I had to have that coat.'

We drove the eleven miles to Winchester, where Imelda and her husband Jonty had their house, in her black BMW with the speedometer hitting numbers that I thought were only on the display for show. To make matters worse, I realized, as I nervously clutched the door handle, Imelda was one of those drivers who looked everywhere but at the road ahead of her. I shut my eyes.

We somehow made it back to the house in the city centre, near the cathedral, without having a horrendous accident or being pulled over by the police for reckless driving.

Jonty was waiting for us inside. He was an architect and Imelda an interior designer, and both were very successful. Muriel had told me that their house was photographed for interiors magazines and used for fashion shoots, and, as I gazed around me in a semi-stupor, I could understand why.

Richie's attempts at interior designing our home had given us the Hotch-Potch House compared to this. This obvious failure of his pleased me now.

Muriel casually threw her weekend bag on the hall floor, which looked to be made of matt black rubber, and disappeared into another room around the side of a big steel screen on wheels.

I stood staring at the gap above me where the middle of the ceiling should've been, and up above that where the middle of the ceiling of the next floor should've been, right up to a glass and steel creation of a dome through which I could see the night sky. There were no stairs that I could see. Instead there was a metal contraption similar to the ones used by window cleaners on the outside of buildings.

'Where do you want me to put my bag?' I asked Imelda when I found my voice.

She pressed the wall behind her with the flat of her hand and a portion of it slid to the side. Inside was domestic chaos: shelves laden with shoes, piles of bags, all shapes and sizes, rows of coats and plastic containers full of cleaning products.

She caught me staring gratefully at the mess and arched her head back and laughed. 'You need somewhere to put everything, don't you, Jonty?' she called out.

'Yes,' came the answer from behind the steel screen. 'Come on through, girls, I'm pouring the poison.'

I stashed my canvas bag behind the sliding portion of wall and we went into the next room. Four shot glasses were sitting on Imelda and Jonty's version of a coffee table, a thick Perspex cube, and Muriel was lounging in some kind of brightly coloured plastic sphere with a scooped-out dip in the middle.

'They're very comfortable,' she assured me.

I grunted dubiously before I could stop myself.

'They are,' Imelda insisted as she sat in another one. 'A friend of ours designed them and we're just road-testing them for him. Aren't they fab?'

I lowered myself into one and leant back into the dip, feeling rigid and conspicuous.

'It's a womb thing,' she told me enthusiastically, apparently seeing nothing strange in describing a plastic chair as a womb. The girl had been out of Waterford too long.

I raised my eyebrows, not sure what kind of reply she was after, and I struggled to find one that sounded interested enough. 'Oh?'

'Dax, the guy who designed it, wanted to pay tribute to his pregnant partner.'

So he made her a *plastic chair* in her likeness! A little cluster of diamonds would've suited me fine. I'd heard all about pregnancy from Hannah: the piles, the veins and the stretch marks. And I'd say that, if I was pregnant, paying tribute to me with that chair would be a mistake.

Jonty handed out the shot glasses I'd spotted earlier, which he'd since filled with tequila, and we all stood up for a toast. 'Let's raise our glasses to the celebration of life,' he said, throwing such an adoring look in Imelda's direction that it made me wince with self-pity.

'Down the hatch,' Imelda suggested, dispensing with the need for any eloquence and showing her roots after all.

We emptied our glasses and Jonty quickly refilled them. 'Muriel, care to do the honours this time?'

Muriel drove the standard up. 'Quoting Oscar Wilde, "It is always nice to be expected, and not to arrive." But here we are anyway,' she grinned at me, 'so let's raise our glasses to arrivals!'

'Hear! hear!'

Jonty refilled the glasses for a third time. 'My turn,' he playfully claimed. 'Not forgetting our friend Oscar, "I like looking at geniuses and listening to beautiful people." So here's to great company.'

We all cheered. 'Hear! hear!'

'Rosie,' he began, heading towards me with the bottle of tequila in his hand.

I grinned at him. 'I won't let the side down.' I could remember one Oscar Wilde quote from school and fortunately it wasn't one that either Muriel or Jonty had used. '"Experience is the name everyone gives to their mistakes." We all know who that's from,' I added. 'So I'd like to propose a toast to my enormous experience. May I put it to good use again some day.'

I emptied the liquid into my mouth and forced it down, ignoring the burning sensation, when a life-size picture of Hank jumped out at me from nowhere and I had to snap my head backwards to get away from it. I blamed it on the tequila.

'And tomorrow night might be just the occasion,' Imelda suggested. 'Muriel, you remember the Hotel de Paris, don't you? That place we took you the last time you were over?'

Muriel nodded enthusiastically. 'Yeah, it was great.'

'Well,' she continued, 'they're doing a special singles evening tomorrow.' Then she caught the aghast expressions on both our faces. 'No, no, it's not at all like you imagine. People even come down from London for it,' she tried to convince us.

I didn't believe a word of it and I didn't need to be sent to a singles party.

'There's excellent food, great wine and really cool people.'

Then why are they single? I found myself wondering before I remembered my own status and Muriel's.

'All my single friends go,' Jonty joined in. 'You've timed your visit well.' He latched on to Muriel, sensing from the razor-sharp tilt of my chin and the unyielding expression on my face that she might be easier to persuade. 'You remember Vince, don't you?'

'Y-e-a-h,' Muriel replied cagily. 'But he's got a girl-friend, that French model.'

'So he does, so he does,' Jonty heartily agreed. Too heartily. 'And where do you think he met her?' he asked.

'There?' She was stunned, which is exactly what he wanted.

'Precisely.'

'He doesn't look the kind to have to resort to a singles event, and she definitely doesn't.'

'That's exactly my point, Muriel, these evenings have class. And the people who go do not consider themselves social lepers just because they're single.'

I didn't consider myself a social leper because I was single; not yet anyway.

Imelda could see that Muriel was wavering. 'We've already booked and paid for the tickets as a little present from us to you,' she said, her *coup de grâce*, and from the Perspex cube she picked up an envelope with both our names on the front, invitingly handwritten in dark-gold ink. 'Here they are.' She held the tickets out to Muriel. The temptress Eve in the Garden of Eden.

I knew that the minute Muriel took them into her hand our fate for tomorrow night would be sealed. 'Don't take the envelope. Don't even touch it,' I mentally told her. But, despite Muriel's other talents, she hadn't yet learnt to read my mind.

'We couldn't possibly accept them,' I said. 'They must've been really expensive.'

Imelda had already decided how she was going to play her next shot. She simply said, 'You're both worth it.' It was a masterstroke. Of course we were worth it. What else could we say?

Muriel took the envelope and by the time we'd had a fifth shot of tequila I felt more comfortable with the idea, and by the time the seventh shot had been downed I couldn't even remember where it was that

188

we were supposed to be going the next night, had taken up permanent residence on the floor, and everything was just fine.

Unfortunately the next day was lost in hangover hell. I just about remembered to get five bottles of St John's Wort, the miracle cure to a broken heart, telling the girl at the cash till in Boots that I had three manic-depressive sisters at home. I also picked up one of those tiny pocket books, called *How to Marry the Woman of Your Dreams*, for Johnny Power – though it didn't say what to do if she was an alcoholic.

'What are you wearing tonight?' Muriel asked me as we sat in a pub sipping Bloody Marys because we'd finally decided to try the hair-of-the-dog remedy to get rid of our hangovers.

'My "Kiss me I'm Irish" T-shirt.'

'You still have that?' We'd bought one each on a school trip to Killarney when we were about fourteen but the teachers wouldn't allow me to wear mine because I was very overdeveloped for my age and men might get the wrong idea, they told me.

'Of course,' I lied. 'What about you?'

'The catsuit I got in Brown Thomas yesterday.'

'The one with the front slashed to the navel?'

'Yep.'

'I'm not really wearing the "Kiss me I'm Irish" T-shirt.'

'I know.'

'We'll have to smarten up our conversation for

tonight,' I said woefully. 'What can you talk know-
ledgeably about?'

'Books.'

'That's a good one.'

'What about you?'

'Deception within the boundaries of marriage.'

'You'll wow them.'

11

Imelda rushed out to meet us in the hallway as we walked through the front door. 'Your mother has called four times,' she said. 'Four times,' she emphasized.

'What's the matter?' I asked, feeling faint with sudden concern. Had Hannah run away with the kids? Or, worse, had she run away without the kids? Did she know about Susan? Had my mother heard what Titch Murphy was saying about me?

'Something about Richie looking for you, urgently.' Imelda sandwiched the last word in inverted commas with two curled fingers, a thick Bulgari ring on one. 'Apparently he's on the warpath and he has been harassing your mother as to your whereabouts. Something to do with a newspaper ad?' She looked puzzled.

'Oh, that.' I breathed an enormous sigh of relief. The newspaper ads must be drawing quite a response, I figured.

'What newspaper ad is that?' Muriel asked.

I confessed.

'Why do you waste your energy on him?' she wanted to know. 'It's senseless behaviour, Rosie.'

'It makes me feel better,' I said. 'I'd better call my mother back. Tell her not to worry.' I laughed at the futility of such a call, my voice bouncing off the rubber flooring, because I knew who would take the worse beating in any kind of encounter between Richie and my mother. Hell hath no fury like a woman whose daughter has been scorned.

About two hours later Muriel sauntered loose-limbed into the bedroom where I was getting ready. 'I feel so much better now,' she declared, zinging with energy because she'd slept while I'd spent my time planning what I could do to Richie next. 'Aren't you ready yet?' She pirouetted gracefully.

'You look great, Muriel.' The black catsuit she was wearing displayed her feminine leanness to perfection. Her long hair was pulled back into a sleek ponytail and thin gold hoops swung from her ears. 'I'm nearly there,' I told her.

My white trouser suit came from my favourite clothes shop. Eilish, Hannah and Carmen had clubbed together to get it for me for Christmas. It had a short tailored jacket and fitted straight-legged trousers, and it made me feel like a million dollars just because I knew it was expensive. Tonight was the perfect occasion for its first sortie. I needed to feel good in front of a roomful of strangers who all knew I was single. It didn't matter that they were single too. I felt more single than them.

Muriel sat on the bed and watched me, trance-like,

as I applied mascara. 'I find it so soothing to watch someone do their make-up.'

'Well, I'm on the last coat of lipstick now,' I warned her, pursing bright-red lips in the mirror. 'You know, they don't look like they belong to me at all.' I tried a few different smiles and gave up. 'I'd be burnt at the stake in another era.'

'Let's go show those Englishmen what they've been missing.' She jumped up off the bed and wandered over to the mirror, where she tried to coax the two sides of the deep slit in her catsuit together to reveal less of an expanse of bare flesh.

'That's a real exercise in futility,' I told her.

She looked at me idly. 'What?'

I pointed. 'There just isn't enough material to go around.'

'No,' she corrected me, in her sensible voice, 'putting those ads in the *Waterford Chronicle* was a real exercise in futility. I just wonder what else you've up your sleeve?'

I didn't tell her.

'That you're going to be too embarrassed to tell me about?'

'I wasn't embarrassed at all. I knew you'd lecture me, that's all.'

'You were too embarrassed by your own behaviour and that's why you didn't tell me.'

'I was *not*.'

'And I understand your thinking.'

'Well, don't bother.'

'And if you are determined to go through with this revenge campaign that you've got going on with Richie then I'll help you.'

'What?'

She'd obviously thought it through because she wore an unhappily resigned look on her face. 'I'm not helping you because I agree with it. I don't. Call it . . . call it . . . Oh, just call it the stuff friends do. OK?'

'OK.'

Jonty dropped us off in front of the Hotel de Paris, a beautiful Georgian building in the heart of the town. He refused to be cajoled into coming inside for a drink with us so that we didn't arrive man-less, which, he assured us, was the object of the evening.

We went on in, somewhat nervously. Muriel handed our tickets to the receptionist seated behind an old-style polished wooden bureau. She took them, smiled pleasantly and told us that aperitifs were being served in the bar. Then she stood up from behind the desk and walked us through the restaurant, two adjoining rooms, old paintings and photos placed haphazardly yet in all the right places on the walls, empty bottles of vintage wine stacked in fireplaces, dark-wood floors and leather-seated chairs. It was a perfect blend of charm and elegance and good taste.

The people sipping drinks in the bar the receptionist showed us to were the opposite of everything I'd decided they would be. Firstly, they didn't have 'DESPERATE' stamped on their foreheads in fire-branded letters. And they didn't seem physically lacking or verbally challenged either.

They were talking, mingling, drinking, and they were normal. There was no sign of any of the awkwardness that I'd expected. Everyone seemed relaxed. I was suddenly delighted that Imelda had talked us into coming here tonight. It didn't feel wrong to be single. It almost felt right.

It was now two weeks since Richie had left me. Two weeks during which I could've stayed in bed day and night and cried, drank myself stupid and barely seen the time pass while nonetheless counting every minute. But I hadn't. I'd got on with life, as unpleasant as it seemed at times. Everyone around me had made sure of it. And I'd discovered something very important. I'd discovered that I get up again when I fall down. I was bruised but I was back on my feet.

As we walked down the stairs into the bar a few heads turned our way, and one or two even nodded in greeting. Muriel was on the step behind me. 'I hope they won't think I'm easy just because I'm showing a lot of flesh.'

She sounded genuinely worried. I turned around to console her and my nose plunged into her bare navel. 'Just make sure they're on the same level as you,' I cautioned her.

We hovered at the bottom of the stairs for a few

seconds, standing close to each other for support and smiling into the crowd at no one in particular. I wasn't sure where to go from there. Was there some kind of special etiquette for evenings like these? Should we walk around and introduce ourselves to everyone or stay put? Should we be prepared to give relationship history? And would it be really bad manners to lie about this?

A waiter delivered us from our quandary. He came up to take our drinks order and suggested that we take a seat by the window. This subtle combination of attentiveness and professionalism meant we promptly did exactly as we were told.

Once seated, Muriel dipped two fingers into a white ceramic bowl on the table and grabbed a plump green olive while looking contentedly around the room. She went to pop the olive into her mouth but it slipped from between her fingers and rolled inside the front of her catsuit. She looked mortified. 'Oh, my God!'

'I bet they didn't warn you about that in Brown Thomas,' I said, and she looked mortified all over again and pushed the offending olive bowl over to the far side of the table.

'You see that guy over there?' I nodded faintly with my head towards the man on the other side of the room. He was wearing a burgundy-coloured shirt, open at the neck, and slim-fitting black trousers. His black hair, tinged with grey just above his ears, was cropped close to his head. He was being very attentive to a doll-like creature in a red sequinned dress, a vivacious Vivien Leigh lookalike.

'You mean Rhett? The one trying to slip his tongue into Scarlett's ear?'

'The very one. He's not bad,' I said, as if it was the biggest compliment in the world that I could pay him.

She laughed, her whole body shaking, and suddenly the olive rolled out of nowhere and continued to roll across the floor, coming to a halt next to a glitzy sandal. 'He's not bad?' she repeated. 'Aren't you still married?' I could tell she was nonetheless delighted that I'd shown an interest at all.

'Hah-hah! Aren't you still a librarian?'

'Not tonight I'm not.' She sat tall and straightened her shoulders. 'Tonight, Matthew, I'm going to be a writer,' she declared.

Muriel wasn't very good at lying, which was the only thing that worried me about her sudden decision to help me with my plans for Richie. 'And will anyone have heard of you?' I asked her, thinking that if she pulled this off I'd have no problem with her helping me out.

'Not unless I tell them I write under the pseudonym of Maeve Binchy,' she quickly replied. 'But you know, I've met writers before and I've always been too embarrassed to say that I've never heard of them, never read any of their books, especially working in a library – and by the way, I'm not really known as a librarian these days; my proper title is information manager.'

'OK.' I wondered what that made me – a transport specialist, perhaps?

'I guarantee you that several people here tonight will have heard of me. A few of them might even have read my books,' she said optimistically. 'What are you going to be?'

Naturally she assumed that I wouldn't own up to working in a taxi office answering the phones. But I decided that I would. 'I'm going to be me.'

'But you're always you. Try something different.'

'I thought you didn't agree with lying.'

'I don't. But this is more like play-acting. Spicing things up.'

'Things are spiced up enough for me at the moment.' I thought about Richie and Ellen Van Damme, about Susan, and about Hank.

Somewhere towards the end of this relay I realized that a man was standing beside the table looking highly amused at our bent heads, purposeful expressions and hushed conversation.

'I'm sorry. I didn't mean to interrupt,' he said as I peered up at him inquisitively.

Of course he'd meant to interrupt. He had a bottle of champagne in his right hand and three glasses dangling upside down in his left one.

Muriel flashed him a smile. 'No apologies needed,'

she said, eyeing the bottle of champagne. 'Would you like to join us?'

'That would be wonderful. I'm Simon, by the way.' He pulled up a low stool, planted the bottle of champagne on the table and handed us a glass each.

Simon raised his glass. 'To new friends.'

It turned out that Simon was very good company, funny and down-to-earth, and that this was his first time at one of these gatherings, too, and he thought they were a damn great idea. We discovered that he was a dermatologist when he complimented Muriel on her beautiful skin – though it wouldn't have taken a dermatologist to notice that.

As Muriel turned in her seat and began joking with two other men standing behind her who'd eagerly engaged her in conversation, I caught Simon peering at my left hand. 'Are you married?' he asked.

I quickly looked at my hand. I wasn't wearing my wedding ring but I did have it in my handbag. I'd loved all that ring had stood for and I just couldn't bring myself to be without it, to get rid of it yet.

He caught my puzzled expression and laughed. 'There's a very faint discolouration of the skin where your ring sits. It's barely noticeable. Only to the expert eye.'

'I'm separated,' I told him, sounding more confident than I felt. It was the first time I'd pronounced my new status aloud.

'I bet you'd be hard to get over.'

I was flattered. 'And I bet you'd be easy to get under.'

'Only if you were her,' he said unexpectedly, pointing with the rim of his glass towards the Vivien Leigh look-alike who was still chatting to Rhett Butler. 'She works as a hygienist for the dentist who rents the rooms on the floor above me. I overheard her talking to the receptionist last week and that's why I'm here. I've come to claim what's mine.'

'Only she doesn't know it yet, right?' I sipped the champagne he'd brought over.

'Spot on.'

Muriel was still laughing up at the two men standing behind her, both of whom were jostling to get the loudest chuckle.

Simon pulled his stool nearer to my chair and whispered, 'Any ideas?'

'Have you tried talking to her?'

He looked at me with a slightly offended expression. 'Of course I've tried talking to her.' I nodded but in my experience that was often the *last* thing men tried. 'Talking to her is the *first* thing I tried,' he assured me. 'I also make sure that I bump into her in the sandwich shop most days. I even left a bad case of acne waiting so I'd get there at the right time last week.' He lifted his shoulders to indicate his helplessness when faced with this woman. 'I smile and make eye contact every time I see her.' He continued to list his 'right behaviour' until I held a hand up.

'Stop, please,' I implored him. 'I'm surprised she hasn't taken an injunction out against you. The poor woman probably thinks she has a stalker.'

He looked aghast. 'Never! I just wanted to make sure that I didn't let any opportunity go by.'

'Have previous girlfriends told you that you were "too nice"?'

'Yes. But it's not in me to be nasty to the women I like. I really don't see the logic in that.'

'There isn't one. Anyway, it's not about logic. It's about creating a bit of desirability. You see, Simon, and this is something that most men do not understand, the . . .' and just as I was about to explain to a very puzzled-looking Simon the inner workings of the female mind, Muriel swung around to face the table again. There was only one man left standing behind her now. The victor was sturdy-looking and tanned. 'Charlie's a garden designer,' she told us, 'and he thinks he saw his sister reading one of my books. Isn't that great?'

'Yeah,' I answered. 'I wonder which one of them it was?'

Muriel turned her face to hide the wicked grin. 'Oops,' she said suddenly as her eyes fixed on the ground, 'the olive's going walkabouts.'

The two men looked at each other, wondering if this was some sort of secret code language we had. I followed Muriel's gaze. The woman with the glitzy sandals had somehow managed to stand on the olive and pierce it with her stiletto heel without squashing it – the finest bit of precision engineering that I'd seen in a long time – and both of them were now headed into the restaurant, where dinner was being served.

Charlie, the garden designer, was not about to agree to being dumped, if that's what all this talk of 'olives going walkabouts' meant, and quickly said, 'Let's all share a table at dinner.'

Simon followed him into the restaurant. 'Good idea.'

Muriel and I followed Simon.

Charlie headed straight for the first table he saw with four free seats, which happened to be the one where Rhett and Scarlett were sitting by themselves, occasionally glancing at the empty chairs beside them and laughing, clearly wondering who would be joining them.

Simon glanced back over his shoulder, his eyes dancing with delight at the prospect of sharing a table with this girl, and whispered, 'By the way, her name's Yvonne. But you must pretend you don't know that, of course.'

'Of course.'

We were a few paces away from the table when Yvonne caught sight of the procession heading her way. Recognition quickly followed by alarm flashed in her eyes when she saw Simon. She smiled weakly at him and mumbled something to Rhett, probably to the effect of, 'Here comes my stalker,' because he whipped his head around to face us and honed in on Simon immediately. By now Simon had overtaken Charlie to take pole position and nab the seat beside Yvonne.

I almost heard her patience snap. She crossed her legs and put a sharp elbow on the table, cupped her chin in her hand and arched her face firmly away from him.

I sat on the chair next to him. 'Don't look so glum,' I cajoled him.

He turned around to look at me. 'I've got serious competition,' he sighed, head-butting the air to his right. 'That's Ken, an American venture capitalist, lives here and works in London. We've a few friends in common and have met before but he doesn't seem to remember me.'

I looked at Ken, examining the hard profile, the intense expression, noticing the expensive watch strapped to a thick wrist. I felt myself flush a little at the undeniable attractiveness of this ... this ... magnificent beast. There was no other way to describe him. He must've sensed my gaze on him because he slid his eyes away from Yvonne and pinned me to my seat with a hard look.

Meanwhile, Yvonne was unfolding her napkin on to her lap with total concentration, encouraging no interruptions from Simon, who was talking to me but was poised and ready to pounce on her at the slightest opportunity.

'A venture capitalist?' I repeated. 'Wow. What a great job!' It had to be a great job. Just look at him! There was no way he could've been, say, a sheet-metal worker.

'Rosie, what does a venture capitalist do?' Simon teased.

'Venture capital?' I guessed.

'Not wholly inaccurate,' he laughed. 'And what does a very successful venture capitalist do?'

'Venture capital very successfully?'

'Correct. And that's Ken.'

'I can tell.' He exuded power from every pore of his primed skin. He was used to controlling and liked nothing more than to be worshipped and obeyed. I could tell. He was arrogant and charming at the same time, and women loved it – it was the kind of behaviour that Simon could never pull off and that Titch Murphy would get arrested for.

I guessed that Ken came to these evenings because they were a perfect playground in which to showcase his skills. As I looked around me I noticed several women throwing enticing looks in his direction, confirming their acceptance even before being asked. I was semi-pulverized by the aura of power that surrounded him. I wasn't used to meeting men like that. They just didn't tend to hang around the taxi offices in Waterford.

Suddenly a rogue thought struck me. Such was its unexpectedness that it made the breath catch in my throat and my head explode in a blinding kaleidoscope of colour. Despite all that Ken had going for him, I found myself thinking that I still fancied Hank more. But how could that be? I'd made it clear to myself for all the obvious reasons that this just wasn't an option.

I made a feeble attempt at eating my starter, pushing the delicious-looking miniature crab cakes around the plate and then stabbing each one with a heavy silver fork. I sat in utter silence, thinking seriously about things, and the dilemma in my head began to unravel itself a little – or to wind itself into a bigger dilemma, depending on which way you looked at it.

I could honestly say that I didn't feel at all uneasy that Susan had started life as a man and was now – a truckload of hormones, a fortune's worth of voice-therapy sessions and one big operation later – a woman. Strangely or not, knowing this did not make me see her as any less of a woman. In fact, I think I admired her more.

However, I did not feel the same way when it came to Hank. I felt uneasy, embarrassed and kind of apprehensive. The reason for this was slowly becoming obvious to me.

Sex.

Sex would never, ever be an issue between Susan and myself. The idea was laughable and absurd. Sex would never be an issue for me and Susan in the same way it would never be an issue for me and Muriel.

But the same wasn't true of Hank. The idea wasn't

laughable and absurd, even though it probably should have been. The idea of sex had somehow super-glued itself to Hank.

Fortunately, Muriel's new garden-designer friend, Charlie, stepped in to save me from too much serious thinking with hilarious stories of well-to-do older ladies who called him in to redesign their gardens and then decided he could tend to more than just the shrubbery.

Muriel was bent over with laughter and the more laughs he got the grittier and more outrageous his recollections became. What Charlie could do on a ten-litre bag of Irish moss peat went beyond the definition of mere acrobatics.

At the other tables, people had swapped seats and were busy chatting to new neighbours, while others stood around in small groups talking and drinking. It was such a pity there was nothing like this back home in Waterford, I mused.

I realized that I'd made the fatal mistake of showing no genuine interest whatsoever in Ken for the last forty-five minutes, making myself very desirable to him, when he suggested to Simon that they trade places.

'So, Rosie,' he drawled, as the waiter discreetly cleared the table in front of us of plates and cutlery, 'what do you do with yourself?'

Suddenly I found myself telling him that I owned a taxi firm in Ireland and he looked so impressed I couldn't resist adding that it was one of a chain of sixteen and that I was rapidly expanding. That would be my nose, Pinocchio-style.

He put one arm across the back of his chair and rested the other one on the table, leaning his well-muscled torso towards me, his nostrils flaring. 'You must be very ambitious. I like ambition in a woman.'

The fact that I felt more attracted to Hank, to whom I shouldn't have been, than to Ken, to whom I probably should have been, was bothering me so I decided to do something about it.

I mirrored his position, one arm slung across the back of the chair, one arm laid on the table, and ran my tongue over my lips provocatively, leaving a sheen of wetness, and a promise of things to come. I was about to put the art into tart.

'Tell me, Ken,' I said smoothly, caressing the rim of my glass with my middle finger, then dipping it in the wine and bringing it to my mouth where I let a droplet trickle on to my bottom lip before deftly catching it with my tongue. 'Tell me what it is you like about my ambition.'

'You obviously reach out for what you want. And I like it when a woman reaches out for what she wants.' His lust-shot eyes pierced mine.

His audacity made me feel bold and wanton. I hadn't felt like that in a while. 'And, Ken,' I said, making sure to use his name, trying to make it sound soft and sexy even though with only two hard consonants and a single vowel there wasn't a lot of room for foreign-sounding manipulations. 'Do you think men should reach out for what they want, too?' I leant forward to take my wine glass, making sure he caught a tantalizing peek of flesh inside my white jacket.

His eyes darkened. 'Most definitely. I reach out for what I want. Say I wanted your glass,' I happened to be sipping from it and nearly choked, 'I would just reach out and take it.' He did just that, and rested his lips at exactly the same spot as I'd just had mine. This was no coincidence.

The buzz of laughter and conversation in the room faded. I could hear only one voice. 'I will take what I want.'

There was no room for any doubt: I was what he wanted. His obviousness was invigorating and even thrilling. But suddenly, deep down, I wasn't so sure that I wanted to be taken – not by Ken. My body was primed but my mind wasn't.

I placed my hands on the table and sat back in my chair. From the abrupt pause in all come-hither signalling Ken sensed that my enthusiasm had waned and looked at me curiously.

It seemed very out of date to admit this but I was hopeless at one-night stands. The thought of them appealed to me but the reality of slinking out of a strange bed, doing my utmost not to let the strange person in the strange bed get a peek at my bottom, was horrible.

And another thing that the one-night stand had against it, I remembered, was that once, in my hurry to get out of a godforsaken hotel room where someone I'd met about five hours earlier had just fallen asleep, I'd slipped on the used condom and badly twisted my ankle. It had been a hard one to explain to my mother while keeping a straight face.

The seconds passed.

'No.'

'No what?'

'No, Ken. No, to this.' I felt awful. Honesty was my only excuse. I chewed on my bottom lip. 'I know I've behaved like a tease. I'm sorry.'

I wasn't going to be too honest and explain what had provoked such action. I didn't owe him that much. 'I'm just out of a long relationship and I'm not ready . . . for anything,' I quickly added before he could tell me that he wasn't interested in a relationship either and I'd have to venture another excuse.

I was relieved that he wasn't pissed off. But on the other hand I could've done with being flattered and watching him crumble when he realized that we wouldn't be spending the night together after all. But that didn't happen. He just shrugged his shoulders and turned again to Yvonne, who immediately shifted her attention back to him, leaving Simon looking bereft.

He swaggered around the table to me, tie loosened, cigar of drug-baron proportions in one hand, balloon glass of liquor in the other. 'You couldn't have held on to him for longer?' he asked me. 'I was just about to get someplace. I could feel it in my bones.'

'My granny could feel things in her bones, too, when she was young. Turned out that it was rickets.'

He covered me in a displeased shroud of cigar smoke.

'I'm not sure dermatologists should smoke,' I coughed.

'She was that close to agreeing to a sandwich some lunchtime.' He pressed his index finger and his thumb together as hard as he could. 'I know it.'

'Which you took to mean that she now fancies you madly?'

'Absolutely. It's further than I've ever got before.'

'Do you mean with Yvonne or any woman?' I laughed, thinking the latter quite possible.

'With Yvonne, Rosie.'

'I'm sure she'll be waiting for you at the sandwich shop on Monday,' I teased him.

'Probably,' he agreed laughingly. 'Anyway, I'm sure she'll see past him,' he said referring to Ken. 'After all, you did.'

I wanted to tell him that I didn't really see past him. It was just that someone else kept blocking my view.

12

It was strange to come home to a house with the lights on, blushing a welcome from within, as they were when the taxi dropped me off from the bus station on Sunday evening. I'd only just got used to arriving home to a dark, empty house.

I'd taken the bus down from the airport with Muriel. It was a monotonous journey with nothing to stare at through the window but my own reflection, the dark night acting as a suitably grim backdrop. We were both exhausted from the weekend and spoke only to complain about how we weren't as young as we once were – which sent the two teenagers sitting in front of us into fits of giggles when they looked back at us, doing nothing to rejuvenate our spirits.

Simon had taken us on to a friend's party after the singles dinner and by the time we made it back to Imelda's Jonty was heading out for a Sunday-morning jog. We collapsed into our beds and Imelda woke us late afternoon when it was time to go to the airport to catch our flight home.

I remembered then that the lights were on because Eilish had helped her nurse friend to move in over the weekend. From now on there would be a nurse's uniform flapping about on the clothesline, her make-up remover on the bathroom shelf, and most import-antly, money in my bank account to help with the mortgage.

'Hello?' I shouted, pushing my head around the door. It came out as a squeak.

'Hi,' Eilish answered, walking out of the kitchen with a cup of coffee in her hand, looking very much at home in my home. 'I wanted to be around when you got back, to introduce you to your new housemate.'

'That's very nice of you.' I pulled my bag up the hallway and left it at the foot of the stairs. 'So where is she?' I was curious despite the tiredness.

'Here I am.'

I simply stared at the person who'd spoken.

'I know what you're thinking and I would like to make it clear right from the start that my mother did teach me how to use a toilet brush. I can cook an egg. And my feet don't smell.'

My new housemate was male. Eilish had sent a guy to live with me. Was she mad? He was about six feet tall, with pale skin the colour of a faded cream-cracker and jet-black hair cut into a wiry crop, and was still wearing his nurse's uniform. Two green eyes laughed knowingly at me from behind a pair of funky rimless glasses.

I'd just presumed, stupidly, naively, that the nurse who was going to share my house with me would be a woman. Now, I knew that not all nurses are women, just like not all men are bastards, but Eilish, who was sheepishly scuffing the floor with her shoe had never said otherwise. And I'd never asked.

'I thought you'd be a woman,' I told him.

'I bet you say that to all the boys.'

'You can say that again.'

'Anyway, I think we can safely assume that I'm not,' he said in a baritone voice.

I didn't tell him that these days I could safely assume nothing of the sort.

'I'm Thomas, by the way. And if it makes you feel any better, I am definitely in touch with my feminine side. I've got five sisters. And to prove it I can perm hair, wax legs and I do a great Dolly Parton rendition of "Jolene" when I've had a few too many.'

Eilish was looking back over her shoulder to where Thomas was standing and was tittering at his witty comments, tucking strands of fine pale hair behind her ears in a girly gesture.

'You've lost an earring,' I noticed. There was only one gold hoop.

'No!' she panicked, her free hand flying up to check both earlobes. When she realized there was nothing hanging off the left one she moaned, 'They were my favourite pair, too. I could've lost it anywhere.'

'When did you get here?' I asked her.

'Five minutes ago,' she said.

'About an hour ago,' Thomas said.

I looked at the two of them. 'Which is it?'

'It must be about an hour ago,' Eilish decided. 'It just feels like five minutes. Time flies when you're having fun.'

I hoped she wasn't suggesting that I join in. I'd had enough fun. 'I'm going to bed.'

'Oh no you're not,' she parried as Thomas pulled out a bottle of champagne from behind his back. 'We're going to drink to new housemates.'

It would've been rude to refuse.

'Are you a very good friend of Eilish's?' I quizzed him the next morning over breakfast and painkillers. 'Because I thought I'd met them all.' It was our first day of sharing a house together and he'd just learnt that I liked my coffee milky and took the top off my boiled egg delicately with a spoon, not with the guillotine-like slash of a knife like he did.

'Well, she's a good friend of mine,' he answered. 'And I'd like to think she'd say I was a good friend of hers too. But you never know,' he faltered and shrugged.

'I'm sure she would.' I felt I had to reassure him. 'She wouldn't have recommended you to me, as a housemate, if she didn't like you.'

'Did she say she liked me?' he asked eagerly.

'She just said she knew a "nice nurse" who was looking for somewhere to live and by "nice nurse" I assumed she meant nice female nurse.'

'Nice, eh?' He sounded disappointed.

'Yeah, nice.' He had the hangdog look of a mutt shunned by a beloved master. 'Thomas, you are aware that Eilish is practically married, aren't you? She's been going out with Jimmy Bible for ten years and has been engaged to him for six of those, though God knows why.' I sighed loudly in exasperation.

'Yeah, I know, I know. What's he like, this Jimmy fella?'

'Oh, he's fine,' I said flatly. 'Jimmy's fine. It's just that he puts his horses before Eilish.'

'What? Is he a vet? Does he have stables or something?' Thomas scratched his wiry crop.

'No, he likes to bet on horses.' It was no secret, even though Eilish downplayed it.

His dark eyebrows shot up his pale forehead and stayed there, urging me on.

'I mean, Eilish is lovely.' I sipped my coffee. 'She could have her pick of any man.'

He nodded in agreement.

'And Jimmy doesn't appreciate her. She's wasting her time on him.'

He was still nodding.

'You know, Eilish has been saving for ages to get a patio built. She puts any spare cash she has into a jar at home and last week or so Jimmy took it and put it on a horse.' I knew I was gossiping but Thomas was absorbing every word and there was no greater incentive to talking than being listened to. Intently.

'I didn't know all this,' he said sadly, the green eyes

worryingly dim. 'She doesn't ever talk about him to me.' Thomas wasn't too up on everything that went on because he'd only arrived in Waterford from Offaly six months earlier.

'Well, don't say anything,' I warned him. I didn't want Eilish to think I was talking about her behind her back, which I was.

Ironically I bumped into Jimmy on my way to work. He was walking to the betting office that opened early at the top of the town. If Eilish wasn't around he had to walk everywhere because he'd lost his driving licence for five years after a second drink-driving incident, where he'd ploughed into a neighbour's wall one night, only two years after taking a short cut through town using the pedestrian streets and being caught.

For no good reason he started to have a go at me, loudly, right there in the middle of the street, using the uneven footpath between the church and the video shop as his battleground. He complained that I'd kept Eilish up all night when she stayed with me at the weekend and now she was tired, and snapping at him the whole time, and wouldn't give him a lift anywhere, and it was all my fault.

Jimmy didn't realize that I'd been away for the weekend because it wasn't mentioned in the *Racing Post*, and I just figured that Eilish had probably stayed with one of her friends because she was still annoyed with him about the patio money and he'd simply misunderstood and thought she was with me. So to keep things simple and get rid of him quickly, I apologized and walked on, swinging the book I'd bought for Johnny Power in a plastic bag in my hand.

'So, did Hank stay over on Wednesday night?' I asked Susan the minute I got to work.

She looked up from the newspaper. 'Don't you mean, "Hello, did you have a nice weekend?"'

'That's exactly what I meant.'

'Yes, I did have a nice weekend, thank you. And no, Hank did not stay over the other night. Can you believe it? After all he drank during the evening he insisted on driving back to Dublin. It takes a man.'

I was unaccountably delighted that he hadn't spent the night with Susan, and launched into a very animated description of my own weekend. Susan interrupted me just as I was about to get to the interesting bit. The bit where I'd filled out a coupon in a men's magazine left lying around Southampton airport requesting information on penile enlargement to be sent to Richie at the shop.

Muriel had slotted it into the post box at the airport as part of her pledge to help me add a bit of discomfort to Richie's life. I knew that the sales girl opened his mail every morning so news would spread around the town like wildfire. She fancied herself as a bit of a personal assistant to Richie and nothing got past her. I used to call her the Berlin Wall.

'We should start answering the phones, Rosie,'

Susan said; they'd begun to get busy. 'By the way, Hank says that you should come out with us the next time he's down from Dublin. Isn't that sweet of him?' She looked genuinely pleased.

'Yes.' But I had no intention of seeing him again. I'd decided that it wouldn't be in my best interest to do so.

By lunchtime Thomas had already phoned to say that he was doing fish fingers and beans for dinner, and I'd had to feign enormous enthusiasm. My mother had left two messages to say that Richie was looking for me again. Richie had phoned to say that he was coming around to have a serious word with me and I'd better open the door or I'd be sorry. Eilish had called to see if everything was going OK with Thomas and to check that I was being nice to him. Carmen had also called to tell me that Hannah was really upset about something big and wouldn't tell anyone what it was but she had a suspicion that my mother knew because they stopped talking any time she walked into the room. And Rory had phoned to say that my mother was acting strangely and could I come around as soon as possible and sort her out?

And to add to all this sometime during the morning Hannah had spoken to Susan and told her that Richie and Ellen Van Damme had paid cash for one of the new five-bedroom executive houses Dennis was subcontracted to work on, and Susan had told me.

So now I knew that they were setting up home together and I felt the tears sting my eyes before I brushed them away. It had to be her money they were using to buy the house. How could she have so much cash? Where did she get it?

In the midst of everything else going on, I hadn't forgotten that today was the day the article I'd written for Myra Barry was due to appear in *Waterford Lights*, the magazine she edited. I imagined that Richie would have something to say about this 'honest exposé' of mine when word of it reached him, which shouldn't take too long as the Berlin Wall's mother was an avid fan of the magazine and she had lunch most days with her daughter in one of the cafés near the shop. He'd know by early afternoon, I reckoned, and I was glad that something would mar the joy of buying a house and setting up home with Ellen Van Damme.

I leant back in my chair and stared up at the discoloured ceiling. After all that had happened I didn't want him back any more. But there were times when I wished that none of this had ever happened, that life could be simple and uncomplicated again, that I could return to my rut. But then the fever would drop, my eyes would stop rolling in my head and my sanity would return. Things could never be the same again.

That afternoon I slipped out for half an hour to see a solicitor about starting divorce proceedings. The

Divorce Act had only become law in 1997, so we had a long way to go in Ireland before we reached the acrimonious heights of the US where I could've sued Richie for emotional distress and hair loss with three loose strands on the pillowcase that morning.

My father would be turning in his grave at the thought of me getting divorced and that made me feel bad. I wanted to talk to him, to explain everything, and for him to tell me that it was all right.

I came back from the appointment shaken to the core because I'd learnt that I had to be living apart from Richie for four to five years before the divorce could go through, whether it was being contested – not very likely – or not.

The upshot of this was that I'd be officially married to Richie for the next four years while he was with Ellen Van Damme, who'd be sporting the enormous knuckleduster from Kneisel's that Susan had seen them look at. Our lives would still be linked, if only on paper, and the idea was appalling.

But apart from that it all seemed very easy. The divorce would be dealt with in the Circuit Court under the Civil Law Bill and if not contested it would only take about five minutes. I didn't even need to employ a solicitor. I could do it myself, a kind of DIY divorce.

'I've got some chocolate in my bag if you want cheering up,' Susan suggested.

I grabbed her bag, dug my hand in and fumbled about, waiting for the tell-tale rustle of foil, and when it didn't come I stretched open the top and peered in. There was a sheet of paper folded with the writing face-up. I knew what it was immediately. Susan had kept a photocopy of the letter she'd received from England, the one from the boy looking for his father, before sending the original back in its trendy bright-orange envelope. I said nothing and quickly found the chocolate bar. My heart ached for her.

Susan realized straight away from my solemn expression that I'd seen the letter. 'I've something to admit,' she said. 'I told my mother not to return the letter when she got it.'

'*What?*' I'd had no idea.

'Yes.' She took a deep breath. 'And I called him. I called the number on the letter.'

'You called him?' It came out as a squawk.

'Yes.' She nodded and smiled. 'We spoke.'

'My God!' I was amazed. Fortunately, I thought, Susan had a voice that was neither deeply masculine nor overtly feminine. It was just kind of husky.

She chuckled at the dumbfounded expression on my face. 'We're going to meet up, Rosie,' she told me excitedly. 'Quite soon. This coming Saturday, in fact. I'm going to arrange for him to pick up his ticket at Heathrow – he lives in London – and we'll spend the day together in Dublin.' Her tone became serious. 'But I'm going to have to go as Terrence.'

I couldn't picture Susan any way other than the way she was. 'How?' This was going to be so complicated.

'I know how,' she assured me. She leant forward and placed both her hands on my knees. 'Rosie, I have a favour to ask.'

I knew what was coming. I could sense it. Since I'd found out about Susan's past I'd felt her draw closer to me and I realized that I'd have extra responsibility in our friendship because of this.

'Will you come with me?' she pleaded. 'We're both off on Saturday. C'mon, please? I'd really like the company for the drive to the airport and I'd be a lot less nervous about meeting him if I knew you were going to be there. You don't have to stay the whole time. Just at the beginning.'

I couldn't let her down. I wouldn't let her down. 'Of course I will,' I agreed, not quite sure what I'd agreed to. It would hardly be a conventional family reunion.

Then all hell broke loose and I had no more time to think about it. Carmen burst through the office door, startling both of us and acting like her life was under threat. 'Is Mam here?' she gasped, shooting rapid glances around the small room. Her dark eye make-up was smeared and her work shirt had come out from the waistband of her pleated skirt.

'No, Carmen, she doesn't usually hang out here,' I laughed, bemused but not overly concerned, and Susan joined in. 'Thankfully,' we both said at the same time.

'*Mierda*. She's not at home either. I've tried. And I

need her advice about something straight away. Do you have any idea where she is?'

'Carmen, you know Monday afternoons are for meditating with Myra Barry.' This wasn't entirely true. Myra meditated in her upstairs room while my mother sat utterly still beside her and planned recipes in her head. Myra had had my mother doing transcendental meditation with her for the past year, which my mother had only recently stopped calling transcontinental meditation.

She slapped her head. 'In all my confusion I'd forgotten.' And then she smiled lamely at her own forgetfulness before the smile disintegrated into a frown. 'Do you know what's happened to me?'

I shook my head.

'I'm going to be fired.' She sucked on her bottom lip. 'I'm definitely going to be fired.'

'What have you done now?' I sighed. Carmen had been fired from her last job in a Chinese restaurant for appalling timekeeping.

She leant against the wall for support. 'Ages ago I booked the banqueting room in the hotel for a company that wanted to do one of those corporate-event evenings, on Valentine's night. I'd given them all the information, answered all their questions, smiled down the phone when I was talking to them, just like they told me to on that course Christie sent me on, and I was delighted when they said they'd go ahead with the booking, only . . .' she buried her face in her hands.

'Only what?' I coaxed her.

'Only I completely forgot to ask them for a deposit, no one checked, and they cancelled this morning. And now Christie is furious and talking about taking it out of my wages, a bit every week. *Que susto* he'll be subtracting till the day I retire,' she moaned. 'That's if he doesn't decide to fire me first.'

Christie owned the hotel where she worked. And he was the one who'd paid for the coffee I'd had in Wino's as I pieced together the newspaper cuttings on Ellen Van Damme, so needless to say Christie was in my good books. 'Ah, Carmel . . .'

'Carmen,' she corrected me irritably, smoothing the dark hair with a tanned hand.

'Car*men*, I'm sure he wouldn't do that,' I soothed her. 'He seems spot on.'

'He might be spot on but he's still a businessman and as hard as nails when he wants.'

'If you think he's as hard as nails you should try the two we've got,' Susan added as she switched between phone calls.

'They're thugs,' Carmen stated flatly. 'At least Christie won't have me sent to the emergency unit.' She'd obviously heard about the taxi driver who ended up with his leg in plaster of Paris.

'No one knows for sure that was them.' I was still feeling loyal to them for their thoughtful gesture of having sent a funeral wreath to Richie. 'So what are you after Mam for?'

'Because she always has a solution for everything,' she declared with an optimism borne of desperation.

Suddenly I had a flash of inspiration. It came to me in a single second of thundering possibilities. Would I dare do it?

'I might be able to help you,' I told her.

Susan's meticulously shaped eyebrows arched.

Carmen's face dissolved into a grateful pool of relief. 'How?'

'I know this is very short notice . . . but I've been thinking about organizing a singles party. It's just what this town needs.' For the next few minutes I tried to persuade them that this was truly a great idea.

Carmen would've been more enthusiastic if I'd suggested burning the hotel down and claiming on the insurance. 'Yeah?' she asked in a tinny voice.

'I really think it could work,' I said. 'There are lots of single people out there. And we could even do it fancy dress for a bit of a laugh.'

She was still looking sceptical.

'I'll do everything I can to help,' Susan assured me, 'but I don't know if the town is ready for this.' She smiled apologetically for saying it. I knew she was only looking out for me, worried about what another failure so soon after the first one – i.e., my marriage – might do to me.

I was having none of it. I'd recently found out that

strength comes and goes in whimsical waves, and a big wave had just come my way. 'I was really sceptical at first too. But when I got there I had a really good time.' I told them about my night out at the Hotel de Paris in Winchester.

'My big problem will be getting people in the door. If I can just get them there the rest will take care of itself.' I was thinking aloud, suddenly brimming with confidence and wanting to make this work. 'I know I can do it.' It felt like it could be the antidote for everything bad that had happened to me lately. I'd show Richie that I was capable of getting on with life, something I was sure he doubted.

'I'm going to take ten people I know,' I decided, 'and get them each to bring ten people they know. No couples.' It was coming to me as I spoke. 'How many people can the banqueting hall seat?'

'One hundred and fifty.'

'And there's a dancefloor too, isn't there?'

'We usually push the tables back.' Carmen glanced questioningly at Susan, looking for reassurance that I hadn't lost my mind. Susan just smiled.

'That'll do. And I suppose you've got the dinner menus planned? For the others who had booked the hall?'

'Eh, yeah, I think so.' Carmen looked uncertain; she hadn't the best mind for small details such as deposits and menus.

'I need to see Christie. Find out whether he'll give

me the hall. After all, he's not going to find anyone else to take it at such short notice.' It was only when I said it that I realized what short notice it was. 'My God, I've only got seven days.'

'Christie will definitely see you,' Carmen said, sounding positive about something for the first time since the conversation had begun. 'He's always asking if you're OK, feels very sorry for you these days.'

'Gee, that's great,' I said laconically. 'He feels sorry for me.'

'Useful, though,' Susan interjected.

'I'll put you down to see him tomorrow morning,' Carmen said.

'That's if you still have a job,' I reminded her.

'Thanks to you, I might. Do you think you could tell him that it was all my idea?'

'Only if it goes wrong,' I promised her.

13

I had to finish work early because I was unable to concentrate on anything other than organizing a party for Valentine's night and the sense of satisfaction it would bring if I could just pull it off and show everyone what I was capable of on my own.

When our regular mystery caller – who, oddly enough, hadn't been in contact for a few weeks – phoned and wanted to check what colour knickers I had on, I was so distracted that I actually answered him. 'Blue.'

'And is that cotton or lace?' he then asked, unable to believe his luck.

'Cotton. Two per cent Lycra.'

'Is that so they fit well? All tight and snug around the bottom?' And with that came the sound of heavy breathing.

'Yeah, and these ones have a small flower at the front.' It wasn't until Susan nudged me hard that I realized what I was saying and hung up.

'Go home,' she ordered me, pushing me out the door.

*

I was sitting opposite Thomas at the kitchen table when the doorbell rang. We both knew it was Richie as he'd warned me earlier that he would be calling around. Thomas and I had already rehearsed the scene that was about to unfold.

'Show time,' I whispered, kind of excitedly. 'Break a leg.' I brushed the tell-tale breadcrumbs from his navy dressing gown, dusting the lapels with my hand. And as he walked down the hall I shrugged off my bathrobe to reveal the towel I'd supposedly 'hastily' wrapped around myself, then I shoved my head under the tap, splashed the water around a bit and quickly raced upstairs. I'd told Thomas to wait until I gave the word before opening the door.

By now Richie had rung on the bell a second time, and a third time, each sharp ring lasting longer than the previous one, as he contemplated the possibility that I had deliberately decided not to be at home when he called around, which I would've done had I not thought of something better to do in the meantime.

'Now,' I instructed Thomas in an urgent whisper. 'And don't forget to sound breathless. But don't do the hound on it,' I warned him.

He gave me the thumbs-up. 'Hello,' he said, sounding puffed, as he pulled open the door, tightening the belt on his dressing gown conspicuously, as if he'd just gotten dressed in a hurry. 'Can I help you?'

Richie was speechless.

It was priceless.

'Can I help you?' Thomas asked again.

Richie peered into the hall over his shoulder. 'I want to see Rosie.'

'Oh? Yeah, OK.' Thomas glanced upstairs with a concerned look, as instructed. 'Listen, now might not be the best time,' he gave a semi-embarrassed laugh, 'if you know what I mean,' and he shamelessly winked at Richie. 'Who should I say wants to see her?'

'It's Richie. *Her husband!*'

I gripped the painted rail of the banister tighter and twisted. The two-timing bastard was still calling himself my husband.

'Hello, I'm Thomas.' Thomas stretched out his hand. 'Sorry about that. Rosie hadn't mentioned that you'd be popping around.'

This was my cue and I bounded down the stairs in my skimpy towel. I wrapped my arms around Thomas's middle and peeked out from behind him, wet tendrils of hair sticking to my cheek. 'Richie? Oh my God.' I tried to sound embarrassed. 'Didn't you say you'd be coming around tomorrow evening?'

'No, Rosie, I said *this* evening.' He glanced past me, his eyes narrowing as he spotted his favourite mirror now sprayed silver. 'Can we have a word?' he asked.

'Sure, Richie, sure,' I replied in my sweetest voice when what I really felt like doing was breaking the mirror into tiny bits and sticking the shards into him, voodoo-doll style.

'I'll leave you two to it,' Thomas said pleasantly. 'Rosie, you know where I'll be if you need me.'

''Course I do. Won't be long.'

Richie was looking at Thomas with a murderous expression on his face as I walked him into the sitting room, tightening my towel around me. 'Well, what can I do for you, Richie?'

'Huh, Titch won't be happy when he hears about this,' he commented dryly, head-butting in the direction of the ceiling towards my bedroom, where he figured Thomas would be. I gave him a rueful smile and he muttered something about spreading myself thin under his breath.

'What exactly was it you wanted?' I asked him.

Out of the pocket of his Burberry wax jacket he pulled a copy of the *Waterford Chronicle*. 'You can explain this,' he said. Then he yanked the latest edition of *Waterford Lights* out of the other pocket. 'And this too. You've become quite the conniver, haven't you?' He was speaking in heated whispers because he didn't want any trouble from Thomas upstairs. His face darkened. 'Ellen is getting very upset with you.'

That was good.

'And I'm getting tired of all your little games. You and that tribe of yours,' he added. I could tell that he meant business because the tiny red dots that appeared at the base of his neck when he was worked up about something were now clearly visible.

I happily wondered what the others had been up to.

'You can tell your mother that there's no point spitting on the doorstep every time she passes in front of the shop. The next time she tries it I'll stick her nose in it,' he promised, trying his best to sound convincing.

Did she do that? *My God!* She hated spitting. When Carmen was little she went through a spitting phase and my mother actually put a plaster over her tiny mouth and spent the next three weeks wracked with guilt because when she pulled it off a minute sliver of translucent lip skin came with it. I was amazed that she would do that for me.

'And that dancing-receptionist sister of yours who thinks she's Mata Hari . . .' That'd be Carmen. 'You can tell her not to bother calling up the local radio using all those different voices to complain about the appalling service she's been getting in the shop. She was doing that awful Dublin accent she does. You know, the one that sounds Bavarian.'

Carmen was doing that for me? I was stunned and thrilled.

'Richie, I have no idea what's been going on.' For once it was true, but he'd never believe me. 'And as for that,' I pointed to his copy of *Waterford Lights*, 'Myra asked me to contribute something and I just wrote an honest account of what happened and how I felt.' There were, of course, several versions of any honest account.

His face took on its murderous expression again

when he heard me calling the article an 'honest account', and I got angry. 'I'm not surprised that you don't like my side being heard,' I told him, 'because it makes you look like a philandering bastard – exactly what you are!'

'Yeah,' he countered, 'and it makes you look like a cross between Mother Teresa and Betty Boo.' His mobile phone rang and he quickly checked the small screen before slamming the 'end call' button. 'And I suppose you don't know what that was about either?' He waved the phone at me. 'All these strange calls I've been getting?'

'No.'

'You have nothing to do with the ads that appeared in here?' he demanded, shoving the newspaper in my face.

I took a step back. 'No.'

'That's what I thought,' he snapped. 'Understandable, I suppose, seeing that I even paid for them myself.'

'Did you?' I asked innocently.

'You know fucking well I did.'

It was time he left. I wanted him gone before we started really fighting. The dull thud of footsteps crossing the landing came at exactly the right time and Richie looked up warily. 'I'm going to say this once and only once,' he hurried. 'No more games, Rosie.'

Thomas walked in just as he'd finished saying this.

'Just on my way out,' Richie told him. 'No need to see me to the door. I know where it is.'

Thomas was very keen to accompany me to my mother's house later that evening, quizzing me several times on the way over about whether Eilish might be there and then feigning total nonchalance, peering innocently out at me from behind his glasses, when I reminded him that he'd already asked me that same question three times, and that Jimmy Bible would do unmentionable things to him if he thought he might have anything other than a professional interest in Eilish, which, unsurprisingly, he swore he hadn't.

Anyway, I obliged him by answering the question, telling him that there was a good chance she would be there. It was as if the lot of us were fettered to the house with elastic bands. We were always in and out, back and forth.

I was going to my mother's to try to 'sort her out' as Rory had asked me to do when he'd called that morning. I'd spoken to her late that afternoon and she'd let it slip that she hadn't been able to get any recipe-planning done during her meditation session with Myra because she'd had things on her mind, what with all this Hannah business, and then she'd backtracked furiously when I asked her what 'Hannah business' exactly.

There was clearly something amiss. Hannah hadn't been in good humour for weeks and now my mother was in on it too.

I used my key to let myself in. Thomas walked in behind me, scanning the framed photos of my sisters and me that covered every spare inch of wall in the hallway, trying to spot the ones with Eilish but pretending he wasn't.

'Whatever you think I'm doing, I'm not,' he told me.

I shook my head at him. He was a lost cause.

My mother was leaning against the kitchen counter drinking a mug of tea with surprising relish. She looked at us over the rim of the mug and indicated with a finger that she'd be right with us. The same finger pointed to the chairs at the kitchen table and we sat down.

'Are you sure that's only tea?' Thomas whispered doubtfully as he watched her tip the mug up towards her nose to drain the last few drops.

'That's more like it,' she gasped with satisfaction and rinsed the cup out at the kitchen sink while I explained to Thomas – who had more than likely noticed but was waiting for the right moment to comment to most effect – that the grunting noises followed by dubious squeaks coming from upstairs were Rory doing his weight-lifting. In one of the back bedrooms they had a black-and-chrome contraption that he paid daily homage to.

'I've met you before,' my mother said to Thomas as she joined us at the kitchen table.

'Yes, once or twice at the hospital,' he said, curiously pleased that she'd remembered him.

'I've been thinking about this Valentine's-party idea of yours,' she said then, turning towards me. 'It's a good one,' she declared, 'as long as it has nothing to do with that wife-swapping thing I heard is going on in the new housing estate.'

I rolled my eyes at Thomas, who looked at my mother in the affectionate way that you do when it's someone else's mother making that kind of comment.

'And Myra thinks it's great, too,' she added, giving it the Myra Barry seal of approval. 'She's on her way here to see you, by the way. Rory said you'd probably be popping by and she's got something to tell you,' she grinned and then clamped her top lip over her bottom one, continuing to grin at me with her eyes but saying no more.

'I've already got ten single people lined up for Rosie's bash,' Thomas piped up, sounding very pleased with himself. 'Eilish told me about it this afternoon in the corridors of pain, after you called her,' he explained.

'That's good,' I told him cautiously, 'but I'm only seeing Christie tomorrow morning to see if he'll give me the hall.' I'd called Eilish to see what she thought of the idea. By now the jungle network would be so hard at work that Christie would know what I had in mind before I even set foot in the door. Any element of surprise would be long gone by tomorrow morning.

Thomas smiled and said, 'I thought I'd get ahead of the game.' Then he looked to my mother for her approval.

'And Carmen has some people lined up, too,' she added, smiling at him. 'She was here earlier and she'd already mentioned it to a few of her friends. She said she'd sent them a text message, something like that anyhow.' Carmen knew enough single girls to keep Cilla Black supplied for the rest of the year. It seemed to be a trend among her group of friends to be single and proud.

'We saw Richie earlier,' I announced.

'That good-for-nothing so and so,' my mother blazed. 'What I'd give to do the umbrella trick on that one.'

I explained for Thomas's benefit: 'The umbrella trick is a little speciality of Mam's. You take a fairly big umbrella, shove it up the person's arse, open it and pull it down again.'

Thomas winced.

I looked at her affectionately. 'I think it might be a bit more difficult to get the umbrella down again than she thinks.'

'I'd use Rory's big golfing umbrella,' she added.

And this time Thomas actually squirmed on his chair.

'Is it true that you've been spitting at Richie?'

She looked disconcerted that she'd been found out. 'He shouldn't be getting away with what he's doing,' she justified herself. 'You know I don't care much for spitting . . . but something just came over me. Ah, I don't know, Rosie, I'm just disgusted by his behaviour and it seemed fitting that I should do something disgusting back.'

'So you spit every time you pass the shop?'

I glanced sideways at Thomas, concerned that he might be perturbed by the direction the conversation was taking, but I needn't have worried – he was engrossed.

'Good Lord, no,' she jumped up, apparently shocked to the core that I might think she spat every time, 'only when the hound is behind the counter. I'd never spit if the Berlin Wall was in there on her own. I've nothing against the girl.'

'And Carmen has been on WLR complaining about the shop?'

'Yes, she's called that consumer programme three times, and this last time they told her that they've been getting a lot of complaints recently about Richie's aggressive sales tactics and terrible after-sales service.'

'Were they all from Carmen?'

'No, Maria – that's her best friend – ' she told Thomas, 'called up twice.'

'At this rate they'll shut him down in no time.'

'If there's a God in Heaven,' she prayed, imploring the skies above with outstretched hands.

'Has Hannah been up to anything that I should know about?'

'Oh, no,' she assured me before she had time to think about what she was saying, 'Hannah's got too much on her mind.'

'What's on her mind?' I asked.

'Nothing, nothing,' she quickly mumbled. 'I just meant with the kids and everything. Have you heard that they're getting an au pair? It might give Dennis and her a bit more time together.'

'No, I hadn't heard. Is there anything else I should know about?'

She shook her head and the doorbell rang. 'That'll be Myra now.'

'I'll go.' I walked out into the hallway, closing the door behind me, and halfway to the door I passed Rory. He was sweating with a towel rolled into a fat oblong wrapped around his neck. 'Well, did you sort your mother out?' he asked me anxiously.

'I didn't find anything really wrong,' I told him.

'There's something up.' He wiped his dripping forehead with one end of the towel. His muscles were hard ridges beneath the surface of his skin, revealed by his cut-away tank top. 'It's not my imagination. She just sits here staring into space when she thinks no one's around.'

'I'll have a chat with her,' I promised him.

'Have I got news for you.' Myra Barry breezed past me and into the kitchen. 'I showed your article to a friend of mine in Dublin.' She pulled a copy of *Waterford Lights* from the vast patchwork bag that

239

accompanied her everywhere. 'The one who's editor of a women's mag . . .'

If she so much as mentions the words 'self-help group' now I'll make a dive for her, I thought.

' . . . and she thought it was excellent.' Myra beamed at everyone in the room. 'Didn't I tell you it was?'

She waited for me to nod, which I did.

'She thought it was so good that she would like to talk to you about making it into a longer article for an edition of the magazine,' she said triumphantly. 'A kind of reader's profile.'

Me? Have something published? *Me?*

'Ooh,' my mother cooed. 'English was always your best subject at school, wasn't it? Remember that time when Mrs Moody told you your essay was like a Mills and Boon?'

'Yeah, but she didn't mean it as a compliment.'

'That was your best work,' she went on as if she hadn't heard me. 'To this day I remember how Daniel *howled* when he had to let go of the rope that Penelope was hanging on to and he thought she had fallen to her death from the cliff-top only to discover that she'd landed on a herd of sheep and both she and her unborn child that he didn't yet know about were saved.'

'Yeah, but how many of the sheep perished?' Thomas asked with such wonderful mock sincerity that my mother mistook it for genuine concern.

'That's the wonderful thing, Thomas. None of them

240

died. Because Rosie made sure when she was writing it that they were a robust breed of mountain sheep.'

He smiled at me, eyes twinkling mischievously, and said, 'You are both a thoughtful person and a gifted writer. Fancy sparing the sheep like that!'

My mother beamed at him while I battled with the upshot of what Myra meant. Could she really be saying that some big magazine wanted to publish something I'd written? That's what it sounded like. *God!*

'I have Angela's number and you're to call her as soon as possible.'

'Are you sure about this, Myra?' It was so unbelievable, so unexpected.

My mother lit the candle beneath the Virgin Mary. 'God never closes a door but he opens a window,' which is exactly what she proceeded to do in an attempt to rid the kitchen of some of the fumes from Myra's cigarette.

'You haven't forced her into talking to me?' I quizzed Myra again.

'What are you talking about?' She shook her head at me. 'They're always looking for interesting reads up there. I did her a favour. Look, just give her a call,' she dangled a piece of paper at me. 'It might not work out but wouldn't it be great if it did?'

'Wouldn't what be great?' Hannah had appeared from next door.

'Your sister's going to get the article she wrote for

Myra published in some big magazine,' my mother told her proudly.

'Everyone's talking about it,' Hannah told me.

'Are they?' I was amazed.

'They're saying that it must've taken some guts to do it.'

'And that Richie sounds like a right bastard,' Myra injected.

'Tell us something that we don't know,' my mother said.

'And that they never knew you could write.'

'How did they think I signed my cheques?'

'Not that way. You know, proper writing.'

Proper writing, as she called it, was very hard. I'd nearly given up several times except that I knew Myra wouldn't let me off the hook. 'Which magazine?' I asked Myra.

'*ME!*' she told me and everyone gasped in admiration. *ME!* was very popular.

'And they want *me*?' I still couldn't quite believe it.

'You owe me one,' she joked, and then got a shade more serious. 'Remember when Johnny Power gave me the lift from your house last week?'

'Yes.'

'You know, he didn't utter a word all the way home,' she told me.

That's because he's of the old brigade, Myra, and your forthright manner probably terrifies him, I thought.

'He was probably a bit in awe of me and a bit shy,' she'd already decided.

'Probably.'

'Which was a bit of a turn-on,' she then declared. She lit another cigarette and blew smoke at me reflectively. 'I'd never thought of him that way before.'

My mother was shocked. 'He's way too old for you.' There wasn't such a big age difference between Myra and Johnny but Myra usually made a point of fancying younger men.

'Maybe I'm ready for something different,' she said. 'There's a lot to be said for the older man.' She gave Thomas a seductive smile. 'I'm sure you'd be the exception to that,' she purred. 'Maybe some day soon, Rosie, I might ask you to put in a good word for me.'

I changed the subject immediately to safeguard Johnny from Myra. 'Hannah, I hear you're getting an au pair.'

Hannah was lost in thought and jumped when she heard her name mentioned, her face turning bright red. 'What? What?'

'I hear you're getting an au pair,' I repeated, wondering why she'd reacted so strangely. 'I hope she's not going to be Swedish,' I joked. 'That would be a terrible move. Everyone knows what they're like.'

'I'm not that stupid,' she snapped and then suddenly burst into tears, mouthing a wet apology at me.

My mother looked disturbed and motioned for

me to say no more. I remembered what Carmen had told me earlier, that she thought there was something really troubling Hannah, something more than usual, more than her troubles with Dennis. It looked as if she was right.

Thomas tactfully suggested that we should leave as he'd promised some friends he'd meet them in the pub, and stood up from the table. I agreed but reluctantly. I wanted to stay and talk to Hannah but I felt that my mother would do a better job.

We were just on our way out the door when Eilish and Jimmy arrived. Eilish was several steps in front of Jimmy, clutching her car keys tightly, her knuckles white. She was wearing low-slung grey sweatpants and a funky gym top.

Suddenly Thomas seemed reluctant to leave and he followed her back into the kitchen while she tersely demanded what he thought he was doing there. He sat back down on the kitchen chair he'd only just vacated and gripped the sides of the seat with his hands, worried that someone might try to haul him out of it. 'Rosie made me come,' he told her, 'to say hello to your mother.'

'I'll bet,' she said scathingly.

Myra and myself exchanged worried glances. 'Eilish, this aggressiveness is not like you at all,' Myra commented.

'I've had it up to here with him,' she said, jabbing a key in Jimmy's direction. 'I want us to go away to the Maldives for ten days but he wants to go to the Cheltenham races.'

'I'll go to the Maldives with you,' Thomas blurted and the room went a deadly quiet. 'That is, if you're looking for a friend to go on holidays with,' he quickly added, but much too late, as the pulse on the side of Jimmy's head had begun to throb.

Eilish stared at him with hang-jaw disbelief. She seemed to be trying to say something but no words would come out.

Hannah and my mother were not involved in this conversation because they were huddled together out in the utility room. Through the pane of glass that separated the two rooms I could make out a lot of head-shaking and shoulder-lifting.

Hannah was holding something in her hand and waving it about. It was a bright-orange envelope, such a distinctive shade. It looked familiar, I thought, and suddenly realized where I'd seen it before. It was exactly the same kind of envelope as Susan had received from that boy in England. How could that be? It made no sense whatsoever. Suddenly they caught me looking and I quickly turned away.

Eilish was still staring at Thomas. I laughed loudly in an attempt to lighten the mood in the kitchen but it was a nervous burst of humour. 'You're hilarious, Thomas. That's a good one, you mad joker.' I'd kill him when we left for undoubtedly getting Eilish into deep trouble with Jimmy.

At that point Thomas decided to get even braver, or stupider, depending on which way you looked at it. 'I wasn't joking.'

Myra eyed him admiringly.

Jimmy stepped up to where Thomas was sitting. 'Mrs Flynn told you about her umbrella trick?'

'Only just,' I answered for Thomas.

'Well,' Jimmy gave him a piercing stare. 'I do pretty much the same thing with this.' He tapped his tightly rolled-up *Racing Post* against Thomas's shoulder. What did Eilish see in this skinny weasel that the rest of us missed? Why did she stay with him? Couldn't she at least find someone with a driving licence?

All this time Thomas was looking at Eilish with an unreadable expression on his face. Right now knowing him for the sum total of twenty-four hours was a hindrance. I couldn't tell what was going through his head.

14

Christie sat behind his desk, smiling pleasantly at me while I tried to sell him my idea for a special singles evening on Valentine's night at the Cosy Inn.

'It'll be brilliant, Christie, honestly.' It was about the fifth time I'd uttered those same words. 'You'd be way ahead of the game around town. Singles parties are going to be all the rage soon. There's no such thing as a committed relationship any more.'

I hadn't slept at all the night before wondering how I would get him to agree to letting me have the banqueting hall next Monday night, especially when I'd be giving him no money up front, couldn't afford to, and as far as he was concerned that's what it was all about. Money. He was, above all, a businessman.

But it was simple, I'd told him. He'd get his cash when the people arrived and paid me for their tickets on the way in. I was being remarkably matter-of-fact because I was trying to hide the truth from him: I didn't know what I was doing and I didn't know what I was talking about. I was used to answering phones all day. And being a wife. That was what I did. And now I had to do something else.

'I hear you want to organize yourself a little do for

the town's rejects.' That was how he'd greeted me first off when I walked in for the ten a.m. appointment that Carmen had set up, wearing a serious-looking navy shift dress and matching coat.

He was leaning back against the wall on the hind legs of his chair. But he keeled forward when he realized what he'd said, and swiftly added, 'Only joking, Rosie.'

'Look, Christie,' I decided to get straight to the point, 'if you don't let me have the venue, you won't get anyone else at this late notice, will you? And what's the worst that could happen?'

'Do you really want me to answer that one?'

'Yes. I mean no.' I didn't need him to. I could imagine. He'd end up way out of pocket and his reputation would take a sharp nosedive. The whole town would be laughing at him and it'd be cold comfort to know that they'd be laughing even harder at me.

'So run it by me again, how you're going to get 150 single people into my banqueting hall with six days to go?' He held a slim gold pen poised above a sheet of blank paper.

'For starters I'm going to get ten single people I know to bring ten single people they know.' I really hoped that I didn't sound too much of a simpleton but I did think that this kind of networking could work quickly.

'Are there that many single people in this town?'

When I'd done the calculation last night I'd been surprised by the growing number of single people I knew. 'Sure there are.' And that wasn't even counting the ones in relationships who acted like they were single. 'And then I'm going to get Waterford Local Radio to run ads for it as well. We mightn't make 150 on the dot but we'll get damn close.' So much confidence, I mused, and most of it a show. 'Rory has agreed to set up the music for me at this late notice and Carmen told me you've already got a menu planned for those people who cancelled. I'm taking bookings in advance and I've already got forty provisional ones,' I lied. I wanted him to come to the conclusion that with all this in place it made more sense to go ahead rather than call a halt. I held my breath.

'You're jumping the gun a bit, Rosie.' The smile turned downwards into a mild frown. He obviously hadn't come to the conclusion I thought he would but at least he was listening to me.

'That's why they're *provisional* bookings, Christie.' I wasn't going to give up.

For the next forty-five minutes we volleyed the pros and cons of such an event across the desk. We haggled over money and discussed as yet hypothetical issues regarding the final arrangements.

'Round tables,' I told him, 'with floor-length white tablecloths, white church candles, no blow-up balloons, a proper three-course meal, not just dollops of prawn cocktail with slabs of lasagne, and reasonable wine for at least the first hour – ' after that no one would notice – 'and dancing.'

I was being very particular and as a result we argued about everything there was to argue about right down to the wattage of the light bulbs. But the more obstacles he put up the more I refused to back down. It was as if my understanding of the word 'no' had disappeared. My determination increased with every passing minute.

It would be such an achievement for me to pull this off on my own. Things could go wrong, I knew, and it would mean a very public failure because all eyes would be on me, waiting to see what I made of this opportunity. But I decided to cross one hurdle at a time, and my first hurdle was convincing Christie.

I redoubled my efforts, mirroring his body language precisely because I remembered Richie telling me that this was a good way to get someone thinking you were on the same wavelength. It felt very unnatural but it must have worked because I suddenly sensed the conversation begin to turn my way as Christie started to jot things down on his notepad.

He put a large question mark beside 'fancy dress' and I leant over and replaced it with an exclamation mark. 'It has to be fancy dress, Christie.' It would ensure that people knew they weren't to take the evening too seriously.

'Well, I don't want a bunch of hairy gorillas turning up in the lobby,' was all he said.

'More like sexy French chambermaids,' I assured him solemnly. 'Or Playboy Bunnies.'

Christie tried not to smile and then out of the blue he named a figure per head. 'I'll barely be covering my costs on this one, Rosie.'

I'd won. To me it meant a whole new beginning. 'I really appreciate it.'

'Just covering costs,' he reminded me again. He didn't mention the money he stood to make on the bar that night – single people were seasoned drinkers and he'd rake in a small fortune on booze, if I'd got the headcount right.

'I'm going out on a limb for you on this one,' he told me. 'It's a bit of a risk.'

'I know.'

'A long time ago,' he continued, 'your father bailed me out of a spot of trouble and I haven't forgotten it.'

'Did he?' I didn't know what my father had done for Christie but it was proof if ever I needed it that he watched over me and could still fix things. I felt a tingle of pleasure. I loved hearing people mention my father. It made me feel somehow closer to him. I missed him every day, as did Hannah, Eilish and Carmen.

'This is for both of you,' Christie then said. 'After that we'll call it quits.'

'OK.'

I left his first-floor office in a daze, took the lift downstairs and walked out through the lobby, only narrowly avoiding an enormous flower arrangement perched on a central marble pedestal. I wasn't thinking about where I was going. In my mind I was already planning ahead.

'Well,' Carmen cornered me on my way out the front door, 'did he go for it?'

'Yes.' I punched the air. The sense of elation I felt really did surprise me. I'd never have thought that this could be me. Maybe Richie had done me a favour when he walked out. He had made me think about achieving something other than a life with him because I couldn't have that.

'My job is spared,' she said dramatically. 'And did you tell him that it was my idea?' she asked hopefully.

I laughed at her expectant expression. 'No, Carmen, I did not.'

'Go back in and tell him that it was all my idea,' she tried to persuade me.

'Some hope.' I ducked under her arm and walked out into the street. I hadn't got far when I noticed someone waving at me from the other side of the street. Johnny Power.

'Hi,' I shouted over and watched as he carefully crossed the road.

'Rosie,' he greeted me cheerfully. 'A soft day, thank God.'

It was true that a light drizzle peppered the air. The fine droplets were undoing the sleek hairdo I'd toiled over for my meeting with Christie but I didn't care. 'I suppose so, Johnny.'

'I need your advice about something.'

'Yes?'

'While you were away over the weekend I took a little trip out to see Lilian.'

By Lilian I knew he meant Mrs Burke. 'And how did it go?' I asked him eagerly. 'Was she surprised to see you?'

'Not really. Then again I've been popping out to see her about once a week anyway for the last few years for a chat and to check that she's OK. But now that I've decided to make my intentions known to her I'm wondering if she can sense a change in me?'

'I don't know, Johnny.' Reading men's minds wouldn't be a strong point of mine. 'Are you behaving any different?'

'I brought her a bunch of flowers this time.'

'And?'

'She was thrilled. Got all flustered.'

'That sounds like a good start,' I told him, thinking how full of hope he sounded.

'And I went out to see her last night, too. That's twice this week. And I've never done twice in the one week before. Do you think she's cottoned on?'

'Probably not yet.'

'But she went off into the bedroom and when she came out she was wearing lipstick.'

I smiled again, at the fact that she wasn't beyond

this kind of coquettish behaviour and that Johnny wasn't beyond noticing her subtle preening. Or maybe it hadn't been so subtle.

'Do you ever talk about the past?' I asked him. 'About you disappearing off like that and her getting married?'

'Never. Actually, there was the one time,' he amended. 'It was a while ago now and I said, "Lil, girl, I apologize for all the bother I caused you," but I shut up then because I could see the tears in her eyes and I didn't want to embarrass her. She's too much of a lady for that.'

'Are you still going ahead with your plans for February the fourteenth?'

'That's what I crossed over to ask you. After much persuasion she's agreed to let me take her out for dinner and I've managed to get us a table somewhere nice. Now, do you think I should pop the question before or after the meal?'

Richie had proposed to me in a Chinese restaurant called the Oriental Garden. He'd somehow managed to have the diamond ring inserted into a fortune cookie and when he handed it to me to crack open at the end of the meal, to discover what the future held for me, the beautiful ring tumbled into my hand. It was everything I'd ever wanted.

'Not sure. But I brought you a book back from the UK. It's in a plastic bag, hanging on the back of the door in the office. It might be useful.'

He raised his eyebrows curiously. 'I'm just on my way over there now. I'll pick it up,' he promised.

Just then Myra Barry drove past in her instantly recognizable turquoise VW Beetle. She rolled down the window and blew a flamboyant kiss in our direction. 'I've got my eye on you, Johnny boy,' she called out.

'You'd better hurry up and get Mrs Burke to make an honest man of you,' I warned him. 'Before *she* gets to you,' I added, nodding towards Myra.

He watched the turquoise car as it careered around the corner. 'That woman should come with a health warning.'

I went straight home after that and phoned ten people I knew to be single. They were friends of mine rather than friends of Richie's and included a few girls I had known since school and some of the younger drivers from the taxi office. I told them about the Valentine's night party and they all agreed to help by rounding up other people. They promised to keep me updated with regular text messages so I could keep track of the numbers.

I sank back against the sofa and sighed contentedly and then I phoned one of Rory's nieces, who worked at Waterford Local Radio, and whose path I often crossed on the way to work as our shifts seemed to coincide, and she promised that she'd make sure the party got a good mention on air during the week.

I thought about calling Christie to tell him that

things were moving along nicely but decided to wait until the numbers began to grow. I called Hannah instead. It was coming up to lunchtime and she was getting food ready and unravelling the budgie from Katie's hair at the same time, so she had the telephone jammed between her chin and shoulder.

'Hi,' I said.

'Oh, hi,' she managed.

'A favour to ask.'

'Ask then.' She dropped the phone, cursed Katie, cursed the budgie, cursed the government for not paying mothers who stayed at home and picked it up again.

'Would Dennis let me use his office equipment to print up some tickets and posters for this singles party I'm organizing?'

'You don't know how to use any of it, Rosie,' she pointed out. 'You only use a phone.'

If I didn't absolutely need her help I would've hung up straight away because there was no need for such a put-down even if she was upset about something. But I bit my tongue. I needed her.

'Well, you'd have to show me. But I'd do all the work,' I promised meekly.

'I suppose so,' she agreed, and I could tell she was already feeling sorry for being so sharp a second earlier. 'When?'

'As soon as possible.'

'What shift are you working?'

'Seven till two.'

'Come over when you're finished.'

Had she lost it altogether? 'What? At two a.m.'

'Yes. Gerry is teething.'

Well I'm not, I wanted to tell her.

'So he's up all night anyway. I won't get time during the day. Dennis is behind with his admin and I'm helping him out, as well as doing everything else here.'

'When is the au pair coming?'

'Not soon enough for me. She'll be here in ten days' time. And before you ask again, she's not Swedish. She's Hungarian.'

'OK. That's good.'

'By the way, has Mam mentioned anything to you about me?'

'About you what?' I'd been waiting for a good time to bring up the orange envelope. It was probably nothing. A coincidence. But it was just such a distinctive colour that I couldn't help but think it strange.

'Anything at all.'

'No. Why would she?' It was an invitation for her to tell me something, if there was something to tell.

She didn't take me up on it. 'No reason. You're just the one she talks to if she wants to talk about anything.'

'I'm not.'

'Yes you are, Rosie.'

'I'm not. She talks to Eilish.'

'She does not. She's way too wary that it'd get back

257

'to Jimmy Bible and everyone at the bookie's would know two minutes later.'

'Oh?'

'Yeah.'

I decided to ask her straight out. 'What was in that orange envelope I saw you with yesterday?'

There was a silence. A long silence. 'Nothing.'

I didn't believe her. I'd ask her again later. Face to face, so I'd be able to read her expression. 'OK. See you at around two.'

'Eh, yeah . . . see you . . . bye.'

There was still one phone call to make. I'd deliberately left it until last. It was Myra Barry's friend in Dublin. I'd put it off because I wanted to savour the feeling of excitement at possibly having an article I'd written published by a big magazine. I was convinced that she'd tell me that Myra had it all wrong, and I wanted to delay that moment.

Suddenly I remembered a box of coloured A4 thin cardboard left over from a promotion for the shop that Richie had done. If I could find it I could bring it over to Hannah's later on, I decided, and we could use it for the tickets. I jumped up off the floor and ran out to the crammed storage space beneath the stairs.

I wrestled my way towards the back, through the boxes of junk, to where Richie kept everything to do with work. But the wooden shelves were bare. All his old paperwork and clutter were gone. When he'd cleared out his stuff, he'd even taken the cardboard. I felt a stab of intense pain quickly followed by a wave of anger.

In the stark light thrown off by the bare light bulb I saw a shroud of black plastic hanging at the end of the narrow tunnel. I knew what it was the second I laid eyes on it, and instantly wished I hadn't seen it. It was my wedding dress and Richie's suit. He'd aptly left his wedding suit behind him when he'd gathered up the rest of his stuff.

I took a few steps forward, grabbed hold of the plastic and pulled it behind me as I kicked boxes to one side on my way out. I didn't want to undo the zipper and look inside. It wouldn't do me any good. But I knew I'd do it anyhow.

It had been a winter wedding, late one December evening. Together with Eilish and Carmen, I'd filled the cosy church on the cliff-top in Crook, a tiny coastal village about ten miles from Waterford, with ivory candles and scattered rose petals all the way up the aisle. I'd opted for a satin dress of the deepest red, flatteringly cut on the bias with long tapered sleeves. Richie had his suit especially made for him and lined in the same satin as my dress. The lying bastard had said it was a symbol of our unity.

I unzipped the cover and looked inside. The contents were still in perfect condition. Was it my imagination or could I still smell the Dunhill aftershave that Richie had worn on the day? It had been his favourite up to about a year ago when he'd suddenly opted for something a lot more imposing on the nostrils. I knew what had sparked the change now and I'd hate that new smell for ever.

With a heavy heart I ran my fingers over the dress. What exactly had I done wrong? Would I ever know? That was one of the hardest things about all this. I closed the cover again and decided to leave it all on the doorstep of the Oxfam shop on my way to work. They'd meant too much at one time to take scissors to them now.

I decided it was time to call Myra's editor friend. 'Hello, may I speak to Angela Walsh, please?' I asked, prepared to be disappointed.

'Speaking.'

'Oh, hello. My name is Rosie Flynn. I'm a friend of Myra Barry's.'

'Yes, yes, of course. The girl who wrote the piece for Myra's mag.'

'Yes.' At least she knew who I was. I steeled myself for rejection nonetheless.

'I'm glad you've called. Did Myra tell you that I'm interested in using you?'

'Yes, but I wasn't sure if . . .'

' . . . Myra was just being Myra?' she continued for me.

'Yes,' I laughed.

'Myra was definitely being Myra when she sent the article to me with a note saying that I should think about using it, but I make my own decisions and I've decided that she's right.'

I could scarcely believe what I was hearing. I was nothing, a nobody, and I was going to get something I'd written, about what had happened to me, published for the whole country to read. I couldn't understand why she thought it deserved the attention.

'There's work to be done on it,' she advised me, 'but I'd like to include it in April's edition of the magazine. We sometimes do a piece that reads like a reader's profile. What do you think?'

'I think that's great,' I stammered with disbelief. 'Really great.'

'Good. Do you think you could make it up to Dublin to see me?'

'Yes . . . definitely . . . great.'

'Let's look at a date. How about February the eighteenth? Come to the office for midday and we'll go somewhere for lunch.'

'That sounds great.' I heard myself using the word 'great' too much and flinched. Some wordsmith I was, but she didn't seem to notice.

She gave me the address of the office and I carefully wrote it down and read it back to her. 'How are you coping with everything now?' she then asked.

I didn't hesitate. 'Great.' Could that be true?

On the way to the taxi office I dropped all that was left of my marriage on to the sheltered doorstep of the Oxfam shop and briskly carried on through the town centre to work. I was looking forward to telling Susan that the meeting with Christie had gone really well and the party was going ahead.

When I did so she immediately responded by saying that she was going to ask Hank to come along and I had to quickly turn my head so that she wouldn't see the ridiculous blush that had appeared on my cheeks. It was a knee-jerk reaction to hearing his name said.

I'd heard of the strange things that people did when they got out of long relationships. But having the hots for a good-looking transsexual was probably the strangest by far and I still didn't know what to do about it.

Several hours later I finished my shift and one of the drivers dropped me off at Hannah's. It was about quarter past two. She opened the door and I could hear the coffee percolator bubbling in the kitchen.

Hannah had been rolling Gerry up and down the hall in his Mamas and Papas checked pram trying to lull him to sleep. His cheeks were traffic-light red, his nose was running and he was trying to put his fist into his mouth and gnaw on his knuckles. They both looked like they hadn't slept in about a year. I felt so sorry for them.

I'd decided not to bother her by bringing up the orange envelope. I'd convinced myself that it was bound to be of absolutely no consequence.

Hannah was feeling remorseful that she'd insisted

I come over so late at night. She tried explaining that when you didn't sleep for nights on end you kind of forgot that other people did.

She rolled Gerry, who was glaring beseechingly at her, into the ground-floor office and I grabbed the glass jug from the percolator and two oversized mugs and followed behind her.

We worked solidly for two hours and I didn't dare to once complain that I was exhausted because compared to Hannah I was the life and soul of the party. The bags under her eyes encompassed her whole face and her skin had a greyish pallor.

She used some graphics program to create the template for the party tickets. We briefly considered using a heart design all around the edge but immediately changed our minds and went for the more appropriate rows of clinking glasses. She printed four tickets per page and I used Dennis's industrial-sized paper-cutter to slice them up. Each time the blade went down I pictured another bit of Richie's anatomy disappearing.

Then we printed out three dozen posters with laughing faces and more clinking glasses to stick up around the town. We called the party Solomania and congratulated ourselves for coming up with such an inspired choice of name at four in the morning.

During all this time Gerry wriggled and fretted and whined, and Hannah expertly soothed and patted and rocked.

I gathered up the results of the night's work and phoned for a taxi to take me home. The phone was answered by Fat Sylvia, who had taken over from me on the two a.m. to ten a.m. shift.

'Triple-A Taxis. If you're drunk hang up now.'

'Hi, Sylvia.' Obviously we didn't dare call her Fat Sylvia to her face. 'It's me, Rosie. Can you send me a car?'

'Rosie, do you know what time it is? Has Titch kicked you out?' She hooted with laughter, the rolls of blubber beneath her chin slapping off each other down the line. 'Got himself a new lack?'

'Titch?'

'Titch Murphy, you old dark horse!' I heard the flick of a lighter. 'He's a fine catch. One of my girls was interested in him.'

'She can have him. I certainly don't want him.'

'That's not what I heard,' she mocked.

'Sylvia, just send a car to Hannah's.' There was no need to give her the address because she knew it just as I knew where all her family lived.

'Yep. Are you on your own?'

'I will be in the company of a male,' I replied suggestively.

Hannah was slumped in the office chair, her eyes shut and her head resting heavily on one arm while she continued to push Gerry with the other. From the basket beneath the pram I managed to grab the tube of Bonjela, a handful of nappies and a bottle of milk. 'Hannah,' I shook her shoulder gently, 'wake up.'

'I'm not asleep,' she moaned. 'I'm just dying.'

'I'm taking Gerry with me.' I had to do something to help her. 'You can call around and collect him in the morning when you've had some sleep. I'm only on in the evening.'

When she heard this her eyes leapt open with gratitude. 'Oh, Rosie, thank you.'

Miraculously, Gerry fell asleep on the way home in the taxi. I carefully lifted him upstairs to my bed and sandwiched him between two walls of pillows, dropping on to the mattress beside him without getting undressed in case I woke him up again.

I slept soundly until nine o'clock. I didn't even hear Thomas get up for work. I awoke to find a small finger worming its way up my nose. I experienced a split second of indescribable panic before I remembered whose it was.

Hannah arrived about an hour later to collect Gerry, looking ten years younger than she had the night before. I handed him over along with a few spare nappies and waved them off before making my way back into the kitchen feeling like the Good Samaritan.

The Rice Krispies that Gerry had spilt all over the floor – the entire contents of a family-size box – crunched and crackled as I walked over them to get to my mobile phone on the counter at the other side. I wanted to check my messages.

Beep after beep erupted from the black Motorola as the screen flashed lists of names at me. Since yesterday my friends had been hard at work publicizing the St Valentine's night party. In the rush to find a pen to jot them all down I slammed my head against the cupboard door and felt no pain. All in all there were twenty-five more names to add to my list for Solomania.

I carefully made a note of them, recognizing most, and the excitement must've sapped my energy because I was suddenly feeling exhausted again even though I'd just got up.

The ringing of the telephone woke me a while later. I'd fallen asleep with my head resting on my arms on the kitchen table, hedged between the empty Rice Krispies box and the ceramic milk jug. I'd never fallen asleep on the kitchen table before.

I didn't make it into the sitting room in time to answer the phone but there was a message from Muriel reminding me about our first flamenco class tonight. I'd forgotten all about it and I moaned loudly as I dialled Susan's number to ask her if she could cover for me at work while I slipped out and made a fool of myself for an hour.

15

Dance class was due to start at seven o'clock at Antonio's mother's dance school in George's Street. Susan had readily agreed to cover for me for the first hour, seemingly finding the idea of me flamenco dancing hilarious, which I could understand.

At quarter to seven I met Muriel outside the library and we walked down Broad Street together and across John Roberts Square, unofficially known as Red Square because of the red paving on the ground, where we turned left down George's Street.

We were only a few metres away from the Oxfam shop where I'd dropped the wedding clothes off yesterday when I heard Muriel gasp. 'Oh my God.'

The stunned tone of her voice was enough to stop me in my tracks.

Her hand was clasped over her mouth and her eyes were perfect ovals as she stared hard at the Oxfam shop window.

'Oh my God,' I repeated when I saw what she was looking at.

'Isn't that your wedding dress?'

'Yes it is.'

'And – '

'And Richie's suit? Yes, it is,' I confirmed, stunned by the sight before me.

'I didn't even know you'd got rid of them.'

'I was just about to tell you.' To be honest I'd been just about to boast about how mature I'd been not hacking them to bits with the nail scissors. 'Needless to say,' I continued, 'if I'd known that Oxfam were planning to use them for their Valentine's Day window-display extravaganza I'd have dumped them in the river instead.' How could they do this to me?

My wedding dress was hanging on a female manne-quin with a stiff Charlie's Angels hairdo. The skirt stopped short at her knees because she was about a foot taller than me. And Richie's suit was on her male counterpart. Someone had stuck a fabric rose in the female mannequin's hair and a cigar between the male mannequin's plastic lips. They were somehow holding hands and all around them floated a constellation of cardboard hearts dangling on different lengths of thread.

And as if we hadn't already gotten the message there was an enormous banner across the window: FOREVER LOVE.

Muriel dissolved into giggles. 'I'm sorry,' she laughed, looking up to the sky and blinking rapidly so that the tears wouldn't ruin her mascara. 'I know it's not funny.'

'You could've fooled me.' I hadn't seen her laugh so hard since she was thirteen and I'd just set fire to the science teacher's tie during an experiment that went wrong.

'Richie will think you've been up to your usual tricks,' she warned me.

'I know.' He'd never allow this to pass, never, and it hadn't even been my fault. Still, I thought, what could he do?

When we got to the dance school Antonio was telling a small group of girls what they should wear to the next class: any kind of a long, wide skirt, so they could get used to the swaying movement of the material, and proper dancing shoes, which he could order from Spain.

He suddenly spotted us hovering on the doorstep. 'Muriel!' he exclaimed, his handsome tanned face brightening. 'I was just about giving up hope of seeing you here this evening.'

Understandably the group of girls he'd been talking to turned towards the door, looking at the two of us, wondering which one was the lucky Muriel whose arrival had fired up such a response from Antonio.

'That's her,' I said helpfully, pointing a thumb at Muriel.

Muriel blushed.

It was hard to know what she should say now, what was expected of her. 'Eh . . . hi,' she mumbled.

Antonio beckoned us in. The sleeves of his crisp white shirt were rolled up to his elbows to reveal brown forearms matted with dark hair. 'Come on through. We're just about to get started. Muriel and Rosie, this is Miranda, Jane, Niamh and Rhona.' Very much the professional, he barely hesitated over their names. 'And this is Michelle and Karen,' he concluded.

We were by far the oldest two there, I realized, and I groaned inwardly. I really did not need the inevitable humiliation that would come of this, no matter how much good Muriel thought it would do me.

Antonio clapped his hands and even that sounded like no ordinary clap. '*Vamos*, let's begin.'

I swallowed hard.

'We'll take it easy this evening,' he promised. 'Just follow me . . . Hands on hips like this.' He placed his hands on his hips accordingly. 'And move your feet like this now.' He brought his right foot forward, tapped the space just behind it with the toe of his left foot and brought both feet back to the spot where he began. Stamp. Stamp. Stamp. Stamp. Four perfect stamps.

I closed my eyes and tried to do the same.

'Rosie,' I heard a voice calling my name and opened my eyes. 'Rosie,' Antonio said, 'let's use the right foot . . . that's it . . . not the left one.'

The rest of the class had stopped and were looking at me, waiting for me to repeat the step – correctly this time. I painfully executed some kind of shuffling foot movement and fervently hoped it would do.

Antonio smiled indulgently. 'I'll let you off this

time. It's not easy on your own, first time around,' he explained to everyone else and beneath the last remaining layer of fake tan I blushed like a disgraced schoolgirl. I'd known this would happen.

Meanwhile Muriel had adopted the resting pose of a ballerina. She'd done classes for years, until she'd grown too tall, and she was now waiting for her next fancy-footwork challenge. The prepubescent Twiglets in attendance looked at her in awe.

'We're going to add a very simple arm movement to that step,' Antonio told us. 'And up.' He raised his arms above his head and rapidly twirled to face us.

I felt distinctly dizzy.

'You weren't that bad,' Muriel tried to console me as she walked me to the office. We broke into a run because by now I was very late. 'I mean, with a bit of extra practice.'

I stopped running. 'Stop right there,' I told her. 'That hole you're digging for yourself is big enough now. I'm not going again. No way.'

'OK, OK,' she conceded. She knew I had a point.

I nodded. 'When's your next day off?'

'Friday.'

'Good, me too.'

'Why?' she asked, sounding wary because she'd just noticed the scheming look on my face.

'Because you and I are going to visit Richie's new house,' I announced. 'Dennis said they've already moved in.' It had hurt when he'd told me. Even though he'd said it in a sarcastic tone, I'd still flinched. 'Ellen's furniture has arrived out of storage and I've got an idea.'

'Well, it had better be legal,' she warned me, only half joking.

I smirked at her. 'Oh, it's legal all right.'

She looked at me expectantly, wanting more detail.

'I'll explain when the time comes,' I pledged. We'd reached the door to the taxi office and I slid it open an inch and glanced in. Susan was manically answering both phones and trying to slide the drivers' rota down the desk towards her with her elbow. 'Looks like there's mass movement around the town tonight,' I groaned. 'I'd better go on in.'

I headed straight home when my shift ended at two a.m. Even if I'd felt like going anywhere else – and I didn't because I was tired – there wasn't a big choice of other places to go at that time of night.

The unexpected smell of fresh paint hit me the minute I opened the front door. Curious, I followed the odour upstairs. Thomas fell out of the door of his room, wearing a pair of pale-blue striped cotton boxer shorts and displaying, to my surprise, a washboard stomach. 'Heard the door,' he yawned. 'Got a surprise for you.'

I was intrigued. I loved surprises. Richie had been brilliant at putting together really nice surprises for me: a new set of sexy underwear hidden at the bottom of the laundry basket for me to find when I was doing the washing; an envelope on the kitchen table on my day off with a wad of cash and a return train ticket to Dublin for an unexpected shopping spree; a relaxing Indian head massage at the local health club when he knew I'd had a particularly trying day at work; and once he'd hired a portable Jacuzzi for the weekend and we'd sat in it for nearly two days solid, drinking, laughing and shrivelling. The conniving bastard.

'Does the surprise smell?' I asked Thomas, because I was absolutely positive that I could smell fresh paint.

He smiled mysteriously and plodded across the landing. 'Taa-daa,' he sang, pushing open the door to my bedroom and bowing in an extravagant gesture. 'Laurence Llewelyn-Bowen, eat your frilly-cuffed heart out.'

I peered inside. Gone were the purple walls that Richie had insisted on. I mean, the walls were still there but the purple colour had disappeared. 'Holy shit,' I stammered. They were now pale buttercup and there was a new matching duvet cover on the bed, with tiny golden embroidered leaves, and even the garish purple silk lampshades had been replaced by strings of delicate glass beads attached to bronze frames.

'God,' I gasped. I wanted to run straight in, shut the door and emerge in ten years' time. 'It's beautiful, so beautiful.'

'You won't be able to sleep in there tonight, though,' he said, reading my mind. 'The paint's still drying.'

'Pity.' I looked around the room again with a wide-eyed delight that I didn't think possible at this unearthly hour. I was amazed by his thoughtfulness and elegant taste. 'Never mind,' I told him, 'I'll use the camp bed in the box room.'

'No, no,' he insisted, 'I'll sleep on the camp bed and you take my bed.'

'No,' I insisted back. 'I'll take the camp bed.' I didn't want to sleep in the bed that Thomas had just vacated. I didn't know him that well.

'I wouldn't hear of it.' He shook his wiry crop vehemently. 'Allow me this single act of chivalry, Rosie. Eilish would kill me if she knew that I'd spoilt the surprise by letting you sleep on the camp bed.'

'What's Eilish got to do with it?' I should've guessed there was a female touch to the room.

'She came up with the idea and did a lot of the work,' he admitted. 'She said you'd always hated that purple bedroom and it couldn't be good for you to sleep in there every night . . .'

'Hang on a minute, why had you two been talking about bedrooms?'

'You know, as you do.'

'Hmm . . . Well, I'm surprised she's talking to you at all, given the trouble you got her into on Monday night. Imagine offering to go away on holidays with her with Jimmy Bible standing right beside you.'

'As I was saying,' he continued, 'Eilish told me that you hated those purple walls and we decided to redo the room as a surprise for you. That's all.' He ran his hand across his bare abdomen. 'Cross my heart.'

'That's nowhere near your heart,' I pointed out. 'No wonder people have their doubts about healthcare in this country.' Either way I was inclined to believe him, even though I didn't say it.

It wasn't that I implicitly trusted Thomas when he told me that he had no interest whatsoever in Eilish other than friendship and a very good professional entente.

No, it was more that Eilish was the single most loyal person I had ever met. In all the years she'd been with Jimmy Bible she'd never once been unfaithful to him, even though he'd given her reason to time and time again, which was something I greatly admired even if I couldn't understand why she bothered. It had taken an awful lot less of what Eilish put up with for Richie to be unfaithful to me – and I still hadn't figured out what exactly that was.

'A penny for them,' Thomas offered.

'You'd make yourself a small fortune in consultation fees,' I told him. 'But I don't have the required leather couch.' I didn't really want to talk about it now. People got very morbid when they started talking about serious things at this time of night. I knew because I'd done it before.

He shrugged and made for the box room. 'You know where I am if you want me,' he called back over his shoulder. 'I have five sisters, remember, and that makes for a lot of experience in these things.'

'Thanks.' I quickly donned my woman-sleeping-on-her-own flannel pyjamas and slouched into Thomas's room, towards his unkempt, still-warm bed. My eyelids were dropping as I inched back the duvet cover and wriggled under the plump softness. The call of sleep was getting louder and louder but just as I was about to slip into the magical world of slumber something cold and sharp wrapped itself around my big toe.

I kicked back the quilt with my leg and almost dislocated my hip. 'Aargh.'

Thomas came thundering across the landing. It took him about three seconds. 'What?'

'*What is this?*' I was massaging my throbbing leg with one hand and holding the object I'd removed from around my toe in the other. I knew perfectly well what it was.

'Well?' I demanded dangling Eilish's gold hoop earring, the one she'd thought she'd lost, from my little finger. 'I'm waiting for an explanation,' I reminded him. 'How did this get here?'

'I don't know.'

'Come off it, Thomas,' I scoffed. 'How long has this been going on?'

Nothing.

'Thomas, I found Eilish's missing earring in your bed.'

Still nothing.

I could feel my patience about to snap. 'Don't tell me that she was tired from all the decorating and took a nap in your bed?'

'No.'

'Aha, so you've found your tongue.' I could barely believe it but the guilty look on Thomas's face was confirmation enough. Eilish and Thomas were carrying on behind everyone's back. I was speechless – and upset, too, because they had duped me. Neither of them had trusted me enough to tell me what was going on. No wonder Eilish had wanted him to move in with me. It was for the sheer convenience.

But why hadn't she said anything? Why hadn't she trusted me enough to tell me? I'd spent years trying to get her to dump Jimmy Bible. I'd have been sympathetic. I would've been a lot more sympathetic before Richie had left me because now I knew what it felt like to be on the receiving end of someone else's unfaithfulness. But surely Jimmy Bible deserved it and I didn't? Surely she could see that?

'I must've been the perfect alibi,' I mumbled dolefully. 'No one would be at all suspicious seeing Eilish come and go here, would they?'

'It wasn't like that.'

'Jimmy Bible will make mincemeat of you,' I warned him dourly. But my head was spinning from everything that was going on and I was reeling from the unexpected turn my life had taken. I could barely take it all in.

Eilish was sleeping with Thomas, in my house, in a bed that I'd bought, and I hadn't known a thing about it.

Richie and Ellen Van Damme were happily ensconced in their new luxury home and I didn't matter to either of them.

Something was eating away at Hannah and we were all feeling the brunt of her mood swings but she wouldn't talk to me about it.

Susan was about to meet the son she never knew she had who was expecting her to be a man, and she was relying on me being there to make it easier.

Johnny Power's future happiness hinged on me because I'd persuaded him to make his feelings known to Mrs Burke.

Titch Murphy, the town's answer to Deuce Bigelow, wanted to get into my drawers and everyone knew about it.

The responsibility for the most talked about party of the year rested solely on my shoulders.

And I fancied a transsexual.

Life had just dealt me a hand of jokers, I decided.

'Oh, why didn't she just do the honourable thing and leave him before taking up with you?' I quipped. 'That's what Richie should've done.'

'She said she'd been with him too long.'

'That's the lamest excuse I've ever heard.'

'Maybe she just doesn't want me badly enough?' Thomas said, suddenly sounding very dejected. 'Maybe she thinks I'm not good enough for her? But surely I'm as good as that other bollocks, Jimmy Bible?' he asked vehemently.

'I don't know about that,' I told him. 'At least Jimmy's love affair is with horses and not other men's women.'

'Ah, Rosie, Rosie, don't be like that. Could I help it if I fell in love with your sister? I mean, man, have you seen her in that uniform?'

'Very funny, Thomas.' I reluctantly accorded him a half-grin because Eilish did look like every man would want a nurse to look like in her uniform and there was no denying it. It went in and out and up and down in all the right places and temperatures rose when she did the rounds with her thermometer.

'Seriously, though,' he said on a more sombre note. 'I'm mad about her. I'd marry the girl in the morning,' he confessed. 'But she won't hear a word of it. I mean, what's a man to do?'

He looked at me expectantly.

It baffled me that I was the one who everyone turned to for help with their problems when I obviously needed far more help than they did. Maybe they just felt a bit better talking to someone they knew was worse at relationships than themselves. If things didn't work out at the taxi office, say if the Furey brothers got a one-eyed donkey in to do my job, I could easily forge myself a new career as an agony aunt.

I opened my mouth to tell him that I was in no position to be giving out advice on these matters but he misunderstood what I was about to say.

'I'll put the kettle on,' he told me as he stumbled down the stairs in anticipation of what he thought I had to tell him about winning Eilish over.

Watching him go I suddenly had a brilliant idea. Something that would help Thomas with his dilemma while at the same time making sure that the singles party would be a big success. I shot down the stairs after him, all signs of fatigue gone, all the things that had been worrying me a few minutes earlier instantly forgotten.

16

It was Friday morning and I was sitting in the California Cyber Café down the street from the Theatre Royal, where Carmen's dance show had taken place, about a five-minute walk from the taxi office.

I was huddled in the corner trying to position my shoulders where they would block the computer screen from prying eyes. I'd just typed in the word 'transsexual' and was waiting apprehensively for the result of the search, praying that nobody I knew would walk in and then come over to talk to me. Because if they glanced at the screen, word would be around town in less time than it'd take me to race to the nearest travel agent and buy a one-way ticket to China that Richie had left me because I harboured secret desires to become a man.

But the real reason I'd decided to do this was curiosity. I just wanted to find out more about transsexuals and their world because I now knew two, which was two more than I ever thought I'd know, and I secretly and inexplicably fancied one of them.

It turned out that there was plenty of information available out there. Ireland had only a few sites but the UK had loads and for the next thirty minutes or

281

so, in between glancing over my shoulder and starting every time the door opened, I learnt all sorts of things that I didn't know before and never thought I would.

When I'd finished I realized that both Hank and Susan were lucky. Both had been able to afford the sex-reassignment surgery that cost an absolute fortune, anywhere from £6,000 to £9,000. And both had totally mastered the body language of their chosen gender. This was what gave a lot of transsexuals away, according to what I'd read. It seemed that running was one of the biggest problems, which was something we had in common, and I now remembered how Susan had baulked when I'd idly suggested a few months ago that we take up jogging to get fit.

'Did you know that transsexualism is actually a real condition? And it affects about 1 in 10,000 people in the UK? And is thought to be caused by a hormonal imbalance in the womb?' I quizzed Muriel on our way to Richie's new house near Faithlegg later that morning. She couldn't possibly know any of this but I was keen to show off my new knowledge.

Muriel didn't take her eyes off the road. 'No, I didn't know that.'

'And did you know that men who become women call themselves T-girls?'

'Really?'

'Absolutely.'

'And did you know that the engine in this Mini

Cooper is actually sideways on to make more room inside?' she then asked me.

'How could I know that?'

'And how could I know that men who become women call themselves T-girls?' she laughed.

I sighed. 'I was just trying to have a serious conversation.'

'About transsexualism?' She raised her eyebrows incredulously. 'Is there anything you want to tell me, Rosie?'

Muriel obviously had no interest whatsoever in the topic so I decided to leave it. 'Can't this thing go any faster?' I muttered. 'They'll probably have moved house again by the time we get there.'

I still hadn't told her exactly what we were going to do when we got there but I had everything we'd need in a bag on the floor, safely clutched between my two feet. I hadn't told her in case she wouldn't agree even though she'd promised to help me.

By now we'd left the town behind and the Mini Cooper chugged along the country road at a worryingly low speed. 'Are you sure there's nothing wrong?' I asked her. 'Does the car need petrol? Does it need a new engine?'

'No,' she said patiently. 'I'm just staying within the speed limit.'

Suddenly I saw a sign in the distance: THE CEDARS. 'Pull in here,' I told her urgently, tugging at the steering wheel until she slapped my fingers away. 'That's the entrance to the housing estate just ahead and I want to explain the plan before we get there.'

Muriel hastily swerved the Mini Cooper into a ditch at the side of the road. 'Sounds like an expensive rehab centre,' she said, looking at the sign. 'Executive housing, eh?'

I had opened the bag at my feet and was pulling out an assortment of objects. 'This,' I told her, handing her the first item, 'is a clipboard. And this,' I said, giving her a sheet of paper, 'is the questionnaire that goes on it.'

She looked at the heading on the questionnaire I'd drawn up on the computer at home. 'Lifestyles of the Wealthy?' she read aloud and grimaced. 'Are you sure about this?'

I nodded firmly but I had to admit it didn't have the same ring to it as when I'd read it out to myself.

'You're going to go knock on Ellen Van Damme's door, tell her that you are doing this questionnaire for some magazine, and ask her if she could spare you five minutes. She's bound to be interested, with all the money she seems to have. Wealthy people always like to talk about their wealth, don't they?' As well as this being Muriel's ruse to get asked in it might also tell me where Ellen Van Damme's money came from.

'This is Faithlegg, Rosie. Hardly the Hamptons,' Muriel deadpanned, looking very dubious now that I'd begun to share my plan with her.

I chose to ignore her. 'She has to invite you into the house.'

'And where will you be all this time?'

'Hiding in the car. She can't see me.'

'But won't she remember me from the theatre?'

'Damn, damn. I hadn't factored that in.' It was an obvious hurdle and I'd overlooked it entirely. I quickly considered a way around the problem. 'You'll just have to be very, very nice to her, Muriel. Act just as surprised to see her. Sorry.' I knew this sounded lame.

Muriel wasn't looking overly happy as she drummed her fingers on the steering wheel.

'You promised to help me,' I reminded her, carefully opening the package on my knees. 'And here's the most important item in your kit,' I said proudly.

She glanced down. '*Stink bombs?*'

'Yes. But they're not going to go off while you're still there,' I assured her.

Richie couldn't stand unpleasant smells. It was his pet hate. We'd had air fresheners and pot pourri in every corner of the house. One time on holiday in Spain we'd moved hotel rooms three times because Richie could detect a smell in each of the rooms that no one else could. I'd just put it down to a sensitive nose and his perfectionist streak, and smiled encouragingly at the hotel staff. I'd been far too lenient on him, I was now realizing.

'I'm just going to prick two of them with this needle,' I told her. 'Leave them behind a cushion or something and that way when they sit down, *pong*.' I scrunched up my nose.

'I'm not sure about this, Rosie.'

'It's harmless really. Just be careful that you don't squash the stink bombs before you get the chance to hide them in the house. Come on, let's go,' I urged her before she changed her mind.

Muriel started up the car, revving the sideways-on engine, and we continued on to the Cedars. There was no one to be seen but it felt like everyone knew we were coming, like we were expected.

The exclusive housing estate was made up of about ten big houses, each one slightly different to the next, and with Dennis's instructions we easily identified Richie's. It was built of red brick and had two large pillars holding up an outside porch. The front door alone was the size of my house.

Muriel stopped the car but not directly outside the house. She gamely took the clipboard and her arsenal of stink bombs, which she slipped into the pocket of her loose coat.

'Muriel, for God's sake, whatever you do, don't sit on your coat,' I warned her. 'Don't pat the pocket and don't lean against anything.'

She gave me a lukewarm smile. She was trying hard to be enthusiastic but it was hard for her because it wasn't in her nature to be spiteful, I knew.

'It'll be over before you know it,' I consoled her. 'Anyway, I'd do it for you, Ms Straight-laced Ryan.'

'I know you would and probably worse,' she grinned.

'Probably,' I agreed.

Ellen Van Damme opened the door immediately and as I peered up from my crouched position I caught the shocked look on her face at seeing Muriel there. But Muriel was all infectious smiles and she soon had Ellen smiling back at her.

On the way out I'd been hoping we'd catch a glimpse of her in a tattered nylon tracksuit, half-hidden behind the front door, with no make-up on. But she was as impeccable as usual, wearing a dark-red polo-neck sweater and matching knee-length skirt with high black boots. Her hair hung in coiffed waves to her shoulders and even from this distance I could see the sheen of matching lipstick. I sighed loudly.

What kind of woman looked perfect at ten-thirty in the morning in the privacy of her own home? I asked myself. It wasn't normal. I remembered Richie's comments on how I never paid attention to my appearance around the house and I begrudgingly admitted that he probably appreciated Ellen Van Damme's attention to grooming.

Suddenly I noticed Muriel almost keel over on the front doorstep. I raised my head an inch and saw her reach out with a hand to steady herself against the wall. I was about to jump from the car and rush to her aid when I realized that it was a ploy to get inside.

It worked. Ellen immediately flung open the door

and ushered her into the hallway, looking genuinely concerned, and then the door closed again and I could no longer follow what was going on. Damn.

I resigned myself to waiting and switched on my mobile phone to check for messages, punching the air when I counted ten more names for Solomania on Monday night. There'd been twenty yesterday and twelve the day before. All in all, I'd now reached the grand total of seventy-five. A few more should show up on the strength of the radio plugs it had been getting all week courtesy of Rory's niece, and when I last spoke to Christie he'd told me that a number of guests had called to say they'd be interested too after Carmen had cleverly included a flyer in their confirmation packages. They were probably all married sales reps looking for a good time, but it was a start.

I noticed that Ellen had planted fragile winter rosebushes in the front garden, along the side of the driveway, and they were beautiful. Richie's tastes had obviously moved on from the potted geraniums we'd had, just as he'd moved on from me. As I realized this a wave of cold anger washed over me. Who did he think he was to cast me aside to be with her when he'd decided that I wasn't good enough any longer?

Admittedly she was wealthy and dressed well but how special did that make her? What was it about her that held such an attraction for him? What stunt had she pulled to make him want to leave me and our life together?

I didn't have the answers and it made me feel powerless. I wanted to spoil their new perfect life together. On impulse I pushed open the door of the car and dashed over to the opposite side of the small estate, where the landscaping had yet to be done, pulled up half a dozen ugly nettle plants from the ground, holding them by their stems so I wouldn't get stung, then ran back to the car.

It looked like no one had seen me. Some of the houses were still being finished but the workers were nowhere to be seen, just empty vans parked in the driveways.

I stared at Richie and Ellen's house without blinking, until my eyes watered, and when I could detect no movement behind any of the front windows I climbed out of the car again. I didn't dare glance back at the house as I quickly yanked the roses from the ground, oblivious to the sharp thorns, and hastily replaced each shrub with a nettle plant. I then dumped the armful of prickly roses I'd collected on to the back seat of Muriel's car.

I was breathing hard and my heart was racing and I really couldn't believe what I'd just done. But I was admittedly feeling slightly smug. I was still lying flat across the two front seats when I heard a sharp tap on the window. I sheepishly lifted my head.

'I saw you, Rosie Flynn.' Titch Murphy was grinning in the window. 'You're a little devil, aren't you?' he said flirtingly.

'Shut up,' I hissed. 'And go away. Go on, get lost.'

He leant against the car. 'Not until you agree to have a drink with me.' He knew he had the edge on me now.

'Never,' I vowed.

'Well, then, I'll just stay here until you-know-who appears and wonders what's happened to her lovely roses.'

I hated him.

'What's it to be?' he asked.

'I'm going to talk to Dennis and get you fired,' I warned him in an angry whisper.

'He'd never fire me. He's too far behind on most of his contracts to be getting rid of his staff like that,' he said confidently and I knew it was true.

'OK, OK,' I gave in. 'Meet me at the Cosy Inn on Monday night. I'm throwing a party there and I'll have a drink with you. Now piss off.'

He saluted me stiffly through the window and it looked like he was having some sort of a seizure. 'Yes, ma'am.'

I buried my face in the seat, bemoaning my misfortune. When I chanced to look up again he had disappeared. 'Thank God,' I breathed.

Suddenly there was the sound of voices and I tried to crouch even lower than I already was.

'Bye, Ellen. Thanks for the tea.' That was Muriel.

'Bye, Muriel. Come around any time with more

Rosie stories.' That was Ellen Van Damme, and she was chortling but in a ladylike manner.

'She was actually quite nice,' Muriel tried to tell me as we drove out of the estate. I was still hiding so it looked like she was talking to herself.

'I really don't want to hear that.'

'A little bit on the precious side but nice nonetheless,' she carried on.

I sunk lower, emotionally and physically.

'But not a patch on you.'

'Really?' I sat up a bit.

'Yes, really.'

'And what did she mean when she said "more Rosie stories"?' I asked her.

'Well, I had to make friends with her so I told her a few stories about you so she'd think we were getting on well.'

'Which ones did you tell her?' She knew most of them.

'I told her about the time you walked the whole way across the pub pulling a trail of toilet paper caught in your tights behind you.' She was smirking as she looked straight ahead, pretending to focus on her driving.

'Oh, God, Muriel,' I groaned, 'not that one.'

'But it's a good one,' she argued. 'And I told her about the time you overdosed on aspirin and had to have your stomach pumped.'

'I hope you told her that I was four at the time?'

'Well, no, I didn't. It wouldn't have sounded as interesting.'

'I'm going to kill you.' What would Ellen Van Damme think of me now?

From there we went to my mother's. It was around lunchtime and both Myra Barry and Eilish were there, eating skirts and kidneys, a kind of offal stew that was a Waterford speciality, which personally I couldn't stomach. I hadn't spoken to Eilish since I found out about Thomas and her. I'd tried but her mobile phone was constantly switched off and there was no answer at home. I knew Thomas would've told her that she'd been found out and she was clearly avoiding me.

She looked up from her stew and nearly choked when she saw me standing beside her. 'What are you doing here?' she spluttered.

'You didn't think you could dodge me for ever, surely?'

My mother motioned with the serving ladle. 'What's going on with you two?'

'I want a word with you,' I said ominously to Eilish. I was going to make her feel so low about being unfaithful to Jimmy, in a way that I'd never got the chance to do with Richie. It wasn't fair but Eilish was going to pay for his mistake.

She looked like she was about to throw up and it gave me a feeling of great power. Muriel, who was the only other one in the kitchen who knew what was going on, gave her a sympathetic smile.

'OK,' she said feebly, following me out into the utility room.

I closed the door behind us and faced Eilish.

'I'm so sorry,' she gushed before I had a chance to say anything. 'I was going to tell you . . . really . . . but then all this Richie business happened . . . and there never seemed to be a right time. You had enough to worry about and I knew how you felt about two-timers.'

That didn't seem to stop anyone else, I thought grimly.

'I never meant to deceive you, Rosie,' she went on. 'This is all very hard for me. I hate doing this to Jimmy. He's been so good to me all along.' And then she started crying.

And my plan to take the moral high ground with her went to smithereens. 'Don't cry, don't cry,' I pleaded. 'There's no real harm done. I wasn't really annoyed with you. I was just upset that you didn't tell me.'

'I want to explain,' she sobbed, the sobs getting louder because I was being nice to her. 'I didn't mean for any of this to happen.'

If Richie had said this I wouldn't have believed him but I did believe Eilish. She surely wouldn't have been able to produce such an impressive quantity of tears if she was lying. 'I know, I know,' I soothed.

My mother and Myra Barry were doing their utmost

not to press their faces against the pane of glass that separated the two rooms, and trying to feign an interest in whatever Muriel was telling them as she threw her hands around to illustrate her point.

'Something just clicked with Thomas straight away when he started working in our unit and next thing I knew we were ripping each other's clothes off in the stock room where we keep the bedpans. That's so unlike me.' She sounded dismayed by her own behaviour.

'Yeah, I know.'

'And now I'm in an awful mess.'

'Do you love him?'

'Which one?'

'Thomas.'

She didn't even hesitate. 'Yes.'

And I knew how Thomas felt about Eilish. We'd spent hours talking about it the other night. He was crazy about her. He said that he'd been holding his breath for years, just waiting for her to come along. And, of course, I knew what he'd planned for Valentine's night, at my suggestion. A man would never come up with an idea like that by himself.

'Leave Jimmy, Eilish. You have to. I mean, OK, so I don't like the fella, but you're not being fair to him all the same. And you're not being fair to yourself or Thomas either.' Needless to say, none of this reasoning in favour of true love could be applied to Richie and Ellen Van Damme.

'I can't,' she sighed.

'Sure you can.'

'No. I can't. You don't know what he did for me. I owe him too much. I'd feel too guilty.'

'What did he ever do for you, Eilish? What? He spends all your money betting on horses.'

'He took my place, Rosie. That night when we drove into the neighbour's wall, I was driving, not him, and I was drunk. We'd had a fight and I'd insisted on driving. But Jimmy took my place when we went into the wall even though he was over the limit and he'd lose his licence. He still took my place to save me.'

I was very impressed with Jimmy's chivalry and he went up a few notches in my esteem right there. 'He did a very noble thing, Eilish. But you still have to leave him. This is life. You only have one shot at it.' Once again, in no way did this reasoning apply to Richie and Ellen Van Damme.

'I knew you wouldn't be able to be mean to her,' Muriel said in my ear when we walked back into the kitchen. 'By the way, your mother was delighted with the roses.' We'd given her the rosebushes from Ellen's garden when we arrived.

'Is Johnny Power going to your party Monday night?' Myra grilled me out of the blue.

'I don't think so.' I remembered his plans to take Mrs Burke out to dinner and propose to her. 'You're not coming, are you?' She'd up the average age by about thirty years.

'Of course I am.'

Then Rory walked in. 'We need to talk about the music for your party.'

'Eighties disco,' I told him adamantly. 'No "Walls of Limerick" . . . no "Haymaker's Jig" . . . no "Siege of Ennis" . . . and no stories of your lost youth in between songs either,' I warned him, because he liked to talk a lot.

He looked into the steaming bowl of skirts and kidneys that my mother had put in front of him. 'Jesus, Rosie,' he said, stirring his stew, 'you're taking all the fun out of it.'

'Trust me, Rory, I know what I'm doing.' I was the only one in the kitchen who didn't laugh out loud when I said this.

I felt my cheeks redden but my tormentors were spared any abuse because my mobile phone rang and I had to answer it because it would be more people for my guest list and that'd show them. 'Rosie Flynn here,' I said as importantly as I could.

'Danny Furey here,' the voice of my boss snapped back, 'and do you know where I am?'

'Eh, no.' Who did he think I was? His keeper? He didn't pay me that much.

'Well, let me tell you. I'm out at Waterford airport.'

There was a congested silence.

'And do you know why I'm here?' he asked impatiently.

It suddenly came to me. Of course I knew why he

was there and I was relieved that I'd remembered in time because I could tell he wasn't in the mood for professional incompetence.

'Yes, yes, I know why you're there. To meet the plane that's bringing in the football team from London to go play golf for the afternoon in Faithlegg. Great golf-course they have out there in Faithlegg House.'

During my shift on Wednesday I'd had a call from the UK, from some travel company that wanted ten taxis to meet the plane coming in from Luton and chauffeur the team around for the afternoon. It had been done before and it would be a lucrative afternoon's work. And Danny Furey was there to lick football arse.

'That's right. I'm here to greet the football team and I've ten cars here at the ready. Except what do you know? There's no football team.'

'*What?*'

'That's right. *No Football Team!*'

'But I got the call,' I insisted. 'And they sounded very professional, very above board, like they knew exactly what they were after,' I argued, desperately trying to remember the exact details of the call. 'I wrote down the name of the travel company and their telephone number.'

'That's right and we've called. And what do you know? It doesn't exist.'

'Oh.' Oh God!

'I'm not happy, Rosie. Not happy at all. I'm

breathing fire here, Rosie.' And with that the line went dead. I didn't know whether he'd hung up on me or the reception had failed.

It didn't take me longer than two seconds to figure out that Richie was behind the bogus call and I had to admit that he'd been very clever. I hadn't suspected a thing. I'd even the score, I vowed, but I wouldn't have time to do it over the next few days. I'd be too busy. I had to go to the airport with Susan and I had the party to finish organizing, and I had to figure out how to get over the crush I had on Hank before I met him again on the night.

The horn honked once, twice and then a third time. I forced an unwilling eye open and looked at the alarm clock on the locker. The figures were blurred. It took a few seconds for them to clear. It was six-fifty a.m. Susan wasn't due to pick me up until seven o'clock to drive to Dublin and I resented her being ten minutes early.

I almost fell out of bed and lumbered painfully over to the bedroom window and poked my head out. My lungs balked at the fresh air. 'You're early,' I wheezed at her.

'I've been here since six-thirty but I've only just honked now. Aren't you ready yet?'

'Nearly,' I lied. 'Two minutes.'

The night before, Thomas had helped me repaint the dining room. It had taken about three coats of

Springwater Blue to obliterate the blood-red colour that Richie had used and while we waited for each coat to dry we'd had a bottle of wine, sitting on the floor and admiring our own handiwork.

Eilish had arrived between the second and third coat and joined in. And when we'd finished the third bottle of wine Thomas went to the night shop and bought two more, and a packet of cigarettes that he swore I'd asked him to get as he left.

But I'd given up smoking. Surely I hadn't asked him to bring me back a pack of twenty cigarettes? And surely I hadn't smoked the whole pack? I sniffed my fingertips and grimaced. There was the whiff of at least sixteen cigarettes. Someone else must've had the other four, I realized gratefully.

I quickly brushed some nice-smelling talc through my hair. It was a tip I thought I remembered reading in some magazine but I wasn't sure. I rubbed cream into my face until it glistened with a false healthiness, and then I got dressed – Gap cords, chunky cardigan, Timberland boots and a woolly hat. Warm, comfortable gear designed to soothe a hangover victim.

Susan looked horrified when I opened the car door. 'You're not going to meet him like that, are you? You look like you're off to milk a herd of cows.'

I looked back at her, even more horrified. 'What have you done to your *hair*?'

'I cut it.'

The beautiful red bob that she was so proud of was

gone and in its place was a military-style crop. The vibrant colour had been toned down too; it was now a staid regiment brown shade.

She shrugged. 'This is more of a man's hairstyle, isn't it? For today?'

'Eh, yeah.' But I didn't understand why she was still wearing women's clothes. A demure long pencil skirt and matching twin set.

'I've brought a different outfit with me to change into,' she explained. 'I only bought it yesterday and it felt horrible. But I'm not doing this for me, am I?'

'Eh, no.' I had no idea how this day would pan out. She was nervous and I was possibly suffering from alcohol poisoning, and we had the monumental task ahead of us of meeting Susan's son and making the right impression. She started up the engine.

I inspected her closely as we drove through the empty town, and along the Quay, and headed for the bridge and the main Dublin road. She wasn't wearing any make-up, and, while she didn't look as glamorous as she usually did, I couldn't say outright that she looked like a man either. God, my head was thumping.

Susan read my mind. 'I've always had innately feminine features,' she said seriously, 'which was quite lucky for me. Fairly soft skin, never really much facial hair, not a very deep voice.'

'You must've been a right namby-pamby. It's a good thing you wanted to be a woman.' It didn't come out as intended.

'How many hours' sleep have you had?' she asked me shrewdly.

'Three.'

'And how much did you have to drink last night?'

'Too much.' The bile rose in my throat. 'Can't remember.'

'And you've been smoking, too, haven't you?'

'Yes. Don't remind me.' I felt myself retch.

'Rosie, Rosie, Rosie,' she cackled.

'Jesus, stop that, you sound like a kookaburra.'

'We're going to pull in at the Long Man in Thomastown and get you a big fried breakfast. That'll put you right.'

'Stop the car. *Now!* I'm going to be sick. *Stop the car.*'

From the public toilet of the petrol station about ten miles from the airport, Susan emerged wearing her new outfit: a pair of dark denims, a white Oxford shirt and a navy V-neck wool sweater with suede loafers. She looked, I don't know . . . wrong.

But then, halfway across the yard, she unexpectedly started to walk differently, taking longer steps, using her shoulders, not her hips, to move forward, and all of a sudden she looked a lot less of a woman. I turned away, then back again, and made myself look at her through different, unfamiliar eyes. There was an immediate difference.

'Wow,' I said, as she got into the car. 'Bit of a stud, aren't you?' I teased.

She gave me a small smile, barely a smile at all. 'Note,' she said indicating her tight mouth, 'men don't do big cheesy grins.'

'Where have your boobs gone?' I quizzed her, noticing the flat chest beneath the wool sweater.

'I've bandaged them down with toupee tape.'

I laughed so hard I thought I was going to throw up again.

There were loads of people milling around the arrivals hall at the airport.

'He said he'd be wearing a baseball cap with sox on the front,' Susan said. She was showing signs of extreme nerves, sweating and trembling. 'A cap with sox on the front,' she repeated herself.

I checked the screen overhead. 'His plane landed twenty minutes ago.' He'd have no luggage with him so I reckoned he'd be through quickly.

'I know, I know.' Susan was by now so nervous that her fingertips had gone pale.

'What did you tell him you'd be wearing?' I was trying to make idle conversation to help pass the time for her.

'I didn't know when I spoke to him. I only just got this outfit yesterday, remember? But I said I'd be with an attractive, petite blonde. He'll hardly recognize you from that description dressed like that, though, will he?'

'Thanks.' I tugged off the woolly hat and made an

attempt to revive my hair. 'Look.' I pointed to the sox baseball cap I'd just spotted wandering, somewhat forlornly, around the arrivals hall. 'There he is, Susan.'

'Don't call me Susan,' she reminded me in an urgent tone.

'I'll never remember,' I panicked. 'Never.'

We were already weaving our way through the crowd. When we got nearer Susan said, 'Harry?'

He turned around with such a hopeful expression on his face that I wanted to hug him myself. 'Yes?'

She held out her hand but then quickly patted his shoulder instead. I knew it was hard for her to know what to do. 'Hello, Harry,' she said. 'I'm Terrence, or Terry.'

We all looked at each other awkwardly. But it was a nervous awkwardness rather than an unpleasant one. We'd planned to go for a quick coffee together and then Susan would take Harry off for lunch on her own and I'd take the bus to town and meet her later, and we'd drive back down to Waterford together and dissect the meeting's every tiny detail during the journey.

Harry and Susan were just looking at each other, trying to spot the resemblances. I couldn't really see any and I hoped that neither of them was too disappointed by this.

'Thanks for the ticket,' Harry said and I knew Susan would be really pleased that he had good manners.

'You're welcome. I'm thrilled that you made it.

There's so much I want to know about you. Let's head to the cafeteria.'

We sat having coffee and listening to Harry talk about growing up in London. Susan couldn't have looked any happier if she was being told the secret of eternal youth. Suddenly he turned to me. 'Are you from the country?'

Susan snorted into her coffee mug and I kicked her under the table.

'Eh, no, no I'm not,' I said, waving my woolly hat at him and grimacing. 'I'm usually very glamorous. Well, I'm not really glamorous, that'd be more Susan than me, but I do look a bit better than this most days.'

'Who's Susan?' he asked.

'Er . . . someone I work with.' I didn't dare look in any direction other than straight at Harry.

'OK.' Then he looked back and forth between Susan and myself. 'Are you going out?'

'God no.' I realized too late that I probably sounded appalled by the idea. 'He wouldn't have me,' I said quickly. 'Who would?'

Luckily, I told myself dryly, there was a singles party coming up in two days' time.

17

My big day arrived: 14 February. The day I was going to show the whole town, and Richie Maloney, what I was really made of. But first I had to go to work.

Susan was smiling when I got to the office. She'd smiled all the way down in the car from Dublin. She'd smiled all through yesterday's shift. And she was still smiling today.

Things had gone very well with Harry on Saturday and they'd agreed to stay in touch with each other. She said that she'd been truthful about most things but missed out on the one big thing and I couldn't really blame her at this stage. She went on and on about what a great job his adopted parents had done in bringing him up so balanced, so well mannered, so caring. The list was endless.

There was another reason she was happy, too. Hank was driving across from Galway, where he was doing some kind of research for a role, she'd said, especially for this evening's party.

Over the last week I'd been telling myself that fancying him really was just one of those silly things that happened when a long-term relationship ended, one of those harmless little things that would pass and that no one else ever had to know about. So I was secretly looking forward to seeing him again – probably as much as Susan was.

'Look what I got today,' I sang as I waved two envelopes at Susan then pulled out the cards that were inside.

'"Happy Valentine's Day to a lovely girl who I love very much,"' I read aloud. '"From her biggest admirer in the whole wide world." Isn't that touching? Now, that one's from my mother . . . even though she did her best to disguise her handwriting,' I explained, sticking it onto the office notice board.

'But this one, this one,' I said examining the beautiful card in my hand, 'I really don't know who sent it.' I was absolutely thrilled to have received a real Valentine's card today, no matter how much I'd scoffed at them in the past.

Susan took the card from my hand and examined it, turning it over and looking at the back. 'Recycled paper,' she commented. 'Know any ecologists?'

'Not likely,' I said. 'Unless they're masquerading as taxi drivers.'

'And what does it say inside?' She opened it. '"Thinking about you." Short but intriguing,' she commented. 'Are you sure it's not from Titch Murphy?'

'Yeah, pretty sure. He'd probably have suggested a quick ride at the building site between the rubbish tip and the bulldozer.' Susan's knowledge of Irish-isms was spot on and she knew exactly the kind of ride I meant.

Johnny Power's voice came over the radio, interrupting the discussion. 'The bridge has gone up,' he told us, 'and I'm stuck with a fare on the other side. We'll be a while.'

In the background we could hear his disgruntled passenger muttering something about how in this day of technology you'd think they could manage to get the water to go down instead of having the bridge go up. We grinned at each other knowingly; it wasn't the first time we'd heard this. And then the phones got busy.

The next time I looked up Muriel had let herself into the office and she was standing beside me. 'I'm here,' she declared.

'So we see,' Susan observed.

She looked at Susan and her mouth dropped. 'What has happened to your hair?' she wailed, automatically putting a hand to her own waist-length tresses. 'Did you have some kind of accident?'

Susan patted her head. She'd been explaining the same thing to people all morning. 'I just wanted a change and it's good for the hair to cut it really short, you know. Makes it grow faster.'

Muriel shook her head firmly. 'You shouldn't believe everything you read, Susan. I don't think I'll be giving that a try. Anyway,' she propped herself up on the desk in front of me, crossing her slim legs, 'just came by to tell you the gossip. I had lunch at the table behind the Berlin Wall and her mother in Loughman's, and I heard her tell her mother that Richie had plans for a penis enlargement.' She was talking in bursts in between bouts of laughter.

The information I'd asked to be sent to Richie while I was in the UK had arrived. Great.

Susan dug her heels into the floor and propelled her chair up to Muriel's knees. 'Tell us more,' she implored excitedly. 'This is almost too good to be true. I'm drooling at the mouth.'

'You know how loudly she talks?'

We both nodded.

'And Loughman's was packed. Lunchtime. All the tables were full. People were queuing all the way down by the counter and her big voice was bouncing off the walls.'

I could see Susan, eyes half-shut, visualizing the setting as Muriel described it.

'And there she was telling the whole place about how she was opening the mail in the shop, when she came across a wad of information on penile enlargement from some clinic in the UK,' Muriel went on. 'Have you ever heard the likes?'

Susan's face was now buried in her hands and she was reeling back and forth with glee. She peeked out at me from between her fingers. 'Rosie, you never said anything.' She'd immediately guessed that I was behind this.

'The art of war,' I told her.

Muriel slid off the desk nimbly. 'Well, I'm off again now. I have to pick up my costume for this evening. I know loads of people who are going, Rosie.' She smiled at me as she walked out the door. '*Loads*.'

Panic seized me by the throat. Would there be enough food and drink for loads of people? And how many did she mean by 'loads' anyway? All of a sudden I was gagging for air. Susan had a brown-paper bag at the ready, which she quickly passed me with one hand while answering the phone with the other.

Throughout the last few days I'd been having overwhelming moments of panic every time I thought about this evening. It was one thing to wax lyrical about organizing a big party for single people on Valentine's night from my office seat but it was another thing to actually do it.

After a few minutes I felt able to talk again. 'I don't even know what I'm doing, Susan. Not really. There's so much to think of.' I had lists of lists and all I ever did was tick the first item and make a new list.

Susan was in the middle of her call. Over the years we'd learnt to have full-scale conversations with each other while being on the phone to someone else at the same time. 'But Carmen said Christie's been telling everyone that you're doing a great job,' she assured me.

'That's because I phone him five times a day with loads of questions so he thinks I've got it all sussed.'

'Yeah, he said you were a bit worried that they'd

forget to fill the toilet-roll holders and you'd run out halfway through the evening.'

'That's a genuine concern,' I told her emphatically. 'I don't know what people do with the stuff but have you ever been anywhere where there's still loo roll left at the end of the night?'

'I always carry some spare.'

'I might've known.'

'You can buy little packs.'

'I've got to see Christie . . . urgently . . . this lunchtime.' I glanced at my watch. It was nearly two. 'Now.'

'When you get back I'm going to buy a computer on hire-purchase,' she said. 'Harry's got e-mail so I'm going to get set up. He said to get myself a Hotmail address. Do you know what he meant?'

'Yes and I'll help you but I've got to go now.' I was lifting my parka off the coat stand.

'He says he's got some great shots of Pamela Anderson that he can send as attachments.'

I fumbled with the zip.

'Won't that be fun?' she added.

I opened the door. 'What are you going to do with Pamela Anderson?'

'I really don't know.'

Then I left.

Carmen was standing behind the reception desk talking to two guests who were complaining about the roughness of the bathroom towels. She was dealing with them with as much customer-friendly cheeriness as she could muster. Her transformation into Rott-weiler was almost complete. I waved at her and kept walking. I could see Christie in the distance, at the end of the long corridor that led to the leisure club.

'Christie? *Chris-tie?*'

He turned around.

It seemed to take for ever to reach him. 'There are loads of people coming,' I echoed Muriel's words.

'That's great, Rosie. Just what I like to hear.' He didn't pick up on the alarm in my voice. 'What do you reckon the final figure will be? Give or take a few?'

I did a very quick calculation based on the list of names I had. One or two friends hadn't managed to find the ten people I'd asked of them because they'd left it too late and the others I'd called had contacted them first. But there had been a good response to the radio ads, plus a few hotel guests were coming, and word of mouth seemed to be working. 'One hundred and twenty-nine people, I reckon, and one gobshite.' That'd be Titch Murphy, who'd conned me into having a drink with him. 'So one hundred and thirty people in total.' I was amazed at the confidence I managed to inject into my voice because I didn't feel like that at all. I was a nervous wreck on the inside. What if they all changed their minds and nobody turned up?

'Come and have a look at the room,' Christie urged me. 'See if everything meets your approval.' He was holding in his hand the sheet of notes he'd taken during our very first meeting and to that he'd added an array of multicoloured Post-it notes representing all the times I'd called him with yet more instructions and questions.

We walked into the banqueting hall. The waiters were already setting the tables and Rory had installed his music equipment that morning. Behind the bar at the far end of the large room shelves were being stacked with bottles.

'We can seat and feed one hundred and fifty people,' Christie said. 'And there'll be no shortage of drink either.' He pointed to the bar. 'We're stocking up.' His mobile phone rang as he was talking to me. 'Excuse me,' he mumbled apologetically and walked towards the door.

I looked around me. The elegant heavy curtains were pulled. The room was lit by three beautiful crystal chandeliers and the round tables were covered with white linen tablecloths and red candles.

'No, not red,' I shouted. Everyone within earshot came to a standstill. 'No red candles. White church candles. That's what I asked for. Who's in charge of candles?'

I spotted one of the waiters discreetly drop a cardboard box and attempt to shove it under the table with his foot. 'You over there.' I was striding towards him, arm outstretched, finger pointing. 'What's in that box?' I was already opening it myself. 'Red candles.'

'That's the box Christie said to use.'

'Well, never mind Christie, I want you to go find me a box with white church candles and replace the red ones.'

'There was only the one box,' he tried to tell me, looking around him for support. But no one said anything, clearly too relieved that they weren't the ones caught with the boxload of red candles.

'Just-find-me-white-church-candles-now-or-else.'

'OK, I'll go look.'

'You've got great management potential, Rosie,' Christie piped up over my shoulder. 'The red candles are for a ruby wedding-anniversary party tomorrow. There's a box of white ones in the stockroom. He'll find them when he opens his eyes and looks around him.'

'And the roses?'

In another of our telephone conversations I'd asked for long-stemmed white roses to be laid in the centre of the tables, as if they'd just floated out of the sky and landed there, to which Christie had muttered something about needless expense.

'They're falling through the atmosphere as we speak,' he now joked.

'Hah, hah! And the menus are going to be typed up on parchment paper and rolled into scrolls and tied with ribbon by this evening?'

'Yes, Rosie.' He looked like he might pull his hair out, or mine, even, if I asked him another question. 'Have you got time for a quick drink?'

I immediately recognized this as an order masquerading as a question. 'Sure, Christie.' Back at the office Susan's nails would be drummed down to the quick, I knew. She'd be impatient to get to the shop, buy her new computer, and get set up online so she could communicate with Harry. She saw every small task now as a measure of her parental ability.

'I've all the time in the world,' I lied, thinking that I'd make it up to her. With just about enough computer knowledge to do it, I'd get her signed up and logged on, and I'd download those uncensored pictures of Pamela Anderson for her.

'Your bosses out of town, are they?' He laughed because the Furey brothers would not be the kind to understand the concept of the long lunch.

'No, but I'm sure they'd be very accommodating,' I lied, crossing my fingers that they wouldn't drop by the office for any reason while I wasn't there.

In his office, Christie sat down opposite me at his desk. 'I've been very impressed with the job you've done so far, Rosie.'

I was impressed that he was impressed.

'You've shown yourself to have a real eye for detail, a good grasp of logistics . . .'

I began to reel from the unexpected praise because I felt like such a novice.

' . . . and a flair for dealing with people that your current employers unquestionably appreciate.'

Quite honestly, I doubted that they'd ever noticed

but it meant a lot more to me to hear Christie say it than the Furey brothers, who belonged among the duckers and divers of this world.

'And obviously good time-management skills, too, given that you've organized all this while holding down a full-time job . . .'

I wasn't going to burst my own bubble by telling him that it wasn't the most taxing of full-time jobs.

' . . . and in such a short space of time.' He placed both hands on the desk, slotted his fingers together and inhaled deeply.

'Rosie, I'll put it to you straight. I'm looking for an events manager and the job's yours if you want it. How about it? Feel like jumping in at the deep end?'

18

I took a last look at myself in the mirror that evening and smiled. Actually, it was more of a big huge grin. I was wearing one of Eilish's old nurse's uniforms, which I'd chopped most of the skirt off, and had the top four buttons undone to reveal a red satin bra and plenty of heaving, *faux*-sun-kissed cleavage, which, along with my sparkly aquamarine eyelids, blushing cheeks and glossy lips, created an overall effect of boudoir chic in the emergency unit. I wondered what Hank would make of it.

'Come on, come on, come on,' I heard Thomas shout up the stairs. 'That is, if you want to get there before everyone else goes home.'

'Don't exaggerate,' I shouted back. 'We're right on time,' I added, glancing at my watch and stepping into the vertiginous stilettos I'd borrowed from Eilish.

Muriel walked into the bedroom dressed as a Playboy Bunny. I'd promised Christie there'd be one and she'd agreed and rented a very authentic-looking costume. We'd created the illusion of a chest by wrapping two chicken fillets in clingfilm and stuffing them down the front of the costume. I was concerned about how she might smell in a few hours' time but she didn't seem to mind.

'Is the taxi here?' she asked.

'Yes, it's outside. Let's go.' I felt jittery. This was my big night. I was sure I'd thought of everything but I worried about what surprises might be in store for me. I'd developed a real aversion to surprises of late.

'OK.'

We ran outside and jumped into the waiting Triple-A Taxi. 'No need to tell me where you lot are off to,' Paddy said, grinning back at us over his shoulder.

'What's the collective noun for a group of butter-flies?' I quizzed Muriel as we pulled away from the kerb. 'Is it a swarm or something? Because I've got one in my stomach I'm so nervous.'

Muriel snapped open her Bunny clutch-bag and pulled out a neatly folded brown-paper bag. 'Just tell me if you need this.'

Paddy looked at us through the rear-view mirror. 'If you're going to throw up, Rosie, tell me and I'll pull over. Don't put the car out of action on me.'

'I'm not going to throw up,' I told him slightly indignantly. 'I'm just going to stop breathing. That's all. So no worries.'

We'd barely pulled out of my street when I was hit by a strong craving. 'I want a cigarette.' I needed something to steady my nerves and nicotine would do.

'No, you don't,' Muriel and Thomas chorused,

neither of them wanting to be accused at a later date of kick-starting my habit.

'I do,' I insisted, leaning forward and tapping Paddy on the shoulder. 'Pull over at a shop.' Paddy was a smoker so he understood the urgency of the situation and pulled over at the first one we came to.

With very little on to protect me from the chilly night air, I quickly ran inside and bought a pack of twenty Silk Cut blue. My mobile phone rang as I had my hand on the handle of the car door ready to climb back in again. I'd switched it on in case of last-minute problems at the Cosy Inn.

'Hello?'

'Hi, it's me.' It was Eilish. 'I can't make it tonight.'

'What do you mean, you can't make it tonight? You have to come. I'm counting on you.' I'd promised Thomas that I'd make sure she was there. We'd arranged it all between us. She couldn't just decide not to come now. It was unacceptable and it thwarted my plans.

'I can't,' she suddenly sobbed. 'I've told Jimmy that there's someone else . . . but not who . . . he'd kill him . . . and I'm just too upset to face anyone.'

'Nonsense,' I told her firmly. 'It'll be just what you need. Weren't you the one who made me show my face in Wino's the night Richie walked out?' I reminded her.

'Eh, yeah . . . but this isn't the same.'

'No, it's not. It's a lot easier.' There's no humiliation involved.

There was a silence.

'Eilish, you've got to come,' I urged her.

'OK, I suppose so . . . but I'm not staying long . . . and don't tell Thomas that I've told Jimmy . . . he'll only get all concerned.'

'Fine.'

I climbed back into the taxi. The gloss on my lips was almost frozen solid from the cold. 'Can I smoke?' I mumbled at Paddy through a semi-paralysed mouth.

'Yeah,' he answered. 'But only 'cause it's you.' He pointed to the red and white no-smoking sign on the windscreen.

I lit up and sank back against the seat waiting for the first rush of nicotine to hit me. 'Eilish has told Jimmy,' I whispered to Thomas.

'Shite tonight,' he exclaimed.

I sucked on the cigarette again. I was turning into Myra Barry. After tonight I'd quit again, I promised myself. 'Bodes well for later on, though,' I told him, 'now Jimmy's out of the way.'

Muriel smiled into the darkness of the taxi. She was the only other person who knew what we were planning. 'I'll be crossing my fingers for you.'

And I was crossing my fingers for Johnny Power, who at this very moment would be collecting Mrs Burke.

Christie was waiting for me, positioned between the reception desk and the enormous bouquet of flowers on the marble pedestal in the middle of the lobby, orchestrating a team of his staff while keeping an eye on the door.

His eyes lit up when he saw Muriel. 'You've brought me a fine Bunny, Rosie.' Then he turned to Thomas. 'And who do we have here?'

'That's Charlie Dimmock,' I said pleasantly, making sure to be very pleasant indeed to him since he'd offered me the job earlier in the day. He'd even accorded me a few days to think it over. There really wasn't a lot to think over. But I'd decided that if Christie thought I should then I wasn't going to try and tell him otherwise.

I looked at Thomas. He made a very good Charlie Dimmock with his wig of straggly strawberry-blonde locks, tight denims, muddy boots and the set of plastic boobs he had strapped on to his bare chest. 'I do a great water feature,' he told Christie, who shook his head in dismay.

'Are these the two helping you out on the door?' he asked.

'Yes. We'll be collecting the money all three of us.'

'Follow me, then.' He showed us to a long table he had set up outside the double doors to the banqueting hall. The felt-covered board on the wall behind us had small sturdy letters stuck to it that read SOLOMANIA. It looked very professional.

Muriel and Thomas both looked at me, waiting for

me to take the lead. 'Yeah, great. Can I sneak a look at the room?'

'Be my guest.' Christie pulled back the door.

The round tables were covered with heavy white-linen cloths that hung neatly to the floor. There were white candles lighting every table, making the silverware and crystal sparkle, and informal arrangements of white roses. The bar appeared to be fully stocked and was lit overhead by a row of small spotlights. There was a line of leather-seated high stools in front of it.

'It's perfect,' I said. Rory was at the top of the room wearing what he usually did for functions: a black shirt and black dress trousers. He was doing a sound check with his headphones on.

Muriel peeped in over my shoulder. 'It looks fantastic,' she gushed.

'Just wait until it's filled with French maids and other Bunnies,' Christie chortled.

'Not to mention all the Bob the Builders and Roman emperors in their bed sheets,' I added and he went off laughing, inspired by my comment to check that there was spare bed linen available to any hotel guest who wanted to join in and fashion themselves a cotton toga.

Thomas and Muriel sat in the two chairs behind the desk and looked to me for orders because I was running the show. For the first time ever I could understand the attraction of being a dictator.

'I'm going to leave you two to it for a few minutes while I whip around and make sure everything is as it should be. Don't stir from the desk in case anyone comes early,' I warned them, heading off to check the toilet-roll holders.

When I got back fifteen minutes later Susan, Carmen and Hannah were standing beside the table. A black-cloaked witch, an Austrian milkmaid and a big green elf. They were huddled together looking at some photo that Hannah held in her hand.

'What's that?' I asked working myself into the circle.

Muriel stepped back. 'It's Hannah's new au pair. She sent a photo.'

'I asked her to,' Hannah explained. 'Now I wish I hadn't.'

I slipped the photo from her grasp and held it up to the light. 'My *God*!'

'Yeah,' Hannah whimpered. 'Isn't she magnificent?'

I was about to lie to comfort her when Thomas said, 'She's a stunner all right.'

'Easy to see that if you're a man, isn't it?' I quipped, wondering how he could be so insensitive to Hannah's feelings. 'What happened to the five sisters? Did they teach you nothing?'

The girl in the photo had the kind of gleaming white-blonde hair that was rare in Ireland and caused gasps of envy. It disappeared past her shoulders. The photo had been taken on a beach somewhere. She was standing with her back to the sea in denim shorts and a halterneck top, tanned and lithe-figured, and with a face that would stop a bus around this town, wide-set eyes, high cheekbones and a mouth that made Angelina Jolie's look like a shrivelled prune.

Thomas was right, she was a stunner. And I felt very sorry for Hannah, standing beside me. She was an exhausted mother of two hyperactive little children, who was convinced that pregnancy and childbirth had destroyed her body for good, with a husband who showed no interest in her.

'You know what, Hannah? I bet she's got no arse whatsoever,' I consoled her. 'You just can't tell from the photo.'

'What's going on here?' a male voice asked over my shoulder and I looked behind me to see Hank standing there dressed in a pristine white officer's uniform, his wild hair tamed to befit a man of regiment, his face freshly shaven, and his mesmerizing slate-grey eyes looking right at me.

I realized that I'd been waiting for him and I reacted immediately to his presence, the more because I knew that I shouldn't. The breath caught in my throat. I began to blush awkwardly from the tips of my toes right the way up. The butterflies that had been in my stomach all evening took to stampeding and my powers of speech deserted me.

Muriel looked to see if I was going to answer the question, quickly ascertained that I wasn't – or, rather, couldn't – so she then smiled at Hank and answered in my place.

'We're just looking at a photo of Hannah's new au pair who gets here on Friday and saying how good-looking she is.' Muriel was probably the only person alive who could say this without the slightest shred of envy in her voice.

Hank bent down to examine the photo I was still holding. His fingers deliberately covered mine as he took it. They felt warm and strong. 'Nah,' he said, 'you couldn't get much better than the company here tonight.' He was looking straight at me again, and making no attempt to hide the fact that this comment was meant for me. I blushed even more.

Hannah and Carmen gawked at him, while Susan gave him an appreciative look for bolstering my self-confidence, and Thomas let rip with a highly amused whoopee.

Suddenly another male voice came booming down the corridor that separated us from the main lobby. 'Rosie Flynn? I came early to see if I could nab you for that drink before the party got started.'

Everyone turned around. Titch Murphy was striding towards us wearing nothing but a motley leopardskin loincloth and a pair of beach sandals. He seemed oblivious to the way the material stretched tight across his middle, creating bulges of skin around his waist and stomach that wobbled as he made his way over.

Carmen exploded with laughter and the mere sight of his near-naked pale body was enough to make Hannah momentarily forget about the au pair. 'I think Tarzan is for you,' she told me.

'Titch, I'm very busy at the moment,' I said flatly when he reached me. 'You'll have to wait. People are going to start arriving soon.'

'Are you supposed to be Fred Flintstone?' Muriel asked innocently.

'I am Tarzan,' he told her. 'Lord of the jungle.'

Eilish showed up just as I'd finished greeting people at the desk and was handing over the cash I'd collected to Christie. We had a full house and I'd sent Muriel and Thomas inside to join everyone else and start having fun.

'Hi,' I said, delighted that she'd come. She was wearing a white paper all-in-one, zipped up the middle, hood up, her small face peering out, and white Wellington boots. She looked like the fifth Teletubby.

'Hi,' she said, glancing around her anxiously. 'Jimmy's not here, is he?'

I shook my head.

'He left the house an hour ago and I just wondered whether he'd put in an appearance here.'

'What are you supposed to be?' I quizzed her.

'A forensic pathologist.'

'OK.'

'Is Charlie Dimmock here?' she then asked of Thomas, her face immediately softening.

'Yes. He's inside with a very handsome naval officer trying to prove that gardeners can hold their drink.'

'Isn't he something else?' she sighed.

'He's the man for you.' I didn't know how I knew this. I just did. Much the same way I knew that Jimmy Bible would never be the man for her.

'I've something to tell you,' she giggled unexpectedly. 'One of the technicians at the hospital said he heard in the pub that Richie is going to the UK for penile-enlargement surgery and liposuction around his middle.'

The liposuction bit was new. Someone must've added it on for the sake of embellishment. 'Yeah, I heard.' I reckoned the whole town had heard by now which is exactly what I intended. He'd have to put up with an awful lot of crotch-gazing over the next few days.

I'd managed to put some emotional distance between Richie and myself, I realized. I could now think about him without wanting to burst into tears. 'Let's go in.'

Most of the tables were full and the waiters had just begun to serve the starters, a fanfare of three different kinds of melon. Eilish and I walked over to the far side of the room and stood beside one of the tall windows.

'I hope this goes OK. I'm too nervous to eat,' I

told her while I checked the waiters' progress around the room.

'And I'm too upset with all this Jimmy business,' she claimed.

I bit my tongue because she didn't look that upset. She had colour in her cheeks and her eyes were twinkling. Eilish, I decided, was probably one of those people who'd mourned the end of her relationship long before it had actually come to an end.

'Let's have a drink instead,' she suggested.

She had a bottle of Ritz, a lovely refreshing drink guaranteed to rip your stomach lining out if you had too many. I had a triple vodka and Sprite. I might kill off a few hundred thousand of my brain cells but at least my stomach lining would remain intact.

Every so often Christie would poke his head around the door to check that all was well then retreat again reassured with a bigger grin on his face than the last time he'd checked. For him the party couldn't be going any better than this. The room was full to capacity and there was a constant stream of people to the bar.

Some guests had already begun doing frog-in-a-blender-style dancing between the tables as they waited for the main meal to be served. Near us a Marilyn Monroe lookalike and Dustin the Turkey were doing a raunchy tango. Marilyn worked in a factory on the industrial estate on the Cork Road and Dustin was a geography teacher in one of the local secondary schools.

Two more guests were engaged in an amorous tussle behind the curtains and the party had only just begun.

Christie poked his head around the door again and beamed some more. 'The same again for these lovely ladies,' he shouted over the din to the bar staff, circling Eilish and myself with a rod-like finger.

'I don't know if I should.'

'Enjoy yourself, Rosie,' Eilish ordered me. 'You've done your bit now and very well if I may say so.' She clinked the neck of her bottle against my glass. 'Well done you.'

Just then, Myra arrived in a cancan-girl outfit made from reams of sumptuous satin and flounces of lace. She struck a pose at the door.

'What's she waiting for?' Eilish wondered out loud.

'For someone to go fetch her,' I laughed. 'I'll do it.'

Lots of people shook hands with me and slapped me on the back as I made my way across the room. It felt every bit as good as I'd hoped.

'It was like watching the Shroud of Turin cross the room,' Myra commented. 'Such reverence, Rosie.'

'Do you want to come have a drink at the bar with Eilish and me, Myra?'

She was looking over my shoulder. 'Who is that cutie-pie over there?' she asked, pointing to Hank.

'Susan's friend. Come on.' I caught her beneath the elbow and guided her to the bar.

'Is Johnny Power here?'

'No, I told you on Friday, he's not coming.'

'Well, I say he is. I had my cards done this morning and there's a cultured older gentleman coming my way. Eilish, sweetheart, don't you look just lovely in your Babygro? Reminds me of when I used to bounce you on my knee.'

Eilish put her straight immediately. 'I'm a forensic pathologist.'

Myra lifted her skirt up to her knee and from behind a fancy garter belt retrieved a folded £20 note. 'Let me buy you two girls a drink.'

'I'll have a Ritz and Rosie is drinking triple vodkas but she'd better just have a single measure because she hasn't noticed that Titch Murphy is heading this way so her senses must be fairly impaired already.'

I quickly turned my head and saw that Eilish was right. Titch 'Tarzan' Murphy was purposefully swaggering this way. Why couldn't he just get lost? He was ruining a wonderful night.

'Are you on for that drink now, Rosie?'

The memory of being caught red-handed pulling up Ellen Van Damme's roses and replacing them with nettle plants was the only thing that prompted me to acquiescence. 'One drink.'

He got himself a pint of Guinness, and another vodka for me, and set about regaling me with talk of how he was going to set up his own contracting company soon and put everyone else out of business.

I'd been deluded about things myself, things like

Richie's faithfulness and the longevity of our marriage, but Titch Murphy was even more deluded. Just when I thought there'd be no escape, Rory lined up 'Come On Eileen'. Within seconds the tables were empty and the dancefloor inundated with Dexy's Midnight Runners wannabes, hands clasped behind their backs.

It was the perfect excuse. 'Thanks for the drink, Titch. I must dance to this song.'

I headed straight for the biggest and noisiest circle on the floor. Hannah, Carmen, Muriel, Susan, Hank, Thomas, Eilish and Myra Barry. My arms swayed above my head and my hips gyrated. With about eight vodkas swilling around inside me I was momentarily transformed into an irresistible goddess of desire.

Within a second I was in the middle of the circle with everyone dancing around me, then I was hoisted on to Hank's shoulders, his handsome face sandwiched between my legs as he laughed loudly. I could feel his skin rubbing against my inside thigh, feel the heat radiating from him, and every nerve end in my body tingled. This was madness, I thought, whatever the reason for it.

The song came to an end and with one smooth movement Hank crouched low to let me off. 'Do you think you and I might talk before the night is out?' he asked me as I slithered down his back.

'Eh, yeah, sure we can.' What exactly did he want to talk to me about? Had he noticed how strangely I began to act when he was around?

Carmen was the first one to make her way back to the table and she picked up a white envelope that someone had left on her seat and waved it at me on the dancefloor, a mildly curious expression on her face.

I shrugged and shook my head indicating that I didn't know what was inside either. I walked over to the nearest table, picked up another of the envelopes and opened it.

Carmen opened hers at the same time and our eyes locked. There was the sound of envelopes being ripped open all around me. I stood motionless, my hand clamped over my mouth, willing myself a thousand miles away to escape the acute embarrassment.

Photos of me that Richie had taken on holiday in Turkey two years ago spilt on to the tables. Only they weren't the usual kind of holiday snaps, frolicking in the waves, sipping cocktails at sunset, sunburnt noses and fuzzy hairdos. These were holiday pictures that were never going to make it into the photo album or be shown to the grandchildren. I should've burnt them.

We'd taken shelter from the blistering sun in our hotel room and Richie had persuaded me to pose for a few naughty shots – readers' wives sort of thing – but for his eyes only, he swore blindly, and just to try out the new camera.

Enlarged copies were now being passed around the room.

19

I glanced at one of them as it was handed across the table next to me. I was standing under the shower, wearing only minuscule bikini bottoms, my thumbs hooked around the sides, trying to follow the instructions that Richie was giving me from a few feet away.

I wanted the ground to open up and swallow me whole. I would make him pay. Public disembowelment was too good for him.

Titch Murphy was the first one to say something to me. 'Love the art work, Rosie. Never knew it was your thing.'

As he said this I could feel a self-preservation instinct kick in. Richie had tried to ruin my evening and discredit me but I wouldn't let him. He wouldn't get to claim this as a victory. I decided to brazen it out.

'That one's my favourite.' I boldly pointed to a photo of me lying on crumpled sheets, back arched, looking impossibly wanton or maybe drugged. We'd had to get them developed in London, where we'd stayed overnight on the way back, because to hand them in to a local shop would've been asking for trouble.

'I like that one too,' Titch agreed.

On the far side of the room, Myra Barry had swiftly taken charge. I saw her do a whirlwind round of all the tables, a blur of righteousness, demanding the return of every photo.

She got to where I was now sitting and gathered up the photos on the table. 'And you,' she said to Titch, 'take that photo out from beneath your loincloth.'

Christie tapped me on the shoulder. 'Here's the culprit,' he told me in a thunderous voice. Beside him stood one of the waiters, ashen-faced.

'I swear I didn't know what was in the envelopes,' he began to argue. 'Some fella out back slipped me £20 to put an envelope out on every chair. He said it was just promotion leaflets for a new sandwich-delivery business.'

Christie rolled his eyes in exasperation. 'Do you believe him, Rosie? I'll leave it up to you. All you've got to say is one word and he's out the door.'

I really hoped Christie wasn't using this as a test of my managerial ruthlessness because I was going to fail. I just couldn't doubt his quivering sincerity and I knew how persuasive Richie could be. 'Yeah, I believe him, Christie.'

Christie shoved him away. 'Off with you and stay well out of my sight for the rest of the night,' he warned. He waited an instant for him to disappear and then said to me, 'I'm sorry about that, Rosie. He should've known better. Can't get good staff anywhere these days.'

I looked around the room. Myra had collected all the photos and everyone had gone back to partying. I shrugged. 'No one else seems to care, so why should I?' I was determined that Richie wouldn't have his hour of glory.

'Good girl.'

I went outside for a cigarette just as the waiters began to bring the food to the tables. The meal was being served a little later than I'd initially planned but no one seemed to notice or even unroll the parchment menus I'd insisted on being tied together with satin ribbon.

Braving the cold in my doctored nurse's uniform, I slipped around the side of the building and huddled into a small doorway. The cigarette packet fell from between my numb fingers. I was about to bend down to retrieve it but another hand got there before mine. I recognized the white cuff of his naval uniform and drew a sharp breath. He must've followed me out here.

The air smelt of the spicy aftershave he wore, accentuated by the coolness of the night. He stood up again, towering over me, and I felt the same immediate attraction as always. My mind wrestled with what I knew as it had done many times before.

This man standing before me, tall, handsome,

broad, and still a mystery to me, was a transsexual, someone who used to be a woman, like me, and yet probably not at all like me, and he affected me in a way I would never have thought possible. His eyes flickered deep and dangerous thoughts into mine of bodies entwined and wayward hands.

I timidly took the cigarette packet he held out and momentarily our fingertips touched, which made him smile.

The moon threw shadows on us and they danced across his face, gypsies of the night casting their spell. We hadn't spoken a word but it felt like I'd just had the conversation of a lifetime. I must've been going mad. The chaos of the last few weeks had finally caught up with me. I turned from him and ran away.

Once inside I headed for the disabled toilet. I needed to be on my own to think. I barely noticed Muriel in the lobby trying to tickle Antonio's face with her Bunny tail. Susan bustled through the oversized toilet door with me. 'Let me come in too,' she urged.

'OK.' What else could I say?

With the door firmly bolted I sank to the cool tiled floor and Susan pulled the toilet seat down and sat there, stretching out her long legs in front of her. 'Great pics,' she said, straightening her witch's cloak. 'Richie's doing?'

'Yeah. It must've cost him a fortune to have all those photos copied,' I figured. 'Eh, how are things going with yourself and Hank?' I asked her gingerly.

I was really hoping there was nothing going on between the two of them to complicate things further.

'You know, Rosie, second base may as well be an island in the South Pacific because as far as Hank is concerned I am *never* going to get there.' She started stoically but by the end I could tell how upset she was.

'Things aren't going all that well in the romantic sense. In fact, they're not going at all,' she revealed. 'At the beginning I thought it was great because he wanted to talk about me the whole time, which was lovely, to have someone so interested – especially when it's taken so much for me to be really me.'

'I see what you mean.' Thank God they weren't involved. It was selfish of me to think that, I knew.

'But he rarely wants to talk about himself. I know nothing about him and I can't even get him to hold my hand.' She looked at her hands to check that there was nothing visibly wrong with them: they weren't overly big, given her original gender, and they were beautifully manicured, nails squared and painted. 'And when I tried to sit on his knee earlier I might as well have been Freddy Kruger. He nearly jumped out of his skin.'

I'd noticed that when I'd been secretly observing them at the time, and I'd thought it looked as if Hank's chair had somehow pressed against a loose wire and an electric shock had seized his entire body. 'I'm sorry.'

'Not your fault.'

I wasn't entirely sure about that. I thought that it probably was my fault in part and I felt dreadful, guilty. I gave her a hug, which was to help me as much as it was to comfort her. She spent a few minutes with her head lowered on to my shoulder and then we both went back to the party.

I craned my neck and scanned the crowd, trying to sneak a glimpse of Hank. He surely hadn't left? I began to panic. I couldn't see him anywhere. As I glanced back towards the main door again I spotted Johnny Power arriving. He was wearing a navy-blue suit that I'd never seen on him before with a white shirt and sombre tie. His tie-pin was positioned too high and needed a woman's touch to slide it slightly lower.

He'd obviously made a special effort to look deb-onair. But he was alone and he didn't look like a man about to announce to the world that he was getting married.

I rushed over to him. 'What happened? Where is she? Did she say no?' What had I started when I'd encouraged him to do this?

'I didn't get that far, Rosie. She was flootered from the word go.'

'I'm sorry.'

'Don't be. I've been fooling myself all these years. The alcohol had well and truly loosened her tongue and she let me know in no uncertain terms that she'd been about to put an end to our courting but didn't bother when I decided to go to sea. She thought she'd just let it die a natural death.'

How many years' worth of illusions had Mrs Burke managed to shatter? 'I'm so, so sorry,' I repeated.

'But you were right,' he told me. 'I had to find out. The person I remember would never have spoken to me the way she did tonight,' he mused sadly. 'Hard to reconcile the two.'

Myra Barry appeared out of the crowd. 'You did come,' she happily exclaimed. 'Rosie, you naughty girl, why did you say he wouldn't? I knew all along you would. The cards are never wrong.'

Johnny stared at her, stuck for words, overawed by her obvious enthusiasm.

'Now,' she said, clutching his reluctant hand, 'we are going to dance and I won't take no for an answer.' She pulled him towards the dancefloor, sashaying her frilled shoulders. 'Do you like my costume, Johnny boy?' I heard her ask him as they slipped into the sea of moving bodies.

Thomas emerged just as they disappeared and made his way towards me. 'It's nearly time,' he told me, reminding me of our plans. 'I've been keeping myself busy by dancing so I wouldn't get too nervous.' He continued shuffling to the rhythm of the music.

'Or too sweaty,' I said dryly, noting the beads of perspiration rolling down his face.

'Where is Eilish anyway? I haven't seen her for ages. You said you'd make sure she wouldn't go anywhere.'

I had said that but babysitting Eilish had dropped down my list of things to do, like sorting out why I felt the way I did about Hank and what to do about it, which had taken precedent. 'I'm not quite sure,' I admitted.

He stopped jigging about, suddenly serious. 'What do you mean, you're not sure? She hasn't gone home has she? Because you said . . .'

'I know what I said. Stay here and I'll find her.' I felt like the human axle on which everyone else's lives revolved and I didn't mean that in any flattering way to myself.

'Have you seen Eilish?' I asked Hannah as she stumbled out of the door to the ladies' loos.

Unsurprisingly Hannah had been drinking solidly all evening and she fixed me with a glassy-eyed stare. The front of her elf costume was wet as if she'd missed her mouth with her glass. 'Who?'

'Eilish,' I said. 'You know, Eilish, your sister,' I prompted.

'Oh yeah,' she snapped her fingers, 'saw her about two minutes ago, said something about taking a look around the leisure club, something about getting fit now that she was single again?' She looked confused, unaware that Eilish had dumped Jimmy.

I moaned inwardly. Thomas wasn't going to be pleased that she considered herself to be single when he clearly thought that she should be his.

'She had a bottle of Ritz in each hand,' she added helpfully.

Please let me find her before she passes out, I prayed. Just a few more minutes of consciousness so Thomas can get on with what he had planned and then she can keel over.

I ran down the corridor but the sign on the leisure club door said it was closed. I rattled the handle to make sure but it still wouldn't open.

'Do you want me to get you the key?' an amused voice asked over my shoulder.

I jumped and my hand flew up to my chest. 'You!' It was Hank.

'You,' he said back to me with a lazy smile. 'I've been looking for you since you ran off.' His unruly hair, forced into orderliness at the beginning of the evening, was beginning to curl again at the nape of his neck. He leant back against the wall and undid the top button of his uniform. 'This is getting uncomfortable. Where've you been hiding yourself?'

'I've been around,' I answered, feeling giddy by now because of his intoxicating presence. I was just happy to be standing beside him, listening to his wisecracks.

He smoothly manoeuvred me against the wall, placed a hand on either side of my shoulders, hemming me in, and leant close. 'Rosie,' he whispered, bending down to me, 'I'd like to say what's on my mind.'

'What's that?' I muttered unsteadily.

'God, your old man was a fool to leave you.'

'Thank you.'

He looked deep into my eyes, delving into my soul. 'So don't you ever feel, because of what he did to you, that you're somehow lacking, because believe you me, you are definitely not lacking.'

I liked how he said that. I hadn't realized how much I really wanted someone to tell me this until he actually said it. How could he have known exactly the right thing to say?

'We're kind of new to each other, aren't we?'

I nodded faintly, not quite daring to believe what was happening.

'But there's something going on between us. I don't know what it is but I want to get it out in the open now.' And then he kissed me.

I'd realized what he was about to do and I did nothing to stop him. I couldn't. I didn't want to. But as the kiss deepened so too did the implications.

'I don't think I could cope with this,' I blurted, pushing him away from me. 'Sorry.' He'd know what I was talking about. I didn't need to explain.

He rubbed a thumb tenderly across my cheek and nodded, and then he changed subjects for me. 'If it's Eilish you're after, she's in the front lobby with Carmen and some guy dressed like a big bird.'

'That'd be Dustin the Turkey. A geography teacher in his spare time,' I tried to make the tone light as if nothing had just happened but I knew I sounded choked.

'Well, Dustin the Turkey was doing his utmost to talk them into a threesome,' Hank said, smiling down at me.

Without delaying any further I rushed off to find Eilish and persuaded her to come back into the party with me where Thomas was waiting for us. He'd taken off his wig and his Charlie Dimmock plastic bust and was wearing a plain white T-shirt over his denims, looking so nervous that he was beginning to make me feel nervous about this too.

He saw me come in with Eilish and nodded purposefully, making his way to the top of the room, where Rory handed him the microphone and stepped back. 'Clear the dancefloor,' Thomas ordered. 'Come on, people, off the dancefloor.'

Word had spread among the revellers that something was going to happen and everyone drifted off the dancefloor as instructed. I made sure Eilish stayed where she was, right in the middle, with a hand firmly on both shoulders. Her reactions were hampered by, I guessed, a dozen or so bottles of Ritz, and she wore a slightly dazed expression until Thomas boomed, 'Eilish Flynn . . .'

And then she jumped. It was only on hearing the sound of her own name echo around her that she realized she was standing on her own in the middle of the dancefloor with everyone looking at her expectantly.

'Eilish Flynn,' Thomas said again with just as much intent. He swallowed hard, the sound amplified by the microphone. 'Words alone cannot say how much *I love you*.' He practically shouted the last three words.

He was looking straight at her and from the undone expression on his face his sincerity could not be doubted. I'd advised him to be bold and he'd gone for it. It was quite a moment.

Eilish gasped, and everyone else did too. Thomas was seemingly forgiven right away for the fact that most people thought Eilish was still with Jimmy Bible and this would be considered as poaching.

'Of course,' Thomas admitted bashfully, 'this might not do the trick either but I'm going to give it a try.' This was greeted by rapturous applause and he didn't look so nervous any more.

A guitarist appeared from behind one of Rory's oversized loudspeakers and walked over to Thomas, who gave him the sign to begin strumming his guitar. Thomas then stood before Eilish and began to sing to her.

He sang with such unbridled emotion that no one noticed he couldn't actually sing very well. I only knew because of the bathroom recitals I had to endure every morning.

His eyes never left hers, not once, during the beautiful love song. Eilish started to cry halfway through and happily sobbed right up to the very end when he dropped down on one knee and took Eilish's hand in his as a current of anticipation zigzagged the big room.

'Eilish Flynn, would you make me the happiest man on this planet and marry me?'

Eilish smiled but didn't answer the question.

Panic suddenly seized me. What if she really didn't want to? What if she was about to say no? What if I'd overestimated the strength of her feelings for Thomas? What if I'd told him this would be a wonderful way for him to prove his feelings to her and it wasn't?

I'd thought a marriage proposal would be the perfect way to end this singles party. I'd only wanted glory and now I was going to pay for it, and Thomas was too. I felt immediately humbled.

A sense of unease began to ripple around the room. The silence was too long. She wasn't going to say yes. I didn't dare look at Thomas. Beside me Muriel whispered, 'He looks crushed.'

Of course he did.

Then suddenly Eilish flung herself at Thomas and screamed at the top of her voice, 'Yes!' Then she looked at me over his shoulder and mouthed, 'Gotcha!'

I clapped harder, shouted louder and jumped higher than anyone else in the room.

From across the room Hank's gaze found mine and I almost felt our hands touch from a distance. What was I going to do?

20

Everyone agreed that the party was a huge success and made me promise to organize another one again soon. I was overwhelmed by their enthusiasm and thrilled that it had turned out so well despite Richie's best efforts to cause trouble.

Eilish moved into the house with Thomas and myself the next day, as Jimmy refused to let her through the front door when he found out, after the whole town, that she was getting married and it wasn't to him. I think it came as a complete shock and for that I pitied him and understood his feelings.

As for me, nobody had cared to warn me what life would be like living with a newly engaged couple with all their *va va voom*. It was only a matter of hours after Eilish's arrival before my whole house was re-zoned for couple use.

From then on, I found myself coughing every time I entered a room in case I inadvertently stumbled across them mating, which was how I preferred to refer to it – any other terms, particularly the more romantic ones, only served to remind me of what I didn't have.

They seemed to be physically fused twenty-four

hours a day. They held hands watching the television. They rubbed feet underneath the kitchen table and made cooing noises. They linked arms as they moved from room to room and shared the middle of their double bed.

This togetherness brought my singleness back to me even more. I came home from work the day after she'd moved in to find her perched on the downstairs loo having a pee while Thomas sat on the floor opposite her, jokingly playing with her toes. They didn't hear me come in, as I'd forgotten to cough, so I sneaked back out again. I felt like a lodger in my own home.

From there I went straight to Susan's, only a few minutes' walk away from me, down the hill. At the end of the party on Monday night Hank had told her that he wouldn't be coming to Waterford again. I didn't know where that left me and I didn't know how much he'd told her. She remembered the serious tone of the conversation as he'd said his goodbyes but she couldn't remember much else. She referred to it as the rum void.

Up to now I hadn't told her about kissing Hank. I felt too awful because she'd liked him so much but more importantly I wouldn't be able to explain it. I wouldn't know how to answer her questions.

'Do you want to stay with me for a bit?' she offered when I told her why I'd fled my home.

'No, it's OK,' I said. 'Thanks anyway.'

'OK. Hey, do you want to see the picture of himself Harry sent me?'

Susan got regular e-mails from Harry, who seemed to preside over his computer at very strange hours – which she'd decided was the norm for most nineteen-year-olds with a computer in their bedroom. Susan had rapidly become an expert on nineteen-year-olds.

We'd downloaded the Pamela Anderson photos he'd sent, amid hysterical laughter, and composed what we thought to be a suitable accolade to her foxiness to send back to him. With hindsight our reply wasn't half hot enough, too soft.

The photo Susan brought up on the screen was a recent picture because he had on the baseball cap she'd bought for him when they met up. 'Isn't he so handsome?' she mused. 'He doesn't really look like me, does he?' She angled her face for me.

'Well, not really,' I agreed, looking back at the screen. 'But there is something familiar about him.' I couldn't put my finger on it. It wasn't anything as obvious as hair or eye colour. It was something more to do with expression.

'He asked me if he looked like his real mother,' she said.

'And does he?'

She shrugged. 'It was a long time ago. And I only met her the once. But it's difficult to say because she had the punk look and nothing was the colour it should've been, you know?' Susan laughed at the memory. 'I thought she looked like a rebel, a bit different, and I felt different, so that's probably what attracted me to her.'

I was very curious about her but Susan seemed detached. 'Would you like to meet her again? Surely Harry's been in contact with her as well?'

She nodded and simply said, 'He's waiting for a reply.'

We sat in a comfortable silence for a minute or two and then Susan spoke again, switching subjects. 'I still can't believe how well the party went. The hangover is only just disappearing,' she laughed. 'Though mine was probably nothing compared to Hannah's. Have you spoken to her?'

'Yes.' Susan had guessed correctly. Hannah was still suffering and feeling too ill to be anything but docile. 'She's trying to persuade Dennis to go to Paris with her for a weekend when the au pair gets here, to kick-start a new beginning for them.' Hannah had been very pleased with herself for having such a good idea.

'So she's still allowing her to come, then?' Susan looked sceptical, remembering how upset Hannah had been when she saw the girl's photo.

'Yeah,' I grinned, 'but she's going to get her a floor-length veil.'

'A burka?'

'Yeah, that's it.'

'The poor thing will suffocate.'

'That's probably the idea.'

My mobile phone rang in my bag and I reached in and answered it. It was Myra Barry. I was hoping it might be Hank, though I hadn't a clue what I would've said had that been the case.

'Just calling to see if you've decided what to wear on Friday?' she asked. 'Presentation is everything, you know.'

Only two days to go before I met Myra's friend in Dublin to talk about publishing the article I'd written. I hadn't thought about it for a few days, what with the Valentine's party, but I now felt a bubble of excitement.

'I'm going to buy something new,' I told her. 'I'll need a few good work outfits now that I'm moving up in the world. I'm going to be the new events manager at the Cosy Inn, Myra. Imagine that?'

Then I explained about Christie's offer of a job and how I'd accepted. Christie had been so pleased with the outcome of Solomania that he'd insisted there and then that I say yes. He thought I was just being modest when I'd truthfully admitted that I wouldn't really know what I was doing, and had brushed off my concerns. 'I'm sure you'll hit the ground running, Rosie,' he said.

When he told me the salary he was offering I nearly fainted. I wanted to explain that he didn't have to pay me that much – that I'd do it for less, that I wasn't worth that much – but stopped myself.

'That's all brilliant news, Rosie,' said Myra. 'Your

mother must be over the moon. She's been so worried about you these last few weeks. And somewhere out there your father is feeling very proud of his little girl. And you'll do well,' she predicted, 'because you're a people's person. Trust me. I know what I'm talking about.'

I really wanted to believe her. 'And,' she added coyly, 'did a certain somebody tell you that we're going out on a date?'

'No,' I replied, 'but I did hear a certain somebody whistle a tune for the first time yesterday.' Johnny Power had come by the office to ask Susan a question about the drivers' rota and while he was waiting for her to get off the phone he'd whistled contentedly, staring out the window and smiling to himself.

I'd spoken to him briefly and it seemed that Mrs Burke's comments had served to make him realize that he had a life to live and shouldn't be spending his time in the past.

'He's a decent man,' Myra sighed happily. 'I think he's ready for a bit of fun in his life.'

We finished our conversation with the promise that I'd call Myra as soon as I got back from Dublin to let her know how the meeting went and then I strolled into the terracotta-tiled kitchen where Susan was emptying a bag of pasta into a saucepan of boiling water.

'I guess you haven't eaten?' she asked and I shook my head.

'It's all change, isn't it?' she smiled, taking out the can opener and shaking it at a tin of tomatoes. 'You, me, everything.'

Susan had decided to leave Triple-A Taxis as well. She said that she couldn't stand the thought of staying on if I was gone. There'd be no one left to call Danny Furey an arse and it was time to try something new.

The Furey brothers had taken the news of this double defection well. They were making us both work a four-week notice period but other than that they didn't seem too unhappy to be losing two employees. I'd overheard Danny use the words 'easily replaced' to one of the drivers and naturally assumed he was talking about us. I later learnt that it had something to do with a fan belt.

Susan wasn't sure what she was going to do but she had managed to put some money aside so she was affording herself the time to think about it, looking forward to the break. She had a few DIY projects planned but that was it.

We worked together in the kitchen in a comfortable silence. She chopped and I stirred. She peppered and I salted. She drained and I served up. We'd done this before.

She lit the candles and I put on the soundtrack to *Stealing Beauty* and we both pretended that we were Liv Tyler. She uncorked and I poured, and we sat down together and raised our glasses.

'I kissed Hank,' I blurted out. Every time I looked at her I remembered and, at the risk of sounding overly Catholic and guilt-ridden, I wanted her absolution to make myself feel better.

She looked at me over the rim of her glass and very calmly said, 'I know.'

'You know?' I spluttered. He must've told her. 'But I thought you said you didn't remember anything of your conversation with Hank? The rum void and all that?'

'I don't. But I'm sure I would if he'd mentioned it.'

So he hadn't said anything. 'Then how did you find out?'

'Carmen dragged me behind the reception desk to get one of the guest sewing kits, useless things. She'd ripped her milkmaid costume dancing and wanted me to put a stitch in it. I saw you on the CCTV screen and nearly subjected poor Carmen to a painful lumbar puncture,' she added. 'Poor kiddo.'

I hadn't even thought of checking for CCTV. It had been the furthest thing from my mind. 'Sorry.' Sorry for kissing him. Sorry that you had to see. Sorry that it made you nearly draw liquid off Carmen's brain through her spinal cord. Sorry for being a lousy friend. 'Sorry.'

'I'm not mad. Not even upset. I've come too far for that.' How could she sound so unruffled? 'I'm just curious.'

'I think I wanted to,' I finally admitted with an

expression that said I thought this might be more than a little strange.

'Well, at least you're being honest. You could've just fobbed me off with the "I was too drunk to know what I was doing" excuse, so thank you.'

I muttered something about not deserving thanks when suddenly a feeling of dread washed over me. It felt like a bucket of ice-cold water had been emptied over my head.

'Don't tell me Carmen saw too?' I groaned. Everyone would know by now. I was surprised it hadn't already worked its way back to me.

'No. She had her back to the screen.'

What a relief!

Susan picked up her fork and began to wind a strip of tagliatelle around the end and paused thoughtfully. 'Hank's a handsome man, Rosie, and a nice one, too, despite the fact that he didn't fancy me. I just wanted him to. It wasn't his fault that he just had friendship in mind.'

'You're so good all the time,' I halfheartedly complained, saying nothing of what I was thinking. 'Why can't you throw the crockery around? Call me a selfish bitch? If I'd caught you kissing someone I fancied I'd be flying the flag of self-righteousness,' I told her.

'I know,' she laughed. 'Anyway, I've got a mobile phone number for him. Do you want it?'

I nearly nodded but then I stopped and thought about it and said, 'It's not something that'd work out.'

'But it does happen,' she pointed out and wound more tagliatelle around her fork. She seemed to want to say more but held herself back. I wondered what it was that she wasn't telling me.

'I know,' I sighed. 'But it's not for me.'

'A man's got to know his limitations, I suppose.'

'Aha, spoken like a true Clint Eastwood fan.' It was meant to sound humorous but came out tinged with sadness.

I was standing in my underwear in one of the small changing rooms of my favourite shop in the town, waiting for the sales assistant to bring me some clothes to try on for tomorrow's meeting in Dublin, when I recognized a voice outside. Ellen Van Damme.

Thankful that she couldn't see me, I cautiously pressed my ear to the curtain and listened. She couldn't know that I was there and I was curious to hear how she handled herself in such an everyday situation.

'Has my suit arrived yet?' she asked pleasantly enough. 'I bought one last week in grey and then ordered it in black.'

What had she on today? Would it be the kind of classy outfit that Richie liked? I parted the curtain a fraction of an inch and peered out.

She was wearing a short, fitted leather jacket in a tan colour, zipped up the middle, with flat-fronted tweed trousers and loafers. I'd never seen her wear the same outfit twice, I realized.

Laura, the sales assistant, leafed through the orders book. Laura lived two doors down from me so I knew her quite well. 'You're in luck,' she smiled, too much of a professional to show her natural bias towards me. 'It arrived in yesterday. We would've called you today.'

'Lovely,' Ellen smiled back, her perfectly made-up face the picture of affability, and she began to unzip her jacket. 'I think I'll try it on. Just to make sure it fits. OK?'

Laura nodded. 'I'll bring it over to the dressing room.' I saw her loosely point to the cubicle next to mine, which was the only other dressing room in the shop, and I suddenly started.

What if she pulls back the wrong curtain? What if she finds me standing here in black popsocks, white knickers and a red bra because I'd gotten dressed in a hurry that morning?

Laura must've been thinking the same thing at the same time because I heard the frantic click-clack of her high heels as she perilously dashed across the shop floor and ushered Ellen into the right dressing room.

I waited until I heard the muted sound of her clothes fall to the floor before I peeked out again. Laura made frantic hand signals telling me to stay where I was, which I had every intention of doing as I would not challenge Ellen Van Damme to a duel in mismatched underwear.

After a short time, I heard her come out, thank

Laura and pay for the suit. Then she was gone. I burst through the curtains fully dressed again. It felt like I had been trapped in there for weeks. 'That woman,' I huffed, half hoping that the indignation in my voice would inspire Laura to tell me what a cow she was and reveal some mean trait of hers that I hadn't spotted.

'She's actually quite nice,' Laura said apologetically, leaning against the cash register, a newspaper folded in two in her hand.

That's what Muriel had said too. And it didn't get any easier to hear. Why did she have to be nice?

'Have you seen the cover of the *Waterford Chronicle*?' Laura asked, waving the paper.

'No.'

'Here take a look. Your party made the front page.' She was walking towards me.

Right in the middle of the front page was a large photo of Eilish and Thomas at the party on Monday night with a caption beneath that read 'Singled out to be happy ever after'. The accompanying text explained that the singles party at the Cosy Inn was a resounding success and the hotel owner, Christie Gallagher, put it all down to the outstanding work of his new events manager, Rosie Flynn.

'That's me, folks,' I grinned, feeling a surge of satisfaction.

'No mention of dodgy holiday snaps in there?' she laughed, pretending to scan the article.

There was no need to mention it because everyone

already knew. 'That's the last time I'll be talked into trying out a new camera,' I vowed.

'I suspect Jimmy Bible will have a thing or two to say when he sees this,' Laura added, turning grim-voiced.

I looked at the smiling face of Eilish, head tilted backwards in laughter, as Thomas held her in his arms. The paper had cut the photo just there and you couldn't see that her legs were actually wrapped around his waist.

'Yeah, I hope he doesn't cause any more trouble,' I said. He hadn't taken the news of Eilish and Thomas well, and I didn't think he'd appreciate this photo either.

Laura nodded in agreement and then she took me by the arm and steered me back towards the changing room. 'Let's get you kitted out for tomorrow's meeting.'

The train arrived at Heuston station and I followed the overhead signs to the taxi rank, giving the driver of the old Mercedes the address of the *ME!* magazine offices. I'd called Angela yesterday to check that she still wanted to see me because I couldn't quite believe that this was happening to me.

While we were on the phone there was a message from Hank: could I please call him; he had something important to talk to me about. And then he gave me the same mobile phone number that Susan had slipped into my bag two days ago.

But I didn't call him and I wasn't sure that I would. For the moment the part of me that was hesitant, afraid and confused controlled the part of me that simply wanted to hear his voice again.

The traffic in Dublin, a regular topic for heated discussion on radio shows, was horrendous. We edged along the banks of the Liffey being overtaken by pedestrians. I leant back against the seat and closed my eyes, and allowed myself to think about how good it could be to be with Hank, if I could find a way around what was holding me back, if I could just make what I presumed to be my small-town attitude disappear.

'Here we are,' the driver finally announced and I paid him, something I hadn't had to do for a taxi ride in a long time.

Angela Walsh's assistant came down to the office's light and airy reception area, with its sparse exotic-flower arrangements in slender tubular vases, to bring me upstairs to Angela's office. She was young, dressed head to foot in tight-fitting black, dark sunglasses holding back a mane of high-lighted hair, and walking towards me with the quick step of someone who worked for a very busy person.

'Hi, I'm Ursula,' she greeted me. 'Would you like to come this way?' She was already stepping backwards, towards the lift.

'Hi. Rosie.' I stretched out a hand and she looked

surprised to see it as if people didn't usually shake her hand. 'I'm sure you're busy. Thanks for coming down,' I added trying my best to be friendly.

'All part of the job,' she assured me and smiled, displaying a small gap between her two front teeth. Very Lauren Hutton, I thought, and very sexy.

'That's a nice coat,' she commented, giving me the once over as we waited for the lift. 'Is it a Max Mara?'

I quickly flipped back the side and looked for a label. 'Yeah, it is.' I was amazed. 'How did you know?' I'd borrowed the beige double-breasted coat from Laura to wear over a knee-length black leather skirt and sleeveless cashmere top that I'd bought yesterday in her shop and would be paying for in instalments. I'd also borrowed high-heeled shoes and a matching short-handled bag from Eilish.

'It's one of their classic designs,' Ursula explained, and by 'classic' I hoped she didn't mean 'ancient' because I knew Laura had had it for a while.

'I worked for the fashion editor before I worked for Angela and you get to know these things. There's the top-stitching around the collar and cuffs. Max Mara make great coats,' she told me.

'They do,' I agreed.

Angela Walsh was also dressed in black. She had a sleek grey bob and angular cheekbones. She was stick-insect thin and I was immediately intimidated. She rushed towards me with her coat in one hand, handbag and mobile phone clutched in the other.

'Gasping for a drink,' she greeted me. 'One of those days,' she then explained. 'So very nearly lunchtime why don't we just head straight out? Not worth getting pernickety about time, is it?'

I had no intention of contradicting her.

'Ursula? Ursula?' she called out. 'Going now . . . going . . . going . . . gone.' Ursula looked incredibly relieved as she waved us off.

Angela put her coat on as we stepped back into the lift I'd only just got out of. 'Comme des Garçons,' she said with utter reverence. 'A nightmare to get my hands on.'

I had no idea what she was talking about. 'Wow.'

'We're going to the Bailey,' she told me. 'You should try their bruschetta. I haven't had better since the Cantinetta Antinori in Firenze last year.'

'Firenze?'

'Florence. It's an amazing place, Rosie. Have you been?'

'Not yet.' But the new me, the one who was stepping outside the footsteps left by her old self, wanted to go to all these places. Florence, New York, Paris and Sydney were all on my list.

'Oh, do go,' she trilled. 'The shopping, the sights, the food, the wine . . .'

I glanced sideways at her and the rapturous look on her face amused me. For a split second she looked innocent and youthful.

We left the building through revolving glass doors.

I stepped out on to the crowded street ahead of her and looked back over my shoulder to see what was keeping Angela only to find her desperately pulling her cherished designer coat from the clutches of the revolving doors. She'd somehow managed to get the material caught and was busy instructing the receptionists to call the maintenance people immediately.

But she managed to work it loose and hugged it around her.

'I'd rather go naked than wear a different coat,' she told me and we both burst out laughing as the same picture sprang to mind: Angela Walsh striding down a busy Dublin street on her way to a fancy lunch wearing only a confident look on her face.

'Where's the Bailey, anyway?' I asked her.

'Near Brown Thomas. Just a quick stroll away.'

I asked her how she knew Myra and she told me that they'd met on a Chinese acupuncture course in Dublin, and immediately clicked, and after that they'd stayed in touch and met up when either of them was in the other one's part of the country.

They must've spoken over the last few days because Angela knew all about Myra's interest in Johnny Power, the success of the singles party, and my new job.

Once in the Bailey, we had to wait to be seated by one of the serving staff dressed in formal black-and-white uniforms. They showed us to our table and Angela ordered a bottle of Dom Perignon and a Caesar salad without even looking at the menu. Following her recommendation, I asked for the bruschetta and hoped the Dom Perignon was for sharing.

Champagne so early in the day felt decadent and luxurious, and I wondered whom to introduce to this pleasure. Everyone, I suddenly decided, with a champagne brunch that I'd host next Sunday. It would be a month since Richie had left me and so much had happened that I'd celebrate it all.

While we waited for the food to arrive we discussed the changes that Angela wanted made to the article. She asked me to make it more upbeat at the end, to show that I was emerging from it all a stronger, more independent person. And then she hinted that she might be interested in more articles, saying she liked my style and was eager to see how it would go down with her readers. I thanked her too many times, way more than was necessary.

While Angela went on to entertain me with stories of models and tantrums, photographers and their foibles and the fighting that went on every month over the colour of the front cover, I munched on my bruschetta.

I had to admit that it was exceptionally tasty for what amounted to tomatoes on crusty bread. I gazed around me in a kind of stupor of delight. Here I was, sipping champagne in this beautiful place, having lunch with the editor of a magazine I'd read all my life.

Suddenly I was stopped in my tracks and my sense

of merry abandonment vanished. I blinked hard, thinking that what I'd seen was just the result of my eyes playing callous tricks on me. I looked again. He was still there. Hank was there. No more than a few tables away.

He was sitting with his by now familiar profile to me, wearing an olive-green corduroy sports jacket with an open-necked shirt underneath, talking to a slightly older man opposite him, who in turn was listening intently and nodding, the white Panama perched on his head dipping up and down.

My heart began to pound. He still had the same effect on me. What was he doing here? And how was I going to explain to Angela Walsh my inevitable panic and hot flushes when he spotted me?

A lump of tomato stuck in my throat and I gulped back nearly a full glass of champagne in an attempt to dislodge it. My eyes began to sting and I could feel myself change colour.

Angela leant across the table, placed her hand on mine with real concern and shook it. 'Rosie, are you all right? You've gone a funny shade of red all of a sudden.'

'Something got caught in my throat,' I croaked. 'But I'm OK now.' I coughed and cleared my throat and then spoke normally. 'See?'

I wouldn't look his way again before we left, I decided, not once. That way I would make myself invisible to him.

'You're all right? Good, because I don't know any

of those fancy techniques – though the staff here are very capable.'

I busied myself with the food on my plate but this ploy barely lasted a minute before my eyes strayed involuntarily over Angela's shoulder to where Hank was sitting, laughing at something his companion had said.

It seemed highly amusing and I found myself smiling along. I liked the way he laughed. He seemed to throw himself wholeheartedly into it.

'Yes?' Angela chirped.

I zoomed in on her again. 'What?'

'Something made you smile?' she said expectantly.

'Life,' I lied and for the next thirty seconds or so Angela was the sole recipient of my attention as she began to explain how she planned to pitch the article within the magazine.

This was something I should've found really interesting and I'm sure I would have done if Hank hadn't been sitting a few tables away unwittingly vying for my attention.

He still hadn't spotted me, too intent on his conversation. A part of me longed for contact with him. But where could it lead? Where was there to go?

'You know, Rosie,' Angela hit the table with the rounded end of her knife handle to get my attention, 'I don't think you're listening to a word I'm saying. There seems to be something far more interesting going on over my left shoulder.'

Then she swung around, dipped her head, and peered out from under her symmetrical fringe. She scrutinized the tables around us with a hawk-like precision.

'That's the only table with any men at it,' she said actually pointing with her finger. 'That's the one,' she then decided.

She seemed to be waiting for me to say something in reply. I sought refuge in my glass and mumbled something, incoherent to both her and me.

'Do you know one of them?'

'No,' I insisted, desperately hoping that she wouldn't do anything to draw attention to us.

'I do.'

'*What?*' She knew Hank? How?

'Yes, that's Jasper O'Neill. He's the editor of the *Sunday Tribune*. He's always wearing that hat, silly man. It's his calling card, you know. Jasper and I go way back.'

'Do you know the other one as well?' I hardly dared ask her this question but I couldn't resist, too eager for any titbit of information about Hank that I might be able to glean from her.

She glanced over her shoulder and then looked back at me. 'Mmmm,' she nodded, 'the publishing world in Dublin is quite small, you know. He's a journalist, a very good one too. Won a big award last year for a report he did on child-labour camps in Myanmar or somewhere. Harrowing reading. But excellent nonetheless.'

She sounded very sure of herself.

'I don't think so,' I told her politely. 'He's a friend of a friend, an actor, and his name is Hank . . .' and then I realized that I didn't even know his last name, when I knew other such important things about him. It didn't seem right. It unsettled me even more.

'No, Rosie, I'm quite sure it's him and he's not an actor. What's his name again?' She tried to remember. 'Ursula met him at that award's ceremony last year . . .'

I raised my eyebrows and she obviously assumed I was incredulous that her lowly assistant would get to attend such a prestigious event.

'I know, I know,' she agreed in a slightly exasperated voice, 'but I get so many of these invitations and I can't attend them all. Sometimes I ask her to go in my place. She loves these things. But really, seen one, seen them all!'

But my dismay had nothing to do with Ursula. It had more to do with the fact that it seemed increasingly likely that Angela knew what she was talking about. But why would Hank lie?

'Anyway,' she carried on, 'Ursula and he got talking and they had a few dates but nothing more ever came of it. I remember it because Ursula was really quite upset.'

'I can imagine.' Had she too found out what I knew? That would explain it.

Angela seemed to think that I needed further convincing. 'Let's settle this for once and for all,' she declared and swung around. 'Jasper, Jasper,' she cooed waving her bony fingers at the table where Jasper O'Neill and Hank sat.

'Stop,' I whispered too late. The expression of horror on my face froze. What happened next was inevitable.

Jasper turned his head and as he spotted Angela a broad smile replaced the previously stern expression. He placed his napkin on the table and said something to Hank, who in turn glanced across the room and saw me.

It was obvious from the look on his face that he was shocked by my unexpected appearance there.

I grimaced apologetically, my heart still racing. I wasn't entirely sure what I was apologizing for. Maybe because I hadn't called him back. Or maybe because I felt I had to rule out a future for us because of his past.

Then he frowned and it hit me like a punch in the stomach.

In the meantime Jasper had crossed over to our table and he was exchanging pleasantries with Angela.

Hank was watching them both closely, too closely.

'Is that the journalist with you who won the award last year, Jasper?' Angela asked, glancing at me as she did so.

I held my breath.

'The one and only,' Jasper replied. 'Nick Baxter.'

2 1

NO! NO! NO! It couldn't be, I wanted to shout. What did this mean?

'He's working on something for me,' Jasper continued while I bit on my bottom lip to stop it from trembling. Had he lied about everything?

'Are you going to tell me what it is?' Angela probed him.

I felt my eyes sting and I refused to look at Hank. Nick. He'd lied about his name. He'd lied about what he did for a living. And instinctively I also knew he'd lied about his past.

'And ruin the surprise?' Jasper joked. 'Not even for you, my lovely.'

Suddenly I had an idea what it was that he was working on for Jasper. It was no coincidence that he'd contacted Susan. He was doing some kind of article that required insider information that only someone with Susan's past could provide. So he'd lied to her to get what he wanted.

I was outraged, incensed, both for her and for me. He'd used us, in different ways, and we were stupid enough to believe him, to let him in. When would I ever learn my lesson? My mouth tightened as my anger increased and the effect he still had on me served only to make me madder.

Suddenly, he said, 'Rosie?'

'Ah, the man himself,' Jasper boomed, turning around to face the mind-numbingly striking Nick Baxter. 'We were just talking about you.'

'I had a feeling you might be,' he said, looking at me, and I realized that the reason he looked so worried when he saw me there was that he guessed his cover was about to be blown.

Angela shrewdly noticed that he'd used my name. 'So you two *do* know each other?'

'No,' I said flatly. 'I don't know him at all.' I picked up my glass from the table but it was empty. I reached for the bottle. Empty, too.

'Sorry,' Angela mouthed.

'Lying bastard,' I hissed under my breath. It couldn't have had more of an immediate result if I'd climbed on to the table and shouted it through a megaphone.

Angela stood up from the table and caught Jasper by the arm. 'Jasper has just offered to buy me a large G and T at the bar and it's an offer I can't refuse. So we'll leave you two to it for a while, and then, Rosie, we should head back to the office and discuss things further.'

Nick waited until they were out of earshot. 'Ah, fuck it, Rosie,' he exclaimed, raking a hand through his thick hair. 'There's an explanation. Don't take it like this,' he said as his grey eyes tried to reach an understanding with mine, captivating me as before.

Damn him to hell for having such an effect on me. 'And just how would you like me to take it?' I fumed, determined not to let this give him the upper hand. 'And how would you like Susan to take it?' I added.

'I'm a journalist, Rosie. I used an ad to reach Susan, and a few others, too, and then I told her the truth. She knew the truth from the start.'

'You didn't,' I argued. 'She would've told me. She thought you were an actor and a transsexual. You used her.'

Nick was shaking his head and standing very close to me. 'You need to check your facts, Rosie.'

'You lied to Susan,' I repeated, 'and now you're going to take the things she told you in confidence and use them for some big article you're writing for Jasper.'

'I never betray confidences . . .'

'Huh,' I interrupted him scathingly, 'in that case you wouldn't have a thing to write about.'

I'd clearly offended him. A dark shadow crossed his face. Richie's good looks had always been lost when he got angry, but Nick's were heightened and the steel-like expression on his face was threatening and thrilling.

He leant down and drew as close to me as possible, as if he wanted to eliminate any possible room for more misunderstandings. 'Rosie, I'm a professional with a work ethic that I'm proud of.'

I felt a frisson from his unexpected nearness. I knew he felt something too because he faltered before he continued.

'If you'd returned my calls, I could've explained everything, and you wouldn't have found out like this.'

Could Susan really have known right from the start? I wondered. Could I trust him to be telling me the truth, after all that had happened recently?

I decided to talk to Susan. 'Excuse me, please,' I said, sliding my mobile phone from my bag. I walked away, but not too far, and hurriedly called Susan, who confirmed exactly what he'd just told me, apologetically saying that she'd promised to keep it to herself. In any case, that night at the singles party he'd told her that he was planning on telling me everything.

I ran back to Nick. 'So you were going to tell me?' I knew I must've sounded ridiculously pleased because he broke into a huge grin.

'Yes.' He sat down and I did the same.

'Why?' I really wanted to hear his answer, especially now that there wasn't a single reason to deny liking him an awful lot.

'Because the situation for me had moved from professional to personal.' He placed his hands on my knees and moved closer. 'I told you before. There's something between the two of us. From the first time I saw you, that night in the wine bar, I haven't been able to get you out of my mind and I'd like to see where all this leads.'

The night he was talking about was the night Richie had first turned up with Ellen Van Damme, which showed that good did sometimes come of bad, as my mother was fond of saying.

Suddenly it all seemed simple. I wanted so much to touch him, to discover what he felt like. 'I'd like to see where it leads, too, Nick.' I liked the sound of that. 'What was with the name Hank, anyway? I mean, couldn't you have chosen a different one?'

He threw his head back and laughed and it almost felt intimate to catch a glimpse of the rough underside of his chin. 'I actually said "Frank" on the phone the first time I spoke to Susan. But she misheard so I just left it and then it became a standing joke between us and I got kind of attached to the name.'

'Just because I'm laughing doesn't mean you're forgiven,' I told him. 'There I was desperately trying to explain to myself how it was that I fancied an actor called Hank who used to be a schoolteacher called Patricia. You bastard!' I playfully threw my napkin at him and he caught it. 'And don't you look so smug. You knew I fancied you.'

'I suppose I did,' he admitted and we smiled madly at each other. 'But what are you doing here? Having lunch with Angela B. Walsh of all people.' He looked impressed. 'The doyenne of the women's magazine. Nobody has actually seen her *eat* in about ten years, you know.'

On the other side of the table the bowl of salad

she'd ordered was untouched. 'I think she takes her nutrition in liquid form.' I was looking at the empty champagne bottle. 'But in answer to your question, I wrote an article that she's interested in publishing.' It felt great to say this, especially to him.

'Really? That's brilliant,' he enthused. 'Can I read it?'

He was sure to find my efforts seriously lacking, compared to the kind of award-winning articles he wrote. 'Nope,' I decided and began to smooth a mountain of imaginary crumbs from my leather skirt.

'Go on,' he coaxed. 'I'm sure it'll be a revelation.'

I placed my chin in my hand and looked at him pointedly. 'No way.' I wondered whether he'd kiss me. 'Anyway, I think it was the subject matter that really caught her eye more than the quality of the writing,' I admitted truthfully. 'The "I've been traded in for an older model" aspect.' I tried to make it sound jokey.

'Rosie, one person is very rarely to blame when things go wrong. It's not your fault,' he said. 'You're great.'

'Well, you don't know me well enough yet to say that. But thank you.'

Nick lifted his hand and lightly stroked my hair reassuringly. 'Don't worry about that, OK?' Well, I would worry about it. I'd worry that the exact same thing would happen again and I'd still be none the wiser as to why.

He continued to stroke my hair. 'Now that you

don't have to worry about me having started out in life as Patricia the schoolteacher, what say we have dinner tonight?'

Damn. 'I can't.'

I really wanted to but Hannah was having a family get-together at her house to welcome the new au pair and I'd promised her faithfully that I'd make it back, and she was so emotional these days that I didn't want to upset her further.

The unfortunate au pair had to take the bus from Hungary to London where she'd change at Victoria station and take another bus to Waterford. It was the cheapest way and Hannah had decided that after such a gruelling journey she should have a proper Irish welcome, code language for a piss-up.

'Are you staying in to wash your hair or is there a real reason?' he asked, sounding slightly unsure of himself for the first time.

'There's a real reason,' I assured him so sincerely that the traces of doubt left his face.

'Another time?'

'Definitely.'

22

The train was late leaving Heuston station but I didn't care.

Instead of consulting my watch every two minutes I used the time to engage in a flirty text-messaging session with Nick, ensconced in some pub beneath the Howth Dart station with two friends, jokingly trying to convince me that he was doing research.

In the end we agreed that he'd drive down from Dublin on Thursday evening and we'd go out for dinner, and I had a plan for what would happen next. I'd invite him to stay over because it would be too late to drive all the way back to Dublin again and I'd get Thomas to let the air out of his tyres while we were out to dinner just to have a back-up plan. I spent the rest of the journey thinking about what would happen after that.

As the train was pulling into Waterford station I quickly called the taxi office and asked for a car to take me straight to Hannah's. I'd miss these freebies when I left the job, and I'd miss Susan's company on a daily basis, but that was all.

It took about fifteen minutes to get there. The front

door was open and I was about to let myself in when I heard someone shout out my name. I looked back over my shoulder.

Myra and Johnny were walking up the path to my mother's house next door. Johnny was looking amused about something Myra had whispered to him. He was also looking more relaxed than I'd ever seen him. They had had their first date last night and I reckoned it must have gone well.

'Just thought we'd pop by and say hello to your mam,' Myra explained as she reached the front door.

'She's in here.' I pointed to Hannah's. 'They're having a kind of welcome party for the new au pair.'

Myra looked mystified. 'But hasn't she only just got here after some horrendous six-month bus journey from Hungary?'

I nodded.

'Poor girl,' she said sympathetically.

'Come on in with me.' I knew they'd be a welcome addition to the party.

The narrow hallway was littered with wooden bricks, empty video cassettes, a plastic dumping truck, stacking cups and some kind of barricade made from stuffed Teletubbies. We carefully stepped over everything and followed the sound of laughter that filtered out from beneath the door at the end of the hallway.

There was a round of applause as we walked into

Hannah's cluttered kitchen-cum-living room and Katie ran up to us with three frilly rosettes with bear faces on them.

'You did my obstacle course. *Yaaaay!* You are now official obstacle-course bears. *Yaaay!*' Hannah couldn't have looked at her with more pride if she'd just finished rowing single-handedly around the world and at that instant I envied her.

Eilish was sitting on Thomas's knee on the well-worn leather sofa and they were both drinking from bottles of Budweiser. Carmen was lying across a pink Barbie beanbag, with some kind of enormous rose in her hair and a bottle of Budweiser clenched between her knees.

Rory and my mother, whiskey drinkers, were talking to Dennis, another whiskey drinker, and Muriel was sitting on a second sofa with her arm around a very young-looking girl with long blonde hair and tear-filled eyes. She looked much more vulnerable than in her photo, and younger too.

'The poor doll has been crying for half an hour,' Hannah told me, handing me a glass of white wine. Her own stood on the low table beside her. 'She phoned home and her mother got upset and that started her off. She was fine up to then. Not a bother. But she's an only child and I think she's worried that her mam will be lonely without her. She's a lovely woman. I spoke to her myself – you know, one mother to another – to try to reassure her that we'd take good care of Katja but she's only got a few words of English.'

I laughed at this turnaround in Hannah's attitude. 'Only a few days ago you were threatening not to let her into the house when she got here.'

Hannah laughed ruefully. 'I was being a bit silly. What with all these problems with Dennis I was just oversensitive about the arrival of an attractive young woman.'

It was rare these days to hear Hannah talk so logically, so calmly. Usually the mere mention of any of her problems would lead to some kind of emotional hullabaloo.

'I mean, yes, she is pretty,' she continued as we both looked over at the lost figure sitting on the couch. Unsurprisingly Muriel had managed to find something to say to make Katja smile.

'She's not much more than a child herself,' Hannah said. 'She's only just gone eighteen. I remember that age . . . though God knows I'd seen more than her.'

I looked at her in bewilderment and wondered what she was talking about. What had she seen at that age?

'But anyway enough of me! How did Dublin go?'

'Great. We went out for lunch to some posh place, drank champagne . . .'

Hannah gave an appropriately envious *ooh!*

' . . . and then back to the magazine's offices, full of gorgeous people and models traipsing in and out.

Would you believe that they're even going to pay me to publish the article? Not a lot. But I wasn't expecting to be paid at all.'

She handed me the bowl of peanuts. 'That's great, Rosie. Here, have some peanuts – you need to fatten yourself up. You need to be more like me,' she grinned, slapping her backside, the very same backside that usually caused her such grief.

I left Hannah stuffing peanuts into her mouth and went over to introduce myself to Katja, who was having trouble remembering everyone's names and the correct pronunciations so Muriel was slowly explaining some mind trick she used when she needed to remember things.

'Here's Rosie,' Muriel said. 'The one who organized the party I was telling you about.'

'Hello,' she greeted me shyly.

'Hello,' I said back.

Muriel cast an approving eye over me. 'Is that new?' I was still wearing the same leather skirt and sleeveless top as earlier and I nodded.

Then Katie appeared and insisted that Katja read her a story, so when they'd settled themselves on the floor I took Katja's place beside Muriel on the couch.

'I saw Hank.' I was still feeling giddy from our encounter. 'It's a bit of a long story but he prefers to be called Nick and he's more of a journalist than an actor.'

'And?' she probed, sensing there was more.

'You had no idea but I actually thought he was a woman,' I told her laughingly and she looked at me as if I'd gone mad. I was bursting to tell her the rest so I just continued without explaining. 'We're going out for dinner on Thursday,' I gushed and felt the grin on my face widen and widen.

'I sensed that he liked you,' she said, looking really pleased for me, and then suddenly nudged me. 'Hey, look at that.'

'What's come over those two?'

Hannah and Dennis were wrapped around each other. He was whispering something in her ear and she was giggling and blushing like a thirteen-year-old. Dennis thought he was being very clever holding a newspaper in his hand but we could clearly see him tickle Hannah beneath her shirt. I honestly couldn't remember the last time I'd seen them have fun together.

Eilish must've noticed what was going on at the same time because she threw a peanut at me and when she got my attention raised her eyebrows quizzically.

I shrugged. Everyone else was looking too, taking in this quietly playful scene, but no one dared say anything in case they stopped and never started again.

My mother and Myra walked over to Muriel and me. 'Just left the boys chatting,' Myra explained, looking affectionately towards Johnny who was talking to Rory.

'Rosie, I think that I have been working towards a

new stage in my life for some time,' Myra announced, as if she needed to explain something to me. 'I appreciate different things now and Johnny sings to my soul,' she continued, trying to demystify her sudden interest in him. 'It takes less time at our age to be able to say when something feels right, against all the odds.'

'I'm happy for you,' I said.

'It's early days yet but I have a good feeling about this.' And then she winked at me.

'Hannah tells us that your meeting went very well,' my mother said, folding her arms across her chest, hidden beneath a floral-patterned blouse. 'Which month will your bit be published in?'

My bit? 'April.'

'I'm so proud of you I could burst at the seams,' she declared and I was so touched by this that I felt the look I gave her could've melted an iceberg.

Thomas appeared then and he perched his lean frame on the arm of the sofa. 'What do you want?' I teased him.

'I've something to tell you,' he grinned and stood up again. 'Over here,' he nodded towards the corner of the room.

'Excuse me a minute,' I said to the others and followed him, intrigued.

He took a long slug from his bottle of beer. 'I was working in the emergency unit today and guess who came in?' Small burp.

'Richie?' I guessed.

'Wrong.'

I guessed again. 'Ellen?'

'Yep.' And then he stopped, to add to the suspense.

'And what happened?' I inevitably had to ask him.

'She was doing some planting in the garden because apparently someone stole her rosebushes. Can you imagine that? Who'd be bothered stealing some shrubs?'

I managed to control the guilty blush. My mother had planted the rosebushes, which she thought had come from Muriel's back garden, in her own. 'Just get on with it.'

'Very unfortunate, this, but she wasn't looking where she was going, stepped on the shovel and the handle flew up and hit her slap bang above the eye. A nasty gash.'

'Couldn't have happened to a nicer person,' I replied but lamely, unconvincingly, and maybe because it was expected of me.

'You don't sound as vicious as usual about her,' Thomas commented. 'Now, this next bit is between you and me,' he warned me. 'While I was attending to her I noticed something, something behind the ears?' he hinted.

I looked at him blankly. 'What, Thomas? *Horns? 666?*'

'No, the signs that she has had a very recent face-lift. I'd say in the last six months.'

'No!'

'Yep! Thought that might give you a bit of a kick.' He wore a satisfied grin on his face.

'Well, all credit to her,' I decided aloud. 'She certainly looks good on it.'

'She does. But, Rosie, this is your cue to start making all sorts of derogatory comments about her suing her surgeon.'

I shook my head and smiled. 'I'll pass this time.' I wondered if this sudden mellowing of attitudes toward Ellen Van Damme could be put down to the fact that there was a fantastic man out there who wanted me. That I was no longer unwanted. Yes, it probably could, I decided and smiled again.

Thomas took another slug of beer and swallowed. 'OK.' But he sounded puzzled. 'I just thought I'd tell you.'

'Thanks.'

Out of the corner of my eye I spotted Dennis tiptoeing out of the room, Katie lying across his shoulder, her eyes shut, the spiky lashes top and bottom fused, and her mouth softly hanging open. She was sound asleep.

I wanted to talk to Hannah. 'I'll catch you later,' I told Thomas. 'We may as well go home together, the three of us.'

'Hi.'

Hannah turned around. There was an industrial-size jar of Nescafé beside her on the kitchen counter and she'd just hit the switch on the kettle to make coffee for everyone, the equivalent of last orders in the pub.

Then came a loud crashing noise from the hallway as Dennis obviously failed Katie's obstacle course trying to get to the stairs. 'No bear rosette for him tonight,' she laughed.

Her usual reaction would've been one of annoyance. She would have rushed out the door, dragged Katie out of his arms, slated him with a long list of all the things he was incapable of doing right, and stormed off to put Katie to bed herself.

But all she said was, 'He'll just have to earn his rosette another way.'

'What's going on?' I was compelled to ask her. 'Tell me, Hannah, because the last time I spoke to you Dennis was either going to agree to go to Paris with you to sort things out or you were leaving him.'

'Well, we've swapped Paris for Kinsale. But that's OK – the food's very good in Kinsale. Gastronomic capital of Ireland.'

'There's more to it than that,' I prompted her.

'Rosie, for the first time in ages, I listened to myself . . . how I was talking . . . what I was saying. And it sounded like I was very seriously thinking about breaking up this family . . .'

I was nodding because that's what it had sounded like to everyone else, too.

' . . . and to be honest that frightened the hell out of me. I have Gerry and Katie to think about too.'

If anything could move Hannah to an act of selflessness it would be those two and I knew that.

'You know what I'd been doing? I'd been mouthing off to everyone else about all these problems I had, about the unbearable situation here at home, and only making halfhearted attempts at talking to the only person who could really help. By that I mean Dennis,' she needlessly pointed out.

'I know.'

'So you know what I did last night?'

All I knew was that it had worked. 'Eh, no.'

'I waited up for him. If he's working late I'm usually in bed knackered after a day with the kids by the time he gets home,' she explained, so that I'd know that waiting up for him was not something she usually did. 'And when he got in I poured him a double whiskey, and myself one too, sat him down and made him talk. Forced him into explaining why he'd locked himself into this cocoon where I couldn't get to him and told him how I honestly felt, which I managed to do without any of the hysteria that usually has him high-tailing it in the other direction . . . Because the stakes were so high this time around.'

'God, Hannah, you're making it sound easy but I know it must've been really hard.' I was full of admiration for her. I should've sat Richie down when I'd first sensed a change in us, which I calculated was just before he met Ellen Van Damme, and made him talk to me, instead of telling myself that it was just a new phase, less than I'd hoped for between us but no real cause for alarm. The outcome might still have been the same. I might still be on my own. But at least I'd understand things a bit better.

'Yes, it was hard. But I'm wiser today than I was yesterday. I'm not saying that everything has been fixed overnight but we're on the way and that's what counts. And we're feeling good again.' The kettle had long since boiled so she hit the switch again. 'I was completely blocking him out, Rosie, and I didn't even realize it. You know, a mother's bond with her kids is so close that it can exclude the need for anyone else . . . and it's a physical bond as well as an emotional one. It was fine while there was just Katie because there was always a snatched moment or two. But then Gerry came along and there was no time left for us whatsoever. Two kids isn't twice the work, it's three times as much.'

I'd half realized this already, because I'd seen the hours that Hannah put in.

'I just didn't get it that Dennis felt completely redundant at home. In work he's in control . . . people depend on him. But here he said it was as if he was a ghost passing through most of the time. Everything functioned without him and he wasn't needed for anything. And it's true. I do all the kids' stuff myself. Yeah, sure I don't need him to change nappies and purée carrots. But I need him for other stuff – the intangible things, Rosie. And now he knows.' She beamed at me.

By this time I was on the verge of tears.

'And there's something else,' she added, sounding kind of shy, which wasn't like her at all. 'I can't talk about it yet ... but it's something that has been on my mind for a long time and I haven't been coping very well with it. But Dennis already knew about that.'

Now I was intrigued. 'What?'

'I'll tell everyone soon.'

23

Susan and I worked the late shift Saturday and Sunday. We started at two a.m. and finished at ten a.m. and at the end of both shifts Susan went straight home to check if there were any e-mails from Harry, now her favourite pastime, and I went home to bed determined to stock up on my beauty sleep before my date with Nick on Thursday night.

Because of the Furey brothers' bad scheduling we changed shifts again on Monday, which meant that I finished one shift at ten a.m. and was due to start another at seven that evening.

I went home, slept for a few hours, got up at around four and went to the library an hour later to see Muriel. It was nearly empty.

'So do you think you can find them?' I'd asked her to look for any articles or reports by Nick. 'I'd like to be able to show an interest in his work.'

Muriel raised an eyebrow.

'Well, I would,' I insisted. 'So?'

'I'll have a look tomorrow, OK? You still have time.'

'That'd be great. I owe you one.'

'Add it to the list.'

'My mother insists that you come for supper tomorrow evening. It's a kind of thank you for the rosebushes.' I still hadn't told my mother the truth about the rosebushes 'I hope mushroom risotto is still your favourite?'

Muriel paled. 'Tell her not to. No, no, *beg* her not to.' She strapped a flat leather satchel to her back as she prepared to leave with me.

My mother was someone who got great pleasure from serving people their favourite dishes, and she kept track of who liked what. The last time Muriel had supper with us she'd had risotto as well but it came from a pack and tasted like stale socks. It had been so bad that Muriel still remembered it – and it was about six years ago, long before food manufacturers had perfected the art of the ready-made risotto.

I zipped up my parka. 'She said she's going to make it herself this time.'

Muriel turned to one of her staff. 'Tina? I'm heading off now. You'll lock up?'

Tina nodded and I momentarily wondered what she made of her boss, who was about a foot taller, three dress sizes smaller and twenty years younger than she was. Muriel had recently promoted Tina from assistant librarian to information officer.

I glanced at my watch. 'I've got one hour and forty-five minutes before I start work. I'm counting the minutes to March the fourteenth.' That was to be my last day at Triple-A Taxis.

Now that I knew I was going I found the discoloured walls of the office closing in on me daily and my patience with the callers who thought they could get one of the drivers to walk their dogs or do their weekly shop for them dwindling whereas I might've laughed about it before.

'I really fancy a drink,' I told her, looking to steel myself for the shift ahead of me.

Muriel shook her long legs one at a time. 'Fine by me but do you mind if we walk for a bit first? I haven't been outside all day.'

We walked through the near-deserted town centre, as everyone had already headed home, and it was Monday, too, which was always quiet. Then we headed down the Quay, making our way towards Richie's shop but not planning it that way at all.

It was a damp, foggy evening and outside the shop door I could just about see the figure of a man struggling to balance a cardboard box on his knee while leafing through some papers.

As we got closer I recognized him as one of the drivers from the courier service that Richie used to get stock down from Dublin, a friendly guy who always carried a wad of photos of his four children around with him and called his wife the Boss.

'Hi, Chaz,' I called out.

'Rosie! Long time no see. How's tricks?' he greeted me warmly.

I reckoned Chaz would've felt a bit more awkward

asking that question if he'd known about Richie and me. 'Great,' I told him.

'Glad you've come along. I've got an urgent delivery here for Richie that he absolutely wanted down here by close of shop today but it looks like I've just missed him. Can you help?'

The temptation was too much. If this really was an urgent delivery, Richie would be waiting for it, consulting his watch every five minutes. He liked things on time and carried out as per his instructions. He was probably in the poky storeroom out back and hadn't heard Chaz knocking.

'I don't have the keys with me, Chaz. Is the box heavy?'

'Not really. Just urgent stock.'

'But probably too heavy for you to take,' Muriel said pointedly.

'If it's too heavy I'll have you to help out,' I replied. 'After all, that's what friends are for.'

She sighed and shook her head and Chaz paid no attention to this slightly strange exchange.

'I'll take it and give it to Richie,' I assured him. 'I'm sure he's not gone far. Where do you want me to sign?' I put my name on the form and waved him off.

'What are you going to do with that now?' Muriel wanted to know.

'I'm going to take it to work with me. Richie will show up once he's called Dublin to find out where his stuff is and they tell him that it's been delivered and signed for by one Rosie Flynn. I can't wait to see the look on his face.'

'But won't you get that nice driver in trouble?'

'Richie will be only too glad to lay all the blame on me. Anyway, I still owe him one for the photographs, remember?' My initial desire to inflict a public disembowelment on him had faded but I still felt that I shouldn't let the incident pass.

'Yeah, I suppose so. Although it might be one of those things that's best laid to rest now.'

I thought I was ready to do this. 'Just one last thing,' I promised her.

We turned around and walked back up the town and headed to T. & H. Doolan's on George's Street. It was dark and comforting inside. I offered to buy the drinks. 'Gin and tonic for you?'

She nodded and took the box from me, hiding it under the low wooden table. I was back two minutes later with the drinks. 'Isn't there something about the way a pub smells that's wonderful?' I inhaled deeply. Life was rosy and pubs smelt great.

'The last time we were in here you said it stank,' she reminded me.

'That was just my frame of mind. It was right after Richie left.'

There was a comfortable silence before Muriel started talking again. 'I really want to do something different,' she told me.

I sipped my drink. 'What do you mean? Cut your hair? Learn a new language?'

'No, none of those things. It's coming up to my thirtieth birthday and I need to do something different, something that I'll only ever do once in my lifetime.' She looked ahead of her, staring unseeingly at the old yellowed map of Waterford city centre that hung on the opposite wall. Then she decided.

'I want to go down Route 66 in a Winnebago van,' she announced.

'Route 66 in a Winnebago?' I liked that idea. 'Sounds brilliant,' I told her, figuring we'd both probably forget all about it.

'Hey, there's Antonio,' I said as I saw him walk in and head for the bar.

Muriel toed the scuffed wooden planks under the table.

'Has he called you yet?' I knew he'd asked Carmen for her number after Muriel had let it be known at the singles party that she liked him.

She looked up. 'No.'

I was surprised. I thought he would've called straight away. He seemed really keen. 'Do you mind?'

'Yes,' she admitted, 'I do.'

'You call him then.'

'Rosie, I rubbed my Bunny tail in his face all night at your party . . .' and her voice trailed off.

'I don't understand.' What was taking him so long? She was gorgeous, funny, intelligent and everything else that men supposedly wanted of a woman, too.

'Me neither. Maybe he thought the chase was going to be more exciting than the kill?'

I was outraged on her behalf. 'Not in your case it wouldn't.'

'How would you know?' she asked, smirking now.

'I'm guessing. And besides,' I added slyly, 'remember that time we went camping to Cornwall and you brought that French guy back to the tent? Well, I lied. I didn't have my earphones on.'

'Is this place getting smaller all the time or is it just my imagination?' I asked Susan because since I'd last been there, which was barely nine hours ago, the walls of the office seemed to have moved in by about another foot.

'If you don't stop going on about that I'm going to bring in the measuring tape.' She was energetically working the foot lever to adjust the height of her chair but to no great effect.

'Must've been a midget on the last shift.' She sounded breathless. 'What's in the box?'

'Something for Richie. I'm expecting a visit.' I tucked the box behind the coat stand.

Susan immediately guessed that he wouldn't be popping by to exchange pleasantries. 'I can't wait,' she said.

The phones rang almost immediately. Susan was

still pumping the chair. 'Can you get that?' she puffed.

'Yeah. Triple-A Taxis.'

'You tell him from me that he's a dead man.' The words were slurred together and were it not for the fact that, as a result of my job, I was very experienced at deciphering this kind of drunken talk over the phone I wouldn't have understood what he was trying to say to me.

'Jimmy?' Why did he have to phone me? What did I have to do with Eilish dumping him? Apart from it being my idea. 'Jimmy is that you?'

'S'nis.'

'Booze won't help, Jimmy.' I tried to be helpful but I just veered towards the patronizing end of the scale. 'It never does, does it?'

'I know you never liked me, Rosie, but you never 'tended you did . . . Not like that sis'er of yours . . . used to 'tend she loved me all the time before *he* came along. Fuckin' big girl's blouse . . . a nurse.' He stopped here for an instant and it sounded like he was slugging from a bottle.

'What kin' a job is that for a man?' he carried on. 'And a BIFFO to boot.' BIFFO stood for Big Ignorant Fucker From Offaly and was in frequent use around the country. It was not a compliment.

At least the BIFFO had got a job, which was more than Jimmy had with his sporadic wins. 'I'm going to hang up now, Jimmy,' I warned him. 'We're very busy here tonight.'

'Yeah, bet Monday night is really the busiest of the week,' he said sarcastically. 'You tell that wiry-haired gobshite that he's dead meat and Jimmy Bible is a man of his word.'

Jimmy Bible a man of his word? There's a first time for everything, I thought. 'I'll be sure to pass on the message.'

'Who was that?' Susan asked when I put the phone down, an inquisitive look on her face.

'Just Jimmy Bible threatening Thomas.'

I must've said something that triggered a recollection because she went on to say, 'I saw Carmen yesterday going into Wino's with that guy from the party. Remember Dustin the Turkey?'

'The geography teacher. She's kept that fairly quiet.' It didn't surprise me because I knew she'd think of a geography teacher as a boring recipient of her affections after a flamenco dancer.

Suddenly the door to the office flew open and Richie barged in. 'I won't be responsible for my actions if you've gotten rid of my box of merchandise.'

He was still wearing the expensive leather jacket I'd given him for Christmas, which I really begrudged him now, and for the first time my heart didn't leap when I saw him.

Susan decided to annoy him a bit more by letting him think that she thought it was her he was addressing so rudely. 'Please do not speak to me in that tone, Richie.'

Richie stared at Susan. 'Where's your hair gone?' he asked bitingly.

I'd grown used to Susan's messy crop and now that she'd dyed it back to its usual red colour I think I even liked it.

She stood up from her chair and casually peered down at the top of Richie's head to where a tiny patch of hairless scalp shone. 'Where's yours?'

I waited with bated breath. What would he say? I used to tease him about going bald and he'd just laugh and say he was working on developing a solar panel for a sex machine. But these were different times.

Richie's face darkened to a telling reddish-purple. That's the problem with having very fair skin: every emotion has its own particular shade. He couldn't hide his indignation at being derided.

First I'd nicked his urgent delivery from under his nose and now Susan was making an assault on his manhood.

'When's the last time you looked in the mirror?' he asked her back.

'At least when I do, no cracks appear,' she replied acidly.

She's really gunning for him tonight, I thought. It was hard to imagine that all the time I was with him she'd actually pretended to like him for my sake. Well, she was making up for lost time.

Richie stepped back from her so she could no longer look down on the offending patch of pink skin.

'You really did climb out of the bucket didn't you, Susan?'

Susan laughed mockingly. 'Is that really all you can find to say, Richie?'

'Actually, it's not, Flipper.'

Susan's large feet were his first target. He licked his lips in anticipation as his eyes searched Susan's person for fodder for his insults. I knew he'd be as cutting as possible and I decided to intervene.

'Let it go, Richie.'

I saw from the stubborn look on his face that he didn't want to be perceived as being weak, as being influenced by something I said, and I suddenly realized then that he had never wanted to admit to any short-comings – in fact, he'd hidden most of them.

But he didn't fool everyone and certainly not my family, who weren't blinkered by any kind of love for him as I'd been for years.

It was only now that I began to see things clearly. He'd disguised possessiveness as closeness and used honesty as an excuse to be as rude as he wanted.

His natural tendency to show off was cleverly hidden behind the label of exuberance and the unending interest he had in all things to do with himself, something I'd always thought of as a by-product of being an only child, wasn't that at all; it was just selfishness. And then I realized what a favour he'd done me when he left.

Without another word I took his box of supplies

from behind the coat stand where I'd hidden them and handed it to him.

'I'm glad you came to your senses,' he said taking the box from my hands.

'I have come to my senses, Richie,' I told him. 'I really have.'

I walked around the block to steady myself and when I got back to the office I found Susan leaning over someone sitting in my chair. I couldn't see who it was because her back was blocking my view.

But then I recognized the Nike trainers that protruded from between her legs. I'd fallen over them at the bottom of the stairs often enough.

'Thomas?' I nudged Susan out of the way. '*Oh God! Oh no!*' Thomas's face was a mess. One eye was closed and the size of a tennis ball. A steady trickle of blood ran from his nose. His top lip was split and both cheeks were bruised and his knuckles were grazed, which meant that he must've managed to hit back at his attacker.

'This is all my fault.' I hadn't taken Jimmy Bible's threatening phone call seriously, hadn't even thought to warn Thomas.

He fixed me unsteadily. 'Don't panic, it looks a lot worse than it is. And I do know what I'm talking about – I'm a nurse . . . and a BIFFO, as your sister's ex-boyfriend so eloquently put it in between blows.'

He winced as Susan continued to clean around his split lip. 'Ouch.'

'Be brave,' she urged him, her voice full of concern.

'Where did it happen?' Had Jimmy called around to the house?

'He pulled me from the Mansion House pub. One of his friends must've let him know that I was there . . . don't know any of them . . . and didn't see it coming . . . I was on my own.' He sounded groggy.

Susan pulled a fresh tissue from her shoulder bag and doused it with mineral water. 'Thugs,' she declared.

Meanwhile the phones were ringing out non-stop and Thomas's face was swelling up even more before our very eyes. It now looked like an overripe tomato. His good eye watered. 'Is anyone going to answer those phones?'

'No,' we replied.

'We'd better call Eilish. Have her look you over.'

'No,' he insisted. 'I don't want to worry her. That's why I came here.'

'Fine,' I sighed. 'Worry me instead.'

Everyone found out about the fight. It would've been nearly impossible to keep it a secret in a town this size. But Jimmy didn't help to keep it contained. He was telling everyone of the 'manly way' – and that's a quote – in which he'd dealt with the 'BIFFO' – and that's another quote – who'd robbed his girl. Dennis heard about it from one of his site workers first thing the next morning, even before the birds started to sing.

In Jimmy's version Thomas had been down on his knees begging for mercy and hadn't got a single blow near Jimmy, which I knew wasn't true because I'd seen the state of Thomas's knuckles.

Dennis called Hannah, who immediately rushed in next door to my mother's to tell her, and she called Eilish to find out who the hell Jimmy Bible thought he was. This domino-like unravelling of Thomas's version of events was very unfortunate, because up to that point he'd been stoically sticking to his story that he'd fallen down the stairs and he'd even persuaded me to say that I'd witnessed the monumental slip.

Eilish didn't really believe either of us but there was nothing she could do as there was no other explanation on offer – until my mother's phone call the next morning.

I was explaining all this to Muriel as my mother scooped generous helpings of mushroom risotto on to the china plates in front of us. Before Muriel had arrived I'd quickly scoured the bin for any empty foolproof risotto sachets and found none, which meant it was homemade as promised.

I tentatively nibbled a fat grain of rice. 'Mmm, this is delicious.'

My mother was indignant. 'Don't sound so surprised.'

Muriel took a mouthful. 'Oh, Mrs Ryan, this is just the best risotto I've ever tasted.'

'Oh, Mrs Ryan, this is just the best risotto I've ever tasted,' I mimicked, including the wide-eyed sincerity, and she poked a pink tongue out at me.

My mother smiled endearingly. 'You'd swear you two were still thirteen.' She sounded delighted by the mere thought of it. 'Anyway, Eilish is giving Jimmy a real run for his money,' she continued the story, tittering to herself. 'Do you know what she's gone and done?'

Two forkfuls of risotto came to a halt in mid-air. 'What?'

'This is so clever.'

It turned out that Eilish had decided to teach Jimmy a lesson by herself. So she took some extra-strength laxative powder from the hospital – those in the know call it dynamite – and went to her old house during her lunch break. She let herself in, went straight to the fridge and mixed the powder into the two-litre carton of fresh milk there. Jimmy drank at least that much in a day. Horse-betting was apparently a thirst-inducing activity.

'The world is about to fall out of Jimmy Bible's bottom,' my mother concluded, quite happily.

Carmen had walked into the kitchen halfway through the story and was listening intently, leaning back against the counter. 'Someone better warn the bookie's,' she laughed.

402

She was dressed up, wearing a smart black trouser suit, a hint of bra showing beneath the jacket. It made a nice change from her usual flamenco-inspired mode of dress. 'Where are you off to like that?' I asked her.

'I'm going out to dinner with Pat.' She didn't sound as excited as her appearance suggested.

'Who?'

'Pat,' she repeated, just as flatly as the first time. 'Oh, you know, Dustin the Turkey . . . the geography teacher,' she explained, tagging on an apologetic grimace. 'We're driving to a restaurant in Wexford.'

Carmen was probably making him drive forty miles so that no one would spot them together, I realized, and Muriel must've come to the same conclusion because she immediately said, 'But he's lovely, Carmen. He's often in the library and a very nice guy. His students love him.'

'Yeah . . . Well, you know,' she muttered.

I watched her study her nails. 'Why did you agree to go if that's all the enthusiasm you can muster?'

'Because, Rosie, no one else has asked. And he's not that bad, I suppose.' She turned to Muriel. 'Has Antonio called you?'

I would've invented a story involving the mysterious theft of my mobile phone and a freak localized storm that had knocked out the telephone lines in the street where I lived, but Muriel replied truthfully. 'No.' She shrugged, looking momentarily very vulnerable and disappointed.

'That's his *modus operandi* all right,' Carmen told us. 'He never calls. I suppose I should be flattered that he never tried it on me.' Maybe she should've been flattered but she certainly didn't sound it.

'Pat is lovely,' I tried to persuade her. 'A decent, dependable kind of guy.' I didn't really know him but this didn't make me any less sincere.

'Well, it certainly beats grappling with one of your best friends' fellas down a dark corridor,' Carmen said then, somewhat smugly.

My mother had gone cross-eyed, she was staring at me so hard. She didn't understand what Carmen meant.

I was blushing furiously so it was too late to attempt to deny it. 'How the hell did you find out about that?' Susan said Carmen had her back to the CCTV screen.

'Someone tried to break the lock into the leisure club that night so Christie and I were reviewing the CCTV tapes and we came across it. Though not literally, of course,' she cunningly added, pulling a face. 'That'd be far too foul to even contemplate . . .'

'Yeah, yeah, I get the picture. And he wasn't exactly Susan's fella.'

'Are you going to see him again?'

'As it so happens, I am. Thursday night. He's taking me out to dinner.' This made the 'grappling down a dark corridor' all right and my mother looked appeased but full of questions.

'You should go,' I told Carmen. 'You're going to be late.'

'He's the kind who would wait.' She sounded comically grief-stricken.

I smiled. 'There's nothing wrong with being the waiting kind.'

She was walking out the door when she swung back again, holding a finger to her forehead. 'I nearly forgot. Pat is organizing a fund-raising event for a school they subsidize in Somalia.' She waved her hand distractedly to indicate that she didn't have a clue where Somalia was. 'And I've volunteered you two to help out. I was sure you wouldn't mind. It'll be a bit of fun.'

Beneath the heavy kohl her eyes twinkled mischievously and it should've been a warning but I ignored it. 'When?'

'Sunday afternoon in the school hall.'

We'd all gone to the same school and the mere mention of the old hall with its waxed floors brought back fond memories of amateur musicals, student fashion shows, lessons in self-defence given by the nuns, and the boundless adolescent enthusiasm we had for life. I was filled with a sentimental longing for those easy days.

'That's good timing. Sunday's my day off and I'm doing a champagne brunch for everyone at my place,' I said by way of invitation. 'We can all go together after that.'

It was actually going to be a cava brunch since I'd calculated how many bottles of champagne I'd need and how much it would cost. 'Bring Pat, by all means.'

'I might just do that.'

Muriel stopped her just as she was about to leave again. 'Carmen, what exactly will we have to do at this charity event? Sell raffle tickets or something?'

'Oh no, nothing that banal for you two. I've got something really special lined up,' she assured us. 'You'll have to wait and see.'

24

I went straight to work shortly after armed with a sachet of two Alka Seltzers tucked into my top pocket.

The mushroom risotto had been followed by the compulsory second helping and after that a wedge of homemade devil's food cake, which was Muriel's favourite pudding when she was about twelve. My mother had put so much thought and effort into this 'all-time favourites' menu that neither Muriel nor myself could bring ourselves to refuse any of it.

For the first time in a long time I was glad I had to go to work. She'd made hazelnut truffles the size of footballs to have with freshly brewed coffee and when I saw them I'd immediately called for a taxi to take me to the office.

It was Johnny Power who came to pick me up. I could barely speak, I'd eaten so much. There was just no room for words to squeeze out past everything else.

'To the office?'

I nodded and swallowed a burp.

'Rosie, I need your help again.' He was looking at me through the rear-view mirror. 'I want to buy Myra a little present. You know, just something.'

I took a deep breath, placed a hand firmly on my stomach and managed to say, 'Turquoise.'

'What?'

Another deep breath. 'It's a semi-precious stone. Myra's favourite.'

'Like that ring she wears?'

I nodded.

'Great idea. Thanks.'

I was very curious about something, curious enough to overcome the congestion in my gut. 'What's happening these days with Mrs Burke?' Had he abandoned her to her misery? Because that's what she seemed to want.

'I still call round, to make sure she's OK,' he replied. 'I've been trying to bring up the subject of going to one of those AA groups but she just laughs. Myra sees her too,' he told me. 'And who knows? Maybe between the two of us we'll get somewhere. But I've a suspicion that'll only happen if Lilian decides it should herself.'

'Fingers crossed.'

'Yeah,' he agreed.

We chatted the rest of the way, about Myra, mostly, and how she made Johnny laugh again, and his sisters loved her, of course. I felt a whole lot better by the time we reached the taxi office, until I saw who was standing outside the front door, glancing at her watch. Ellen Van Damme.

Johnny kindly offered to drive around the town

until she got fed up waiting and left again but I decided to get out and talk to her. He stopped the car outside the butcher's shop and I climbed out.

I walked up to her, surprised not to feel in the slightest bit intimidated and not to feel like a cast-off either. The gash above her eyebrow from her gardening accident was still quite noticeable. I felt a stab of guilt.

'Sorry to disturb you at the office.'

'It's OK,' I assured her. 'It's not as if you're inter-rupting rocket scientists at work.' I noticed the vertical blinds on the window sway slightly, and between two of the plastic slats an eye appeared then a flash of red hair.

Ellen Van Damme's appearance was as immaculate as ever, right down to the pointed tips of her black patent high-heeled shoes. Beneath her oyster-coloured wool coat she was wearing the black trouser suit she'd bought in Laura's clothes shop last Thursday when I'd been there. 'You must think I'm really awful to have done what I did.' She shook her head slowly, sounding genuinely contrite.

Yeah, I did, but less and less so. Richie was mostly to blame. He was the married one. Despite myself I admired her courage in coming here on her own to talk to me. Two of Eilish's nursing friends walked past and openly gaped at us.

'Rosie, I'm not going to beat around the bush. I've come to ask you to call some kind of truce. Believe me,' she continued suddenly sounding tired, 'we should all have better things to be doing.'

I guessed my constant interfering in their lives was causing some strain, which was what I'd originally intended.

Rory drove by at that moment in his white van and nearly slammed into the car in front of him when he saw us standing together on the footpath.

'I know it's an awful lot to ask,' she conceded.

Calling a truce wasn't the same thing as forgiving Richie, I decided. I didn't feel ready to forgive him yet, but I was ready to get on with life without him. I was even looking forward to it.

'OK,' I said.

The strained expression on her face lifted like a paper bag in a brisk wind and she did something that I wasn't expecting. She reached out to shake my hand. It was the first time there was any physical contact between us and with her hand in mine it felt like a bridge had been crossed, a bridge from the otherworldly, where I'd placed her, to the human.

'It sounds ridiculous to say this,' she smiled encouragingly, 'and I have so little right to, but I hope we can all move on for the better now.'

Rory had obviously done a quick U-turn further along John Street because he now drove up the other side of the road, his window fully rolled down and his face peering out anxiously at me.

'I have no excuse for what happened. I'm not going to lie and say that I didn't know Richie was married. He was honest . . .'

'To you but not to me,' I interrupted her. Maybe she would see this as a warning of how quickly, and unnoticeably, Richie's loyalties could change.

'Yes.' I was glad that she didn't apologize here because I would've found it demeaning. 'I know things have gone on recently,' she continued, 'and no one has had it easy.'

On that I disagreed. I thought that Richie had had it fairly easy. But I did realize that she probably hadn't. To be with Richie, she'd come to a town where she didn't know anyone and where I knew nearly everyone. She'd come knowing that she'd be the butt of people's toy-boy jokes and be cast as the wicked witch in this particular story. And she'd accepted all this. She must really love him. Just as I once did.

'There is one good thing to come of all this,' she said, very seriously.

'What's that?' I was intrigued. I'd found Nick but she couldn't know about that.

'No bunnies got boiled,' and her face creased into a wicked smile. 'Remember the film?'

I nodded. A sense of humour was the one thing I hadn't reckoned on and I found myself thinking that I could like this woman. 'I just couldn't find a pot big enough for all the bunnies I wanted to boil,' I told her and smiled back.

We contemplated each other in silence for a few seconds.

'I have to go in now,' I said.

Inside Susan was on the phone and she began gesturing madly when she saw me. 'What did she want?' she asked.

'To bury the hatchet.'

'In the side of her head,' she quipped. 'She's got some cheek.'

I unzipped my parka. 'She's probably right, Susan. It is time to move on.' I adjusted the height of the chair, lined up my pens, and rubbed the telephone handset with a scented wet-wipe.

There was an envelope on the desk with my name on it in Muriel's handwriting, which meant that she'd managed to find some articles by Nick as I'd asked her to. Bedtime reading, I thought.

'You're already moving on,' Susan assured me.

'Yeah, I guess I am. I've a new job and a date Thursday night.' That I was really looking forward to. 'Have you had any news from Harry today?'

'Yeah. He's had a reply from the second letter he sent to the address for his biological mother that the agency gave him, and I think he's quite excited, though he's trying to play it down.'

'Brilliant. I wonder what his adoptive parents make of all this?'

I answered the phone, sent a car out, and we took

up the conversation from exactly where we'd left off without missing a beat.

'He told me that they're really cool about it all. It was never a secret that he was adopted. They've three other kids and they're all adopted too. Two of them aren't interested in looking up their real parents and two of them are.' She looked me squarely in the eye and declared, 'This is one of the best things that has ever happened to me. I know we have some, ahem, issues to get around but I have enormous hope that everything will work out. I will make it work out.'

Sheer determination had gotten Susan where she was today – and I don't mean working for the Furey brothers. It had seen her through the kind of drastic changes that would've destroyed a lesser person. If she wanted to make this work, then I knew she would.

She started fiddling with the gold chain around her neck, sliding the small medal that hung on it from side to side. 'And here comes the really weird bit . . .'

For my part things were weird enough as they were.

' . . . the letter Harry got back from his mother was from Waterford, not Harrow.'

My elbow, resting on the edge of the desk, slipped right off. 'What? How could that be?'

'He called it a coincidence himself.'

'But you said . . .' I was determined to uncover the flaw in her story.

'When I said an address in Harrow I assumed that the girl and her family had moved from Dublin –

413

that's where she said she lived – to London, and now it seems she must've moved here at some stage. People don't stay put these days, do they?' she mused. 'I chose to come here, why not someone else?'

'Because not everyone moves somewhere because they're a big fan of the local crystal.'

'True. But there's also the beautiful coastline and the lively pub scene.'

'Susan, can you remember the girl's name?' I hardly dared ask her this question but I had to because I was suddenly beginning to realize what it was that was so familiar about Harry's face, that up to now I hadn't been able to put my finger on.

I didn't want to be right because of what it would mean. But I knew. Somehow I just knew that my instincts were not going to be wrong.

'It was Marsha.'

Marsha! This answer didn't make me feel any better. Before the Brady Bunch had become the Booby Bunch, we'd all adopted one of the girls' names for a laugh.

Hannah's had been Marsha.

The phone was ringing but I couldn't move. I looked down at my fingers and they were trembling. I clasped my hands between my knees to steady them.

I remembered Hannah and my mother standing huddled in the utility room in tears and Hannah stuffing the bright-orange envelope into her pocket, and I remembered the mysterious long stay with my aunt in London that I'd been so envious of at the time, and I remembered Hannah aged sixteen with dyed black hair, purple lipstick and a white powdered face, unrecognizable to the way she was today.

And the other night Hannah had said to me that she had something big to tell me but she wasn't ready yet.

Everything was slotting into place. '*Oh God.*'

This was more than just a coincidence as Harry had said. This was a collision of destinies.

'What's wrong? Do you know a Marsha living in Waterford?' Susan asked warily. It wasn't a common name. 'I don't think I'd recognize her.'

Up to now, you haven't, I felt like telling her. And she certainly hasn't recognized you.

I spent the rest of the night and all the next day grappling with what I'd found out and wondering just what to do about it. I had to do something. What? The answer still hadn't come to me by Thursday but at least my ongoing struggle with the question was peppered with the excitement of going out on a date with Nick that night.

It was my first proper date with anyone in years and I hoped that people still did pretty much the same thing as before: went out, drank far too much and stumbled home to bed, or the sofa if the stairs proved too tricky, with said drinking partner.

I'd read the articles Muriel had copied for me and

was more resolved than ever not to show Nick my journalistic efforts. My essay on the aftermath of Richie walking out seemed like a ditty compared to his exposé of child-labour camps in Myanmar.

I began counting the hours until I saw him again.

When I got home from work I listened to a message on the machine from Angela Walsh asking me to send her the changes to the article we'd discussed, which I couldn't do because I hadn't yet started them. Working in a taxi office meant the word deadline held no meaning for me whatsoever.

There was a second message, from Nick. I recognized his voice straight away and began to smile. By the end of the message I was no longer smiling. Something had come up. He couldn't make it. He'd call again.

With his way with words was this the best he could do? I fumed. I'd been dumped. I wasn't even properly his to dump and I'd been dumped anyway.

Common sense prevailed for an instant and I hit the erase button so that I wouldn't be able to replay the message and analyse the exact tone of his voice and then I sank into the sofa and resisted the urge to cry.

I heard the key turn in the lock and I knew that Eilish and Thomas were home from work armed with their ever-growing bundle of glossy wedding magazines.

Ever since last Friday, or, to pinpoint the exact moment, since seeing Nick last Friday, their togetherness hadn't bothered me so much. But now I suddenly found it hard to deal with again.

I quickly slid off the sofa, shoved my feet back into my work shoes that I'd discarded only minutes earlier, picked my parka up off the floor, grabbed my bag from the bottom step of the stairs and breezed out past them.

'Can't stop now. Out to dinner.'

'Isn't tonight your big date?' I heard Eilish shout after me, excited on my behalf.

Bits of broken terracotta were still scattered here and there on the garden path. It seemed like an eternity since I'd thrown the flowerpot at Richie and yet I could so clearly remember the look on his face as I barely missed.

It was a good thing to walk. I didn't know where I was going but by the time I'd pounded the footpaths for twenty minutes I was feeling better. Better enough to give Nick the benefit of the doubt. Maybe he would call me again. But it wasn't the end of the world if he didn't. I'd get over it.

Without realizing it I'd meandered towards Susan's. I decided that I'd ring the front doorbell and if she was in then I'd suggest going out for a few drinks and if she wasn't I'd walk a bit further, to Hannah's.

It wasn't as exciting as the evening I had originally planned, and it hardly called for the red Betty Jackson dress that Laura had lent me to wear, but in terms of entertainment it was light years ahead of sitting on the sofa at home, trying to block out the sound of Thomas and Eilish slurping at each other.

There was no answer at Susan's so I headed back up the steep Folly Hill towards Hannah's.

I hadn't got very far when Titch Murphy drove past, came to a screeching halt and leant out of the window of his Ford Escort to offer me a lift. I refused because I would've walked to Dublin barefoot, over a bed of crushed glass, rather than get in the car with him.

I spent the rest of the walk to Hannah's, a mile or so, trying to think of a good way to bring up the subject of Harry without her suspecting that I already knew something. In the end, the subject brought itself up.

Hannah sent me over to the unit beside the hob, where her cookery books were housed, because I was looking for a recipe for soda bread to have with smoked salmon on Sunday for brunch.

I edged the biggest one out from between two others and as I did so two orange envelopes flittered to the floor.

We were on our own in the kitchen. Dennis was still at work and Katja was upstairs with the children having a pig-in-a-slaughter-house squealing competition, judging by the noise that filtered down through the walls.

The envelopes seemed to fall in slow motion, with both of us watching them.

Now, I told myself, say something now.

But Hannah beat me to it. She wiped her wet hands on the front of her oversized Oxford shirt, bent down and picked them up. 'I'm going to tell you something, Rosie, and apart from Mam, and Dennis, of course, you're the first person I've told.'

I was actually nervous for her. I could feel my heart beating faster.

She took a deep breath. 'Remember that time when I went to stay with Auntie Jane in London . . .' and so she began.

By the time she'd finished both of us were crying. Katja had walked in with Gerry and Katie and went straight back out again, sensing we needed to be on our own.

'I've thought about him every day,' she confided. 'You have no idea how hard it was. I have a recent photo. Would you like to see?'

I nodded, still unable to tell her I'd already seen him. 'Is he going to come and visit?'

She took a deep breath. 'I'm going to go there first. I thought it might be easier for him if we met on his territory. But I do want him to meet you all when he feels up to it.'

She crossed over to her red tote bag, unzipped a small pocket on the inside and took out a photo. She held it to her lips before she passed it to me.

It was the same photo that Susan had. The one

with Harry wearing the baseball cap she'd bought for him, grinning at the camera.

'We've spoken. And the strangest thing ever is that he says his biological father is now living in Waterford. I mean, of all the places to show up. Can you believe that?' she said incredulously. 'Talk about coincidences. How come I've never run into him?'

It was definitely time to say something. 'Hannah, you have,' I told her and she stared blankly at me. 'Get Katja to bring Gerry and Katie in next door to Mam's to sleep over. This is going to be a long night.'

There was something in my tone of voice that made her do what I said straight away without asking any questions. She glanced over her shoulder at me with a worried expression as she quickly ushered them down the hall towards the front door.

Hannah's phone hung on the wall beside photos of the kids stuck on to a green-felt notice board with multicoloured drawing pins. I picked it up and called Susan on her mobile phone. She answered almost at once.

'Susan, I'm at Hannah's.'

'Yeah?' There was a lot of noise in the background. It sounded as if she was at the bottom of a rugby scrum, though it was more likely that she was in a pub.

There was only one way to say this. 'I've found Marsha.'

There was a long silence as she digested this. 'OK.'

'Oh God, Susan, I hope you're ready for all this because there's no way around it.'

Hannah's head appeared around the door. '*Messes and Muddles?*'

I just stared at her. '*What?*'

'Have you seen the Teletubbies *Messes and Muddles* video? Katie won't go without it.'

'No.' *Messes and Muddles*, I thought. How very apt.

Then Susan spoke in a clear voice. 'I'm ready, Rosie. This is who I am,' she told me very calmly. 'I'm on my way over there now. Don't move.'

25

Over the next two days I talked myself hoarse. We'd stayed at Hannah's until very late Thursday night discussing everything and then on Friday we told the rest of the family. They were, of course, shocked, but were more concerned about how Hannah and Susan were feeling than about the unbelievable news itself and when Hannah took out her photo of Harry they showered it with all sorts of compliments.

Then Susan and Hannah took the very brave decision to let the whole truth come out, no more lies and no more hiding, and by the next day most of the town knew about Susan's past and Hannah's baby, and about the twist of fate that linked them together. No one would be talking about Richie and me again for a while.

What had seemed to me to be an awful mess when I'd been the only one to know the full story, the keeper of secrets, suddenly became life as we knew it. Nothing more. Nothing less. Despite the potential for recrimination, regret, bitterness and anger, there was none.

That Sunday, the day of the brunch, was one of those beautiful winter days when everything outside looked three shades lighter than the day before due to the icy cold. The grass in the garden resembled a metallic carpet and the branches on the bare trees brittle crystal rods. The only exception was the three cranberry-tipped noses that sped up the garden path like miniature heat-seeking missiles: Rory, my mother and Carmen.

I watched through a slit in the front door and pulled it open only at the very last minute. 'Quick, quick, inside.' I shuffled them in to the warmth.

'I should've stayed in bed,' Carmen said unequivocally. 'It's like the Antarctic out there. They said it'd be unseasonably mild but it's Siberia. I'm practically Mediterranean,' she told us, 'and not made for these climes.'

We all threw our eyes up to the ceiling.

Rory unzipped his battered fighter-pilot bomber jacket, the arsenal of badges on the front clinking against one another, while my mother watched Carmen unbutton her coat.

'Carmen Flynn,' she sighed, exasperated. 'How many times do I have to warn you about going out with no clothes on?'

Carmen did have clothes on, light, skimpy ones, and she tried to flatten the goose-pimples on her bare forearms by patting them. 'You can't let temperature take precedence over fashion, Mother.'

'No, but I'd have thought you'd at least have let your health.'

Carmen muttered something in reply.

I immediately recognized the onset of a familiar scene.

My mother would declare that Carmen had absolutely no respect for herself because she didn't eat properly, didn't wear warm clothes, drank too much and stayed out too late, to which Carmen would respond by laughing hysterically and my mother would get even more upset.

I quickly intervened. 'Welcome, everyone.'

Eilish stuck her head around the kitchen door and said, 'This way for the bubbly.' Behind her Thomas waved two empty glasses invitingly and the others went towards him.

I stayed by the front door because I'd heard the distinctive chug of Myra's Beetle as it pulled up outside the house. Johnny and she scurried up the garden path towards the front door and he gallantly let Myra through first and stepped in after her.

'It's so invigorating out there,' Myra chimed with a full-body tremble.

Johnny smiled indulgently at her. 'Don't you just see the good in everything?'

I noticed a new turquoise fob that hung from a long silver chain around her neck. Johnny and Myra seemed good together and I vaguely wondered whether there'd be another happy couple to add to the list that already included Thomas and Eilish.

I'd caught them playing tiddlywinks naked in the

sitting room this morning when they thought I'd gone out to get the papers. It was like living on the set of *Carry On Frolicking* these days.

Muriel had arrived early to help me prepare the food because I couldn't be sure that my housemates wouldn't get sidetracked. We piled smoked salmon on to toast, because I'd never found the recipe for soda bread the other night at Hannah's, and we spooned creamy scrambled eggs and slices of bacon on to small plates. In addition to which there was enough chilled cava to float the *QEII*.

Hannah, Dennis, Katja and the kids had arrived in their military-style people-mover just before my mother, Rory and Carmen had.

The small house was bulging with people but there was still one more person to fit in: Susan, now part of the family. Because of the people involved and how well liked they were, everyone who knew was doing a brilliant job at pretending that this was undeniably the most ordinary of situations they'd ever encountered.

The Irish ability to unearth the humour in most situations certainly helped and in any case the scenario was so unbelievable that there was little room for any kind of awkwardness.

This point was perfectly illustrated by Rory when he'd asked Susan outright last night what they did with the bits they'd chopped off. He'd wondered if she still had them tucked away in a jar somewhere. Susan laughed so hard at the earnest question that I thought we'd have a medical emergency on our hands.

And from all this had sprung a common resolve not to lie to each other about anything again. I gave it thirty-six hours.

I itched to call Nick and tell him what was happening but I didn't because he hadn't yet called me.

Susan arrived about ten minutes after Myra and Johnny and was greeted with such enthusiasm that she couldn't be in any doubt that she was welcome here. I could tell that she was touched, and fighting back tears, by the way she kept on putting her hand to her throat.

As I looked round the house I realized I had never been prouder of my family.

I listened in on the different conversations around the room. Myra and Muriel were discussing how amazingly adaptable the human psyche was and how we all underestimated it. I sneaked past them.

Eilish and Carmen were on the topic of bridesmaids' dresses. I heard Eilish say 'emerald-green satin' and nearly choked. Carmen tactfully tried to suggest an oyster-coloured Vera Wang dress that she'd seen in a magazine and Eilish suggested that Carmen pay for her own dress.

Beside them Hannah was doing her best to explain to Katja that the nappy bag she'd brought along for Gerry actually needed to contain nappies and my mother was telling Susan how we didn't rule life, it ruled us, and Susan was trying to disagree.

Rory, Dennis and Thomas were standing in front of the flat-screen Sony television, a football match playing, the volume turned down.

I looked around the room. The old-fashioned bronze reading lamp in the corner was a wedding present. The oak-effect laminate flooring had been laid by Richie and myself one wet weekend. The cream walls, the cream sofa and armchair and the shaggy cream rug were all part of the mono colour scheme Richie had wanted for the room. The books on the shelves were chosen by both of us but there were now conspicuous gaps where Richie had taken his favourites.

I was tripping over memories. That's all I was doing here in this house.

I swallowed the last few drops of cava in my glass and beckoned for Eilish to follow me out of the room. We stood by the foot of the stairs and talked. We were back in the room again in less than five minutes, both smiling at the outcome of our discussion. I knew I was doing the right thing.

I tapped the side of my glass until I had everyone's attention. 'Given that we've all turned over a new leaf and decided to be honest with one another . . .'

Someone giggled.

' . . . I feel I should tell everyone that I've made a decision.'

They all cheered and clapped as if I'd just announced that I'd won the lottery and was dividing

427

it equally between everyone there. I glanced at Eilish who'd crossed the room to Thomas, who smiled and nodded at me to go ahead.

'I've decided to sell the house. Eilish and Thomas are set to become the proud new owners. They've already baptized every room so they may as well own it.'

There was the briefest of surprised silences, followed by more cheering and clapping. It seemed like everyone thought it was a good idea for me to move on.

'They're getting all the furniture too.' I didn't want any of it. Besides I'd be making a profit on the house so I thought it would be a nice gesture to them.

The house had gone up in value since we'd bought it and I'd offered to call in three estate agents for quotes and let Eilish and Thomas have it for the lowest one with everything included.

There was something thrilling about making a snap decision of this magnitude. I felt carefree all of a sudden. I didn't know where I was going to live but it didn't matter. I'd be able to find someplace nice thanks to the generous wages Christie would be paying me when I started my new job.

The charity event that Pat, the teacher Carmen was dating, was organizing to raise funds for the school in Somalia kicked off at two o'clock and we were there a little before that.

Carmen had asked Pat to come along to my brunch but he was busy setting up the school hall with some of the 'involved' parents who'd offered to help. I'd had to assure Carmen over and over again during the morning that this was not just an excuse; because as soon as he'd actually declined her invitation, she'd suddenly decided that she really did want him there after all.

Muriel put forward the theory that he was using reverse psychology on her and Carmen had crash-landed her glass on to the floor, a panic-stricken look on her face.

At the school hall someone had hauled all the gym benches into the black-and-white-tiled corridor outside and they were stacked on top of each other, a very good imitation of the Leaning Tower of Pisa.

The old padded gym mats were rolled high in another corner and a bunch of kids were bouncing on them, effortlessly ignoring their parents' orders to get down at once. Since Hannah had had Katie and Gerry I'd discovered that selective hearing was something pioneered by small children, not deliberately inattentive adults.

Carmen had refused to tell Muriel and me what she had lined up for us when she'd asked us to help out but as we walked into the big hall, the three of us side by side, we spotted two wooden booths.

They were conspicuously parked in front of the big

stage, a square window cut out of each one, and somehow I knew they were intended for us.

Carmen began to titter when she saw me looking at them, and Pat was walking over to us saying, 'It's really game of you to do this,' and looking appreciatively from Muriel to me. 'It'll be a bit of fun. You know, coming up with different ideas for these things is a bit of a challenge but then Carmen had this great idea. You'll be the star attraction here this afternoon,' he promised us. 'Two attractive girls like yourselves.'

What was he talking about? There was a pained expression on my face as I tried to remain cheery and my jaw began to ache from holding a smile I didn't feel. Muriel's arm pressed against mine, harder and harder.

A laughter tear escaped from the corner of Carmen's eye and she quickly wiped it away with the back of her hand. 'Look,' she said, pointing. 'The sign's going up.'

A hand-painted banner flapped as it was hoisted up to its position of prominence between the two booths. I read aloud. 'Kiss the girls! Only 50p!'

Now everyone would think I needed charity as an excuse to be kissed. How humiliating.

Muriel surreptitiously placed her heel on my toe and bore down with all her force. 'Surely the nuns won't allow this,' I ventured. 'This is a convent school after all.'

'It's cheek only,' Pat laughed.

'There's a queue starting already,' Carmen enthused and I stared hard at her.

Huddled in the area in front of the booths were four skinny teenagers, skittishly pulling on one another's sweatshirts and throwing mock punches. They weren't in line for one booth in particular and I guessed they didn't want to commit themselves before they saw who'd be ensconced therein. After all, it might've been the Reverend Mother.

Muriel spoke up. 'Look, Pat, I'm kind of worried about something . . .'

'Yeah, I know and I'm sorry,' Pat interrupted her. 'Fifty pence isn't a lot, but they're only schoolkids and I didn't really feel I could ask for more.'

I pointed towards the booths. 'And what about their fathers?' The two latest additions to the group, middle-aged males, couldn't by any stretch of the imagination pass for schoolkids except in the enthusiasm stakes.

Anyway, it wasn't the money she had a problem with. She was worried about being eaten alive.

The big hall was nearly full by now and up on the stage the school band had started playing. The noise was deafening. 'Show time,' Carmen said.

Pat bumped Muriel forward a few steps. 'Go get 'em.'

We stomped towards the two booths. Muriel was looking straight ahead, poker-faced. 'How dead is

Carmen?' she asked through gritted teeth, displaying none of her usual temperance.

'So dead she's already a fossil.'

She nodded. The answer satisfied her. 'That school in Somalia had better produce an Einstein or two.'

We forked and went into our separate MDF booths. On the floor beneath the window was a plastic bucket for money. I waited a few minutes but no one came.

Where the hell was everyone? Surely even those teenagers could afford a measly 50p? Their trainers had probably cost £90. I leant forward and looked out.

Everyone was queuing outside Muriel's booth.

There wasn't even an overexcited, sex-starved father of ten to be found shuffling his way up to my window. I withdrew my head and dropped to the floor to hide.

Suddenly there were three short knocks and the entire wooden frame shook. I shot up.

'Yes?' I was so relieved that someone had come that I couldn't help but sound overtly grateful.

Nick was standing there, hands stuffed into the pockets of his khaki trousers, trying hard not to look amused, and looking better than he'd ever looked before to me. My heart did a somersault.

'It's very considerate of you to hide yourself away to make sure that Muriel gets some customers,' he said, his broad shoulders shaking with laughter.

'It's very considerate of you to let me think you might think that,' I shot back, 'and even though you are an exceptionally good liar, the smirk on your face is giving you away.'

He yanked a battered leather wallet from his trousers. 'Do you think if I put this,' he waved a crisp £20 note at me, 'into your bucket that you'd be relieved of your duties for the afternoon?'

That was the equivalent of forty kisses, I calculated – and, ironically, I would've paid him for the pleasure.

I nodded. 'And maybe a little explanation as to what exactly came up on Thursday night that prevented you from taking me out to dinner?' I prompted, trying to pout but too thrilled to see him to feign authentic displeasure. My hormones were doing back-flips.

'Something did come up,' he assured me with twinkling eyes. 'An American editor wanted to have dinner to discuss a new project he'd like me to work on. It's a big opportunity for me and he could only make that night, so . . .' he shrugged helplessly. 'But I'm here now to make it up to you.'

I found myself blushing uncontrollably as I imagined all the ways I could get him to make it up to me.

'I phoned your house on the way down,' he then said, explaining how he'd tracked me down, 'and spoke to your sister, Eilish, is it?'

I nodded.

'Yeah,' he went on, 'and she said you'd just left and

433

told me where to find you.' He looked around the hall, grinning. 'Is this what people do in this part of the world on Sunday afternoons?'

Compared to his Sunday afternoons skiving around Dublin this must seem very parochial.

'It's for a very good cause,' I claimed defensively. 'Usually I go skydiving or potholing.'

He laughed, the familiar volcanic rumble. 'I'm going to put my money in the bucket now and then you're going to come out of that hut and say a proper hello to me.'

I felt myself go giddy.

The note floated in wide arcs into the bucket and when it landed I dashed around the side of the booth.

'Come here,' he said and lifted me up off my feet.

I squirmed with pleasure as all five feet two inches of me locked against his solid frame. 'Is that some kind of a twitch?' he teased before he brought his face down, placed his lips on mine and kissed me. Neither of us was prepared for how quickly the kiss would escalate from dreamy sensuality to a harder, more erotic level.

We snapped apart, breathless, and decided to leave immediately.

As per small-town dictum it was impossible to cross from one side of the hall to the other one without stopping to talk to someone.

First was Christie with his wife, both there because their youngest daughter, Sienna – named after her place of conception long before it became tasteless to do so – was one of Pat's geography students. I hadn't spoken to Christie since the day after the party, when he'd called me up about his job offer, and I'd said yes, and we'd decided on a start date and ended on a promise to do the paperwork nearer the date.

'Rosie, the very person I wanted to talk to,' Christie greeted me, stepping out in front of me so that I had to stop. 'My new events manager, eh?' he chuckled, smoothing his thick grey hair.

I wasn't too concerned that the idea of me being his events manager made him laugh because he wouldn't have given me the job if he didn't think I was up to it.

'When is your first day again?' he asked.

'March the twentieth,' I told him. That's what we had decided.

'That's what I thought. We're going to have to rethink . . .'

'But, Christie,' I interrupted him, 'I've already handed in my notice at the office.' And I wasn't staying on at Triple-A Taxis one minute longer than necessary.

'Good, good,' he mumbled distractedly. 'The thing is that we've managed to free up some funds and we've decided to close for renovation work for the months of April and May. It makes sense to do it then before the busy season kicks in.'

'Oh.' I felt deflated. Did this mean that he was going back on his offer of a job? Nick squeezed my hand reassuringly.

Christie's wife prodded him sharply and his face puckered up in pain. 'But this being said, Rosie, given the inconvenience of you finishing work for the supposed start date, I think it's only fair that I pay you your salary for these months.'

His wife beamed with satisfaction and I knew immediately whose idea it was.

It sounded too good to be true. 'So you're going to pay me not to work for April and May?' I checked. I couldn't believe my luck.

'Yeah, that's about it. She's a clever one all right, isn't she?' Christie said to Nick.

'Beauty and brains,' he replied, draping his arm around my shoulders.

'That's settled, then.' Christie rubbed his hands together, his enormous signet ring catching the light. 'Drop by the office and we'll run up the paperwork,' he told me. 'Now,' he said, lightly clasping his wife's arm and gazing around him. 'Who are we saving today? Ah, yes . . . the school in Somalia. Well, let's go do some good, dear.'

We watched them wander off. Two months' paid holiday. It was unbelievable. 'Two months' paid holiday,' I mouthed at Nick. I was going to be paid to do nothing.

'Hello, Rosie.'

I didn't need to look around. I knew that voice. I'd heard it every day for the last four years, longer if you count the time before we were married.

'We just popped by because Pat's parents are our new neighbours and we thought we'd show our support,' Richie explained in a tightly controlled voice.

I turned around. 'Hi.'

Richie stood with Ellen. I stood with Nick. We were only two steps away from each other yet we were worlds apart.

'Richie, Ellen . . . this is Nick.' I introduced him into the bizarre triangle we formed. But I was actually saying a lot more than that.

Nick greeted everyone with effortless charm and Ellen smiled back warmly. 'Hello, Nick. Nice to meet you.'

My stomach lurched. I didn't want to see the faintest flicker of attraction register on his face when he looked at her. Not even of the purely objective kind when faced with a good-looking member of the opposite sex – if attraction could ever be objective. Because Ellen Van Damme wasn't just any good-looking member of the opposite sex, she was the woman who had what it took to take my husband from me.

Nick accepted the greeting with a polite inclination of his head. There was no sign whatsoever of him being bewitched by Ellen. I wanted to wrap my arms around his neck and kiss him.

'We're just on our way out,' I told them. 'Richie, there's one last thing.' This sounded more ominous than I intended. 'I've decided to sell the house and you should get back what you put into it.'

Richie looked elated. I guessed he thought he'd have to fight me for it.

But Ellen quickly spoke up. 'To be honest, Rosie, we don't need the money. I really think you should keep it, all of it. What do you say, Richie?'

She wasn't really giving him the choice and I wondered if Richie would have as much control over her as he had over me. I didn't think so and I was very pleased about this.

Richie was noticeably wrestling with his facial expressions. He couldn't help but look pained but he wasn't going to let himself down in front of his new love and fall short of her expectations.

'That's a great idea, Ellen,' he agreed shallowly.

'I knew you'd think so,' she sighed contentedly.

Nick tapped the thick face of his watch. 'Rosie, I think we should get a move on.' Then his hand found mine again, dangling by my side, and he held it. 'OK?'

'Yeah, OK.' I turned to face Richie. There was only one thing left to say.

'Goodbye, Richie.'

Outside, the weather was still freezing. I tilted my head upwards and inhaled deeply. Air rushed in and filled my lungs. It was like crushed ice – both numbing and invigorating.

I thought back over everything that had happened in the time since Richie had left me, and I turned to Nick. 'Stranger than fiction, all this.'

'What do you mean?' he asked, pulling me close to him and kissing my upturned face.

'So much has changed,' I mused. 'It's as if Richie walking out on me was just the start of something and not the end, like I'd feared.'

It had been the start to a new life that I'd built with the help of everyone who had rallied round me when I'd needed them, everyone from the Furey brothers, who had sent Richie the funeral wreath, to Christie, who'd offered me an interesting new job, and my mother, who used to spit on the doorstep of Richie's shop, and, of course, Muriel, who'd got our friendship back on track and stood by me throughout everything.

'I've moved on, Nick, to somewhere wonderful.' I really meant that. I'd entered a world of new possibilities and wider horizons and I'd learnt a lot on the way. I'd learnt that life's blows would make me stronger and that extraordinary things can happen to ordinary people.

Four Weeks Later

The busy Aer Lingus flight from Dublin to Chicago O'Hare landed smoothly on the runway of terminal five some point mid-afternoon local time.

It was the day after Muriel's thirtieth birthday and we were about to embark on a two-month trip down Route 66, the Mother Road, in a rented Winnebago van, just like she'd told me she wanted to. Neither of us had slept for the last week, turned insomniacs with excitement.

Muriel had taken unpaid leave from the library and I was taking advantage of the fact that Christie's wife had bullied him into paying me my full salary for April and May when the hotel would be closed.

But I'd also had to dip into the money I'd made on the sale of the house, because renting a Winnebago van was not the cheap option I'd first thought when I offered to pay for it as a birthday present to Muriel.

Our plan was to collect the Winnebago at the airport and head to downtown Chicago, which we reckoned from the map to be about eighteen miles away, and hit the official start of Route 66, currently on Adams Street at Michigan Avenue. We'd read that it had moved quite a few times, which was something

I found hilarious because a road either started some-where or it didn't.

Route 66 stretched all the way from Illinois to California and covered 2,448 miles. I couldn't even hazard a guess at how many times you'd have to zigzag across Ireland to make up this kind of distance.

It crossed eight states and three time zones, and we had to drive from east to west because the opposite direction was historically wrong and a lot harder to do since all the books and maps went the right way.

According to our guide book all 2,448 miles of it could be run in about four months – needless to say, not by either Muriel or myself. We figured we could easily drive it in two.

However, no amount of planning could have pre-pared us for the sight of the rented Winnebago van, the Minnie® 29N complete with Meadowbrook interior, that we were taken to at the airport when we landed and cleared immigration. It'd sounded fancy from the description the car-hire people sent us but that didn't come close to describing the hotel suite on wheels that stood before us, gleaming in the sun.

It had a galley with a stainless-steel sink, microwave and a three-burner hob for cooking, a separate bedroom with double wardrobes and a queen-size bed, and a nineteen-inch television and VCR that was satellite-system ready, the rental agent told us.

'My God,' Muriel gasped in awe. 'Do people actually give them back?'

'Yes ma'am,' he guaranteed her, 'they sure do, because we have their credit-card details.'

She walked around the spacious interior with her arms outstretched, and sighed happily. 'I could live here for ever.'

I followed her. 'It probably has a gym, too.' I was only half joking.

'Well, at least there'll be plenty of room when Nick gets here. We won't be tripping over each other.'

I grinned at her.

Nick had begun working on a project for the American editor he'd met the month before in Dublin and he was now in New Orleans doing research on voodoo culture.

He was going to meet up with us for the last leg of the journey, Flagstaff to LA, and then he was taking me to Acapulco for a week to celebrate the success of the reader's profile in *ME!* magazine, which had been a real hit. I'd even received fan mail, to which I'd personally replied because I was so thrilled. And Angela wanted to talk to me about doing some more articles when I got back from travelling.

I was beginning to think I was the luckiest girl alive.

We quickly loaded our luggage and giggled excitedly as we climbed into the roomy front cab of the Winnebago.

We'd spun a coin on the plane and I was first up behind the wheel but the sheer size of the van suddenly made it far more daunting than I'd expected. But we